ABSENCE OF MIND

H.C.H. RITZ

grey gecko press

Published by Grey Gecko Press, Katy, Texas.

www.greygeckopress.com

Printed in the United States of America

Library of Congress Cataloging-in-Publication Data
Ritz, H. C. H.
Absence of mind / H. C. H. Ritz
Library of Congress Control Number: 2015936649
ISBN   978-1-9388217-9-0
First Edition

To Lisa

**My beloved mother-in-law,
who was "Granny Day Care" for my son
so that I could write.**

ONE

My Navi reads the news to me inside my head. It has a smooth, masculine voice, which I chose, but also a robotic intonation that they've never been able to fix.

<< Tensions continue to escalate as Chinese officials refuse to respond to allegations that China is continuing to re-develop its nuclear weapons program twelve years after its defeat and disarma—>>

< Next. >

Sunlight sweeps across my vision as my automatic car makes a right turn, and the game of GlowDisc I'm playing in my heads-up display almost winks out in the bright light, then returns.

<< Entertainment conglomerates Peake International, Big Wave, and Kimberley Corp posted record profits for the fourth straight quarter. >>

< Next. >

<< It's official: Elephants have gone the way of the dodo, joining the list of nineteen major mammals to—>>

< Oh God. Next. You know what, Navi? Don't show me sad news about animals anymore. >

<< Preferences updated. >>

It's early afternoon on a Monday, and Tobi—my blond German Shepherd—and I are heading to the dog park. I scritch Tobi's head as I watch my six opponents make their moves in rapid sequence. Then I mentally direct a yellow disc on top of a blue disc, and the neighboring red discs obediently turn green.

<< Call from work. >>

< Ignore. >

It's my weekend, which sometimes corresponds to the actual weekend, depending on what they do with my schedule at the hospital.

After the others take their turns, I shift a blue disc onto a red one. I grin as purple cascades across the playing board and my opponents shower me with rude comments and praise.

<< Smart drug Allivan proven effective in treating schizophrenia. The last of the most common neurological disorders has fallen victim to the newest smart drug produced by global drug manufacturer New-Phase, which expects the new drug to become commercially available within six months. >>

Well, that's cool. I can look forward to better treatment for the schizos in my ward.

Hmm . . . Nope. If I split the orange discs, I'll lose too many green discs . . .

<< Call from Family. >>

< Ugh. Ignore. >

"Family" means it's someone from back home in my family's weird community. Since it's a shared landline phone, my Navi can't tell me exactly who it is.

< Gimme more news. >

I feel Tobi's cold, wet nose on my hand and pet him some more as I consider splitting the brown discs into red and green.

Then I hear Jamie's voice. When messages are personal, they come through in that individual's voice, accompanied by a video image of their face in the corner of my display. Jamie is my youngest brother, out of the five of us, and my only family member here in Atlanta.

>> Okay, Phoebe, so are you too cool to come by my birthday party tonight? >>

< No, dorkamous. Of course I'll stop by. Glad you reminded me, though, because I forgot. Why don't you have your party on a Friday or Saturday night like a normal human being? >

Nearly everything on the GlowDisc game board shifts to blue, and I glare. I lost. I start a new game with new opponents.

<< Because today is my actual birthday. Duh. And only old people like you have to wake up in the morning anyway. >>

I snort.

< Only old people like me make actual money, you know. >

<< I make money. I earn scholarships. Unlike some, ahem, people I know. >>

< Bookworm. Nerd. >

I'm only teasing him. I'm proud of how well he's been doing in schoo—

Suddenly, the brakes squeal, and something big flashes past by my left window. A massive crunching sound batters my eardrums. Everything goes up into the air and comes back down again.

When things settle, my head is still swimming. I blink a few times. My eyes refocus from my heads-up display to the world around me—the cars, the buildings, the bright blue sky and green trees.

Obediently following my attention, my Navi goes to text mode. The display disappears in the center, leaving only the notification and news feed panels on the right periphery of my vision.

Tobi collided with the front panel of the passenger compartment with the impact, but he looks okay. I give him a couple of pats with shaking hands while I twist to look out of the front window. There's a car to the right front corner of my own car. A tall, blonde woman gets out of it. I unbuckle my seatbelt and open my door, my mind still reeling.

Emergency messages in bold red appear at the bottom of my display and flash.

!!! There's been an accident. !!!

!!! Stay where you are. !!!

!!! Emergency responders have been contacted. !!!

I walk around the car unsteadily, looking.

Messages from Jamie and Sara appear in my notifications panel, in text.

| Jamie: You do realize those were all compliments, right? News flash: smart is in. |

| Sara: We need you to come in. Dr. Foret said he called you. |

The corners of each of our cars are crumpled. It doesn't look too bad. Other vehicles are driving carefully around us. We're right in the middle of the intersection.

I approach the woman and extend the digital handshake. Nothing. I glance at her in surprise.

| Target is not equipped with a Navi. |

I blink again. For a moment, I don't quite know what to do.

| Sara: We're super busy over here. |

The woman is studying her car and mine, frowning.

"Um, I'm Phoebe Bernhart," I say. "Are you hurt?" My voice rasps and I cough. I'm unaccustomed to speaking aloud.

"Uncertain," the woman says. "But unlikely, given the rates of speed, angle of impact, and safety systems of my vehicle."

Another message flashes red at the bottom of my vision, demanding my attention.

!!! Distance Insurance: You have been in an accident. Please enable video permissions to Distance Insurance for visual review of the accident. !!!

Christ on a—

I sit down somewhat abruptly. I feel dizzy, and I dimly recognize that I'm more unbalanced by this little wreck than I probably ought to be.

I glance over at my messages in the panel on the right, to remind myself of what they were, and I reply to Sara.

< I had a small car accident. I'll get back to you in a minute. >

"Oh, no!" I realize I left my car door open. *Tobi. Tobi, Tobi*—
I'm in my car, checking the passenger compartment. No dog. I jump back out and scan the horizon. No dog. My heart's pounding.
If he gets run over—
"No, no, no . . ."

| Sara: Oh, wow, really? Are you okay?|

I remember that I had Tobi ID-chipped.

< Navi, find Tobi. Please, please, please . . . >

The woman is looking at me from across the car. "What's wrong?"

"My dog!" I shout, my voice hitting a higher octave than I thought it could.

| Tobi is northeast, fifty yards. |

A bull's-eye appears in my vision to the left.

"Help me get him!" I shout.

The woman's eyebrows go up at the prospect. I don't care. This is my dog, the sweetest, most adorable dog ever whom I rescued from the city pound and who deserves nothing like getting hit by a car because I was stupid enough to leave the door open. "Help me get my dog!" I'm shrieking while I run, and my tone leaves no room for argument.

The woman is wearing pants and flats, at least, and she starts running, too.

Actually, she's faster than I am. She overtakes me quickly and then looks back for me to point to where my Navi tells me Tobi ought to be. Which is right in the middle of about six lanes of moderately busy traffic.

I hear car horns and screeching brakes in the distance, and I'm hyperventilating as I run. And praying for all I'm freaking worth. *Dear God, I'll stop drinking, and I won't have any more premarital sex, I swear to God, please, please, save Tobi, please please please—*

Car horns, sirens now, cars everywhere, my feet hitting the pavement hard, sending jolts up my legs, it's hot, the sun is blinding me, I'm between lanes with cars flying by me, which is dangerous and stupid, people are swerving—

I see the blonde woman bending over up ahead. I see yellow fur on the ground in front of her. My heart stops. Then she wheels around. She's got Tobi's collar in her hand, and she's dragging the dog along—Tobi's panicked and confused and throwing himself around, paws scrabbling at the air, trying to get away from the car horns. I don't see any blood.

A moment later, I'm there, too—

!!! Atlanta Police Department: Ma'am, this is
the police. Please return to your vehicle. !!!

—wrestling Tobi, panting, looking for a break in the traffic, and then pulling him along, the blonde woman still with one hand on his collar, too, the nearness of the stranger awkward, and then we have him off the side of the road, in a parking lot. Safe.

!!! Please enable video permissions to Distance
Insurance for visual review of the accident. !!!

I hug Tobi for all I'm worth. He's shaking. So am I. Tears fill my eyes.

| Sara: So are you okay or what? |

I look up, and everything seems to grind to a halt as I finally look at this woman whose car I hit and who rescued my dog anyway. The sunlight frames her curly blonde hair. Her pale skin glows. Her eyes are ice blue. I realize that I'm staring.

| This might be an excellent time
for a CoffeeBreak caffè mocha.
There's a CoffeeBreak twenty feet
ahead on your left. |

"Thank you. So much," I stammer. "I don't even know how to repay you for this."
I feel chunky and plain right now. She's slender and lovely. I'm envious. I look away, feeling awkward.
"We should go back," she says.

!!! APD: Ma'am, return to your car immediately,
please. !!!

< I'm on my way. I'm sorry, my dog got loose and I had
to get him. >

I get up and make sure I have an iron grip on Tobi's collar.

!!! Your vehicle is blocking traffic, ma'am. !!!

< As I said, I'm on my way. >

We head back to the scene of the accident.

"I'm sorry I hit you. Wait, *did* my car hit yours, or did your car hit mine?" I realize I don't know what happened.

"Your car was supposed to yield. You had a left-turn-yield."

"That's so weird. I don't know why that happened. I've never had my car do anything like that before. It usually does everything just fine."

"I'm sure."

I glance over at her. Her tone is aggravated, but her expression is placid.

It's so strange to be talking out loud.

!!! Distance Insurance: If you do not enable video
review, you will be required to wait for an insurance adjuster to be dispatched to the scene. !!!

"I don't know your name," I say.

"No, you don't."

That was kind of cold. "Well, thank you again," I mumble. "Thank you for rescuing Tobi. He's important to me. And to Mrs. Jones."

"Mrs. Jones?"

"My neighbor. He's Mrs. Jones's, too. We time-share him."

Silence. Then, "You time-share a dog?"

"I'm never home. I work twelve-hour shifts at the hospital. Mrs. Jones is this old retired lady who's always home. It works out." I sound defensive, I realize.

We walk the rest of the way to the cars in silence while I reply to the messages that have been stacking up in my notification panel, including questions from the cops waiting at my car. I eye the messages from Sara with annoyance, because all I want to do right now is go get a drink, but eventually my sense of duty wins out and I tell her I'll come in as soon as I can.

Once we're back at the scene of the accident, I get Tobi settled in the back of my car again, and then it takes about half an hour to get all the details sorted out. I enable video review from Distance Insurance, and they direct me to walk around the car to give them a complete picture of the damage and to submit the video from the few minutes before, during, and after the accident. The claim gets processed, and I go ahead and request a tow truck to come take my car. I'll take the light rail system for a couple of days.

At the same time, I get a chance to observe the woman, whose name turns out to be Mila Bremer (she pronounces it "mee-luh breh-mer"), and how she interacts with the cops. Normally, conversations are private, because they're Navi-to-Navi, but they're having to speak out loud, so I know everything that the cops know. I know her address, her phone number, her date of birth, and even the name of her insurance agent, who eventually has to show up in person. And it's all being recorded by my Navi, of course, since I have the Memory app running.

I notice that one of the cops speaks slowly and loudly, as if Mila were intellectually disabled or partially deaf. It makes me mad. She seems odd, but it's clear that she's intelligent, and it's not her fault that she can't take a Navi.

At least, I'm assuming she's non-Navable—a "Nonnie"—one of the 0.5 percent whose bodies still reject the implant, despite all the efforts of modern medicine. She doesn't seem like the sort of person who would voluntarily go without one. Those people are on the fringe of the fringe, like neo-Luddites . . . and like my family back home.

Next, the cop asks her, loudly and slowly, "Do you suppose you missed the light turning red?"

I'm confused until I realize that she was *driving*: hers is a manual-drive car. I wonder if maybe Nonnies can't use smartcars. Then I wonder, too, if it was even true that my car hit hers and not the other way around. It seems much more likely that a Nonnie would react too slowly or not see something than that a smartcar would malfunction.

"The light was green," Mila answers.

"You're only human," the cop says. "You may be confused. You may have thought you saw something besides what you saw." His condescending tone makes me regret my own thoughts along those lines.

Mila doesn't even blink. "Check the video from the smartcar."

"Okay. You know what? We'll do that." His chin goes up in the air as he turns to my vehicle.

We all wait, most of us reviewing messages on our Navis in the meantime.

After a moment, the cop says, "Both of your vehicles are drivable. I recommend you get them out of the path of traffic. Ma'am"—looking at me—"your vehicle's CPU has been reset and its drive path realigned. You should be good to go." Then he turns away.

What a jerk. Obviously, the video proved Mila was right, and he won't admit it.

Both cops leave right as the tow truck shows up. A moment later, without another word, Mila is getting into her car.

I find myself calling out to her, not wanting her to disappear.

"Wait . . . Mila! Can I buy you a meal? As a thank-you for helping me rescue Tobi?"

I don't know why I do it. I feel like I owe her one, and also, something about her seems interesting to me. Maybe that she's a Nonnie. That's pretty weird, after all. Or maybe I feel sorry for her because of how that cop treated her.

Those pale blue eyes consider me for a moment. "Fine. Did you record my number?"

"Yeah . . . well, my Navi did, yeah."

"Then you can try calling me. But I only have a land line, I'm not home much, and I don't have voice mail." Her tone is final. It seems to say, *Don't bother.*

She closes her door and starts the car, but then she pauses and looks at me through the glass. She rolls down her window. Her tone sounds as if she's conceding an argument. "Usually, I'm home by eight, though." She rolls the window back up and drives off.

I sigh heavily and study my hands. They're still trembling, but not as badly. I need a drink. But I promised Sara I'd come in, and I will, even though I'm not happy about it.

First, I have to get Tobi back home. I start to look around for a rail station before I remember that I can't take Tobi on the rail. I have my Navi request an automatic cab, warning the dispatch that I have a big dog with me, and I sit at a bus stop to wait.

I pet Tobi feverishly. I'm still weirded out that my car crashed like that, but I'm more freaked out that I almost lost my dog because of a moment of inattention. At least Tobi seems to have forgotten the whole thing already. He's just happy to be petted.

My Navi knows that whenever I'm not doing anything else that's auditory in nature, it can go back to audible mode, so it starts reading to me in that smooth, masculine voice again.

> << Breaking news: Great Britain has declared sanctions against China for the third time since the China War. >>

I groan.

> < No. Skip it. >

I review my notifications to make sure I haven't missed any messages. Whenever I've gotten behind, the messages are always there waiting for me. I also review my news feed panel, below the notifications panel that is reserved for personal messages, to see what global updates I've missed while my Navi was in text mode.

There's random news, email newsletters, and then the social updates from people I knew in high school back in Ohio, old coworkers at my last hospital, random people who share my interests, and then the current coworkers. Together, I call them the Collective. It's a deliberate reference to the fact that most of the time, it doesn't even matter who said what. It's just nice to know you're not alone.

I make a post.

> < Had a car wreck today. Yup, an actual car wreck.
> My car decided yielding on the left turn was optional.

Nobody got hurt, though. And the other driver? Was a Nonnie. But no, the accident wasn't her fault. Some sort of bug in my car's software, I guess. >

I use my Memory app to pull a few seconds of video of the accident, from when I got out of the car to when I sat down on the curb, and attach it to the post.

Almost immediately, responses come in.

<< Ian: Wow, she's hot. She's a Nonnie? >>

<< Shannon: Oh no . . . glad you're okay. >>

<< Wayne: I saw a Nonnie once at the grocery store. I mean, it had to have been a Nonnie. She paid a cashier—with a physical credit card. >>

<< Alyssa: Oh, I went to school with a guy who was a Nonnie. He used a laptop computer for all his schoolwork. >>

<< Chris: Wild. Aren't there, like, almost no car accidents anymore? Is your car defective? Are they going to replace it? >>

I chuckle. The automated cab pulls up, and I get in with Tobi.

< Navi, have the cab take me home, please. >

< Ian, ha. Eat your heart out, I'm going to have dinner with her. >

< Chris, no, they're not replacing it. They reset the CPU and something about the drive path. Said it should work fine now. >

<< Ian: You have a date with the Nonnie?! >>

< No, Ian, it's not a date. Sheesh. >

<< Shannon: Well, then, why are you having dinner with her? That's kinda weird. >>

>> Ian: You sure you're not gay? Come to think of it, you've never dated anybody, man or woman, that I know of. >>

< Why is it weird, Shannon? I mean, I owe her. I wrecked her car, and then she saved my dog's life. >

<< Alyssa: What, what, what?! What about Tobi?! >>

< Sorry, forgot to mention. Tobi got out of the car and almost got run over. She helped me get him back. >

I rub Tobi's ears even more vigorously than before.

<< Wayne: She used to date me. She's not gay. I can TESTIFY. >>

< Wayne, STFU. >

<< Wayne: *laughing* Anyway, what're you going to talk to her about? She's a Nonnie. >>

< Same stuff I'd talk to anyone about. Just because she doesn't have her smartphone implanted in her head doesn't mean she lives on a different planet. >

<< Patti: She kind of does, though, doesn't she? I mean, could you imagine not being able to get your messages real-time? Not having conversations like this one? It must be so lonely. >>

I have to stop for a moment. Patti's comment makes me think about my family back home, none of them with Navis—not because they're Nonnies, but because of their religion.

I hate how different my family is and how I never feel like I can talk to anyone about them, or about my weird childhood, without feeling embarrassed. But I don't like how Wayne and Patti make it sound like Mila must be some sort of alien or reject because she's a Nonnie. That would make all my family back home aliens and rejects. I may think of them that way myself sometimes, but that doesn't mean other people get to.

> < She can use a phone, you know. She's not that different just because she talks out loud instead of with her thoughts. >

> << Patti: I guess. >>

> << Ian: So, Wayne, tell me more. What does Phoebe like in bed? >>

> < OMG STFU you two. Seriously. >

> << Ian: Eat your heart out, you said. Gonna make you sorry you said that . . . >>

> < That's it! Done! >

I end the conversation, blocking any further comments, even though I'm giggling at the same time.

So maybe it is weird that I asked Mila to go to dinner. She is kind of strange. She didn't seem friendly, either, so I'm not sure what the point was.

I go ahead and review my Memory app to find the phone number, and then I make the call, even though I feel nervous about it. She should be home by now, I figure.

But I don't get an answer.

My Navi interrupts me.

> << You have arrived at home. Should the cab wait? >>

> < Yes, please. I'll be right back down. >

I get Tobi upstairs and settled, and then I head back down and climb back into the taxi, still listening and responding to messages as I go. A few minutes later, I get another message directly from my Navi.

<< A Burger Boy is one minute ahead. The Baco-Burger
meal is on special for $9.99. Would you like to stop? >>

Hmm . . . I *am* hungry, I realize.

< Sure. Make it a #6 with a Coke. >

<< Deducting $10.81 from your primary checking ac-
count and redirecting the cab. >>

Moments later, the car drives through and lowers the window
for me to pick up the food. I down it fast and then lick the french-
fry salt from my fingers in a state of pure bliss.

About three minutes later, I'm kicking myself. I wish fast food
didn't hit my brain's reward center so perfectly. I keep meaning to
give it up, but it isn't happening yet. In fact, every time I eat it, I
think about ordering my Navi to stop telling me about my proximity
to fast-food restaurants—the advertising messages can be adjusted
so that they're less annoying—but I can never manage it. Fast food is
good, and I jog enough to keep my weight down.

Or so I rationalize.

As the cab turns in to Grady Hospital a few minutes later, I call
Mila again. But still no answer. Oh well. I'll try again later.

As I cross the threshold of the hospital, my Navi badges me
in and automatically turns to text mode. I think that's because I do
service work with actual people. Information workers are probably
always on auditory mode. Of course, they don't have to go into a
workplace anymore, either. Navis broke the chains that bound previous generations to their desks for their entire lives.

At the same time that I cross the threshold, I also enter the hospital communications network, and I start getting general broadcast
messages from my coworkers. I note that the tone of the conversation
is unusual.

As I ride an elevator and two travelators through the 1.2 million square feet of hospital to get to the neuro ward on the seventh
floor, I read with interest.

| Derrick: Y'all, we've got another
live one. Room #730. Acute para-
noia. |

| Sara: Does anyone know if they're
calling in extra doctors? |

| Abhay: They're saying we might
hit drive-by in the next few days
if this keeps up. |

My eyebrows go up. "Drive-by" means that if an ambulance
or a cop is bringing someone in, they're supposed to keep right on
driving, because our beds are full and we aren't taking anybody.

| Tolony: Wow, drive-by? Do we
ever get that, even on Halloween?
I mean, even during a full moon
on Halloween? I've heard that's
the busy time. |

| Rhonda: I've never seen a neuro
ward on drive-by. Not even here at
Grady. |

< Hey, peeps. I'm here to help. What's got everybody
so busy? >

| Deonte: A lot of aggressive and
paranoid people in the last twenty-
four hours. |

| Melita: It's seriously weird. |

| Sara: Oh, good, Phoebe. I've got
seventeen new cases to give you. |

< Wow—you've had seventeen new cases since yester-
day? >

| Sara: No, we've had twenty-nine.
These seventeen are the ones I need
to give you. |

Ugh. My stomach sinks. I'm about to be overwhelmed. Dealing with "neurologically impaired" patients is stressful at best, and this is going to be a hell of an evening.

| Sara: Don't get written up again,
Phoebe. |

I glower. Is she reading my mind now?

< Okay, now I'm regretting that I even told you about those write-ups. Sheesh. Mind your own beeswax. >

I'm only aggravated because she's right. I have a history of getting angry with the doctors when I'm already stressed and I think they're not acting in the best interests of the patients, which I think half a dozen times a day.

| Sara: Just sayin'. Didn't you tell
me you've gotten fired from two
other hospitals already? |

< *One*, woman. *One*. >

| Sara: Didn't management recom-
mend an attitude-improvement
plan? |

< That's it. I'm never telling you anything ever again. >

Grumbling all the way, I head to the break room and fix myself some coffee in the biggest mug I can find. I down it, and then I fix myself another cup to take with me.

I hate those Navi-based attitude-improvement plans. I tried one once, for maybe forty-five minutes, before I couldn't stand it anymore.

As I head down to my ward, I notice that I'm experiencing tightness in my chest and mild heart palpitations. I've had this almost daily for a couple of weeks now. The symptoms probably say something about how stressful my work is.

They may also say something about the sheer quantity of coffee I drink.

A few minutes later, I'm finishing the handover of extra cases from Sara in the south wing. My side of the ward—the north side—now has fifty-seven total patients, which is a lot for me, two LVNs, and three techs. We have only three beds left. Hopefully, Dr. Pienaar can get some of these folks moved out tonight. But I'm super curious about why there are so many.

Sara is the other day-shift RN in my ward, but she handles the south side. The LVNs—Licensed Vocational Nurses—and technicians handle most of the work, with us RNs supervising, but when things are this busy, we still have to do a lot of hands-on work ourselves.

I begin my day with a room-by-room environmental check for plastic bags, glass, fire-making materials, etc. I don't trust my techs or LVNs to do it carefully enough. Next, I supervise the initial dispensing of any new meds that the LVNs can't handle by themselves and double-check all the med pulls. I've had patients suffer serious adverse reactions because they got the wrong meds, and I hate it.

Then, I start my rounds. I have my Navi calculate how many minutes I have with each patient morning and afternoon—today, it's 4.35 minutes, which is absurd. Normally, I try to breeze through the patients when I can so that I can spend an extra couple of minutes with those who are distressed and wanting to talk, but today, I'm going to be sprinting from room to room.

All the while, I'm getting more messages.

> | Bourey: What I wanna know is, why are all the new patients either pissed off or scared to death? Are hallucinations not trendy anymore or what? |

| Derrick: I feel ya, man. Not
a single one who's suicidal or
obsessive, either. |

| Melita: FYI, shift change told me
#719 almost managed to set a fire
again last night.|

I grimace. Patient #719 has summoned firefighters three times in two weeks.

< Is night shift handing out lighters now or something? >

| Bourey: Yeah, yeah, yeah. |

| Thiago: Anyone else scared spitless
of #712? I don't believe in demons,
mind you, but that man is *possessed*. |

< Yes. He is creepy as hell. It's gotta be a biotech mod, right? >

His eyes light up red. It was seriously unsettling when I saw it for the first time, especially given that he was cackling maniacally and screaming into my Navi, "You will burn in the fires of hell!" Especially given that I was raised by an ultra-conservative religious family.

!!! Emergency message—All available personnel:
Room #717. !!!

I'm just leaving #728, so I'm available. I book it.

Two

Shouting comes to my ears as I round the corner toward #717. I get almost to the doorway, and then there's a man-sized shape in a hospital gown and a blur of motion. An impact knocks the breath out of me. I hit the wall, then the floor, and scramble for footing.

My Navi sounds a siren in the front of my mind, as if I didn't know already.

!!! Danger! Personal risk of injury! Run away! !!!

Strong hands grab my arms, the pressure painful. I grit my teeth, unwilling to cry out. His eyes are red-rimmed, his face contorted. Then there are others around me, helping to pull the man away. My Navi identifies him before I do—Paul Davis—and delivers his messages. Since we're face-to-face, it goes back to audible mode.

<< Get away from me! Get away! >>

I pull on all my reserves of empathy instead of getting defensive.

< What's wrong? What do you need? >

Davis wrestles against the techs, fighting hard. Bourey, an LVN, is approaching with a jet injector.

<< You're not going to hurt me. No one is going to hurt me! >>

< You're afraid. Something is scaring you. >

It sounds simplistic, but I learned a long time ago that this kind of language calms people down quickly.

Davis suddenly goes limp, collapsing like a toddler about to have a tantrum. Bourey hasn't even hit him with the sedative yet. I kneel next to Davis.

< You're scared. Tell me what's scaring you. >

He doesn't respond. He's broken down into sobs, wrapped in a fetal position, now rocking himself back and forth.

Bourey kneels, too, and taps the injector against the side of Davis's neck. He cries out once and then tries to scrabble back into a corner. The techs stay close but let him get to the corner. Once there, he huddles, abject. I keep my distance.

< Navi, include Bourey and Douglas with Davis. >

This will send any messages that I send to Davis to the other two as well.

< Davis, tell me what's scaring you. We'll keep you safe, I promise. >

He doesn't reply. He cowers with his arms over his head as if he's expecting a beating.

< You're so frightened. So frightened. >

He looks up at me, some sort of expression on his face. The medication starts to kick in. His pupils dilate.

< Can you tell me what's scaring you? >

<< Everything. Everything. >>

< Okay. Everything is scary. I can see that. Can we go into this room over here where you'll be safer than in the hallway? >

After he looks around and sees where I'm pointing, he seems to evaluate and then nods. He scrambles into the room and hides behind the bed. Like a frightened child, he peeks up from behind the bed.

<< Who are you? Where am I? >>

< This is Grady Hospital. I'm Nurse Phoebe. >

I come into the room and sit on a chair opposite the bed, minimizing any movements that might seem threatening. It's amazing how my attitude problems vanish when I'm genuinely needed. I wave off the techs, the real excitement over for now.

<< Am I sick? Oh God . . . what do I have? >>

< There's something wrong with your brain, and it's causing you to be frightened. We can help you, though. We'll fix it. >

<< Oh no . . . I'm going to die. >>

Davis collapses to the floor, his hands over his face, crying again.

< No, sir, you're not going to die. We're going to fix your brain. >

He peeks out again.

<< Do you promise? >>

< Yes, I promise. >

I'm not even lying. The new smart drugs, coupled with Navi guidance, have made psychiatric issues eminently treatable. The hardest part is getting people into treatment.

He sits up slowly.

> < How are you feeling now? Are you still as fright-
> ened? >

> << No . . . I feel better. >>

> < Will you sit on the bed so I can check your blood
> pressure? >

It takes me a few moments to coax him up off the floor. I have
to show him that I don't have any weapons and point out that I'm a
smallish and not-very-strong woman before he lets me come close.
His paranoia seems all-encompassing.

I check all his vitals, ask Bourey what medicine he gave him,
and notice that eight hours have passed since he was last dosed. The
sedatives tend to run in seven to eight hours, so his had probably
worn off.

> < The doctor will be in to see you shortly. He was al-
> ready scheduled to see you about now. >

I grimace when I see that it's Dr. Green on the schedule. Dr.
Green is a thin, dark man with short, black hair and condescending
nostrils. He's not regularly assigned to us, but when we're short on
staff, we get him. His knowledge of brain disorders is twenty years
out of date, and he regularly makes decisions the entire nursing staff
thinks are bad.

Davis messages me again.

> << Are there germs in here? Diseases? Anything con-
> tagious? I don't want to touch anything. >>

> < No. This is the neuro ward, so people don't generally
> come in here with anything contagious. >

He goes back to staring intently around the room, looking for
hazards and occasionally wiping away tears. Despite the sedation,
he seems ready to spring into action if he faces any new threats.

I'm trapped. I don't think I can leave him here alone. But luckily, after a moment, Dr. Green steps into the room.

< Ah, Dr. Green, here you are. >

<< Here I am, indeed. >>

There's always a sneer in his voice.

Meanwhile, Davis has dived behind the bed again.

I give Dr. Green a quick update, including a sped-up video of the last few minutes, and then talk the patient back up off the floor so that Dr. Green can talk to him.

Dr. Green puts Davis through the standard evaluation questionnaires and screening tools. As I listen to the responses, I realize that something strange is going on here. The patient claims to have had no prior symptoms. No voices in his head and no visual or tactile or olfactory sensations. No prior violence. No unusual stress, no anxiety, no depression, and no notable mood swings. Minimal alcohol use and no drug use. No pain, illnesses, medications, surgeries, or disabilities. No family history of brain disorders. He said he was watching a scary movie late last night and then became terrified and has been trying to protect himself from all the threats in the world ever since.

Most notably, he's afraid of everything, but he's not expressing any delusions. He's not convinced that we're out to get him, he's just terrified that we might be. It's basically the most intense anxiety I've ever seen, and that's on high doses of Callex and Altipar.

< You guys, are you noticing that these new patients
have none of the usual onset factors? >

| Bourey: We aren't total simpletons, you know. |

| Rhonda: Bourey, be nice. Yes,
Phoebe, we're noticing it. |

< And is #717 the only one who's barely responding
to Callex and Altipar? >

| Bourey: Nope. |

| Allan: No. |

| Abhay: Not at all. |

I frown, wondering what in the world is going on.
Meanwhile, Dr. Green posts an update.

<< Paul Davis. Dx paranoid schizophrenia. Rx Ifothal,
450 mg twice daily, Movatase 5 mg twice daily. Continue hospitalization. >>

Whoa. Wow. This is probably the worst call I've ever seen him
make.

< Doctor. Hold up.>

I gather my thoughts and then message him again.

< Ifothal has been superceded by better drugs for five
years. And if this is paranoid schizophrenia, it's wildly
atypical. There are no delusions or hallucinations. >

Dr. Green turns and looks directly at me.

<< Questioning me again, Phoebe? >>

< Ifothal has high risk of neuroleptic malignant syn-
drome, especially when given when not needed. That's
why it's not a go-to drug anymore. >

<< Phoebe, would you like to be reminded that you are
a nurse and I am the doctor? >>

< Doctor, neuroleptic malignant syndrome? Coma?
Seizure? This ringing a bell? >

<< So observe the patient for any issues, *Nurse.* >>

And with that, the doctor sweeps out of the room.

Even though Navi communications don't require proximity, I follow him out of the room, staring at his back as he goes down the hallway.

< That's an irresponsible diagnosis and prescription, and I refuse to administer it. >

He turns and faces me again.

<< Honor it or I'll write you up. >>

My fists clench, and I feel adrenaline shoot through my veins.

< I will report this to the charge nurse. >

He steps closer to me, his beady little eyes searching mine. He speaks out loud, but almost in a whisper, mindful of the other people passing by in the hallway. "And I will write you up, Nurse. So do as I tell you. I am the doctor here. You are the one who changes bedpans."

And then he walks away.

I grind my teeth, feeling my mouth twist in anger. Without another word, I go back to Davis, make sure he's reasonably stable, and administer the required medication. It's a good thing he doesn't want to talk, since I'm struggling to push down my seething rage and probably can't manage anything multisyllabic. I also request the live stream from the security camera in Davis's room and pin it to my display so I can keep an eye on him.

Most doctors, in my experience, are not like Dr. Green. Well, they all respond equally badly to being challenged, and many of them are dismissive toward nurses, so in that regard, they're all the same. But few of them would go for the jugular like he just did.

And I can't do anything about it. Sure, my Navi recorded the whole exchange, but nothing—not even video evidence—will convince hospital administration to ignore a doctor's write-up. It's not how things work in hospitals, at least not in the hospitals I've worked in.

Mostly, I'm upset because I wasn't able to convince the doctor to prescribe something else. I see myself as my patients' best advocate most of the time, and this time, I've failed. If Davis starts going into seizures or a coma, it's going to be partly my fault, because I couldn't be tactful and persuasive when he needed me to be.

As my rage settles down, though, and I rush through the remainder of my round in a futile attempt to make up lost time, it dawns on me that I've been an idiot. I glance at the clock in my Navi display and see that Davis and I only have to make it four more hours without a negative reaction. Then I'll be able to recommend to the night-shift doctor that he reevaluate and re-prescribe. And if it's the regular doctor—Dr. Pienaar—I'm confident that he'll make a better call.

I mentally kick myself. I may have been right, but I didn't have to burn that bridge.

As I continue to hurry from patient to patient, I realize that my heart rate is racing more than it should, even given the recent drama. It feels like palpitations. I pause outside a patient's door to self-evaluate.

Overly irritable . . . chest tightness . . . heart palpitations . . . lots of stress . . . two large cups of coffee in less than an hour.

Hmmm.

Okay, I hate to admit it to myself, but I'm not doing myself any favors with the coffee. I think it may be time for me to quit.

At almost ten o'clock, I get permission to go home, but only by agreeing to come back at eight in the morning on what was supposed to be a day off. We don't have enough staff for this many patients.

I'm relieved that Davis made it through and that Dr. Pienaar wrinkled his forehead, cursed Dr. Green in two different South African languages, and prescribed something different and much safer. But I'm still haunted by Davis's case, along with all the other new cases that don't fit the usual profile.

It's not that psychosis doesn't happen right out of the blue. It does. But it's rare for it to happen to someone who doesn't have any stressors in his life or any family history or any personal history, and yet be strong enough to provoke physical violence, and then fail to respond to the meds the way it should. And with dozens of cases all at once, we've got a weird situation on our hands.

I sigh and try to stop thinking about it. I can easily spend all my time either at work or thinking about work, which is a bad habit.

I toy with the idea of showing up to Jamie's party late—my Navi reminded me about the party a few hours ago—but I'm just too tired. I already sent him an apology for not going, so I leave it at that. I'm about to tell my Navi to surprise me with a short film based on my past preferences when Mila springs to my mind. Those ice-blue eyes. Such a strange person. I wonder what makes her the way she is.

I go ahead and call her again. I don't know why I call her, other than that maybe I'm a glutton for punishment. Or, I suppose, because I am curious about her.

She surprises me by answering. Her voice is dry and cool, like autumn leaves. "Hello?"

I speak subvocally. "Hi. Hello. This is Phoebe, the woman who ran into your car, and you rescued my dog? Sorry." I wince, not even sure why I tacked the apology onto the end of that.

"Yes?"

"Um. I was calling because I said I was going to buy you dinner as a thank-you."

"Yes, I remember." She doesn't say this in an encouraging tone of voice. In fact, she sounds like she's being sentenced to prison.

"Um, okay." I'm suddenly hot all over, and I wipe my forehead. This is definitely rating high on my list of awkward conversations. "So, is there a good time and place for you? For this dinner?"

There's a pause, and then she says, "Why don't we go out and get some pie and coffee right now, and then you can be done with the thank-you?"

Wow. I sit there stunned, at a loss for words.

I ping my Collective.

> < I guess you all are right. This Nonnie is weird. And rude. >

I hear a sigh on the other end of the line, a strange artifact of calls with physical telephones. Apparently, she's noticed my silence. "I apologize if that was rude," she says. There's another pause. "But pie and coffee tonight would be good with me if you're up for it. There's Cat's Diner off I-20."

I'm reconsidering the whole thing, frankly, but I forge ahead. "Actually, I just got off work, and I have to be up early in the morning. So tomorrow night is better for me. I get off work at eight, so how's nine o'clock?"

"Yes, thank you much, and I will meet you there then." She hangs up without waiting for a reply.

I feel like I've had my self-esteem trampled by a herd of elephants. *Extinct* elephants, I remind myself. As the warm wash of embarrassment passes, I get back to my Collective, who've been replying with eager questions.

> < She didn't do anything particularly weird. We set up coffee plans. She's just . . . not friendly. I guess. >

> << Dominick: I can't wait to hear about this coffee thing. You're brave. >>

> << George: I don't see why you're bothering. >>

Yeah, me, neither. For a few minutes, I wonder if I should even show up tomorrow night. Mila doesn't seem like she's looking forward to it. In fact, I would probably be doing her a favor by standing her up.

It suddenly occurs to me what might be going on. Mila could have Asperger's Syndrome. Usually, people's Navis help diagnose them early, and the apps we have now are excellent at providing real-time feedback to help them develop their social skills, but Mila has probably never had a Navi. And if she doesn't interact with people much, maybe no one would've ever realized.

Well, I know I can't diagnose anyone, certainly not after two brief conversations. But now, I want to know more about her, and I'm almost prepared to feel for her, rather than be offended by her, if she does have an untreated neuro disorder.

>> It's time to wake up, Phoebe. <<

>> It's time to wake up, Phoebe. <<

>> It's time to wake up, Phoebe. <<

I groan and bury my head under my pillow. Naturally, that doesn't work.

>> It's time to wake up, Phoebe. <<

< Shut up, Navi. >

>> You have thirty-five minutes remaining to leave for work. Your commute is longer, because you are taking the rail to work today. You must shower now. <<

< Snooze. Snooze snooze snooze. >

>> You have been written up twice already for insubordination. You cannot afford to be late. You will be fired. <<

The reminder is like being dunked in cold water. I told my Navi word-for-word what to tell me to get me up, and I chose well. It always works like a charm, and I hate it every time.

So I drag myself out of bed, exhausted and angry, as I do most mornings, and trudge into the kitchen with the intention of downing a cup of coffee. But this time, when I get there, the coffeepot is dormant and cold.

< Coffeepot, WTF? >

My Navi replies.

<< I have overridden the coffeepot's instructions. Last night, you decided to give up coffee. >>

< No way. >

I'm practically reeling, yet I do now remember something about this from yesterday . . . something about heart palpitations . . . but I don't care right now. That was yesterday's problem.

< Navi, make me some freaking coffee! >

<< Last night, you decided to give up coffee. >>

Argh.
There's got to be some manual way of making coffee. Some buttons or something. I look for buttons on the pot, but I don't find anything. There's a power button, but it doesn't make the coffee start brewing.

<< You have twenty-five minutes remaining to leave for work. Your commute is longer because you are taking the rail to work today. You must shower now. >>

< Son of a *bitch*. >

<< You have now donated $10 to Citizens Against Science. Every time you curse, you donate $10 to a charity you hate. >>

Oh, oh—oh—I can't think of a protest that doesn't involve cursing.

< I cursed to *you*! That shouldn't count! >

<< Instructions unclear. Please try again. >>

I lean on the kitchen counter and grind my teeth. Today is off to a stellar start.

> << You have twenty-two minutes remaining to leave
> for work. Your commute is longer because you are tak-
> ing the rail to work today. You must shower now. >>

I groan and stagger off to the shower, making plans for how I'm
going to get a coffee on my way to work . . . or at the break room at
work . . . or something . . . but I know that it's futile. My Navi is always watching me through my own eyes, always there to keep me on
track—unless, of course, I disable the instructions I'd set up. But, as
I recall, I always bury my self-help programming under three or four
layers of security so I'll find it too difficult to change later.

I'm too smart for my own good sometimes.

So, Past-Phoebe thought it was a great idea to give up coffee,
did she? Well, Present-Phoebe would like to kill Past-Phoebe.

Instead, I take a big dose of ibuprofen on my way out the door,
to combat the caffeine-withdrawal headache I'm bound to have in a
couple of hours otherwise.

> < Navi, please remind me WTF I was thinking when
> I decided to give up coffee. >

It recites the information I dimly remember assembling and
giving to it yesterday.

> << Coffee interferes with insulin production, poten-
> tially contributing to Type II diabetes. Coffee elicits
> excess cortisol, worsening stress. Withdrawal symp-
> toms from coffee are quite unpleasant and start within
> a few hours. Coffee lowers serotonin synthesis, pos-
> sibly contributing to depression. Coffee unbalances
> electrolytes. >>

> < All right, all right. That's enough. Shut up. >

As the light rail takes me to work, I review the notifications
that stacked up in my panels while I was fighting with my Navi. I
staunchly ignore the messages about fast-food places offering breakfast along the way.

The first thing I do when I get to my ward is go into the break room to get coffee like I always do, because I've already forgotten. But as I approach, my Navi flashes an emergency message.

!!! Warning! Action not consistent with personal goals. !!!

| You have decided to give up coffee. |

I mentally kick myself, because I can't imagine how I managed to forget that so quickly, and then I stare forlornly at the full pot of hot brew right there in front of me.

I don't remember what I told my Navi to do to me if I try to drink the coffee, but I think it was extreme. I think I told it to go to full Red Mode if necessary.

I decide to test the boundaries a bit.

I edge a few steps closer, eying the coffee.

!!! Warning! Action not consistent with personal goals. !!!

| Activating Personal Persuader app. |

Uh-oh. The Personal Persuader app is good.

I don't answer. I take a coffee mug from the cabinet and step cautiously toward the coffeepot.

| You don't want to drink coffee anymore. |

| Coffee is bad for you. |

| You only need to wait thirty-three more hours to beat this addiction. |

| In thirty-three hours, you will have much more energy than normal. |

| You will also sleep better. |

I falter.

| Will you please drink a big glass
of water instead? |

| You will feel much better, I
promise. |

< I don't believe you. >

| Please, give it a try? |

I sigh, groan, whimper, and then put down the coffee mug and grab a glass for water. My Navi erupts in cheers and applause, and a big "Congratulations, Phoebe!" flashes in the emergency notifications area. I experience a short battle between rolling my eyes and grinning and seem to manage to do both at once. But I make sure the grumpy expression has the last word. Screw Past-Phoebe and all her good intentions.

That afternoon, Mila walks into the Lovely Pines rest home with slow steps, her head down and her face drawn. As she approaches the front desk, the security guard, Jerry Armstead, stares into his Navi display, oblivious to her presence. She taps on the desk.

His eyes refocus. "Sorry, Ms. Bremer, I kinda got lost in my Bible study. Sorry about that." He looks her over and then tilts his head in concern. "You doin' all right today?" As he speaks, he pulls out a clipboard and pencil.

Mila signs in on the clipboard. "No, Jerry. I don't feel well."

He shakes his head. "Well, don't give your momma any germs, now. Lord knows all these old people don't need to be gettin' sick."

"No, I don't believe I'm contagious. I . . . feel unwell . . . in my head."

"Well, hold up." Jerry looks at her intently for a moment and then says, "Nope, Susan don't see nothin'—nothin' diagnosable, anyway. Guess you can't be too bad off."

"Susan?"

"My Navi. I like her to have a sexy name. Gave her a sexy voice, too—wish you could hear it." He grins widely.

Mila shakes her head, not quite cracking a smile. Her head down again, she moves slowly down the hallway, through double doors, and into the main recreation area. She scans the room, which contains a number of older folks in various stages of decay, and then approaches a plump, silver-haired woman in a wheelchair in the far corner. The woman's head tilts down at a sharp angle, practically hanging from the neck bone, her chin resting on her chest.

"Mrs. Bremer?"

The woman doesn't respond. Mila sees that her eyes are closed. She straightens up and glances around as if to see whether anyone has noticed her, whether she can perhaps leave. She rubs her hands over her face. But then she shakes the woman gently by the shoulder. "Mrs. Bremer . . . you have a visitor."

The woman's eyes open slowly, and she looks up, seemingly confused at first and then brightening. "Oh my. It's so nice to have a visitor. Sit down, won't you?"

Mila pulls up a chair and sits. She rubs her temples as if suffering from a headache. "How are you feeling today?" she asks without interest.

"Oh, I can't complain, can't ever complain," Mrs. Bremer says placidly. She eyes Mila, obviously trying to place her. "You look so much like my daughter. But you're a few years too old, of course. My Mila went off to college. And her hair is short. She likes having a short cut to her hair. The magazines call it a pixie cut."

"Yes, ma'am. I'm a friend of Mila's. Mila will be visiting tomorrow, but she wanted me to stop by and see you."

"Oh my, that's sweet. That's so sweet of her." Mrs. Bremer eyes her, noting her slumped shoulders and drawn face. "Are you feeling all right, sugar?"

"I don't feel well. It's not important. Mila says to tell you she got a 4.0 again."

"Oh, wonderful! Do you know her from college?"

"Yes, ma'am. I'm a teaching assistant working on my master's degree. That's how I met her."

"Oh, good. Good. So Mila has a friend? That's so good. You know, I have always worried about Mila making friends. She has never seen the point in it, you know. She has always had her head in a book or in a computer. But I have always told her, you have got to have friends. Otherwise, you get old, like me, and you don't have a soul to come and see you."

Mila doesn't say anything. Her face has a pained expression. "Do you want to play a card game?"

"Oh, yes. I love card games. Do you—"

Mila interrupts, sounding too exhausted to keep up the charade. "Cribbage? I love cribbage. Let's play cribbage."

"Oh, wonderful! I was going to say, I *love* cribbage. Here, let's ask these nice people for the cribbage board and cards . . ."

Mila gets up and goes right to where they're kept on a bookshelf on a nearby wall. When Mrs. Bremer studies her curiously, Mila says, "I've visited other people here before."

"Oh, that's nice," Mrs. Bremer says. "So you like to volunteer at places like this?"

"Yes," Mila says. She shuffles quickly and places the deck face down, and both she and her mother choose a card. Mila comes out the dealer, and she starts counting out cards.

"That's thoughtful," Mrs. Bremer says. "So many of the old folks here don't get any visitors. It can be a sad place here, you know."

Mila clenches her jaw. "I know."

The two women look at their cards. Then Mrs. Bremer flips over the starter card. "Oh look, it's a Jack. You get his heels."

"Yes, ma'am." Mila puts her elbows on the table and hunches forward as she moves her peg two spots up the cribbage board. Then she rests her head on one hand as she surveys her cards.

They've started counting out cards and making pairs and runs when Mila groans. "I'm sorry, Mo—Mrs. Bremer. I'm not feeling so good. I have to go, I'm sorry."

She bolts up from the table, leaving Mrs. Bremer sitting open-mouthed, and runs to the women's restroom, where she is briefly sick. Then she flushes the toilet, rinses her mouth, and washes and dries her face, which remains inscrutable all the while. Her hands tremble.

Not long afterward, Mila walks to her apartment with the slow, cautious movements of someone who is feeling horrible, and she lets herself in. She steps into the kitchen and pours some apple juice from the fridge. She takes a wary sip of it.

Taking a box of crackers from the pantry, she walks back into the living room. Her gray cat mews from the sofa, and Mila sits carefully beside her.

"Something happened to me today, and I don't know what it is." She nibbles at a cracker and stares at the cat, who stares back. "I don't feel good at all, and I don't know why I don't feel good. And I can't even remember how it started, really."

The cat mews. She stretches out one paw toward Mila and squeezes her eyes shut in that universal cat expression of affection.

Mila strokes the cat slowly, then takes a few more nibbles of the cracker. She swallows hard and takes another sip of juice. Then, putting a hand to her forehead, she winces.

"I know I had a meeting with my boss. But I don't remember the meeting well. I had such a headache. I think. And after that . . ." She trails off. "This has never happened to me before, and I don't see why it would have happened, and I don't like it at all. But something . . . something is happening to me."

The cat puts her head down on the sofa.

"I left work early, since I was feeling bad. I went to see Mom at the nursing home."

The cat doesn't respond.

"She always talks about me making friends. I'm getting tired of hearing it."

The two sit silently for a bit.

"But I'm trying. You know? Oh. I didn't even tell you. I met someone yesterday, in fact." Now there's distress in her tone. "Her name is Phoebe."

Mew. The cat looks up.

"I'm not sure what to do about it," Mila says. "It's a problem."

The cat begins to purr loudly, and Mila rests her hand against the cat's throat as if to feel the vibrations.

"It would be fine if she didn't want to have dinner with me. But she does, tonight. So, yeah. Phoebe."

The cat mews again.

Mila sighs and rubs her throat, under her jaw. "Maybe my glands are swollen. But it only hurts on this one side."

Mila falls silent after that. She eats several more crackers and finishes her juice while petting the cat.

The apartment becomes so quiet that only the hum of the air conditioning unit can be heard. Then the refrigerator comes on and adds its hum to the stillness. The apartment grows quite dark as the sun sets outside, until Mila and the cat are only dark shapes on the light-colored sofa.

"I'm going to go take a nap," Mila tells the cat quietly, standing up. "Sleep this off before I have to meet Phoebe at nine o'clock." The kitty purrs again and leaps off the sofa to follow her to the bedroom.

A few hours later, Mila stands outside Cat's Diner, looking about for Phoebe. As she watches silent people approach and leave the restaurant, she shrugs and rolls her shoulders periodically as if trying to loosen tension. The day is windy and overcast, making it chillier than one would expect for Atlanta in May.

Phoebe appears from around the corner of the building, her curviness and straight brown hair easily recognizable from a distance. She approaches Mila, smiles, and says, "Hi."

"Hello," Mila replies, unsmiling.

After a moment, during which her smile fades, Phoebe says, "I guess we should go inside." She gestures toward the diner.

Once inside, Mila steps up to the hostess and says, "I'll need a server to come take my order."

The hostess's eyes widen in surprise, and then she says aloud, with the over-eager tone of someone trying too hard to be accommodating to a person with a disability, "Of course, ma'am. That's no problem at all. No problem. Will you be needing a physical menu also?"

"No, I know what I want."

"I can order for you if you want," Phoebe offers.

Mila shrugs.

The waitress glances from one woman to the other. "Do you still want the server to come take your order, ma'am?"

"No, it's fine," Mila says.

The server leads them to a booth. Mila takes a seat, unfolds her paper napkin, and then places it in her lap. Phoebe follows suit.

The restaurant is quiet other than some light pop music in the background and the sounds of some young children in other booths. Everyone over age six speaks to one another via Navi.

Phoebe clears her throat and asks, "So, what are you planning to order?"

A few people look over at the sound of the out-loud voice.

Mila looks up. "I'm sorry?"

"Oh. I was asking what your favorite meal here is. What you like best."

Mila rubs a spot under her jaw. "I always order pecan pie and coffee."

"Oh," Phoebe says.

Mila starts to sigh and then redirects the movement toward refolding her napkin.

Some of the other patrons' gazes have become pitying. They've realized that at least one of the women is a Nonnie.

Mila offers reluctantly, "And at other places, I always get a baked potato and a salad with Ranch dressing."

"I guess no one can screw that up, huh?"

"Right."

There's a moment of silence. Phoebe's eyes move about as she looks at something on her display. Mila looks off to the side, toward the windows and the night sky outside. A few minutes pass. Then Phoebe focuses on Mila again.

"I placed our orders. Um . . . So, I wanted to tell you, thank you for saving my dog."

"You said that already."

Phoebe's cheeks flush slightly. "So I did." She straightens the napkin in her lap and takes a drink of her water. Then she asks, "So, what do you do?"

"With what?"

"I mean, for a living."

"I'm a computer programmer."

"Oh." A moment passes. "I'm a nurse. In the neuro ward of Grady Hospital." She looks hopeful that perhaps this information will provoke some conversation.

"Ah," Mila says.

Phoebe stifles a sigh. Again, her gaze unfocuses, giving her the same blank look that almost every other person in the restaurant has. Mila glares at her briefly and then goes back to looking out of the window.

Phoebe refolds her napkin again—aggressively this time—and straightens up in her chair. The set of her shoulders suggests that she's made up her mind about something. She begins, "We've been having a busy couple of days, since I met you. There have been dozens more new cases than normal, and the cases are bizarre, too. People are coming in with extreme anxiety or aggressiveness. I've also seen some—"

The waiter brings their food and sets it on the table.

Resolutely, Phoebe continues. "—some cases of extreme addiction to bizarre behaviors." She takes a bite of her scrambled eggs. "One person was addicted to video games to the point of not eating or sleeping or going to work, and that's not unusual, but another person came in because he was so addicted to candy that he wouldn't eat anything else and he wasn't doing anything else other than buying and eating candy. I've never had to help someone detox from candy binging before." She takes another bite.

Mila only picks at her pecan pie, but Phoebe doesn't notice.

Phoebe grimaces. "So, tell me about your computer programming. Where do you work, what kinds of things do you work on, and do you like the work?" Her tone is commanding. She seems determined to have a pleasant conversation.

Mila sighs and takes a tiny sip of coffee. Then she settles back in her chair resignedly. "I work at a company called ENI. I code to unit tests. A unit of code is a small piece of programming that is supposed to bring about a highly specific result. The unit test places this bit of code into an artificial context, supplying test inputs and ensuring that the output is correct. If each unit of code works correctly, then the final product will work properly in the end-user's experience."

Phoebe blinks slowly and nods. "So you put pieces of the program into isolation. That makes sense."

Mila tilts her head to the side and raises her eyebrows. "Most people don't understand anything I just said the first time through."

Phoebe smiles. "Do you like your work?"

Mila pauses. Finally, after taking another reluctant bite, she says, "If I were a shark, programming would be the ocean."

Phoebe's eyes widen and she nods slowly. "Nicely put." Then her eyes refocus on her Navi.

A few moments pass while Mila stares at Phoebe, unnoticed.

Phoebe giggles at something she's hearing or reading, and Mila grimaces and looks away. She eats a couple of small bites of pie and rubs the place under her jaw again.

After a bit, Phoebe's eyes refocus on the eggs and pancakes cooling and congealing on her plate. Then she looks at Mila, her eyes wide. "Oh, I'm sorry. I got distracted with some messages. I didn't mean to do that. I'm sorry. I'm a jerk." She sounds alarmed. "I hope that wasn't too insensitive to your . . . condition."

Mila grimaces again and doesn't answer.

"I mean, I'm assuming you can't take a Navi. Right?" She sounds cautious, afraid of being snapped at. "I mean, it's not by choice?"

"That's correct."

Phoebe nods. "But you don't use a smartphone, either."

Mila says nothing.

Her eyebrows knit, Phoebe asks tentatively, "Is it for religious reasons?"

Mila tilts her head to the side again. "No, of course not. Why would it be religious?"

Phoebe's forehead smoothes out. "Well, there are some people like that. My family, actually. They're called 'Plain people.' Have you ever heard of that?"

"No."

"They used to be called Old Order Mennonites, but my family belongs to a sect that branched out from the Mennonites. Anyway, they avoid modern technology. No Navis, no TVs, no computers. No cars, either. And they're called 'Plain people' because they wear simple clothes and have simple homes and furnishings and stuff."

Mila doesn't respond.

"My family lives in Zanesville, Ohio. Little town about an hour from Cleveland. About twenty thousand people. My people own a bunch of land and have farms and gardens and such. They don't interact with the outside world other than the mail carrier and whoever else they can't avoid. Most people think it's weird . . . I don't usually tell people about them . . . actually."

"It sounds peaceful." Mila takes a sip of her coffee. "I like it quiet. That's why I don't have technology. I like it with me and my cat."

"Ah."

They fall silent again.

Phoebe's eyes unfocus as she interacts with her Navi some more. Mila stabs at her pie.

"I'm sorry," Phoebe says for at least the third time in the last thirty minutes, but this time, her voice is strained, her face stricken. "I got an emergency message about my little brother. He's in the emergency room. I need to go the hospital. I'm sorry, I'm going to have to go now."

She stands up as she speaks, and then she stops, her eyes widening.

"I forgot. Damn it!" She squeezes her eyes shut and freezes for a moment. Then she comes back. "I forgot that my car is in the shop and I took the rail here. I hate to ask, but can I please, please, please get a ride from you?"

Mila stares at her, unblinking.

"It's that it'll take more than an hour to get to the hospital from here by rail, and it'll take forever to get a cab here . . ."

"Yes, I can give you a ride," Mila replies. "But we do have to pay." She unzips her backpack and starts to dig in it.

"No, no. I'll handle it." She taps her forehead, suggesting that she'll pay by Navi. "I'm supposed to be paying for you anyway, remember? I want to get to the hospital. Please?"

Mila zips the backpack closed again. "Fine. Let's go."

THREE

I've already messaged Jamie four times, and he's not replying. My heart is pounding, my stomach is sick, and now I'm wishing I hadn't eaten anything. I authorize payment for our meal at Cat's Diner, and then I direct my Navi to connect me to the ER. Once I'm connected, I verify my identity, confirm my relationship to Jamie, and pull up the ER report. As I do so, I hardly notice Mila taking me by the elbow and leading me to her car. She directs me toward the seat, and I grope for the belt buckle.

> !!! Warning. You are about to ride in a manual-
> drive car. !!!

> !!! Such vehicles are responsible for over five
> thousand deaths and forty-three thousand
> injuries annually. !!!

As if I don't have anything more important to think about right now.

I read the ER report.

Jamie's not hurt, but he's sick. In a nutshell, it says he's uncontrollably violent and forced to wear restraints, which makes no sense to me at all, because Jamie doesn't have a hint of violence in him.

Jamie's only eighteen, a sweet kid in his freshman year of college at Georgia State, and the only blond in the family. He left home about six months ago. He followed me here, out into "the world," as my community puts it, after I left them all behind in Ohio. He was the other one to turn away from the ways of my family and religion, and it was surely because of my influence. I have yet to figure out whether I feel guilty or happy about that. But my parents will never forgive me.

Jamie and I are the only ones who have Navis, and that didn't go over well, either. If I'd known better, I never would have told my parents. They would never have found out otherwise. There's no tell-tale sign. I can take a phone call in my head the same as I could out loud. There's never any background noise on the call, but otherwise . . .

I'm just trying to distract myself from what's happening now.

Oh, how I wish I'd gone to his party last night. But then a surge of anger hits me as I piece together what must have happened to Jamie. Somebody must have given him street drugs that resulted in a psychotic break. My big-sister protectiveness sets in, and I'm ready to kick some ass. Just as soon as I know whose ass to kick . . . but for that, I've got to get a clear story out of Jamie.

I connect with one of the nurses I know who's on duty at the ER.

> < Darla, my little brother Jamie is there in the ER.
> Can you please look at him and patch me in? >

> << Sure, sugar. Just a minute. >>

I wait impatiently, tapping my fingers on my knees.
No, I can't handle waiting. I look at my notifications.
In addition to the usual, there are two voice mail messages from my family members. They've found out about Jamie somehow.

> < Navi, reply to all messages about Jamie that I'm on
> my way to the hospital to handle the situation. Then
> go to busy mode. >

> | Busy mode confirmed. |

> | Reply-all messages confirmed. |

Busy mode is brutal, and I hate to ever use it. It goes to text mode, turns off my news feed, and filters out all personal notifications unless they come from people I've favorited and also contain certain keywords that I've spent quite a bit of time setting up. Or unless I initiate the conversation. It will, however, auto-reply to the other personal notifications, letting them know I'm on busy mode.

The worst part, though, is that when I turn busy mode back off, there are a lot of messages that I still won't see. Because I'll be so far behind, it'll only catch me up on personal notifications and broadcast items from my favorited people—and then only the ones that are also about my topics of interest. Important items always get lost.

Finally, the message from Darla.

<< Are you sure you want to see? It isn't pretty. >>

< Yes. >

| Authorize live video feed from
Darla? |

< Yes. >

The live video appears in my heads-up display, and if I weren't an experienced nurse who sees this daily, I would recoil. Even with the sedation, Jamie is screaming into his gag and throwing himself violently against his restraints. His eyes are rolling in his head. Bruises and blood discolor his face, and his clothing is torn. He's had quite a fistfight, by the look of it, and he's wild with aggression. Normally a peaceful, sweet, handsome kid, he looks like a convincing case for demonic possession.

I let out a slow breath as I look at the situation analytically.

It has to be street drugs. There's no other possibility for something like this. Unless he's experiencing the onset of schizophrenia. Or bipolar disorder. But this doesn't look quite like either one.

Then my mind goes to the epidemic of new cases that I've seen in the past few days. There have been several who looked like this—looked like Jamie. Those cases had just been a curiosity a few hours ago, but now they feel malevolent, terrifying. Now I need to know what's going on.

> < Okay, thank you, Darla. I'll be there in a few minutes. >

I feel a light touch on my arm and look over. Mila is gesturing, telling me that, actually, we've arrived at Grady's ER. "Thank you—so much," I say as I get out of the car. I try not to run as I go in. There's no point in running. My Navi checks me in at the door, and I head straight to Jamie's bed.

In person, it's no better, although it's also no worse.

There's a tech sitting by him, watching him. Legally, nobody can be left alone while restrained. Even Navi surveillance isn't considered good enough.

I send him another couple of messages.

> << Jamie, are you in there somewhere? >>

> << Can you register this, Jamie? >>

No reply, no sign that he's getting the messages.

I lean over the bed and try to get eye contact. His gaze passes over me, but he doesn't seem to register that I'm there.

I check the report again to see which doctor he's assigned to. Thank God it's not Green. It's a Dr. Birer. I know it's unprofessional, but I recklessly ping her.

> < What's the status on bed #18? He's my brother. >

The response comes back almost instantly.

> << Read the report. >>

Gee, thanks, Doc.

I reconsider what I'm asking and then go straight to the source. First things first: determine whether it's street drugs or not. I have my Navi locate the lab, and I send them a message.

< When will the results be back from the blood draw on ER patient James Bernhart? >

Meanwhile, I message Dr. Birer again.

< When can he get another dose of Callex? He's uncomfortable. I'm happy to handle it. I'm an RN from Neuro. >

<< I'll tell his nurse. >>

Fine. I go hover around the dispensary until someone pulls the meds. On the way back, I realize that Mila is standing there, looking acutely miserable as she watches Jamie writhe in the restraints. I feel awful. I didn't even realize she followed me in.

"You don't have to be here," I say as the nurse administers the Callex to Jamie. I watch for any sign that it's taking hold. "You can go home. I'm sorry. I didn't mean to drag you into this."

Mila says, "Okay," and starts walking away.

"Wait," I call out, and I get a sense of déjà vu. "Can I have your email address?"

Mila stares with her frosty blue eyes. "Why?"

She's so damned unfriendly that I grit my teeth. "I was going to send you a thank-you for giving me a ride, but you know what? I guess I don't have to."

"No, you don't."

We lock gazes, but then I feel tears spring into my eyes and look away. As if I need this on top of everything else. Why am I even trying to connect with this person, who is more of a machine than a person anyway?

Mila answers reluctantly. "It's my work email address. I don't have personal email. Mila@ENI.com."

"That's okay, thanks anyway." I've already decided I'm never contacting her again. What kind of weird person doesn't have email, anyway?

When I look back up, Mila is gone. Fine. Whatever.

<< Priority call from Family. >>

< I'm busy. >

Oh, hell. Who am I kidding?

< No, I'll pick up. >

I pull up a doctor's stool next to Jamie's bed and speak subvocally. "Hello?"

It's my dad, of course. "Hello, Phoebe Esther. What's happened to James?"

"They don't know yet. He's okay right now, though, all right? He's resting comfortably."

I say this while I watch Jamie writhe and scream. It's a good thing phone calls via Navi don't have any background noise.

At least he's beginning to settle down. The second dose of Callex is helping.

"What do you mean by resting comfortably? What's wrong with him? Your mother said they couldn't give any real information over the phone. They said we had to come in, but you know how difficult that would be for us."

My people only drive with horse and buggy, although they'll ride in cars that others drive and even take airplanes. But it's a last resort, and Zanesville is ten hours away by car.

Honestly, if it weren't me or Jamie, they'd probably come anyway. But I know they won't come here for either of us. We're damned.

"They don't know, Dad. That's what I'm saying. Look, he's been admitted, and they're still running diagnostics."

"Do you know what happened? An accident, an injury, a sickness?"

"Oh, sorry. I didn't realize they didn't even—"

"Phoebe Esther, we are sitting here not knowing a thing about what's going on over there. Use your common sense. How could we know what's happening there in Atlanta?"

I close my eyes and take a deep breath. "He's not injured. I don't think there was an accident. Judging by the signs, I think it's probably a neuro problem of some—"

"Talk in plain language, Phoebe."

I take a second deep breath. "Something is interfering with his normal brain—with how his brain works."

There's a moment of silence while Dad tries to put this together with his limited medical knowledge. "You mean he's having a stroke or a seizure or something?"

"Yes, something like that. We don't know yet. Look, where is Mom?" I always prefer to talk to my mom over my dad.

"She's not available right now," he says in a commanding tone. "You can talk to me. Now, what are you doing for my son?"

I grit my teeth again. I'm rapidly losing all of my remaining patience, which has already been stretched to its limits. "We're doing everything we can, Dad. First, we have to wait for the blood test results to come back. That's the first step, and it takes time."

"Do you have competent doctors over there?"

"Yes, we have excellent doctors over here. You know perfectly well—" I stop and grind my teeth. It's not a good idea for me to lose my temper at my dad. Our relationship is strained enough as it is. "As you know, this is Atlanta's largest hospital and one of the best hospitals in the nation. I'll have more information for you soon."

"This never would have happened if he hadn't followed you out into the world. Nothing good could ever come of this. You led him into the world of Satan. I consider you personally responsible for everything that happens to him."

I don't even know what to say. I feel like I should want to cry, but I feel empty. My dad's guilt trips always feel like a stealth attack, and yet they should never be a surprise at this point.

<< Priority message from LabTech. Display? >>

"I got the message from the lab. I'll let you know when I know more." I disconnect, with a stab of guilt and defiance twisting my mouth on its way to my gut.

< Show me the report. >

I scan it quickly. It turns out that Jamie hasn't had anything. He hasn't even been smoking pot.

I can't decide whether I'm happy or dismayed, because that means it's neuro, just like the guys in my ward. It's the only thing left.

I take a deep breath. I should be reassured. Just yesterday, I was telling Davis that neuro disorders are eminently treatable.

Still, I hate this. For me, when I have to deal with these crazies day in and day out, there's always a certain amount of comfort in being able to say, "Well, at least it isn't me or anybody I love." Well, so much for that.

Dr. Birer seems to materialize at my side.

<< He's had two doses of Callex and he's still like this? >>

< Yes, ma'am. >

I stand up. Jamie is still writhing and muttering and fighting the restraints.

<< Well, let's see what we've got. >>

She leans over him and establishes eye contact. After a few minutes, she gingerly removes his gag. I imagine she's speaking to him via Navi, but she doesn't have me patched in, so I don't know what they're saying.

He laughs bitterly and starts shaking his head. He yanks against his restraints again, and after she makes sure she doesn't have any hair or loose clothing where he can reach them, she leans back over him.

Not being able to hear what they're saying is killing me.

After a couple of minutes, Jamie starts talking out loud again. "Get me out! Let me go! Right now!"

He flails around, and his eyes land on me. He freezes for a moment. This time, he seems to be calm enough to process what he's seeing.

<< Sis? >>

< Yeah, Jamie. I'm here. >

<< Let me outta here. You gotta let me out. I can't take this. >>

< If you can promise to be quiet and still, then we can let you go. I'm sorry, I know that's really frustrating, but you have to promise not to fight. >

<< Oh, screw you. >>

I blink and raise an eyebrow. That's not Jamie at all.

< Jamie, I'm serious. They aren't allowed to let you go until they know it's safe for all of us. >

<< I'm not going to hurt anyone. >>

<< Dr. Birer: Patch me in, please. >>

I grimace.

< Navi, include Dr. Birer with Jamie. >

< Jamie, you said that you wouldn't hurt anyone. Will you promise to be quiet and still and calm? >

<< Yeah. I promise. >>

His eyes are still wild. He's still breathing hard. But that could be the restraints—they make people upset and frustrated. They make some people claustrophobic.

Dr. Birer waves a couple of techs over, and they release Jamie from the restraints.

The moment they do so, he jumps off the bed, howls like a wild monkey, and runs, knocking over medical equipment as he goes.

I start running after him, along with everyone else. At least the sedatives have him slowed down, and he doesn't get far. Mostly, though, that's because on his route out of the room, he gets distracted by a beautiful red-headed technician and throws himself at her, knocking her to the floor, pawing at her chest, and trying to kiss her. She flails and shrieks.

I scream in my head.

< Jamie, no! Stop that! >

The techs pull him off her and onto the floor. Each one of them grabs an arm or a leg, and they haul him back to his bed. I shadow them. In their wake, nurses pick up the medical equipment he's spilled and examine it for damage.

Jamie howls, and I scold him via Navi as the techs tie him back down. Then I put my hands over my face. I can feel that I'm beet red.

This may be the most mortifying moment of my life. I've seen plenty of humans rendered hypersexual, hyperaggressive beasts by their misfiring brains, but I've never seen it happen to someone I know and love. I have a whole new perspective now.

A few hours later, Jamie is upstairs in my ward, but on the south side. He's been given a court order for involuntary confinement, and the night shift doctor, Dr. Abadi, has ordered him kept in restraints for the next few hours.

Of course, his Navi has been put on lockdown, too—the same thing he'd get if he were in prison. He can't interface with the outside world, only use apps that he already has installed in his Navi that don't require internet access. And he can only message people who are hospital staff who have the appropriate medical clearance or visitors who are inside his room.

Applying lockdown is something only the doctors can do, but it's a simple-enough procedure, judging by the fact that they glance over at the patient for a moment and then make the note in the chart that it's been done.

We've gone through a modified repetition of the earlier excitement four times. Each time we give him a high enough dose of Callex—and now Altipar, too—to calm him down, he asks to be released. And since we know better by now, we talk him through a whole litany of promises to behave, but he loses his patience with that after a few minutes and gets hyperaggressive again, proving we can't release him.

I don't think I can handle going through it again.

It's illegal to hold him in restraints for more than four hours, though, so we'll turn him loose in one of the padded rooms shortly so he can move about, restore normal blood flow, and all of that.

I'm afraid to have him given higher doses of the sedatives, because he's already approaching the limits of what can be given without risk of long-term brain damage. But I'm also afraid that if we can't interrupt the cycle of misfiring that his brain is locked into, it'll become deeply entrenched.

Dr. Abadi hasn't been in yet to render a diagnosis and provide a prescription, and I'm slowly going crazy myself. I pace his room in a state of acute misery.

Dad was right. This is my fault. If I hadn't let Jamie come here . . .

No. I shake off the self-blaming. If something was going to happen to Jamie's brain, it would have happened no matter where he was living.

Unless he was under tremendous stress here that I didn't know about. Maybe college in the big city was proving to be too much, and he didn't think he could tell his big sister.

Which would mean it was my fault after all.

I realize that I haven't updated my family in several hours, and I summon up the force of will necessary to call my dad.

< Call Family. >

My dad picks up on the first ring, which means he's waiting by the phone, which is remarkable, given that the phone isn't even in his house. It's in the bishop's house, where the religious authorities can monitor its use. Voicemail messages are transcribed by the bishop and delivered by his children to the relevant house, and unless there's an emergency like this one, calls have to be scheduled with the bishop. "Inconvenient" barely touches it.

"It's about time, Phoebe. We've all been waiting to hear. You do know we're worried sick."

"There's no news, Dad. Nothing new to tell you. He's still the same as he was. We're waiting on the doctor to get here to make a diagnosis."

"After all—"

I cut him off. "I'll call back when there's something to tell you." And I end the call.

I'm grateful that Dad doesn't have a Navi. He can call and leave a voicemail message—that's the extent to which he can invade my brain, and that's enough. I can even have my Navi block his calls and auto-delete his messages if I need to. I hope it'll never come to that, but let's face it, I already had to leave the state of Ohio because of that man.

Well, that's not fair. My whole family is a product of the religious community they were raised in. It's the community I hate, and everything about the community that expresses itself in my dad— the control, the guilt trips, the judgment . . . especially the judgment.

Living Biblically, according to the Plain people, requires what I consider to be superhuman feats of self-discipline and self-denial on a daily basis—plain clothing, head coverings, no art, no musical instruments or recorded music, no computers, no TV, no dancing, no alcohol, and most of your time spent working or praying. If you deviate for a moment, you're unworthy of God's grace and sure to forfeit salvation. And if you go out into "the world" as Jamie and I have . . . well, the world is ruled by Satan. Enough said.

Well, whatever. There's nothing I can do about my family or my community finding me unworthy. All I can do is put as much distance between us as I can. Whether God will find me unworthy is something I try not to think about, although I always thought that a god who would make you a rebellious, free-spirited person and then punish you for it was kind of a jerk.

Dr. Abadi finally comes in with the night-shift RN for the south wing, Deonte, behind her, and I breathe a huge sigh of relief. It's funny how my perception of the doctor shifts when I'm a patient's family member instead of a nurse. Suddenly, the doctor looks like a savior instead of the pain in my rear end.

Dr. Abadi observes Jamie for a moment and probably runs through his chart via Navi. Then she surprises me by patching me in to her conversation with Jamie.

<< Hi there, Jamie. How are you feeling? >>

<< I'm getting tired, Doc. >>

<< That's good. We need you to rest. You're going to feel a whole lot better afterward. Tell me, what are you feeling right now? >>

<< Amped up. Super amped up. I'm so bored and pissed off about being tied up like this. I want out real bad. >>

<< Okay, I hear that you want to get out of those restraints, and we're going to do everything we can do get you out of them as soon as we can, all right? But I have to ask you a lot of questions, and it's going to get boring. I need you to stay patient with me, all right? >>

Jamie nods.

The doctor runs through the standard intake questionnaire and screening tools that I've witnessed hundreds of times. By the time we're halfway through, it's clear to me that this is another case like Davis—another case like all the other new ones we've been swamped with in the past couple of days.

| Deonte: I just got the word. We're officially on drive-by. |

< God bless. >

I put my head in my hands. A dozen questions later, Jamie reaches the end of his patience and starts thrashing around like a wild animal again. Nearly in tears, I shake my head. I want this to stop. I want Jamie to go back to being the adorable brat I know and love, not this monster who has devoured Jamie's brain and is taking up his body.

As a matter of protocol, Dr. Abadi gives Jamie the option of signing in to the neuro ward as a voluntary patient, and, of course, Jamie reacts with screaming and curses, so the doctor renews the involuntary commitment and leaves. Then, two techs come in and escort Jamie to a padded room, which he's going to have to share with another patient, because we're running out of rooms.

Once the room is empty, I lose it. I bawl like a baby.

I tell myself that I'm just not used to this. Normally, I meet patients when they're seriously ill and then get to watch them turn into reasonable human beings as the medications start working and they get discharged. I'm not used to seeing it go the other way.

But it's not just that. It's the fact that something is going on. Something is happening in Atlanta, something mysterious and horrible. But I tell myself that I might as well assume that Jamie and all the others will respond to treatment normally, regardless of what's causing it, and I get the tears under control.

I can't bear to call my dad again. I send a voice mail message to the bishop's phone with assurances that Jamie has been given medication that'll kick in quickly and that he'll be in good shape within a few days.

I hope that was all true.

I try to patch into the live feed to Jamie's room, so that I can keep an eye on him, but the system won't let me. I'm only authorized to watch the rooms on my wing.

Well, it's probably better that way. There's nothing else I can do right now. It's in the hands of other professionals.

I realize that I'm exhausted, so I stand up with the intention of going home to a well-deserved mindless movie and a good night's sleep.

Naturally, that's when the message comes in from the charge nurse.

> << Sorry to do this, Phoebe, but we need you here. We
> got put on drive-by, and we can't handle the workload
> without you. It's all hands on deck. >>

I squeeze my eyes closed and groan.

< Amusingly enough, I'll be there in about three minutes. >

The charge nurse, Mary Anne, calls a meeting with Sara, Deonte, myself, and the other night shift RN to catch us up on what's going on. The hospital administration reported the influx of cases to the State of Georgia this morning, and they, in turn, informed the CDC—the Centers for Disease Control and Prevention. They're headquartered in Atlanta, not that that does us any good. Anyway, they've done some initial assessment to confirm that there's an outbreak, and an epidemiologist from the CDC has already given the syndrome a name of its own: UAAD, Unspecified Anxiety and Aggression Disorder.

As I pointed out to Dr. Green, most of these patients aren't having delusions or hallucinations or any of the usual accompanying symptoms that would aid in a conventional diagnosis. There are also the extreme addicts I'd mentioned to Mila, but right now, no one is sure what to think about them, and apparently, nobody's up to adding another A to the acronym.

Then Mary Anne confirms my worst, secret fear. We've now had enough time with the earliest-admitted patients, like Davis, to know that not everyone is responding to the meds in the usual ways. Some patients are proving nonresponsive, and others are having unusual side effects.

"We're about to start a series of molecular MRIs to determine what's going on with these patients. Also, the CDC is sending us a panel of investigators to hunt for common elements that would suggest cause or mode of transmission. They'll be looking at possible diseases, environmental exposures, food supply, medical history commonalities—the whole nine yards. Cooperate with them, please, even though they're going to slow us down during a time when we can't afford that."

Then Mary Anne hits us with the scariest part. This may be happening nationwide. Houston is seeing similar cases. I think all of us leave the meeting with a feeling of apprehension.

I team up with the night shift RN on my wing, and we dive in. The next few hours are a whirlwind. I spend a lot of it jogging from one task to another, one emergency to the next. At first, I tell my Navi to let job-related messages through as they come, but within fifteen minutes, I'm forced to put it on sleep mode—otherwise, I wouldn't be able to finish a thought, let alone a task. In sleep mode, nothing comes through except emergency messages.

Even though I'm busy and I shouldn't, every time I finish a task, I go back to normal text mode and look at all my messages, even the social ones. I reply to a few of the most enticing each time. It eats up a few minutes, and I feel guilty, but I'm helpless to resist the siren call. I hate being out of touch, knowing that there are unread messages piling up out there in the ether somewhere.

My Navi flags me around two in the morning to tell me that I haven't eaten in too long, and I stop by the break room. I get some snacks from the vending machines and then eye the coffee. I've been running on adrenaline so far, but I'm going to wear out soon. And then me and Past-Phoebe are going to have a little chat about coffee.

> < You guys, I quit coffee this week. I don't know why
> I did that. Why did I do that??? >

I get a surprising amount of commiseration, given the late hour.
I glare at the coffeepot.
Wait. I never promised I wouldn't take caffeine in pill form.
Take that, Past-Phoebe. Shoulda been more specific, Past-Phoebe.

> < Aha! Caffeine pills FTW! >

I run down to the gift shop/pharmacy and grab some pills with caffeine and B12. Then I get back to work.

Around four in the morning, the charge nurse broadcasts a priority message, not bothering to try to get us all in one place for a meeting this time.

> << Functional M-MRIs are showing excess activity
> in the amygdalae of patients with UAAD. Eight out
> of eight scanned so far. >>

> << Allan: Then it's got to be either a disease or an en-
> vironmental thing. >>

Both possibilities make me nervous. I want to know what's
going on with Jamie.

> << Tolony: Could it be a mass hysteria thing? Or is
> that even an actual thing? >>

> << Allan: I dunno. Could be. >>

> << Sara: Okay, maybe this is crazy all by itself, but
> could it be a Navi malfunction? With the program-
> ming? >>

That's an interesting thought, although an odd one. I remember
that Navis had some strange issues in the first year or so, like making
people lose their short-term memory for a few hours. Of course, by
the time I got mine about seven years ago—when I was eighteen—
they were already perfected. The Navis were so exciting, so desir-
able, that the pressure to get them error-free and highly secure was
intense enough to guarantee all the funding the companies needed
to fix them fast.

> << Mary Anne: Not likely. That's like blaming a pace-
> maker for heart disease. >>

Dang. Quite the shut-down.

Mary Anne's answer makes sense, though. The Navis are an
audio/visual tool and nothing more. That's why it's called a NAVI:
Native Audio/Visual Interface—although the rumor is that the programmers who developed it borrowed the name from an old anime
called *Serial Experiments Lain*.

Anyway, the functionality is limited by design: pieces of the
Navi are installed into each optic nerve and each cochlear nerve to

make sure the signals can't go wandering around in the brain. Well, to be fair, there's also the subvocal receiver in the larynx. Not that I'm an expert on this stuff, but everybody gets the spiel right before they get the implant, and from what I remember of the diagram, no part of the Navi has any business doing anything to the amygdalae, which are in a different part of the brain.

By eight in the morning, the disorder's name has been changed from UAAD to UOAD: Unspecified Overactive Amygdalae Disorder. And yes, the hyper-addicted people have it, too.

It drives me crazy how new diseases get renamed half a dozen times before everyone settles on something. Hospital staff pick their favorites and then fight about it. I'm confident that at least three people on my ward will refuse to stop calling it UAAD on general principle.

I think only briefly about telling my Collective about what's going on here at Grady, and I'm surprised at myself when I dismiss the idea. Normally, I tell my Collective all my personal news, no matter how trivial. I think it's denial, like if I don't tell anyone, it isn't real, and Jamie will go back to normal soon.

At nine o'clock in the morning, we're released, and the alternate-shift people are called in. We're all going to be trading twelve-hour shifts each day until this situation is resolved.

The moment I clock out, I go check on Jamie, and I send up a prayer of gratitude when I see that he's sleeping.

I start to head home. As always happens when I work an overnight shift, I'm confused to discover that it's daylight outside.

Then I put on my sunglasses and head toward the parking lot and go right to where I normally park and stare at the empty parking spaces for an embarrassingly long time before I remember that my car is still at the shop.

And then I remember Mila. It all feels like it happened years ago and to someone else.

I head to the nearest metro stop. At least, now that it's tomorrow, with all its bright sunshine, the light rail has resumed its daytime schedule. A few minutes later, I'm on board a train.

I turn off busy mode at last, and I let my Navi tell me how many messages I missed, just to torture myself. It's one hundred seventy-three. It's so painful, everything I've been missing, but I know from past experience that it's not possible to catch back up once I'm this far under.

With busy mode off, I have about thirty-five messages that pop up that meet my criteria of favorited people and topics. I scan them, but I'm too wiped out to respond to them.

< Navi, give me your best romantic comedy. >

A few minutes later, my display fills with the opening frames of a movie, and my ears fill with a soundtrack designed to help me ignore my aching, exhausted body and anxious mind.

As I get off the light rail, my Navi informs me that Sunlight bakery has hot, fresh donuts half a block down. It tells me this every time I get off night shift, but these last few months, I seem to have no willpower. I go down there and get a dozen donut holes.

My Navi gives me increasingly dire warnings about going over my allotted calories for this twenty-four-hour period while I eat every last one.

Screw you, Navi.

The next day—Wednesday—I wake up early in the afternoon. Still sitting up in bed, I immediately check Jamie's patient records. Since I'm family, I have access. What the records say is that he awoke at around ten in the morning with no emotions at all.

FOUR

On top of having a *flat affect*—inability to feel or express emotions—Jamie also has memory impairments. He woke up not knowing where he was or what had happened recently. But he's totally docile and apathetic, so he didn't even ask. They had to ask him.

< Go dark, Navi. >

I bury my face in my arms as my Navi shuts down all optical input and puts me into a blackout.

I try to decide just how bad this is. At least he isn't suffering. He's not unhappy. But he will experience no joy, no pleasure, until some kind of treatment can be devised.

With the expert pessimism I've honed, I start to think of other problems. If he doesn't feel strongly about anything, he may become suggestible, and if his empathy is also impaired, he may continue to act anti-socially. And with the memory deficits to consider—well, he can't be left on his own.

It's irrational, but I'm convinced that I've lost him, that I'm never going to have Jamie back the way I knew him. The certainty settles into my stomach, and I want to be sick. I give Tobi a big hug, as if that's going to take away the pain or the anxiety, and it doesn't. Then, immediately, my mind is working again, trying to figure out what's going on and how to fix it.

How could he possibly have shifted so dramatically overnight?

< Navi, go bright. >

Once my vision fades in, I notice that his chart also shows that he's been scheduled for another M-MRI and CAT scan. I also see a notation that he had his court appearance this morning by video conference. On the recommendation of Dr. Abadi and another doctor—two psychiatrists have to agree to any commitment—his court order has been extended for seven days. Ironically, by the time the court appearance happened, he was agreeable to staying in the hospital, but they still made the commitment involuntary on the basis that his condition is "unstable."

Which means they have no idea what's going on with him.

I check my messages to see whether anyone from the hospital has sent out any new information about the disorder. Nothing new. Then I message my counterpart at the hospital to ask what they've learned today. After that, I do a media search to see whether there's any news about it yet, but I don't find anything. I set up a TellMe-When trigger to let me know if anything comes out about it.

Finally, with a heavy heart, I go ahead and turn on busy mode. I can't handle any distractions right now.

< Navi, Info-me about the relationship between emotion, memory, and the amygdalae. >

The awesome Info-me app assembles the most relevant and best-validated information on any subject for me to scan. A few minutes later, I'm reminded that a lack of emotion and memory impairment can both be caused by severe damage to the amygdalae. The research talks about diminished fear and anxiety as well as effects on the reward center, which impacts motivation and motivation-based learning. Having a flat affect also happens with schizophrenia, which implicates the amygdalae, too, but schizophrenia has already been ruled out with these UOAD cases. And memory impairment is also common with amygdalae damage.

I rub my face and try to figure out how Jamie could have gotten his brain damaged without anyone noticing. Plus, this doesn't explain why he started off with heightened emotion and then flipped over to none at all.

An errant impulse has been tugging at me. I want to check on all those messages I'm missing. Busy mode is an effort to hold off messages until I can focus on them, but right now, I'm more bothered by being out of communication. I'm not at work today, so I might as well release the floodgates again.

< Text mode. >

| Text mode confirmed. |

I go ahead and scan through the old messages and give my Navi instructions. I group-reply to half a dozen messages that Jamie slept peacefully and is better today. I'm not ready to tell them the truth yet . . . although, technically, I do think a flat affect is better than outright psychosis. Then I delete about half the remaining messages, make a couple of one-time payments, and unsubscribe from a couple of newsletters.

Then a headline in my news feed catches my attention: "Atlanta Police Shoot 3 Suspects to Death in 72 Hours." I select the story.

Atlanta Police Shoot 3 Suspects to Death in 72 Hours

Area Assaults, Homicides Up 120%

According to an unnamed source within the Atlanta Police Department, police have shot and killed a record 3 suspected violent offenders in the past 72 hours. The shootings, for which no official statements have so far been made, coincide with an unprecedented 120% increase in violent crimes such as assaults and homicides in the Atlanta metro area.

Our source, who is a law enforcement officer, states that the uptick in crime is primarily in "unmanageable perpetrators such as what we'd typically see in PCP drug users." He could not comment as to whether those sorts of suspects are the same as those shot by police in recent days.

Police Commissioner Robert Nguyen was not immediately available for comment.

I rub my face with my hands. I just realized that Jamie is one of the lucky ones. He got brought to the hospital before he got shot by the cops.

I'm chilled by the realization that they're shooting people who have neurological disorders. Not that this sort of thing doesn't happen normally—anyone who attacks a cop is going to get shot, regardless of whether it's a medical problem, a drug problem, or a judgment problem—but my God . . . And then my vision focuses in on the unexpected name of Mila Bremer in my notifications panel.

I stare for a moment, reading and rereading the name and the single line next to it: "How is your brother doing?"

Not shot by the cops, I want to say. *So at least there's that.*

I heave a sigh.

I don't know how I feel about Mila contacting me.

I don't know how I *should* feel about Mila contacting me.

I remember how I found her forlornly standing there staring at my writhing, screaming brother yesterday and then how she said "Okay" and walked out when I said she could go. I remember the awkward-doesn't-even-start-to-cover-it dinner in which she was all but monosyllabic. But she did give me a ride to the hospital when there was nothing else in the world more important to me. And there's still a chance that she has some sort of neuro disorder of her own, which means I shouldn't take any of it personally.

And she had to have looked up my email address somehow. I didn't give it to her.

I decide that I owe her cordiality, at least.

< He's improving, thank you. Thank you for the ride yesterday. It meant a lot to me. >

There. Done. And done with all the outstanding messages. Not that that ever lasts more than a nanosecond.

I dive back in to my research.

| Call from Family. |

< Ignore. Navi, Info-me about diseases affecting the
amygdalae. >

I read about Urbach-Wiethe syndrome, Kluver-Bucy syndrome,
and herpes simplex encephalitis. UW is a slow-onset degenerative
illness—definitely not what's happening here. KB can happen as a
result of the herpes simplex encephalitis or after a stroke. I blink a
few times, wondering whether Jamie could have had a stroke overnight. I'm sure someone would've noticed.

KB has a lot of other bizarre contributing factors, none of which
seem relevant to Jamie. The encephalitis, though . . . I don't know
much about that. I scan the information and compare the sympto-
mology with Jamie's file. He has psychiatric symptoms, obviously,
but that's it—that we know of. His records don't mention fever,
seizures, vomiting, or focal weakness, and they would have. He
might not self-report headache or memory loss. Still, though, with
no other matching symptoms, this one seems unlikely.

Mila's name in my notification panel draws my eye.

| Mila: What's wrong with him? |

Okay. I hadn't expected that.

I wonder how disturbed she might have been by seeing him in
that state. I think about it for a moment and realize that while I may
be jaded about seeing people in that state, other people might get
freaked out about it. Mila seems like a calm person, though.

< It was psychosis. Now it's a flat affect and memory
deficits. Functional M-MRIs show too much activity
in the amygdalae. >

I get up and pad to the kitchen with Tobi behind me. I glare
at my cold, inanimate coffeepot and take a caffeine pill. It's a poor
freaking substitute, but I am going to need caffeine to get through
this week.

I head toward the shower.

| Before you shower, you should go
for a run. |

| You have requested reminders to
jog before breakfast. |

< No. Leave me alone. >

| Exercise boosts mood, improves
sleep, and helps resist stress. |

< Navi, *leave me alone*. I am *not* going for a freaking
jog this morning. >

| If you do it, you will be glad you
did later. |

I stop walking halfway down the hallway and put my hands
over my ears, as if it'll help. It won't. I know I've already lost. I'm
going to go freaking jogging.

I lose this fight on all my days off. I don't know why I continue
resisting. Aren't people supposed to develop a hardwired habit after
thirty days of repetition? It's been *months* for me, and I still want to
take a jog right off an overpass when I get the reminder.

I go get dressed in my running suit and put the leash on Tobi,
who rewards me with bounding excitement, and we head out.

As we run along the path my Navi has set for me, following the
directions in my display, I turn off busy mode and send a message to
my Collective. It takes me a few tries to figure out how to phrase it.

< For those who don't know, my youngest brother
Jamie is in my hospital—Grady Hospital—with
some kind of neuro disorder. No, he's not in my wing,
but the other one. Prognosis is somewhat uncertain
right now. There's a new disorder of some kind going
around, and he seems to be part of it. But don't panic.

No reason to think there's anything contagious going around. Anyway, I'm worried about him, but hopefully he'll be all right soon. >

I post it and wait only seconds before the supportive messages start to come in from my Collective, making me smile despite all the stress. It's good to know that people care. I soon post a clarification.

< He can't receive messages right now due to his fragile mental state. But if you send them to me, I'll read them to him next time I see him. >

That results in a few more messages specifically for Jamie, which also makes me feel good.

Along with the other responses comes another message from Mila.

<< What's causing it? >>

< I'm not sure. There are theories. Maybe environmental, maybe a disease. Someone proposed that it could be the Navis, but that doesn't make sense. >

Her response comes surprisingly quickly this time.

<< Why doesn't that make sense? >>

< Because Navis don't interface with the amygdalae. >

I remind myself that she doesn't have a Navi. She's probably never heard the spiel that everybody gets right before the implant process.

< I know you don't have one, but trust me. The CPU and the SRUs—Send/Receive Units—make sure no signals go anywhere else in the brain. It's hardwired to be impossible. >

<< No, it isn't. >>

I wrinkle my forehead and think for a moment.

> < What do you mean, no, it isn't? >

> << It's not hardwired. >>

I count slowly to ten—or at least try. I get to three.

> < Why are you saying that? Everyone knows that
> they're hardwired. >

> << Everyone is wrong. >>

I stop running long enough to shriek in frustration. Tobi cowers, since he usually only hears that sound when I catch him chewing up another pair of my shoes. I pet him reassuringly and compose a remarkably (I think) patient reply.

> < Could you please explain in detail, because I don't
> know what you're talking about, and it's important to
> me, and I would very much like to understand what
> you're saying. >

But I can't help the follow-up.

> < And how would you know, since you don't even have
> a Navi? >

I sit and wait for a moment. No reply.

> << Heart rate dropping below maximally beneficial
> level. >>

I groan and push off again. For a moment, I feel and enjoy the sensation of the warm summer air against my sweaty skin and the piston-like pumping of my legs propelling me along. That lasts about three seconds, and then I'm scanning updates from my Collective. Cute puppy videos, silly optical illusions, cupcake recipes—anything distracting is fine by me right now.

<< Speaking of cupcakes, there is a Red Velvet bakery on the corner one block away. They are offering a 25 percent-off coupon for only the next ten minutes. >>

< Shut up, Navi. >

God, I'd love a cupcake from Red Velvet right now.

Finally, the email comes in. It's quite long, and I convert it to text on a semi-opaque background so I can scan it quickly. I can still see the sidewalk behind the text, so I don't have to worry about accidentally jogging off into the street. Besides, my Navi would warn me if there were any obstacles or dangers ahead.

> When Navis were first released, there were numerous security holes which occasioned numerous lawsuits, as you may recall. As the software became more sophisticated and the risks decreased, attorneys for the manufacturers argued that these devices were "secure" to the point that they could begin to defeat claims for negligence, and some part of that discussion caused the non-tech-savvy judges to misinterpret them as saying that the security was "hard-wired."

> This was to the advantage of the companies, so they never clarified. It was written that way into the legislation and into judicial opinions and then into news stories, and so it became common parlance. Those who deal with Navi security know better.

> The reality is that Navis are extremely secure for a consumer device but still hackable. Successful hacking happens, albeit rarely. The manufacturers settle the lawsuits out of court in exchange for non-disclosure agreements.

> The electrical impulses that travel the nerves are managed by the SRUs, as you said, to ensure that they are confined to the auditory and visual nerves. But the

SRUs can be reprogrammed to fail to do their job or to do it differently. Impulses can go anywhere in the brain if they are so directed.

And I program Navis for a living.

I trip over something—maybe my own feet—catch myself, and stop running, bending forward with my hands on my knees as I catch my breath and try to reconcile myself to this new information that the implant I put in my brain isn't secure. I suddenly have the disconcerting feeling that there are eyes and ears inside my head, listening to every word, watching every action I take.

I mean, besides the eyes and ears I put there myself.

I feel queasy.

I have the instinctual desire to rip the implant out of my head here and now. Of course, that's impossible to do on the spot. Each of the nine pieces are nestled into my brain tissue, humming along, integrated. But I've heard of people having them removed. It's not supposed to be difficult. It can be done through the tear ducts once the installation nanobots are directed to break down the components. I start to wonder how much it costs, how much it hurts, and how quickly I can schedule it.

Then good old rational thinking kicks in to protect me. Sure, Navis may not be safe, but everybody has one. They can't be that bad. Mila said hacking was rare. And I've never known a single person to have a problem with their Navi.

Unless UOAD turns out to be a problem.

I tell my Navi I'm going home early. I've passed the fifteen-minute minimum I originally imposed on the programming, so it obediently routes me back toward home, and I start jogging along again, Tobi still trotting by my side.

I realize that I wouldn't even know how to get home right now without my Navi. I look around. There's a skyscraper on my left, a mid-rise apartment building and a strip mall on my right. Some restaurants, a salon. I don't recognize a single landmark. Why would I? I always have my Navi to orient me, to tell me whether there's anything important for me to look at. And I don't drive myself—my smartcar drives me. I've hardly ever made note of my surroundings since I was a teenager, since I got my new best friend installed.

How in the world does Mila even program Navis if she doesn't have one? She can't test them.

Then I remember what she told me before—unit coding. Each piece of software is programmed in isolation. As long as it produces the right outputs, the overall application will do what the end user needs it to do.

The bouncing is making my stomach feel even worse, but it'll take forever to walk home, so I keep running.

I tell myself that there's no reason to suspect that it's the Navis. The CDC is looking for an environmental or disease-based cause. They'll find something.

I don't want it to be the Navis.

An hour later, showered and dressed and with two cupcakes from Red Velvet in my belly, I turn Tobi over to Mrs. Jones, take the light rail to finally pick up my smartcar from the body shop, and then head to the hospital to see Jamie. In his current state, it probably doesn't matter to him whether I'm there or not, but I want to see him. Medical charts never tell you what an in-person visit does.

On the way, I feel the familiar heart palpitations and tightness in my chest and realize that giving up coffee wasn't enough—at least not while all of this is going on. I ask my Navi for a suggestion for anxiety, and it reminds me that meditation is a good, science-based intervention, proven more effective than drugs.

> < Navi, silence everything and give me a calming meditation. In fact, always remind me to do this when I head into work. Starting as soon as I check my messages in the morning and stopping when I get to work. >

> << Preferences updated. >>

<< What image would you like for the meditation? >>

Hmm . . .

< The beach. >

My vision and hearing are blotted out entirely, replaced by a video. Waves wash up peacefully, and palm trees sway in a gentle wind. Gulls sound out.

Tension drains from my body. All that's missing is the smell of the salt water, but I can imagine it easily enough.

I make it about eight seconds before I'm itching to check my message feed again. I tell myself that the ride to work is only about fifteen minutes.

Fifteen minutes sounds like a long time right about now.

I try to settle my mind again and look at the scene. The rolling waves are nice. I take long breaths.

Then I can't stand it anymore.

< OK, Navi, end meditation. >

<< You have not arrived at work. >>

< I know that. How long has it been, though? >

<< Four minutes. >>

< Are you freaking kidding me? >

<< I am not programmed to possess a sense of humor. >>

< Okay, I'll do three more minutes. >

That sounds heroic to me.

And, in fact, it feels like twenty more minutes before my Navi interrupts me. My vision and hearing slowly return to the usual, and I heave a sigh.

As my smartcar pulls up at work, the crowds and lights out front pull my attention. Four police cars ring the entrance to the hospital, their lights flashing, the cops leaning against their cars and survey-

ing the situation. Three media vans sit on the walkway with reporters in front of lights and cameras. Throngs of people cluster near the
reporters or stand around aimlessly.

My heart sinks. I'm pretty sure I know what this is about. I ping
the charge nurse anyway.

> < What's going on at Grady? What's with the cops
> and media? >

I don't get an answer right away. I imagine she's busy. I join the
cluster of people near a reporter and listen in. Soon enough, I hear
that it is, in fact, about our favorite amygdalae disease, which has
now been renamed to Hyper-Aggression Disorder, or HAD.

I can imagine the jokes now. "I've been had, she's been had, we
all have HAD."

The reporter intones, "The hospitals here in Atlanta have been
overwhelmed. Every neurological disorder ward has been filled to
capacity and then overflowed. Grady Hospital is the first to reded-
icate portions of other wards to handle the influx of patients, but
other hospitals are expected to follow suit in the next twenty-four
hours. Hospital administrator Bruce Atwell is scheduled to give a
press conference here at eleven o'clock, and his assistants tell me
that he plans to detail the efforts of the Centers for Disease Control
to identify the cause of the disorder. Meanwhile, if you observe
anyone with unusually aggressive, anxious, or repetitive behaviors,
hospital staff urge you to keep your distance and call 911."

Things are getting serious around here. I don't like this at all.

A few minutes later, as I'm heading up the elevators, my TellMe-
When trigger starts sounding off. The news reports start coming in
with headlines like "Mystery Brain Disease Strikes Atlanta with
Aggression, Anxiety" and "Atlanta Area Hospitals Overwhelmed
with New Neurological Disorder."

Then the blog posts and the retweets and the reposts start flooding in faster than I can read them. As I'm walking down the hallway
to Jamie's room, people are putting in so many "I've seen it, too"
comments from around the country that it becomes clear it's a na-

tionwide problem, not an Atlanta-specific one. There are a few references to potential cases overseas, too.

I modify the TellMeWhen trigger to only ping me when there's new information, something I haven't heard yet.

My heart is thudding in my chest again. Now I feel anxious, and feeling anxious makes me feel more anxious. Am I feeling anxious because I'm having problems with anxiety in general or because there's some bizarre neurological epidemic happening . . . or because I'm coming down with the bizarre neurological epidemic myself?

I tell myself that it's the first option.

Naturally, the moment the news comes out, my Collective starts pinging me, wanting to know whether I've seen this at my hospital, whether it's what Jamie has, and what's causing it. They want the inside scoop. I group-reply that it's what the news articles are saying—nothing else to add. I pretend to miss the part about Jamie.

For the first time, it occurs to me to wonder what this disorder looks like as it first hits. Out of morbid curiosity, I do a search. I soon find a series of videos tagged HAD. New videos are being added by the minute, with hundreds of alternately mocking and panicked comments.

There's a series of short clips with one woman in a clothing store. This one shows the addiction aspect rather than the aggression or paranoia. As the video starts, she carries an armful of dresses across the line that automatically tallies the total and deducts the money from a credit or bank account via Navi, and she drops the armful of clothing directly on top of a shopping cart already full of items. As she does, she flushes and her face takes on an expression of wide-eyed bliss. She stops and closes her eyes, apparently basking in joy.

The person taking the video adds a quiet comment, "This is the fourth time she's come through to buy stuff." The view shifts over and shows another basket next to the first one, also heaped with clothing. "That's all her stuff. She keeps going around and getting more stuff and putting it in the baskets. I mean, what the hell? I guess she won a shopping spree or something."

The video jumps, and it's the same woman with another armful of clothing coming through and putting it into the basket. She stops again with the same expression of bliss.

Then again. And again. The commentator says, "This is trip number six. Look at all that stuff. She's probably spent a couple thousand bucks."

Twice more. The woman's cheeks are permanently flushed now, her eyes glittering wildly.

The next time, a male store employee approaches the woman. They appear to speak via Navi. The man puts his hands on one of the baskets as if to push it away, and the woman's face twists into an ugly scowl. Things happen too fast to follow, and then the woman slaps at him viciously with both hands, and the man tries to fend her off. The commentator cheers on the fight.

I stop the video, feeling nauseated. I scan the headlines of other videos.

> "This guy gets thrown out of Wal-Mart for trying to eat everything in the cookie aisle."

> "Even a bucket of ice water won't get this kid to stop playing Slipdaisy."

> "WATCH: Granny goes after Grandpa with an axe."

Okay, that one would be freaking hilarious if it wasn't so disturbing.

When I go in Jamie's room, he's sitting placidly in one of the chairs next to the bed, probably looking at something on his display. His blond hair is unkempt, giving him a just-woke-up kind of look. He glances up at me, and his face remains blank.

I sit down gingerly on the edge of the bed, avoiding any fast movements.

He messages me.

> << Hi, Phoebe. You're new. But you're not a nurse. >>

I don't say anything for a moment. I'm trying to come up with some other interpretation of his words, some way to convince myself that he still knows who I am. His Navi would have told him my name. I'm not sure it would bother to mention that I'm his sister. Usually, people already know these things.

I have that feeling you get when there's a step down that you didn't notice and so you unexpectedly drop those few inches.

< Actually, I am a nurse at this hospital, but I'm not in my uniform, because I'm just here to visit you. >

<< Oh, okay. Thanks for visiting. >>

His eyes resume the distant look people get when they're engrossed in their Navis.

< Can I ask you some questions? >

<< Sure. >>

< Where do your parents live? >

His brow furrows, and he tilts his head a bit.

<< I don't remember. Isn't that funny? I'm not sure. >>

< Do you remember anything about yesterday? >

He looks thoughtful.

<< What's today? >>

< This is Wednesday. Do you remember your birthday party on Monday? >

His eyes get a faraway look.

<< Yeah. I think so. There were a lot of people. I played music. So I think so. >>

I debate my next question for a moment. The Jamie I know and remember will be unhappy with me over this . . . if he ever comes back, and if he ever finds out . . . but I'm asking for his own good.

< May I review your Navi archive from these last few
days to see if anything unusual happened? >

<< Okay. >>

Yeah, definitely not the Jamie I remember.

I take a deep breath and turn on my disinterested-nurse mind-
set, just in case I learn something I don't want to know about my
littlest brother. Then I request access via his Navi and back up to
Monday morning. All Navis keep recordings of the past 72 hours for
exactly this reason, in case it's needed by law enforcement or medical
personnel.

A few minutes later, I'm both disappointed and relieved to know
that Jamie is—or at least was—the bratty but sweet kid I thought he
was.

He didn't have any Monday classes, so he did laundry and
cleaned up his apartment. Then his party was fun but not crazy,
without drugs or too much drinking on his part. The only surprise
is the visit from the girlfriend I didn't even know he had. The little
twerp has been keeping one secret. But even watching that part
makes me smile. The two of them are sweet together.

Then people leave, and they start making out. I grimace and
fast-forward.

Tuesday seemed like an uneventful day at first. He attended his
3D rendering class and a biology class via Navi, told some folks he
was going to eat dinner in the college cafeteria, headed over there—
and started assaulting people.

As I'd expected by this point, I can't see any provocation. I back
up and rewatch the thirty-minute transition from normal Jamie to
wild-animal Jamie several times, but there's no reason for him to
flip out.

What bothers me more at this point is why he's flipped over to a
flat affect and memory loss. Is this going to happen to other victims
of HAD, too?

I sigh and disconnect the feed. Jamie still sits placidly. I recon-
nect long enough to look at what he's doing right now: watching

an old action movie from the hospital's library, which is accessible specifically to people on lock-down.

<< Call from Family. >>

Ugh. I let it go to voicemail, which I hear a couple of minutes later. I learn that my family has heard the news about HAD somehow, probably from interacting with shoppers in their community store or maybe from the mail carrier. They want to know whether it's what Jamie has.

After thinking it through carefully, I dictate a voicemail—one of the best uses of a Navi, in my opinion—that says that the media is hyping it up and it's not all that, but yes, he has it, and yes, I'm confident that he'll be released from the hospital soon.

A smidgen of that isn't a lie.

I focus back on Jamie.

< How are you feeling in general? Do you feel okay? >

<< Sure, I guess. My wrists are kinda sore. And my stomach is tender for some reason. >>

Sore wrists would be from fighting the restraints, and the stomach tenderness is probably from the fistfights he got into yesterday.

< Well, you can message me if you need anything, okay? I'm here at the hospital a lot. >

He doesn't reply.

Once I'm outside the room, I lean against the wall, my stomach feeling like a stone.

I desperately want to reach out to someone, to tell someone what's happening, to gain that comfort and reassurance. But where would I post that my youngest brother doesn't know who I am anymore? It's too painful, too frightening to say to my Collective. I'm not ready to tell any family members. It'll break my parents' hearts if they find out, because if he doesn't know me, he won't know them either. So who can I tell? I don't have any friends who are that close, with whom I would entrust this kind of secret.

For some reason that I don't fully understand, I message Mila.

< Jamie doesn't recognize me anymore. He doesn't know me. >

With that message released into cyberspace—with someone else knowing—it's more real, and I feel tears start in the corners of my eyes. I rub them back, frustrated with myself. I cried yesterday. That was enough. No more crying. No pity parties here. Jamie's not suffering, and he's only one of thousands who are affected by this thing. It's a freaking pandemic, and I can be part of solving it. I decide to put on my scrubs and go see if the CDC people can use my help before I have to report in at 8 p.m.

At about seven thirty, my Navi forces me to stop and eat something, so I go down to the hospital cafeteria and load up on a veggie pasta and check the news. Stories about HAD are coming in from cities across the United States, and reports of HAD overseas keep coming in, too. The number of victims is going up by the minute.

A news video shot here in Atlanta says, "Although officials continue to assure the public that there is no evidence as yet that the disorder is contagious, many people are withdrawing into their homes."

The video cuts to an older lady, who tells us, "I came out to pick up some groceries, and I promise you I'm goin' right back home afterwards, and ain't nothin' gettin' me back out 'till they find out what's doin' it. I don't want to catch it, whatever it is."

The newscaster goes on. "Numerous people have had sightings of those afflicted with the disease, and fear is gripping the city."

A middle-aged man this time. "I saw a guy sitting there in his car. It was a manual-drive car, but he was just sitting there, blocking traffic. Finally, somebody came to see what was going on and if he was okay, and he busted out of there and started swinging. He took out the other guy like it was nothing. And then he sat back down, right there on the ground, and—and did nothin'. Sat there."

Back to the newscaster. "According to officials, the man was playing an online poker game rather than driving, and he didn't want to be interrupted."

Ugh.

For my part, I've been helping give questionnaires to patients and their friends and family members while other CDC team members have been analyzing microbes and any traces of physical substances left on clothing and in people's homes. I've talked to several CDC workers, and the universal answer has been that, so far, they have no idea what's causing this.

Meanwhile, the CDC and the World Health Organization are doing regression analysis and demographic analysis, and other than that, they're hand-waving and saying that they're "exploring possibilities."

I asked three people from the CDC whether the Navis could be implicated. They all looked at me like I was crazy and tried to explain to me that Navis are hardwired to be incapable of *yadda yadda yadda*. To two of them, I relayed what Mila had said. They both looked thoughtful and serious in response, but then they had to move right on to the next activity before they had time to respond. Regardless, it's obvious that no one is planning to investigate the Navis as a serious possibility, at least not yet.

As I finish the bread that came with my pasta, I decide that it's time I try to do something with this information Mila gave me.

Dr. Abadi should be arriving for night shift. Of course, I don't have to see her in person to talk to her, but I've noticed that Navi messages delivered by someone standing nearby seem to carry a greater urgency. And I think this is urgent.

I find Dr. Abadi in the locker room, praying in front of a *murti* image in the door of her locker, and I wait for her to finish. When she walks toward me, I hold the door open for her.

> < Sorry to bother you, Dr. Abadi. May I give you some information and ask a question? >

> << Go ahead. >>

She doesn't look at me as she heads out into the hallways. I follow one step behind her.

> < I was discussing the emergence of HAD with someone who programs Navis for a living. She assured me that although this is not common knowledge, it's possible for people to hack into Navis. >

Dr. Abadi halts briefly in front of the nurses station, probably telling them something via Navi.

> < She says it happens, though rarely, and the manufacturers settle the lawsuits out of court and have the victims sign non-disclosure agreements. >

Dr. Abadi is in motion again, and I follow.

> < The CDC workers tell me that they aren't finding anything that could explain this disorder. I think we should investigate the possibility that the Navis are implicated. >

Dr. Abadi pauses outside a patient's door and looks at me.

> << What would this investigation look like? >>

I think quickly, since I hadn't thought this through in detail yet. As I do, I feel a massive headache coming on.

> < We'd probably need a Navi installation technician, maybe the Navi programmer I mentioned. The Navi technician and programmer would probably have to drive the investigation, since it's a technical issue rather than a medical one. >

> << I don't have time to deal with this, so you set it up. Be sure you get patient consent or family consent for each patient. You're merely looking for issues and not

> providing any treatment. As soon as you need a doctor, notify me. Don't shirk your own duties. >>

> < Understood. Thank you. >

> << Oh, and make it legit. You have to get a properly licensed and bonded technician in here, not some random Navi programmer you know. >>

She's already stepping into the patient's room.

I let out a long, slow breath and rub my aching head. Okay. I hadn't intended to end up in charge of this, but I guess it makes sense, given that it was my idea. I mentally gear up to face an even heavier workload than I was going to be facing already.

First things first.

> < Mila, we need a technician who is licensed, bonded, etc. to do Navi troubleshooting to come out and investigate your suggestion that the Navis are implicated in the amygdalae disease. Can you recommend someone? >

This headache has intensified. It's making me nauseated, and I'm starting to get the vision flares that mean it's going to become a migraine soon. I think back and realize that I haven't taken a caffeine pill in a while, so I take one plus a few ibuprofen and curse Past-Phoebe again. I have no idea what she was thinking, giving up coffee.

FIVE

Half an hour later, Mila plays a hand of cribbage at a table in the Lovely Pines Rest Home across from her mother. Mila's face is tight and tense. The wrinkles in her forehead suggest that she still isn't feeling well. She's currently winning the round, with her peg about eight places ahead of Mrs. Bremer's.

They've been talking for a while, and now there's a break in the conversation. Mila plays a seven of clubs, and her mother says, "That's twenty-three," and plays a seven of hearts. "And two points for me." She chuckles gleefully and moves her peg.

Mila finally speaks, her voice reluctant.

"There has been a new disease happening. Nothing to worry about, nothing contagious. But I know one of the nurses at Grady Hospital, and she asked for some help with it."

"Oh, now, is that right? Do you mean she was asking you for help? Are you a doctor or something like that, honey?"

"No, I happen to be an expert on a particular type of industrial material, and they think that might be what's making people sick."

"Oh, now that's awful. That kind of thing used to happen years ago, back when they used . . . What did it used to be called? Something in the insulation?"

"Asbestos," Mila says, playing a two of diamonds.

"Oh, that's twenty-five. Yes, they used asbestos. But all that finished off when I was still younger. The last of the people that got sick with it died. They didn't know, of course, back when they were using it, that it would do any harm."

"Yes, this is like that."

"Well, you're going to help, aren't you, dear?" Mrs. Bremer's eyes widen expectantly, creating more wrinkles.

"I could ask one of my coworkers to help. It doesn't have to be me."

Mrs. Bremer studies her hand and then says, "That's it for me. It's 'Go' to you, sweetie. Now, can your coworkers help as well as you can?"

Mila frowns and admits, "Well, no. Probably not." She plays a five of spades.

"I'll bet you're about the best there is at whatever it is you do." Mrs. Bremer nods with a sidelong glance. "You are one smart girl. I can tell that from talking to you for this little while."

Mila shrugs.

"So if you're the best one to solve the problem, then you ought to do it, especially if people are sick. I tell you what, no one ever appreciates their health until they lose it, and then they realize that there is nothing more precious in this world. Nothing else matters when you're in pain or when you can't get around or don't feel good. It might as well all be over."

Mila looks at her cards, and Mrs. Bremer gives her another perceptive look. "You don't want to do it, do you?"

"No, not especially. I don't like to get out of my routine. I like how my days are. I go to work, I come visit—" She catches herself. "I go visit someone in a hospital or nursing home who might like some company, and then I go home to my cat. I like things how they are."

Mrs. Bremer chuckles. "Oh, honey. One thing I have learned in my time—things don't stay the way they are. Not for long at all. You might as well get used to that. And if things change because someone needs help, then that's a whole lot better than the alternative."

Mila says, "Yes, ma'am," but it sounds like courtesy, not agreement.

"So you'll help those nurses out?"

"It isn't my problem," Mila argues. "I shouldn't have to do it. It's nothing but trouble for me."

Her mother gives her a look. "I know you're not my child, but if it was my daughter I was talking to, I would say you ought to be ashamed of yourself if there's something you can do to help someone and you don't do it. That's what I would say."

Mila looks like she's being sentenced to a long prison term.

"If we only live for ourselves," Mrs. Bremer says, "we aren't living at all."

"Okay. I will help," Mila says, though it sounds like it may be through gritted teeth.

Mrs. Bremer beams. "Thatta girl. You'll be glad you did it."

When I wake up the next afternoon—Thursday—the first thought that hits me is, *Whoa. Jamie's girlfriend.*

Jamie has been cut off from his girlfriend and his other friends for at least a full day and probably no one has told any of them what's going on. Not unless someone in my Collective overlaps with someone in his—but let's be honest, what little brother would let that happen? Not mine.

I direct my Memory app to go back to yesterday's visit to Jamie, to when I was reviewing his memories of the weekend. From my video of his video, I pick out the girl's name and send her a message, although I have to take a few minutes to decide how to phrase it.

> < Tonya, this is Jamie's older sister. Jamie has been out of touch because he's in the hospital. He's okay at the moment, just a problem with how his brain is functioning, but while he's in the hospital, he's not allowed to talk to anyone. It should only be a few more days. I can let you know when he's been released or you can wait for him to contact you again. Please spread the word to Jamie's friends. >

This is an absurdly optimistic message, but I cross my fingers that it'll end up being that simple.

I realize that I'm exhausted. I've been working a lot in the past two days.

Before I can even form the next thought, Tonya has written me back. Seven times.

<< OMG HOLY CRAP >>

<< I HAVE BEEN CRYING MY EYES OUT >>

<< I thought he BROKE UP WITH ME >>

<< he didn't talk to me for TWO DAYS >>

<< I was so MAD >>

<< OMG OMG OMG >>

<< thank you for writing me >>

Okay then.

I'm so glad I'm not seventeen anymore.

When I left work this morning, it seemed that the wave of new patients had crested for the moment. The problem is that we're having trouble getting them discharged. The regular medications aren't working reliably, and Jamie is no longer the only patient who has flipped from hyper-aggressive to a blank slate. In fact, it seems to be a typical progression, affecting about fifteen to twenty percent of the patients.

I check my other new messages, and I spot one from Mila.

<< I will help. I've already talked to my supervisors about it and obtained the necessary approval to do the troubleshooting. I can come after work. Where do I go? >>

I blink in surprise.

< I thought you were a programmer. >

<< I hold a Class IV Navi Interface License from the DEA and a Georgia Department of Health certification with an in-situ repair rating. I started as a technician before I worked my way up to being a programmer. But my license and bond are still current. >>

My heart sinks for two reasons—first, that she wants to be the one to help, and second, that she didn't even respond to my message about how my brother doesn't know me anymore. Her offer to help is devoid of all emotion, just business. I do think that she might be on the autism spectrum somewhere.

Well, that's fine. At least I feel like she's a known quantity at this point. If she's on the spectrum, then I can rest assured that she probably doesn't mean to be rude. And it means that I don't have to worry about small talk or other social niceties. I can keep things simple and straightforward. I can't expect emotional responses, and that's fine, I tell myself. Why would I need anything else from this particular woman?

I message her some directions for tonight, and as I do, the headache from yesterday makes a vicious resurgence. I wonder if I'm having rebound headaches from taking too much ibuprofen the last few days. Or maybe I'm taking too much caffeine and this is withdrawal from the overnight break without a dose. I decide I'm going to have to taper off both caffeine and ibuprofen, and that's going to make the next couple of days even more special. For now, though, I go ahead and take some of both.

Heading off the annoying Navi reminder before it can even get started, I go for a quick run, but sans Tobi, since he's still with Mrs. Jones.

Just as I start off, my TellMeWhen trigger goes off, and I listen as my Navi reads to me.

I knew it wouldn't take long for someone to connect HAD with the police shootings, and I was right.

Preliminary reports show that over two dozen violent offenders have been shot and killed across multiple metro areas since the onset of Hyper-Aggression Disorder (HAD), which began on Monday and has swept the nation with over three thousand cases reported so far.

In most cases, the suspected offenders have been shot two or more times in the chest or face following or during an assault, armed burglary, or homicide or in the attempt of those crimes.

The police commissioner of Atlanta, Robert Nguyen, has issued a statement that police "always regret the taking of a life."

"Our law enforcement officials are trained to recognize threats of various types and to respond with lethal force only when they have no alternative and only to protect themselves or innocent bystanders."

The commissioner said that while they recognize that "the taking of lives of those suffering from neurological disorders is always tragic," sometimes such actions are unavoidable to protect the public.

Commissioner Nguyen has confirmed the deployment of police dogs and the utilization of riot gear, rifles, and shields in the public's defense against HAD.

Other metropolitan areas, including Houston, New York, and Los Angeles, have followed suit.

The dramatic increase in violent offenders—as high as 300% in some areas—is taxing resources, according to an anonymous source from within the APD.

"Now that we've recognized that these offenders are suffering from HAD, we are sending the survivors to neuro wards in hospitals for treatment," said the source.

The "survivors"?

I do not like for neuro patients to get shot. They need treatment, not riot gear.

My jaw clenched, I ask my Navi what else is new, but there's nothing. Hospitals are doing press conferences that echo one another's statements about being overwhelmed with patients and looking into possible causes, but nothing plausible has come up yet.

My Collective is officially freaking out. "Hyper-Aggression Disorder" is the top searched term on social media today. Some people are already wearing gloves and surgical masks or refusing to leave their homes, even though there's no indication so far that HAD is contagious.

But they're also coming up with jokes about the epidemic, like, "I think my girlfriend has HAD. She was strangling me, and our safeword wasn't working."

Ba-dum-tsh.

Actually, my favorite comment, in light of the above article, is "HAD + APD = DOA."

Amid the comedy and the hysteria, there are already some pretty stupid conspiracy theories out there. Since this seems to be somewhat US-centric so far, of course there are people saying that it's a government-created virus designed for population control. Others say it's terrorism, with one guy making a detailed outline of how it all goes back to the Lord's Resistance Army—never mind that it's been defunct since James Kony, the group's leader, died fifteen years ago.

Of course, I'm most interested in the Navi theories, but they're too crackpot for me. One lady with too many facial piercings says it's the Singularity. Our Navis have come alive and are trying to suppress the inferior intelligence of their hosts. I kind of like that one.

Another Navi theory is that it's an early attempt at mind control. We're all assured that they'll refine the process later on. Whoever "they" are.

For my part, I post calming reminders about the bird flu and the other pandemic scares we've had in the past thirty years. "Did everyone end up dying of Ebola?" I ask rhetorically. "No, we're still here. Don't panic."

I leave unsaid the fact that I'm investigating the Navis myself. I don't want to end up sounding like one of the conspiracy nuts.

When I get home after my run, my Navi prods me to go to the grocery store, clean my apartment, and do some laundry, but I tell it to leave me alone. Normally, I'm all over these chores, thanks to being trained by my parents to help around the house from age three, but I'm too overwhelmed right now. Lucky for me, these are low-intensity reminders, not the ones I programmed to be unavoidable.

I end up at the hospital hours before my shift is due to start, so I visit Jamie, who is the same as he was yesterday—disinterested in my existence and without personality. I miss my brother. He was a pain in the ass, but at least he was a person.

I check his chart and note that a new M-MRI has been run. The report says that both of his amygdalae show indications of deep lesions. That makes me feel sick. There's actual brain damage happening here. But what in the world could be causing it? I hate it that something is injuring his brain while he's sitting right here in the hospital, surrounded by medical staff who are unable to do a damn thing about it.

My forehead deeply wrinkled, I dive back into my project. I arrange for the assistance of a Navi install technician and write up the consents for the investigation that we'll be doing. Then I start going patient-to-patient to request the consents, trying to ignore the renewed pounding of my head as I do so. Of course, I have Jamie sign one of the consent forms, and he's agreeable, confirming my suspicion that he can't be discharged. I can easily imagine him letting other students walk into his dorm room and take anything they want.

I've collected eleven consents when I get a message from the nurse's station that Mila is there waiting for me.

Despite my worry, when I get there, I smile at her for some pointless reason. "Hi. Thanks for coming to help."

"Where are the patients to examine?" Mila asks, unsmiling.

"This way." As I lead her, I notice that I'm not offended by her lack of a greeting. I think I've come to terms with her neurodivergence.

We start with Jamie, even though I waver about it initially. If I admit it, maybe I'm afraid that Mila might accidentally do something that'll make it worse. But my strongest impulse is to help Jamie as quickly as I possibly can. Some part of me hopes against all reason that it'll be easy and fast.

"How are you planning to investigate, exactly? I mean, how do you gain access to someone else's Navi?"

She pats her canvas backpack. "I have a laptop computer in here."

"Oh," I say, feeling foolish. "So you can use the internet to talk to the Navis?"

"Yes. More or less. It's a wireless connection to the Personal Area Network."

"How do you get in? I mean, there's security, right?"

"Of course. I'll show you when we get there."

I clutch my head as we walk. This headache is a doozy. I notice I'm having some dizziness as well.

We hit a small hiccup when we try to start. That is, as soon as we walk in and get Jamie's attention, he starts heading for the door.

<< Gonna go out. >>

< Um, hold up, Jamie. You have to stay here. >

I get between him and door.

<< Don't wanna stay here. >>

He starts to push past me, and I have to strong-arm him a bit.

< Is there something in particular you need? I can bring it to you. >

<< I wanna go out. >>

< Jamie! Stop this instant. Go sit down! >

His expression doesn't change, but he hesitates, and then he goes and sits down on his bed. I let out a breath. I was worried for a moment there that we were going to end up in a fistfight.

Once he explains that he's just hungry, I order up some room service. A few minutes after that, I've made brief introductions between Mila and Jamie, and Mila has sat down and opened her slim, silver laptop in her lap. I scoot a chair over next to her and watch.

"Tell your Navi to open the Navi port, please," Mila commands Jamie. "Tell it, open 6284."

Jamie doesn't so much as twitch, but apparently it happens since she begins working.

It both fascinates and frustrates me to watch Mila interact with her laptop. It seems so painfully slow that she has to use her hands to interact with the device. She taps on an icon, types in a password, taps on "All discoverable devices," types in a "B," scrolls through a list and taps on "James Bernhart," taps "Request access," waits a moment, and then tells Jamie, "Approve the access request, please." A moment later, she sees "Access granted" and taps on "Open Navi interface."

"You can't give voice commands?" I ask, still clutching my head and still aghast at how time-consuming this is.

"I could, but it hurts my throat to talk all day. I'd rather use my hands."

I message my Collective.

<< You guys be grateful for your Navis. The old way is downright painful. >>

What she does after that loses me. She opens a black window and types nonsense words into it, and equally nonsensical responses scroll by too quickly for me to read. The brightness of the display makes me squint.

"What are you doing now?" I ask.

"Evaluating the processes that are running, to look for anything out of the ordinary."

"What does that mean?"

She looks directly at me with her pale-blue eyes, and I feel like I've been skewered with something sharp. I realize that I'm disturbing her. "Sorry. I'm going to go . . . do . . . nurse things. Just tell someone at the nurse's station when you need me again."

She goes back to scanning the text, and I leave the room. I'm practically staggering. Nausea hits in waves, and I almost duck into a restroom, but I decide it's not quite that bad yet.

I know I said I was going to taper off the painkillers, but I can hardly function at this point. I head toward the break room to get some water and take another couple of ibuprofen, but by the time I get there, my head has decided to start getting better. Whatever.

Two hours later, I'm able to catch a break and go visit Mila and Jamie. When I walk in, she's frowning and hammering at the keys on her laptop.

"Things going okay?" I ask.

"No," she replies.

I sit down and wait for a bit, but when it becomes apparent that nothing else is forthcoming, I ask, "What's wrong?"

Mila stops typing abruptly and sighs. "There's definitely some malware here that's been added to the Navi's security module and encrypted so that I can't get to it with the normal Navi security access."

She glances over at me, and I probably look confused, since she explains. "Navis have two main parts, the security module and the CPU—although the security module has its own processing chip. The security module manages security, obviously, and the power supply.

"Since Navis are powered by blood flow, there's no external power switch. There's no way to turn them off. When you tell your Navi to turn off, the main CPU just stops responding to anything but an order from the security module to 'turn back on' or resume normal functioning.

"The security module serves as the gateway to the rest of the Navi's functioning. It's also the same part that doctors and law enforcement use to reduce the Navi's range and functionality in a situation like this." She gestures at my oblivious brother.

I nod. My headache is coming back, and I rub the back of my neck.

"That's how the whole misconception came up about the security of Navis being hard-wired. When the manufacturers created the security module and separated it from the CPU and built a wall between them so that the CPU wasn't accessible without going through the security unit, it got interpreted as 'hard-wired security.' A misconception, though, as you can see."

Mila sighs again and stretches, reaching her pale, slender hands upward and arching her back. Her curly blonde hair swings back, and her chest rises, and I find myself staring. I quickly look away. She collapses again and goes on, "The point is, code has been added in that section that's referenced only from the CPU, and I can't get to it yet. But I can tell you this." She looks straight at me. "It's not what I thought it was. I told you in my email that the signals can simply be redirected elsewhere, but that's not what's happening. What I have been able to determine is this: the installation nanobots are missing."

I blink. "Missing?"

"Missing. Not docked where they're supposed to be."

My mind races. "Why didn't the M-MRIs pick up the location of the nanobots?"

"The nanobots are made of bio-identical substances and flexible polymers. They wouldn't show up in an M-MRI scan."

I get up and start pacing. "The nanobots are used during the installation process, I remember that. Do you know the details?"

"They unpack the components, assemble them, and send them to the appropriate locations in the brain. Beyond that, installation isn't my area of expertise. I troubleshoot function, not installation."

"I know who'll know." I message the installation technician I'd recruited earlier, and I patch him into my video and audio. Then I speak aloud so that Mila will know what I'm saying, even though every movement of my face is causing pain to radiate from my upper chest to the top of my skull.

"Abhishek, is this a good time for a couple of questions?"

<< Sure, go on ahead. >>

"What role do the nanobots have in the installation process?"

I repeat Abhishek's message out loud for Mila. "The installation takes place, as you know, through the carotid artery via hydraulic injection. All the components have to be assembled by nanobots as they enter the bloodstream. Then, the nanobots ping the optical and auditory cortexes to find the best installation locations—two at the cochlear nerves and two where the fibers cross where the optic cortex meets the eyes.

"Same thing for the auditory and optical processing chips on the sylvian fissure and occipital cortex, and the primary CPU on the motor strip."

< Abhishek, okay, so the nanobots "ping the nerves" to find good locations for installation. What does "ping" mean in this context? >

I read his answer out loud again.

"Those nerves aren't accustomed to receiving data input from those locations, so they have to be electrically stimulated to pick up the signals at first. Then they're able to learn to do it themselves afterward. The nanobots locate the most receptive spots on the nerves for the installation by giving them small electrical shocks and seeing which ones respond best.

"They also position the subvocal SRU and the power source, which remains alongside the carotid artery, using blood flow for the power for the whole system."

I'm already connecting dots. "So the nanobots can send out electrical shocks. If the nanobots went somewhere they shouldn't, then could that same electrical stimulation they use to find the optimal location cause problems?"

Ugh. Another wave of nausea hits. I get up and fill a paper cup with water from the room's sink, lean back against the counter, and take three ibuprofen.

Abhishek replies, and I read the message out loud. "I don't know for sure, but it seems unlikely to me. The intensity of the stimulation is quite mild."

I look at Mila. "So where does that leave us?"

"I can't tell you anything else yet. Only that they aren't where they belong."

"Okay," I say. "Thanks, Abhishek. I'll get back to you later if there's anything new."

> << Actually, I'm about to go home. I'm not feeling so well. But you can message me anytime if it's important. >>

> < Okay, thanks. >

I groan out loud with the intensity of my headache, and Mila looks at me.

"Sorry," I say. "I'm having a hell of a migraine. I think—"

Things go sideways, and I clutch at the counter, gasping. Then they go right-side-up again.

Mila is staring now. Even poor Jamie is looking at me.

"I think I might actually have to go home."

I'm trying to figure out how to get my legs to work properly when the door swings open and Dr. Green—he of the condescending nostrils—sweeps in dramatically.

"Stop what you're doing," he snaps.

Mila, Jamie, and I all look at him with what I imagine are equally blank faces.

"Your research here has not been approved by the ethics board, and it is not permitted to go forward. Nurse, get this civilian out of here." He waves toward Mila.

Civilian? Is this the military all of a sudden?

Mila snaps her laptop closed and stands up.

"Wait!" I say. A wave of rage is quickly eclipsing my agony and nausea, though the dizziness tells me it's a profoundly bad idea to let go of the counter. "Mila, don't go anywhere. Doctor, I have approval from Dr. Abadi to do this." Then I wince and grab my head.

As if on command, Dr. Abadi stalks in. She, too, speaks aloud, her voice low and tense. "This isn't a formal research study, Dr. Green. Your department doesn't need to approve it."

I freeze. I'm about to watch two doctors fight.

"Wrong, *Doctor*. They are researching a medical issue in live human patients. That is explicitly in the domain of formal research, and the ethics committee for the protection of human subjects must be involved. End of story."

"How is this formal research?" Dr. Abadi demands. "We have a licensed, bonded technician sent by ENI troubleshooting the code of the medical device. Troubleshooting is done by technicians all the time for all sorts—"

"I am sending you both a copy of the formal complaint right now," Dr. Green snapped. "Read it. With a formal complaint lodged, the research must cease until it has been thoroughly investigated. Those are the rules, and you know them as well as I do."

Dr. Abadi is obviously scanning the document at the same time that I am, because her olive face is turning crimson. "You filed this complaint yourself."

"So I did." He folds his arms.

"So revoke it!" Dr. Abadi said. "What reason do you have to oppose this? It will take months for a formal research study to be set up, and you know it. Explain this!"

The room seems to lurch around me, but all I see is Jamie's placid, staring face seeming to plead with me, and suddenly, I'm like Daniel entering the lion's den. "These patients don't have months. Something is happening to their brains right now, as we stand here. They are deteriorating. Something has to be done."

Dr. Green's nose turns up even further. "Need I remind you what will happen to you if you get another write-up, Nurse?"

My vision goes red—literally. It's my Navi flashing a red hue into my display, warning me. At the bottom of my vision, a message blinks urgently. This is the beginning of Red Mode.

> !!! Warning. Behavior not consistent with
> personal goals. You are having an
> argument with a superior. !!!

Some part of me whispers *Oh no*, but the rest of me doesn't care. Doesn't care at all. What I care about is my family and my patient, and with the kind of feeling you get when you're about to do something that's both courageous and idiotic, I step up to Dr. Green.

When I speak, my voice is low with rage. "Listen to me, you worthless son of a bitch."

My Navi shrills an alarm at me and my vision flashes a brighter red.

> | You have donated $10 to the
> Animal Control and
> Depopulation Society. |

I stick my finger right in his face. I can barely hear my own words over the shrieking of the siren. "I am going to find out what's wrong with my brother, and you had better not *dream* of getting in my way. I am going to—"

Dr. Green laughs. Loudly. And slaps my hand down to my side. "You can consider yourself fired, Nurse. Your supervisor will be processing the paperwork in a matter of moments."

And with that, he sweeps out of the room.

Dr. Abadi looks at me.

<< That was stupid. >>

Mila walks smoothly alongside me as I stagger down the hallway. I can't believe what happened, what I did. Normally, I would never, ever get involved in a dispute between doctors. Those strike hospital staff like the Apocalypse—everyone takes cover until it's over. I wasn't thinking because of how sick I feel.

My heart is hammering, and my breath is high in my chest. On top of that, I'm still dizzy, and my head feels like it might explode. I practically pant with the pain as I speak to Mila. "I shouldn't have done that. I really shouldn't have done that."

"No, you shouldn't have done that," Mila says calmly.

"Thanks. Thanks a lot for that very helpful confirmation."

She looks at me, and I think I might see a touch of amusement in the way she raises her eyebrows. "Well, you shouldn't have done that."

"Thanks again," I mutter, and I clutch my head again.

Right on schedule, I get the notification.

| Priority message from Grady Hospital Administration. |

I groan, but there's nothing I can do but suck it up.

< Show it. >

Dear Phebe Bernhart, Grady Hospital regrets to inform you that your employment has been terminated effective immediately. Please collect your personal items and depart from the premises. Your badge will be withdrawn in thirty minutes, and security will escort you out at that time if necessary. We thank you for your 1 years of service and wish you profitable employment elsewhere.

Screw you, Grady.

But my anger is weak, because I know this is my fault. My stupid bad temper has ruined any chance I had of being able to help my brother or any of the other patients. I tell myself I deserve every agonizing throb of my head and more.

<< Deonte: Dude, did you really get fired? >>

< How the hell did you find out already? >

<< What did you do this time? >>

< I can't even talk about it right now. >

<< Sara: Did you really just get fired? >>

I groan.

"Can you transfer him somewhere else?" Mila asks.

I stare at her. "Do what?"

"Can you transfer your brother somewhere else?"

I stop walking and stare some more. My brain is firing awfully slowly, but I see what she means, and I'm stunned that she thought of it already and I didn't.

She misunderstands my silence and explains, "The doctor's refusal to let you continue can only be enforced in this one hospital, right? If you can move him to another facility where they don't mind the research, then we can carry on."

"You're a freaking genius," I say.

Mila pauses, then nods.

> << Sara: Did you really cuss out Dr. Green? I would've loved to have seen that. >>

> << Thiago: Did you really get fired? That sucks. >>

Maybe Mila is a genius.

That gives me a shred of insight into the blonde woman. Maybe she's not an Aspie—or maybe she is, but maybe it's not that she doesn't understand social cues so much as she's simply too smart to be bothered with them.

All of that aside, she's right about what we should do.

And I already know who to ask.

> < Dr. Abadi, I would like to apologize for being an idiot and getting myself fired. >

> << Not my problem. >>

I wince.

> < The research we were doing is, however, crucial. Mila had determined that the nanobots used during the Navi installation process are missing. These rogue nanobots could be related to the problems the HAD

patients are having. Further investigation is warrant-
ed. Do you agree? >

<< I do. >>

< May I ask that we transfer the patients to a differ-
ent facility that is amenable to our efforts? >

<< Yes. Do so. >>

I blink in surprise.
She messages me again an instant later.

<< Forgot you were fired. I'll have Deonte handle
it. You can locate an alternate facility, though. First
check with Browning Charity Hospital. I'm there on
Thursdays and Fridays. >>

< Roger wilco, over and out. >

I couldn't help that last bit. I think it's the hysteria. Or, at least,
the hysteria I would be having if I were the hysterical type.

I stagger as things go sideways again, and Mila takes my arm
and lets me lean on her. "You don't seem to be doing well," she says.
"Do you have the amygdalae disorder?"

"Not that I know of, thank you very much," I mumble. "But if
I start punching you in the face or trying to have wild animal sex
with you, then you'll know."

I suddenly realize that with her so close to me, that last bit was
terribly inappropriate.

"Sorry," I say. "It's the hysteria."

Mila doesn't even answer. I think she's decided that I'm not
much use to talk to.

A few minutes later, she's carrying my box of personal effects
to my car for me, even though I'm feeling better. All the ibuprofen
has kicked in at last.

Tentatively, I ask, "So, just to confirm, you're going to keep
helping us with the research?"

"Yes." She says it somewhat grudgingly.

I can't understand why. Not that Mila doesn't seem to care about people, but . . . to be honest, she doesn't seem to care about people.

"Please don't let me talk you out of it, but why?"

"The code they introduced is poorly implemented," Mila says. "It annoys me. I want to take it out."

"Ah." I feel chilled by how right I was. I don't think it matters to Mila that there are human beings on the receiving end of that code. "Well . . ."

There's an awkward silence.

"Goodbye," Mila says. "Please keep me informed as to where and when we can continue. Meanwhile, I've got a copy of the malware running on a virtual machine on my laptop, and I'll take it to someone with a quantum computer so we can crack the encryption."

"Is it safe for you to carry it around on your laptop?" I ask dubiously.

"Yes."

As she walks away and gets into her own car without another word, I feel let down. I keep having that feeling with Mila. It's as if I want something more from her beyond normal courtesy. But there's nothing else that I ought to want from her.

Six

By Friday morning, I have provided sufficient details to the charge nurse at Browning Charity Hospital and have received permission to continue our work there. I spend the next couple of hours replaying videos of Jamie from my Memory app and trying not to cry.

We both got our Navis at age seventeen and both when we left home, but we were almost a decade apart. Jamie just got his eight months ago.

Other kids these days get theirs starting at age six, when their neurology is stable enough. Their parents throw them Navi parties. The parents love being able to track their kids' movements and listen in on their conversations—minors don't have any right to privacy under the law—but even so, the kids love having them. The constant connectivity, the games, the nonstop entertainment—it's a win/win for everybody.

As I run through my videos from my few visits home over the years, I stumble across one that I'd starred. I watch as we all head out to the horse-and-buggy to go into town for an errand of some sort. Jamie, who's around thirteen here, is dancing around like a maniac and won't settle down. Dad hitches up the horses to the buggy, a process that takes several minutes and a number of steps, and then takes hold of the door handle and pulls it open.

As he turns toward us to tell us to take our seats, the buggy collapses in on itself like a house of cards. Even the wheels fall over.

The horses startle and look around in confusion. Everyone stares in shock except Jamie, who howls with laughter. Just howls.

I start laughing through my tears as I watch.

Then Dad lunges at Jamie, yelling about whipping him good, and Jamie runs for it, still laughing. The rest of us watch them go around the inside of the house twice.

Then Dad stops, red-faced and panting, and gets serious. He summons Jamie with That Voice that you just don't disobey, and I stop the video. I don't want to see the lashing.

Jamie gets it for five days straight, one day for each hour it takes him and Dad to put the buggy back together, but Jamie told me later that it was worth every lash, and I believe it.

Jamie has always been such an immature pain in the ass. But I don't care. I want him back.

I spend Friday evening in Jamie's room. There's no point in it, as we both just stare into our Navis, but I feel better being near him.

As I scan the news, a headline catches my attention:

"Homeless Man, Suspected of HAD,
Murdered and Burned by Mob."

My stomach lurches, but I can't help but read the rest of the article.

> A 45-year-old African American man was pulled from a NiteRx drugstore and beaten to death, then his body set on fire, by a mob of patrons and employees who reportedly believed he was suffering from Hyper-Aggression Disorder or HAD, the epidemic of aggression and paranoia with over four thousand cases in the past four days.

> The incident occurred in a suburb of Philadelphia that historically has had a violent crime rate lower than surrounding areas. The attackers were primarily middle-class citizens.

An eyewitness said that Noah Greg Manning, who was indigent, became belligerent with a NiteRx staff member when she refused to unlock the restroom for him. When he shouted at her and pushed product off a shelf, someone shouted, "He's got HAD!" and a mob quickly formed.

Before police arrived, Manning was killed with tire irons and his body set on fire in the parking lot, reportedly in an attempt to halt the spread of HAD.

Two arrests were made. Neither of the two suspects are currently believed to be sufferers of HAD.

Following the attack, the Centers for Disease Control issued a statement that "there is, as yet, no reason to believe that HAD is a communicable disease. It may be arising from an environmental cause or it may be a spontaneously occurring neurological disorder. Therefore, we reiterate the pleas of law enforcement officials nationwide: avoid and report potential victims of HAD, but leave actions to the officials."

Within minutes, it becomes a social media thing: #avoidandreport.

I get up and walk to the cafeteria for a snack. I can't deal with this anymore without chocolate.

On my way back up, I see a report on the demographics of people affected by HAD. I read it eagerly.

Factors reported so far: there are more men than women, ages range from school-age children to the elderly, all races are affected equally, and—victims include people who don't have Navis as well as those who do.

I shake my head in dismay and then forward the article to Mila along with the note, "Guess we're on the wrong track. If people without Navis have HAD, then the Navis aren't causing it, right?"

I stand up and pace Jamie's room. My heart has sunk to my toes. I pull up a game of GlowDisc and halfheartedly turn colored tiles. Before, I had hope that we were going to find something, and now I have none.

But then Mila's reply comes in.

> That's not definitive. Consider the following: there's widespread alarm about HAD, its cause is unknown, and it's behavioral, with no detectable physical symptoms. Therefore, it's inevitable that some cases will be instances of mass psychogenic illness. Until the non-Navi cases of HAD are confirmed with brain scans showing the damage to their amygdalae, we can't be certain that those are true cases of HAD.

Of course. I should have thought of that myself. Mass psychogenic disorder—what used to be called mass hysteria—often muddies the water when it comes to outbreaks of disease. There are all the people who have the disease, and then there are the ones who just talk themselves into having the symptoms. If I weren't so tired, I would have recognized that.

I take a breath, and hope surges again.

< So we stay on the case? >

<< We do, indeed. >>

Deonte handles the confinement hearings and paperwork via Navi, and by Saturday morning, he's able to transfer five of the patients who had originally consented to the Navi troubleshooting, including Jamie.

Browning is an old, small charity hospital with a lot of children as patients, located on the far-east side of Atlanta, more than thirty minutes from my apartment. Our assigned nurse is Honor Thompson, a pretty but serious nurse with old-fashioned waves in her dark hair. She's new to Browning, too.

Saturday around noon, I notify Mila that we're back on the job. She tells me that she cracked the encryption last night, and we both head to Browning Hospital to work for the rest of the day.

Speaking of jobs, my savings account is empty, and my checking account is low. I ask my Navi to project my account balance into the next few weeks, and I figure I have about a week to spare. If I don't have a job by then, I'll soon have to throw myself on the mercy of my landlord or else put my things in storage and start asking people if I can sleep on their sofa. And I would like to avoid that, to put it mildly, but on the other hand, another job would pull me away from Jamie, and I need to give him all my attention for as long as I can.

My ace in the hole is that I think I can get another job nearly on the spot once I apply—even without a good reference—simply because of this crisis with HAD.

I hope.

While Mila works, I talk to my dad by phone again. I tell him that Jamie's improving and will be released soon. I feel guilty for lying, but I still can't bring myself to tell him the truth.

Saturday night, I have a late hospital-cafeteria dinner of mashed potatoes and faux pork chops. I still remember the taste of real meat from my childhood, and I miss it, but it's become too expensive for ordinary consumption. People have to go to specialty shops for it now.

While I eat, I scan more news stories. Despite my TellMeWhen trigger, I watch the news feeds obsessively. There's something new every time I look.

Naturally, more suspected victims of HAD have been mobbed, killed, and burned—because, come on, these are human beings we're dealing with here. Ignorance and fear are immune to reason.

Also, sales of guns and applications for concealed-carry permits have both hit an all-time high, which is just what we need. I wonder whether the guns are to protect against the people who have HAD, the mobs who think you have HAD, or the cops who will shoot you if you do have HAD.

An absurd number of people are wearing gloves and surgical masks, even though there's no compelling reason to believe they'll help. Poorer people are wearing the kind of mask you buy for the fumes when you're painting your house. Those will do no good at all.

Most interestingly, despite the officials saying it's still considered non-communicable, there are small concentrations of the disorder popping up in schools, nursing homes, and in certain workplaces, especially high-stress workplaces. As a result, they're theorizing that stress could have something to do with it.

The news media has latched onto the CDC's comment yesterday about HAD maybe being a "spontaneously occurring neurological disorder," so the media's catchphrases have become "a product of modern civilization" and "perhaps inevitable." Everyone's talking about information overload and general overwhelm.

From what Mila told me yesterday, I'm wondering whether these little pockets of HAD could be mass psychogenic disorder again. If even one person in a school has it—or thinks they do—their symptoms could be psychologically contagious and tear through that facility within hours.

Meanwhile, of course, those locations are being shut down or boycotted or both—schools, nursing homes, and workplaces left as ghost towns of HAD. A symbol that refers to HAD is being painted on doors to signify the threat.

All told, though, I think I'm actually impressed. Thousands of people have been affected over five days' time, and society hasn't completely fallen apart. The vast majority of people are going about their business like usual. Even if they are wearing painting masks and packing heat while they do it.

When I finally finish my meal, which sits in my stomach like a lead weight, I go back upstairs with a to-go meal for Mila. I place it in front of her: a baked potato and a salad with a small container of Ranch dressing. I remembered it from when she mentioned it at Cat's Diner. She raises an eyebrow at me and then nods. "Thanks."

I sit for a while and then pace for a while as I watch videos, send messages, read blog posts, and play games all at the same time. But beneath the steady rush of stimulation, I feel even more antsy and unsettled than I would have expected. I finally darken my display and give myself a moment to figure out what's bothering me.

I'm useless here. That's the problem.

"Isn't there anything I can do to help?"

"No," Mila says.

I grimace. "Are you sure?"

"Yes," she says. But it's obvious to me that this is an automatic dismissal with no real thought behind it.

I pull a chair over and sit right in front of her. "Listen to me," I say.

She looks up with reluctance on her face.

"Think about it, okay? I know I'm probably not as smart as you are, and I know I don't know anything about programming, but I *am* smart, all right? I'm smart, and I have a Navi, which is good at all kinds of information processing. Are you sure there isn't anything you can give me to do that might help? Take a few minutes and *think* about it."

Mila sighs heavily and looks back at her laptop screen with a frown. "All right. Give me a moment."

About ten minutes go by, during which time I've defaulted to watching a stupid sitcom, and then she speaks again. "I've already run it through a disassembler and bypassed the debugger check, and now I'm looking for specific variables I've identified as being used by the malware. I'm sending your Navi a file of about two gigabytes of code and a text document titled 'searchme.' Tell your Navi to install the XNET+ developer's dictionary, since that's what Navi programming is written in, and then set up a search for the variables in the text document. I need to find every subroutine that uses them. I could do it myself, but I have a lot of documents to review, and at least if we're both searching at the same time, it will go faster." She sounds disgruntled.

"Great," I say. I've already turned on busy mode, and I'm already following her instructions. As I do, I start to get another godforsaken headache—my first since Friday. I get some water in a paper cup and take more ibuprofen.

An hour or so later, despite the stabbing migraine that has only been dulled by the pain reliever, I'm able to send her fourteen subroutines using those variables. She reviews them quickly, without comment, and then sends me another batch of files with a different searchme document, and I continue my work after a brief break to respond to my Collective. Then I do my work lying down on the fold-out bed in the hospital room, with my palms pressed over my eyes. It helps somewhat with the headache.

We repeat this process twice more. At midnight, she snaps her laptop shut and stretches languorously, like a cat. She says, "Tomorrow, I think I will have a complete picture of the malware." She stands up and starts walking out but pauses long enough to say, with evident reluctance, "You were useful." Then the door closes behind her.

Tired but triumphant, I smile.

The next morning—Sunday—Mila keeps me busy tracing the variables through more subroutines, trying to find all the affected modules. Then, while she continues to work, I go down to the cafeteria for my lunch and bring up a salad and baked potato for her like I did yesterday.

At the same time, I take a call from my dad and try to convince him that Jamie will be out any day now. He threatens to catch a plane down here and see to the situation himself. I tell him that he would be no use at all.

I kind of enjoy that part.

Then I resume helping Mila.

I also resort to Tylenol with Codeine for my headache and Dramamine for the dizziness, both of which work reasonably well. Somewhere in the back of my mind, a small voice complains that I probably need to get an M-MRI of my own. Persistent headaches, nausea, and dizziness could mean something. I ignore the voice. Taking care of myself is a low priority.

At about two-thirty, my TellMeWhen trigger goes off, and I check the news. Immediately, a headline jumps out at me: "Hyper-Aggression Disorder: Second Wave."

A brunette reports gravely in a video. "City and state officials nationwide are now confirming a second wave of Hyper-Aggression Disorder as of about three hours ago, with over a thousand additional victims identified during that time. With only about 10 percent of victims from the first wave so far released from prisons or hospitals, the second wave is straining medical and law enforcement resources. The governors of New York, Texas, California, Pennsylvania, Ohio, and Florida have activated the National Guard, with Illinois expected to follow shortly. Ohio, Texas, New York, and Florida have also requested assistance from the Red Cross.

"Citizens are asked to remain at home whenever possible and to avoid areas with large numbers of people until the danger has passed. Curfews have been instituted in localized areas where rioting and looting have been most prevalent.

"The Centers for Disease Control continue to tell us that no cause of the disorder has been determined, though they have so far ruled out dozens of potential environmental causes. They hasten to assure citizens that at this time, there is no evidence that the disorder is contagious, and they request that citizens merely avoid and report suspected victims."

"There's a second wave," I tell Mila. "Thousands more patients. Still no known cause."

She nods and keeps working.

I scan through more news stories. Numbers have been slow to come in, but the international impact seems to be about the same as it is here in the United States. So much for the idea that it's terrorists—not unless they're out to get all of humanity.

Not much later, Jamie again decides that he's bored and heads for the door. It's right after Mila stepped out for a restroom break, so it's just me and him. Again, I hurry between him and the door.

< Jamie, what do you need? Are you hungry? Thirsty? I'll get you whatever you want. >

<< I'm bored. I want to go out. >>

He tries to push me aside, and I put one hand against each side of the door jamb and stiffen my arms, keeping him inside.

< You can't leave, Jamie. I'm sorry. We can find you some new games or movies or something. >

But he gets amused by the experience of playing Red Rover with me. He starts laughing in a wild, unhinged sort of way as he shoves against me harder and harder.

!!! Warning. Situation is escalating.
Walk away. !!!

Gee, thanks, Personal Safety Monitor. You've always got my back.

I'm trying to find this funny, this throwback to being kids and fighting over what we want, but my body is getting tense, my breathing harsh. It's not fun.

He throws his body against me, knocking me back a step and catching me in the shoulder with an elbow.

< Ow, Jamie, you're hurting me. Back away from the door! >

I notify the nurses station that I need help.

< Nurses station, room #223, code 22. >

He looks at me with a big grin and throws his hand awkwardly into my face—almost a slap, almost a punch. I cry out and put my hand up to my face. He laughs and does it again.

My display is flashing red.

!!! Warning. You are under attack. Run away. !!!

Suddenly I'm a teenager again, with my stupid little brother hitting me just because he can, just to make me cry.

I punch him in the chest, hard.

His mouth opens in surprise, and then he laughs. "Oww . . ." he says, and he laughs again.

Then he slaps me in the face.

I gasp and scream at him, my throat tearing raw with force of it. "Stop hitting me!"

Tears are in my eyes. My face is hot.

Techs push past me and grab Jamie and restrain him on the bed. He's flailing and fighting but laughing the whole time. Nurse Thompson is there a moment later, administering a sedative with a jet injector.

I stand back, gasping, holding my face. I glance in the big mirror against the wall—there are big red finger marks on my face, and my hair is disheveled. I fight back tears.

Mila peers into the room from the doorway, her eyebrows up.

I can't bring myself to say anything to her, and she doesn't ask. She steps back and waits in the hallway.

A few moments later, Jamie is settling down, although he's still giggling sometimes. After Nurse Thompson makes sure he's calmed down, she has the techs release him from the restraints.

> < Jamie, you have to stay in the room, okay? Please? And don't hit me anymore, ever. >

> << Okay, Nurse Phoebe. >>

His muscles have gone slack. He chuckles again.

> << That was fun. Exciting. >>

I say nothing.

When the staff leave, Mila comes back in and takes her seat. "Everything okay now?"

"Yeah," I say. "I think so."

She looks at my face appraisingly. "You'll have bruises."

I shrug. I'm still trying to calm down and not cry. I don't want to cry in front of Mila.

She looks at Jamie and then back at me. "We're making progress," she says.

I nod.

I take a walk after that. I have to work off the adrenaline. I pull up a first-person shooter video game and blast the crap out of a bunch of zombies until I can focus on work again.

Later, when I tell Mila that I'm going down to the cafeteria for dinner, she surprises me by saying, "I'll go, too."

We walk down the hallway together, and I sneak sidelong glances at her. We've spent a lot of time together in these last two days. I know she eats light meals, drinks hot tea from her own thermos, taps her fingernails on her keyboard when she's thinking, and stretches like a cat, lithe and languorous. Other than that, she's still an enigma to me, but I already feel closer to her than I did.

As we walk, she doesn't look at me at all. I wonder whether she's made any observations about me or whether she feels any of the same closeness I do.

I doubt it.

As we get into the elevator, she asks, "Have you found another job?"

I let out a breath as the familiar chill of my financial situation hits me. "Not yet. Honestly, I'm not even looking yet. I have a few more days before I really have to panic, and I want to focus on Jamie as long as I can."

"What is your bank account balance?"

That's usually considered a rude question, but this is Mila, after all. "Oh, it's not looking so good. Like I said, I have a few days . . ."

"How much money do you need to live per week?"

I can't see why she would need to know, but as we get off the elevator, I say, "Well, hold on. Let me do the math." Actually, I ask my Navi to do the math. Then I report, "About $2,500. Why?"

Mila looks contemplative, then nods. "I'll pay you that much, then. Until we're done here."

I stare at her blankly. "I'm sorry? What?" I stop walking, and she stops, too.

"You've proven to be useful to me in carrying out my work," Mila says dispassionately. "You'll be more useful if you aren't working elsewhere."

"Okay, but . . . but . . . no, Mila, I can't accept— it's not—"

She looks right at me. "What's wrong with the idea?"

I hesitate. Then I decide that spelling things out is probably best with Mila. All her other oddities aside, she strikes me as someone who's quite capable with the truth.

"Because I feel awkward about accepting large amounts of money from someone I don't know well."

Mila looks away and blinks, then looks back at me. "You are eager to accept large amounts of money from an employer who presumably won't know you well before he or she hires you."

"It's different because that's an employer. You're not an employer. And it's different, because for an actual job, I would be supplying at least forty-eight hours a week of skilled labor that's worth that kind of money, and I don't know that those factors would apply in this situation. And also, the employer presumably has a large enough budget to pay people, and most private individuals can't afford to do that, so it feels like it would be unfair for me to impoverish you by that amount of money." I grind to a halt.

"Are those all of your objections?"

"I think so."

"One: People become employers by employing others, and I'm offering to employ you, thus making myself an employer. Two: Your work product is valued by your employer. I would value your work product at more than $2,500 a week, so I'm getting a bargain. Three: I have a great deal of money. I make an excellent income and I don't spend it and it amuses me to let it accumulate in my bank account. I feel like a dragon sitting on her hoard."

That last line was probably the most personality I've ever seen Mila exhibit.

"So I will not be impoverished by paying you $2,500 a week for a few weeks. Does that resolve all of your objections?"

I feel like a mouse stuck in a nice trap with a lot of good cheese. It doesn't seem right somehow. "But you're the one helping me. With my brother. I should be paying you, not the other way around."

"We've both agreed that this work needs to be done, and we're both doing it. I don't need to be paid to do it, but you do. I can pay you, and no one else is offering to do so. So it only makes sense for me, the person with the money, to give some of it to you, the one who needs it."

No rational objection is coming to mind. "I feel awkward about this arrangement. Accepting your money because I need it."

"Can you ignore these awkward feelings long enough to accept the money?"

"Uh . . . hell. I guess so."

"Then let's consider the issue resolved. I will transfer the first payment to you tomorrow."

She goes into the cafeteria and picks up a tray and starts looking at the food choices.

I follow, my mind still a confused mess. I'm not sure what happened here or what to think about it.

A few minutes later, as I'm following her back upstairs with a to-go order of mock turkey, green beans, and rolls, I decide not to fight it. A smile creeps across my face as I realize this is one of the nicest things anyone has ever done for me. It's also a confirmation that I've learned how to be useful to Mila, and, for whatever reason, I love that.

As we approach Jamie's room, Mila asks, "Can we rename you?"

"I'm sorry, what?" I wrinkle my forehead.

"Rename you."

I don't react, because I have no idea what to say. As we walk in and sit down, I look for any clues in her facial expression. As usual, there aren't any.

She opens her laptop without looking at me. "You see, I already have a cat whose name is Phoebe, and it's awkward having to call you the same thing."

I briefly contemplate laughing, but I can't quite work up the energy. "Are you serious? You want to—you don't like for me to share your cat's name?"

"It's awkward," Mila says.

"Well, I'm sorry it's awkward, but Phoebe is my name and I like it. More or less. And I don't want to change it. And, by the way, I was first. I'm older than your cat. I'm pretty sure."

Mila frowns but doesn't look up.

More irritated responses are coming to mind, but I'm trying to keep them inside. Finally, I manage a chuckle. I can't believe this woman.

An alarming thought suddenly occurs to me. "This isn't part of the deal of you paying me, is it?"

Mila shakes her head.

I sigh and start eating my dinner.

After a few bites of her meal, Mila says, "I'm going to have to call you person-Phoebe."

I stare at her some more. "Say again?"

"Person-Phoebe. To distinguish you from cat-Phoebe."

I say nothing for a moment. Then, "Whatever works for you, person-Mila."

Mila looks at me uneasily. "Is there a cat-Mila?"

"Somewhere in the world, probably, yes."

Mila eats half her baked potato with her forehead wrinkled. Then she says, "But you don't need to distinguish me from a cat-Mila if you don't know a—"

I groan. "Never mind. It was a joke. Of sorts." I shake my head.

Her forehead is still wrinkled. "If you *do* know a cat-Mila, then it's okay if—"

"Joke, Mila! Joke!" I say loudly.

Jamie perks up, apparently hoping for some more excitement. I shoot him a glare, and he grins.

I'm surrounded by lunatics.

Early on Monday afternoon, Mila sits on her sofa with her laptop open, working with her cat beside her, when her doorbell rings. She looks up, her expression concerned, and then returns to her programming. The doorbell rings again, twice . . . then three times.

With a sigh, she stands up and looks through the peephole. After a moment of deliberation, she opens the door.

Three men in dark suits gaze at her. The one on the right, a middle-aged guy with televangelist hair, says, "Ms. Bremer, your employer at ENI, Mr. Brockman, sent us. We need to have a word with you."

"Then come in," she says reluctantly.

Mila's cat scurries to the back room. Mila perches on the edge of her sofa with one of the men next to her, while the other two men settle in Mila's armchairs across from them.

The men glance at activity in their Navi displays. Their Adam's apples quiver as they speak subvocally—perhaps to one another, perhaps to third parties.

"We need you do something for us." This from the man on the left, a red-faced man with a thick neck.

"Oh?"

"You've become bit of a problem to us. And so has your little friend, Ms. Phoebe Bernhart." This from the third man, a squirrely, wiry fellow.

"Oh, are you the ones with the shitty code?"

Neck narrows his eyes at Mila, but none of the men speak.

"So, what about it?" Mila asks, glancing from one of them to the other.

"We need you to play bit dumb for us," Televangelist says. "Stop being quite so effective at figuring out what's going on, but stick close to Ms. Bernhart. At some point, we may need you to pass some misinformation to her."

"Why would I do that?"

"Why wouldn't you do that?"

Mila pauses. "Allow me to repeat myself more slowly, since you seem not to have heard or perhaps not to have understood me. Why would I do that?"

"My apologies," Televangelist says smoothly. "I don't mean to be obtuse. The question is simply this: what would motivate you to do this for us?"

Mila pauses. "Why do you care about Phoebe? She's an out-of-work nurse. What threat is she?"

Televangelist answers. "She's an out-of-work nurse with a strong interest in solving what's wrong with her little brother and every intention of revealing what she learns to the world. Don't you think?"

"So, why don't you just scramble her brain? Since scrambling brains seems to be your favorite thing to do?"

The three men look at each other.

Mila laughs shortly. "Ah, so you can't. Your code is broadcast to Navis by some algorithm. You can't select specific Navis."

Neck says, "Get back to the question. What kind of payment do you want in order to cooperate?"

Mila shrugs. "I can't think of anything."

The men also pause for a moment. Then Squirrel asks, "What do you like? What are you into? Cars? Clothes? Bling? We can give you whatever you want."

"I don't care about any of that."

"Then name a price, and we'll see how close we can come," Televangelist says.

"I don't care about that, either."

"Ms. Bremer, are you being deliberately stubborn?" This is from Neck, with a threatening tone in his voice.

"No." Her tone is flat.

Televangelist tries to soothe. "Would you like to not have to work for a long time? Perhaps early retirement . . . or simply a long vacation?"

"No. I like my work. And fixing your shitty code."

Televangelist grimaces and stands up, paces to the fireplace mantel, and leans on it. "Let's turn this around, Ms. Bremer. Why are you objecting to our request? Do you care about this woman, this Phoebe Bernhart?"

Mila's chin goes up and she glances at him briefly. "Of course not."

"Do you care about the project itself? What Ms. Bernhart is up to?"

"No."

"So why not do what we say?" Neck demands.

"I don't feel like doing you any favors. I don't like you. And I don't like your shitty code."

"We'd like to clarify that it's not our code, and it's not our project," Televangelist says, folding his arms. "It's merely a project that we're interested in. But it's important to us that you stop making progress on your side of things."

"It's important to me that I do make progress," Mila says.

Neck clenches his jaw. All three men are silent for a moment, probably communicating via Navi.

"Then let's turn this a third direction, Ms. Bremer." Neck's tone has become cold, and he leans forward again. "What wouldn't you like to have happen, if you don't cooperate?"

Televangelist steps forward, his height imposing. "Let your imagination supply you with possible scenarios. Anything you wouldn't like much."

Mila's shoulders tense. A long moment passes in perfect stillness. "I don't know which of my theoretical responses you might be capable of."

"Assume that we're capable of all of them," Televangelist says.

"Some of them are illegal, some unethical, some stupid—and some would take a lot of money and effort to implement," Mila says.

"None of those things present an obstacle to us," Televangelist says.

Mila takes a long breath and lets it out slowly. "You're going to have to be more explicit. I don't do guessing games. If you don't know what I—"

"Your mother," Neck says.

Mila's mouth stops moving in mid-sentence.

Neck continues, "The nursing home. You visit almost every day. You pay her bills."

Televangelist nods. "It's no secret that you love her very much."

It looks like Mila has to work to get the words out. "I don't love her."

Televangelist raises an eyebrow, sits down on the edge of his chair. "So you wouldn't mind if something . . . unfortunate . . . happened to her?"

Mila is perfectly still for almost half a minute. No one speaks.

At last, Mila says, "I don't negotiate with terrorists."

Televangelist raises both eyebrows, and the men look at each other.

"This is the only card you have to play," Mila says. "Once you've played it, you're done. So you go ahead and kill my mother. I still won't have done what you asked, and then there's no way to force me to accomplish it."

Neck shifts forward. "You stupid bitch. You think we're bluffing."

"I know for a fact that you're bluffing," Mila says. "What good will killing her do when I've already said no? Succumbing to coercion like this is criminally stupid. Once you agree, the other party has control of you for the rest of your life, because they can bring up the same threat again and again. The only way to win is not to play. One of my favorite people said that."

The three men freeze for a long moment, and then, as if on cue, they lunge at Mila.

Mrs. Bremer's voice comes through the receiver. It's unnaturally loud, the sound distorted and buzzing. "Mila, everything is fine here. I'm very comfortable here in the new facility. There are lots of cedar trees out in the park where we can walk."

Mila's eyes hurt from the bright, white light around her. She squints as she tries to make out where the light is coming from. Her living room distorts and wavers as if she were viewing it through a curved bit of glass. The colors are too bright, too vivid. Her head hurts, and her upper arms. She tries to rub them, but she can't lift her hands. Three shadows stand above her, shifting and undulating.

Her head hurts. It *hurts*.

"Mila, do you understand me?"

"Yes, Mom. I'm glad."

Mila is falling now, everything flashing past.

"Mom, where are you? Aren't you at the . . . Pines . . ."

"No, these nice men moved me yesterday. Moved me in here to this place with the cedar trees." Her voice is curiously flat. "You had better do with they say, don't you think? Those men?"

"Yes . . . Okay. Mom?" The light is fading into blackness. The image of Mrs. Bremer in Mila's mind is getting swallowed up into the darkness. "Don't get lost, Mom. Mom?"

Everything is getting lost.

Her eye hurts.

Mila Bremer reclines on the sofa in her living room. The three men in suits surround her, Televangelist on the edge of the sofa and the other two standing. Their faces are flushed and tense. One man has a red mark across his throat, beginning to fade.

Mila straightens up and wipes a trembling hand across her face, smoothes back her blonde hair, looks around.

Televangelist says, "Is everything clear now?"

"What happens next?" Mila asks. Her voice is hoarse, her tone distracted. "I don't . . . I don't remember . . ." She rubs one eye, which is tearing up. She looks at that hand and sees a smear of blood.

"Do you remember speaking to your mother now?" Televangelist asks.

"Yes . . ."

"How she said she was safe in our facility?"

Mila nods slowly.

"Do you understand that we'll hurt her? Severely? On every day that you do not follow our instructions? That it will not be a one-time thing or a quick death?"

Mila looks away.

"No harm will come to her as long as you fail to make any further progress on your project and follow any other instructions we give you. Do you understand?"

"I understand."

Televangelist nods. "That's a good girl. This will all be over soon, and then she'll be transferred back to her facility. And as long as you report every day, she'll be perfectly safe and happy. We have no reason to mistreat her, you understand?"

Mila nods.

"This is the number." Squirrel holds out a card.

Mila leans forward cautiously to take it.

"One more thing," Televangelist says. "We may need you to exert some influence on Ms. Bernhart. So we suggest you get close to her, in case you need to be able to persuade her. Under no circumstances may you quit this project until we say so. Keep close to Ms. Bernhart."

Mila looks away. "You couldn't possibly have chosen a worse person for this," she says quietly.

"I'm beginning to agree, given your . . . warm and approachable personality," Neck says sarcastically. "But you're going to have try anyway. See if you can get her . . . interest." He leers.

Mila shrinks into the sofa. Her voice is a whisper. "I don't like people."

"Try harder," Televangelist says, standing up.

"I don't think you work for ENI," Mila says.

The three men laugh. "Of course not," Squirrel says as he opens the front door.

They leave.

Mila hurries after them to close and lock the door. Then she leans back against it, her face drawn. A moment later, she slides down the wall. She rubs her eye again and looks at her hand. No blood this time.

The scene is silent and still for a few moments. Then Mila's cat slips out from behind the sofa. She trots over, purring audibly. She headbutts Mila's hand, and the blonde woman strokes her weakly.

Mila swallows hard and speaks in a hoarse whisper. "They have my mother."

Mew. The cat flops down on her side and flicks her tail, demanding more pets.

Mila's eyes are full of tears. She blinks a few times, and they're gone.

"They're doing something to me. They have to be doing something to me, but I don't know what it is. Because I don't remember everything.

"Did you . . . did you hear what happened? What we said?" She looks down at the cat, who doesn't answer. "No, I don't think so. I think you were in the bedroom for most of it. I don't remember when you came in . . ." She swallows and feels a place under her jaw on one side. "And now I'm trapped. I'm trapped in this thing. My mom . . ."

Mila holds out her other hand. It's trembling. A visible shudder runs through her body. "Why do I feel so sick?"

Seven

When Mila shows up in Jamie's room Monday evening, I can tell immediately that she's not feeling well. Her normally pale skin is even more wan, and her face is drawn and pinched.

"What's wrong?" I ask. I've dispensed with ordinary greetings, as I've figured out that those are wasted on Mila anyway.

"Nothing," she says.

"Liar."

"I don't feel well." Her tone is abrupt.

"I can see that. What feels bad?"

"It doesn't matter. Let's get to work." She sits down and opens her laptop.

I feel rebuffed, but I tell myself to let it go. She seems so bad-tempered right now, I decide that caution is the better part of valor, or whatever that saying is. Anyway, if I have the right to battle agonizing migraines and dizziness without getting myself looked at, I suppose she has a right to feel bad in peace, too.

I ought to get myself looked at.

| Call from Family. |

I think quickly. I haven't talked to anybody in a day or two. I probably can't get away with letting it go to voicemail. I pick up.

"Hello?" I ask subvocally.

"Daughter," my dad acknowledges, his voice somber, as always. "What news about Jamie?"

"Nothing, Dad. If there was news, I would have called you and told you."

"Has his condition not improved? You said he would be leaving the hospital by now."

"Well, I think it might be another couple of days now."

"You said that before, Daughter. To fail to speak the utmost truth to one's parents is to displease God."

I squeeze my eyes shut. "I'm not lying," I lie. "A couple more days, Dad. I'm pretty sure. As soon as there's something new, I'll tell you—I promise." I sigh again. "Let me talk to Mom."

I hear the receiver being handed over. My mother's voice trembles. "Phoebe, is Jamie going to be okay?"

"Yes, Mom," I lie. Well, I *hope* I'm not lying. "Could you please tell Dad that he doesn't need to call me? It's a distraction when I'm trying to take care of Jamie. I'll call him when things change."

"I'll try, Phoebe. You know it's all I can do."

"I know, Mom." I tell her silently that I love her. I never tell her out loud. She won't reciprocate. "Goodbye."

I hear the click of the receiver, and I rub my aching head. I'm aggravated and hurt at the same time. This is why I don't talk to my parents.

I catch Mila looking at me. "What?" I ask.

"You have headaches a lot."

"Yeah?" I shrug defensively.

"How long has that been going on?"

"Not long. A week or so." As if she has any right to bug me about it.

She studies me. "What other symptoms do you have?"

"Just the headaches. And dizziness. It's no big deal," I lie again.

She doesn't say anything. After a moment, she goes back to her laptop.

I shrug it off and check the news about HAD. I know I have the TellMeWhen trigger set up, but I can't just sit around and wait for it to tell me if something new happens. It makes me feel twitchy to think I might be missing something.

I find a news video with a male newscaster who I decide is overdoing the "serious newscaster" tone.

"We're on day eight of the mysterious neurological illness the Centers for Disease Control have dubbed Hyper-Aggression Disorder, with hallmarks of fear, aggression, and repetitive behaviors, and along with Day Eight comes an estimate of eight thousand victims in total, with nearly three thousand of those occurring in the last twenty-four hours.

"Law enforcement officials, in conjunction with the National Guard, have worked overnight without sleep to create temporary detention centers nationwide, most of them in school gymnasiums, community centers, and temporary buildings, for the influx of patients that have overburdened hospitals and overwhelmed jails.

"No information has been supplied to the news media about conditions within these detention facilities or the treatment of the victims, nor is it clear whether they are considered medical patients or offenders under arrest. Numerous lawsuits have already been filed for illegal confinement. City officials have had no official response, other than from Mayor Frederick Brown of Cincinnati. He issued a statement saying that 'the safety of the public and the continued functioning of American society is our top priority at this time.'

"The Centers for Disease Control continue to rule out possible causes, but without finding any plausible explanation for the epidemic. For now, all the world can do is watch and wait."

I close the video and go back to my work.

I think I've had enough of HAD.

Two hours later, Mila says, "We're almost there. I can almost touch it. I've traced most of the functioning of the code, and I'm very close to understanding how it all works together."

I let out a long, slow breath. I hadn't even realized how stressed I've been until I feel the weight on my shoulders lighten a little. "Progress is fantastic news, Mila."

I contemplate the fact that she's paying my bills and living expenses while she spends her evenings here trying to figure out what's wrong with my brother and all the other thousands of affected patients. She could be the one person who solves this whole thing. She looks like a hero to me. I swear there's a halo. My heart seems to swell.

"You know, Mila . . ."

She looks up from her laptop, her gaze neutral.

"I wanted to say thank you. The CDC still has no other leads as to what could be causing this disorder. We would all be at a complete loss without you. Thank you so much for doing this."

Her gaze sharpens, and for some reason that I do not fathom, she snaps at me, "Yeah, whatever. You can keep your gratitude. I don't care about any of this. It's not my goddamned problem, and I don't even know why I'm here." Her gaze returns to her laptop screen, and she hammers something on the keyboard.

I feel like I've been slapped. I look at what's currently showing on my Navi, as if I'll just return to my work, but I feel my breath coming faster and faster and my heart stepping up its rhythm, and I become certain that I'm about to say hurtful and damaging things that will probably cause Mila to stop helping me.

The only way to prevent it is to leave. Now. I stand up so rapidly, I knock over my chair, then I dash out of the room. I want to slam the door, but I don't. Then I stomp down the hallway, tears burning their way out of their ducts.

"Son of a *bitch*."

> | You have donated $10 to the
> North American Man/Boy Love
> Association. |

I put my hands over my face and scream in my mind.

> < That is *not* helping! Navi, calm me down. Please. I
> am so angry right now. >

> | Would you like a calming medi-
> tation? |

< No. Yes. No. That's not going to help. >

I message my entire Collective.

< This Nonnie pisses me off sooooo bad. >

| Would you like a cheerful video? |

< *No.* Nevermind. Leave me alone. >

I pace rapidly up and down the hall.

<< Dominick: What did she do this time? >>

<< Shannon: Are you still hanging out with her? >>

I hear a sound behind me, and I turn to see Mila stepping out of Jamie's room.

Her shoulders are drawn and her face tense, and she looks frail and vulnerable. "I'm sorry that I hurt you," she says. Her tone is curt, but it's the only emotional statement I've ever heard from her.

I don't even know what to say.

"I don't even know what to say," I tell her. "That was so *mean*. Why would you say something like that? What is *with* you?"

"I'm sorry. I don't want you to be mad. Please don't be mad." She still isn't looking at me.

I stop my pacing.

< She's helping me with a personal project that's important to me. And she said that she doesn't even know why she's bothering. >

<< Laura: Okay, what? Then why is she? >>

<< Megan: Yeah, that's rude. >>

The instant support from my Collective helps calm me down, but a part of me still wants to lash out at Mila. "That was an awful thing to say. Why did you say it?"

Her mouth opens and tries to form words, but she fails. Finally, she says, "I don't know. I shouldn't have. I'm sorry."

<< Erik: She's a Nonnie. What do you expect? Weird people are weird. >>

It's Mila's third repetition of the apology that gets through to me. I take deep breaths for a moment while we stand there in the hallway. My head is throbbing again. Medical staff and family members of patients eye us as they pass by, making me feel awkward.

<< Shannon: Well, as long as she's still helping, right? >>

< Well, now she's apologizing. >

"All I wanted was to say 'thank you,'" I grumble. "I mean, this is my brother's *life* we're talking about." I realize Mila was right a moment ago—I'm not angry. I'm hurt.

She pauses. "You're welcome?"

It's so pathetic, so halting, that I start laughing. It's either that or start bawling.

She looks at me for a moment, and then, slowly, a smile spreads across her face. It's the only time I've ever seen her smile, and for a moment, she's breathtaking.

I shake my head. "Yes, that's what you're supposed to say. 'You're welcome.' Next time, try that, okay?"

"Okay."

<< Shannon: She'd better apologize. >>

<< Dominick: Better be a good apology, too. >>

I study her for a moment longer. I'm still hurt about what she said. She meant it. That's the thing.

"You know, you don't have to help," I say. "I mean, I'm screwed without you, honestly. But maybe you know someone else who could do it instead of you if you resent it so much."

She looks away, the furrowed eyebrows making their return. Then she takes a step closer to me. "I want to help. I'm not feeling well, and it made me angry. But I want to help you." The words are halting, uncertain. Along with them, she places one delicate, warm hand on my arm, and those icy blue eyes regard me apprehensively.

The final traces of my resistance melt. "It's okay," I mutter helplessly.

We go back into the room. I pick up my chair and set it right.

> < She apologized, and she said she wasn't feeling well.
> Not a great excuse, but whatever. >

Jamie surprises me by messaging me.

> << Why are you fighting? >>

> < No good reason, Jamie. Don't worry. We're done fighting now. >

> << Okay. It was exciting for a second there. >>

He goes back to his video game or movie or whatever he's doing, and Mila and I sit back down and resume our work in quiet companionship.

Some time later, Mila asks in a subdued tone, "Is your mother important to you?"

I look at up beseechingly, as if God were going to help me out here. I wish I *ever* understood where she was coming from with these random questions and comments. "Yes, of course she is."

When no reply is forthcoming, I elaborate. "My father is kind of harsh, kind of severe. Not likeable. My mother is serious, too. Neither of them are happy people, I guess. But my mother is generous with her spirit. I know she would do anything for me—or any of her kids. But even more than that, I think she would do anything for anyone. She's a compassionate person. Even if it weren't taught by our community that we're supposed to help each other, which we are."

"Do you love her?" Mila asks, her tone absent-minded.

I sigh. "Of course I do." I remember how I can't say it to her out loud, and my heart hurts again. I pull up a photo of her and email it to Mila. It's a candid photo taken by my Navi without her knowledge, since my community eschews photography. Too close to "graven images," forbidden by God in the Bible. Too likely to encourage egotism. In my own experience since leaving home, I've found photographs more likely to inspire self-hatred. But maybe that's just me.

I wait for a while, but Mila doesn't say anything. I see her bring up the photo of my mother on her screen, but she doesn't comment.

"Why do you ask?" I prompt.

"No reason." She types for a moment and then says, "My mother is senile."

"Really? How old is she?" I've always thought Mila was about my age. Her mother ought to be too young to be senile.

"She's fifty-six. But she had early onset Alzheimer's. She was forty-six when it started."

Ten years ago . . . that was about three years before the Alzheimer's smart drugs were perfected. Mila's mom just missed the window where she could have had her mind given back to her good as new. "Damn it, Mila. I'm sorry. That's tough."

If Mila's as old as I am, then her mother started losing her mind when Mila was a teenager. Suddenly, some of Mila's strangeness makes more sense to me.

"Were you her primary caregiver at first?"

Mila doesn't answer.

I wait several minutes, and then I give up and go back to work. Apparently, the conversation is over.

It's almost two o'clock in the morning when Mila jerks bolt upright in her bed, gasping and whimpering. She flails for a moment, then manages to catch the lamp in her hand and fumbles for the light switch. Yellow light pushes back the darkness, and she looks around with wide eyes, her body rigidly upright.

Her cat mews from beside her. Mila looks at the cat for a moment, but her body doesn't relax. She scrambles out of bed and goes into the kitchen and gets a drink of water. She goes around and turns on all the lights in the apartment. Then she stands in the center of the living room in her silk pajamas, staring into the distance and rubbing the spot under her jaw.

Then she goes into the bathroom and looks at that spot. A pale bruise, roughly the circumference of a quarter, is apparent under the bright light.

Mila's eyes widen. She backs away from the mirror, her breath coming fast. "No," she says. "No, no, no."

She goes back into the bedroom, where her cat has gone back to sleep on Mila's pillow. Mila stares at nothing, her face stricken.

Then she dives for her purse, on the bedside table, and scrambles for her notepad. She looks up a number, grabs the phone by the bed, and dials with trembling fingers.

The phone rings, rings again, and rings a third time.

A sleepy voice comes over the line. "Mila? Is that you?" It's Phoebe.

"Yes. I need you to do something for me. Please."

"Okay . . . what is it?"

"I need an M-MRI scan. I need to know if anything has been put into my brain."

There's a pause. "Okay. Is this an emergency?"

"Yes, it is." Mila's voice is distressed.

"Okay . . . um. Okay, but things are kind of crazy in emergency rooms and M-MRI labs right now because of HAD." Phoebe's voice strengthens and gains clarity as she wakes up. "I don't know if you would be able to get a scan anytime soon. Can I come take a look at you? I might be able to figure some things out."

Mila hesitates only a moment. "Okay. I'll just come to you. Actually, let's meet somewhere in the middle. It will be faster."

The two women make arrangements to meet in a parking lot of a twenty-four-hour restaurant. Fifteen minutes later, they both arrive.

Phoebe approaches as if she might hug the other woman, but she stops at the last moment. "So, what's happening?" she asks. She looks alert and concerned.

"I have a sore bruise at the implant site for Navis. I'm worried that they've installed a Navi without my knowledge."

"Who's 'they'?"

"I don't know. People. Someone. Anyone."

Phoebe nods, despite looking at Mila askance. "Let me scan you with my Navi." A moment later, she reports, "There are no detectable devices within range. You don't have a Personal Area Network. So if you do have a Navi, it's not turned on. What other symptoms do you have?"

"I've had memory issues, where I can't remember parts of conversations, and episodes of weakness, shaking, nausea, and headache that lasted a day. This has happened twice. And pain at the corner of my eye and here at the site of the bruise."

Phoebe looks again. "My Navi doesn't detect anything wrong with your pupils, breathing, temperature, or heart rate. If you had a Navi and your body was going to reject it, you would know quickly, right?"

Mila nods slowly. "I guess so. I got a Navi when I was seventeen. I had an acute rejection reaction. Dizziness, headaches, and nausea at first . . . Three hours later, I blacked out and started having convulsions. My mom said I convulsed for an hour before they got the Navi out. I don't remember it . . . I remember the recovery afterward. I've never felt that bad before or since."

Phoebe nods sympathetically. "I don't see any signs of a Navi or of a rejection reaction. And like I said, it's going to be a nightmare at an emergency room. If you're not obviously in immediate danger, you would probably wait for days. Let me and my Navi keep an eye on you. We know what to watch out for this time. If you start to have a reaction, I can get you to an emergency room and make sure you get the appropriate treatment."

Mila takes a deep breath and then nods.

"We might as well have a good breakfast while we wait," Phoebe says. She gestures toward the restaurant.

Inside, there are virtually no customers or wait staff. The hostess seems surprised to see them. "Business is way down with this HAD thing going on," she says.

Phoebe orders a full breakfast, but Mila orders toast and doesn't eat it. She gives monosyllabic responses to Phoebe's attempts at conversation, and after a while, Phoebe turns to her Navi to pass the time. Mila just stares into space, waiting.

Eventually, as pale morning light comes in through the windows, Mila gets up and pays their bill. When she returns, she says, "So far, so good. We might as well sleep."

"Okay," Phoebe said.

They walk slowly to the entrance, and Mila pauses just outside. "You didn't have to do this, and it was a lot of trouble for you, but you did it anyway. So, thank you."

Phoebe touches her on the arm and smiles slightly. "Hey, what are friends for?"

Mila puts one hand on Phoebe's arm and squeezes lightly before she turns away.

Late the next morning—Tuesday morning—Mila shows up at Lovely Pines rest home. Two police cars are parked out front with their lights on. Seven geriatric folks wait for pickup at the curb with boxes of their possessions around them. A large impromptu sign says, "Lovely Pines remains open for business and appreciates its customers."

Inside, Jerry Armstead is standing at the security desk, telling a middle-aged couple that they have nothing to worry about. "We've had two cases here. Two. It ain't no problem here at Lovely Pines." The woman in the couple insists that they want to bring Dad home just as soon as someone is available to help them.

Jerry's gaze catches Mila. "Hey, what're you doin' here? I didn't figure I'd ever be seein' you again with your mama gone."

"I know, Jerry. I need to ask the facility manager on duty some questions about that."

"Ms. Peterson? Sure, I can call her over if you want. Things are a little crazy, though. People movin' out."

"Yes, please." Mila leans on the desk and runs her hands through her hair with a forlorn expression.

Jerry glances at his Navi display and then looks back at Mila. "Everything goin' okay?"

Mila shakes her head and turns away. "Long story."

The man looks as if he'd like to inquire, but then he seems to think better of it.

A moment later, a graying woman approaches with an unsmiling face. She stops in front of Mila. "Yes, ma'am, what can I help you with?" Her tone is defensive.

"I need all the details you can give me regarding the transfer of my mother, Joanna Bremer, out of your facility."

"Well, Ms. Bremer, I'm not clear about what you're asking—since you're the one who authorized the request?"

Mila's eyebrows go up and then back down. "Would you mind humoring me and printing out the request?"

"Of course. As her legal guardian, you're entitled to all your mother's records." Ms. Peterson gives Mila a sidelong look, as if doubting her sanity.

As if on cue, a printer on the reception desk begins to whir.

"That's all I needed, Ms. Peterson. Thank you."

"You're welcome," the older woman says, and she turns and walks away.

Jerry has been looking back and forth between the two women with interest. Now, as he hands her the printout, he asks, "Is something goin' on?"

"Were you on duty yesterday when she was transferred?"

"You mean this morning?"

"This morning?" Mila's voice rises. She scans the date and time of the request. It says that Mila made the request by Navi at 3:28

p.m. the previous day. That was during the time the three men were at Mila's apartment. The request is verified by the normal biometric signature used by Nonnies. The paperwork released Mrs. Bremer from the Lovely Pines into the care of a Bruce Donovan, no company name listed. "What time did they come?"

"About nine-fifteen, I'd say. About . . . two hours ago."

Mila groans and rubs her face.

"What's going on, Mila?"

Mila sighs. "Can you forward me a photo of the people who came and took her? And the vehicle they were in?"

"Well, sure." His eyes flit across his display.

As he does, he speaks slowly. "It was two men that came for her. White men with short, dark hair. Dark suits. And there was a nurse with them. Dark-haired woman."

He pauses as he focuses on his task.

"They told me about the transfer request, and I called for Ms. Peterson, told her about it. She sent out a nurse with a couple boxes of Mrs. Bremer's personal effects and then another nurse with Mrs. Bremer."

Stopping again, he tilts his head as if looking at something that's angled. "I asked your mama where she was headed, but of course she didn't know. She acted like she was okay with it all, though. I asked the men where she was going, and they said it was a private facility closer to you. I thought it was funny that you weren't here, but I figured you just wanted her out on account of HAD, like all these other folks."

He glances rapidly from one spot to another. "That was all. They loaded her up into a van and took off." His eyes focus on Mila again. "What's your email address?"

Mila gives him the address "mab287a239@anony.net," and a few moments later, he says, "Sent it off."

"Thank you," Mila says and turns to leave.

"Wait, wait—hold up. You can't leave like that. What's going on with your mama?"

Mila hesitates. "I don't know what to tell you. I don't think you ought to worry about it."

"If something's goin' on with your mama, I want to know about it, you hear? Hell, I'm the security guy." He taps his badge. "If something happened right under my nose, I damn sure want to do something about it."

Mila looks away, her eyes darting about as she thinks. "I have no reason to believe that she's in any danger. And I don't know of any way that you can help. But if I think of something, I will tell you, all right?"

Jerry nods slowly. "All right, Mila. All right. If that's what you want." But his expression is unmoved.

Mila walks out with her shoulders bowed.

I sleep late into the afternoon that day. I wake up thinking of Mila. I know I dreamed about her icy eyes and her pale, drawn face, but the dream slips away as I open my eyes.

I saw a new side of her last night. It's sort of a relief to discover that she does have emotions. And in a moment that she was plainly terrified, she turned to me.

I wonder whether she has anyone else to turn to. I know she isn't talking to anyone by Navi while we're working, and I've never seen her place a phone call. In any given evening, I talk to dozens of people. She talks only to me.

I call her while I shower. She doesn't answer, and I'm forced to wonder where she might be if she's not at home. I never think about that with any of my Collective. It doesn't matter where they are or what they're doing because they'll get my message within a few minutes, usually.

As I get out of the shower, I receive a notification that James Bernhardt has been issued a transfer order to detention facility #110. Immediately, I'm on the phone with hospital staff even as I'm getting dressed and driving to the hospital. I can't let Jamie go to one of those places—partly because I won't be able to continue my research and partly because I don't trust the idea any farther than I can throw it.

The administrator I talk to is sympathetic and quickly places a call to Dr. Abadi to verify my research project. By the time I arrive, they've confirmed that neither Jamie nor any of the other four patients will be transferred.

"They're doing this across the country," the staff person tells me. "The hospitals are running out of sedatives, and apparently, these detention centers have the security they need to manage the patients. So all HAD patients are going to the facilities. But you do have a legitimate exception. Dr. Abadi has gotten approval to use some of the remaining sedatives at Browning on your five patients, too."

I feel as if we've dodged a bullet.

When I arrive, Mila is already there, working. She has more color in her cheeks than she did yesterday. I tell her that we nearly lost all of our patients, but she doesn't react. She never reacts.

Once she gives me my instructions, we settle down into our normal routine—me on the foldout bed with my eyes closed and her in the chair with her silver laptop. As usual, Jamie sits and stares into his Navi. And as usual, within half an hour or so, I'm having to dose up on the Tylenol with Codeine and Dramamine.

I decide that I'm officially going to get looked at. I message my regular doctor.

> < Doc, can I get an M-MRI approved? Recurrent migraines, dizziness, nausea, flares in vision, for about a week, almost daily. >

I don't expect a response anytime soon. Not with our current health care crisis.

About four hours later, Mila performs one of her arresting catlike stretches and declares, "I've solved it."

I set my Navi to text mode to give her my full attention.

"The malware allows servers to give new instructions to the nanobots to alter their behavior and location in the brain. The new instructions are cached—and it's lucky I was able to find them before the RAM was overwritten. Probably something the hackers overlooked during development. I will give you one guess as to the nanobots' new location."

"The amygdalae?"

"Correct."

I look at my mindless, emotionless brother sitting placidly in his hospital bed, probably watching another movie, and I feel a flush coming up my neck and cheeks. My heart pounds, and my fists seem to clench of their own accord. "Someone is deliberately doing this?"

Mila nods. "It is deliberate. There is no doubt."

I stand up and begin to pace, my fists still clenched. My face twists. "How are the nanobots doing harm to the brain? Abhishek said that the stimulation was weak."

"That's part of how they've been reprogrammed. They've been set to deliver much stronger electrical impulses than is normal."

I stare at Jamie. "They're frying his brain."

I rub my temples as the constant migraine threatens to overcome the medication. "But why? Why would anyone do this to random people? Is it terrorism?"

Mila is looking at her laptop screen with a raised eyebrow and a new expression—a flat, blank glare that seems out of place.

"It isn't random," Mila says slowly. "It's directed." She pauses. "But I haven't figured it all out yet. I need to make a call. Excuse me."

She snaps her laptop shut and hurries out. I'm too busy being freaked out about my brother to pay much attention.

I reach out to the nurses station.

> < Do you have a Navi installation technician at this hospital? I need #223's Navi uninstalled right now. Immediately. >

I sit down and try not to wring my hands. I try to tell myself that it won't hurt him any more to have the Navi in for another hour or two. It's already been . . . God, it's already been two weeks. I try not to hyperventilate.

<< We don't have any Navi technicians available right now. We'll send his doctor to evaluate. >>

I glower at no one.

< When? >

No immediate response.
I message Dr. Abadi, closing my eyes to try to ease the migraine.

< We found out that HAD is definitely caused by the Navis. The Navi installation nanobots have been relocated to the amygdalae and are providing extra-strong stimulation there. We need to get every one of those Navis uninstalled right away. >

<< How many patients have you confirmed it with? >>

I pause, taken aback, but I understand her question.

< Jamie so far. We'll start confirming in other patients immediately. >

<< Please do and keep me posted. Let me know when you've reviewed all five patients. >>

< Please tell me you are going to act on this information immediately? >

<< Uninstallation is not that easy or quick, and people will be resistant. I can't justify advising this if we aren't sure. >>

I clench my fists again.

< They are having their *brains fried*, Doctor. *As we speak.* >

I wince. I probably shouldn't have shouted. I wait for an angry response for several painful moments, but all I hear is the humming of the air conditioning in the hospital room, and all I feel is the damned throbbing in my head.

< Sorry for shouting. We'll confirm as quickly as we can. >

When Mila leaves the room, she goes to the nurses station and asks Nurse Thompson to give her a phone and some privacy. Once the nurse steps away, Mila takes the card from her purse and dials with trembling fingers.

The phone rings only once.

A man's voice. An unfamiliar one. "Hello?"

Mila doesn't speak at first.

"Hello?" the man asks again.

"Yes. It's Mila Bremer. I got an email telling me to call."

"You aren't following instructions, Ms. Bremer."

Mila says nothing. Her face is pale and pinched.

"Seems like you didn't take us seriously. I guess you didn't know we were watching you."

"Through Phoebe's Navi," Mila says.

"Can we trust that now that you know you can get away with nothing, you'll keep your end of the bargain? Or bad things will happen to your mother?"

Mila closes her eyes. "Yes."

"Do what you're told. And keep working on seducing Ms. Bernhart."

"I want to speak to my mother. Every day."

"We'll put her on tomorrow."

The line goes dead.

Eight

Mila comes back in with an unusually stormy expression on her face. I'm still busy freaking out, and the increased blood flow from the adrenaline is making my head pound worse than ever.

"Mila, how quickly can we confirm the same problem in the other patients?"

She thinks for a moment while she looks at her screen and heaves a sigh. "Assuming that all the patients are using the same code and the same security algorithms, it should only take a few . . . days."

"A few days? Jesus." I wanted it to be a lot faster than that. I rub my temples.

<< Dr. Abadi: Is hacking involved? >>

< Yes. >

<< Can your programmer stop the hacking instead of removing the Navis? >>

"Dr. Abadi wants to know if you can take out the virus or whatever it is," I say.

She closes her eyes for a moment. "Yes, I . . . think I will be able to remove the malware. It will take some time to be sure, and then it will take longer to accomplish."

"How much time? To be more specific, will removing the malware take less time than confirming the hacking in four more patients?"

Mila shakes her head slowly. "Unknown, but unlikely. The malware is written into existing code using overloaded variables. It can't be taken out like taking meatballs out of a pan. It's more like trying to take a specific strand of spaghetti out of the whole pot. Everything's tangled together, and everything is fragile."

"Damn it!"

| You have donated $10 to Exodus International. |

"Oh, shut up!"

Mila raises her eyebrows.

"Not you. My Navi." I heave a sigh. That order I gave my Navi, to auto-donate to an organization I despise every time I curse, seems ridiculous with everything that's going on. So I'm cursing. Well, it's a good thing thousands of people aren't dying from a bizarre pandemic. Oh wait, they are.

I started pacing, and now I stop because it's making my head throb worse. "So, are you saying that we can't remove the malware?"

"I'm saying that it's difficult. I can start by removing the malware from the version on my virtual machine here on my laptop and looking for any unintended consequences of what I do. It is risky to perform the same operation on a live subject. I would want to replicate it at least a dozen times with other cases on my virtual machine before I attempted it on a person."

I grind my teeth. Dr. Green was jumping the gun before, but this degree of operation on a live subject without oversight probably would be illegal and unethical. "What are the proper channels for this sort of thing now that we've identified the problem?"

I answer my own question. "If we can get it confirmed in enough cases, Dr. Abadi will help us get the Navis uninstalled for all the patients, and I imagine she'll spread the word to the CDC, who will relay it to everyone else. Uninstalling or even just turning off the Navis will stop the problem, right?"

Mila nods. "That's assuming you can convince people to go without their Navis." She sounds a little bitter. "Good luck."

"Shouldn't we alert the manufacturers or software programmers who normally work on Navis? I mean, no offense, but wouldn't they be able to solve this a lot faster than you by yourself?"

She stares at her laptop screen. "I wouldn't count on it."

"What do you mean?"

"Let's say that's probably not going to work and leave it at that for the moment. I'll work on confirming the malware in the other Navis in order to satisfy your Dr. Abadi. I think that's the best thing to do right now."

I don't understand why she's dismissing the manufacturers, but Navi hardware and programming is her domain, not mine.

"Listen, if this all takes more than another day, I'm going to want to have Jamie's Navi removed. I can't risk him getting any worse."

She doesn't answer, but I'm confident that she heard me.

I pace for a few more moments and then ask, "Is there something I can do to help?"

"Get me the list of Navi IDs for the other patients."

I nod and message our nurse, Honor Thompson, with the request.

About thirty minutes later, Mila says, "It would be easier for me to do this if I could pinpoint some details about the installation of the Navis, since that's how the nanobots are usually deployed. Is there an installation technician I can talk to?"

"They already said there wasn't anyone," I reply. "But let me ask again."

The nurses station takes a good forty-five minutes to reply, but around midnight, we finally have a young technician bring the jet injector to Mila. He's not an installation technician, but he's familiar enough with the device to show it to her. He lets her handle it and review the specifications that scroll across the tiny screen on the side of the device.

I note that he's rubbing his forehead like I am. "You don't look so good," I comment.

"Yeah, I'm about done for," he answers. "Guess I'm coming down with something. Got headaches and maybe some fever. Going back home after this." He turns back to Mila. "Did you get what you needed?"

"It would be good if I could hang on to it for an hour or two," she says.

"Sure," he says with a shrug. "I mean, my boss wouldn't be happy, but don't tell anybody." He winks, briefly summoning up enough energy to flirt, but Mila doesn't even seem to notice.

We both work until three-thirty in the morning, when Mila snaps her laptop shut and says, "My effectiveness has dwindled past the point of diminishing returns. I need to sleep."

That happened to me about an hour ago. This kind of Navi work is a lot harder to concentrate on than nursing, and the migraines make it even worse. Instead of helping, I've been watching the news about HAD. There's really nothing new. More schools and business are being shut down by the day. The medication shortages I found out about this morning are just hitting the news.

Now that I'm really thinking about it, I wonder what it's like inside those detention facilities if there are no sedatives. Are they tying people to stakes like dogs and letting them flail and scream? It would be Bedlam, but I can't figure out what other choice they would have. It's horrifying.

"How close are we?" I ask.

"I don't know," Mila says, not looking at me as she stretches and rubs her eyes.

We walk out together, and for the first time, she says "Good night" as we approach our cars.

"Good night to you, too," I say. "Listen, I know you have a real job, too, but is there any way you can take some time off to keep working on this? I think you get how important this is . . . to a lot of people."

She hesitates at her car door. Then she says, "I guess I can. None of my projects at work are urgent, and I have time off available."

I let out a breath. "Thank you," I say.

Her expression is inscrutable as she looks out into the distance. "Thank me when I'm able to help," she says.

When Mila gets home, she pets cat-Phoebe for a few minutes and brews more hot tea. Then she opens her laptop again, despite her bloodshot eyes. She pulls up the email from Jerry Armstead at the nursing home and studies the photos of the men who took her mother away. They are, unmistakably, Neck and Televangelist.

Also included in the photos is the nurse. Her face is turned partly away from the camera, but Mila knows her instantly. It's Nurse Thompson from the hospital they're in right now.

Mila rubs her hands over her face. "Great," she whispers.

Next, Mila looks at the photo of the van. A portion of the license plate is visible: X89-Z.

She thinks for a few minutes, tapping her fingernails on her keyboard as she gazes into the distance. Then she opens a browser window and navigates to the website for Atlanta's Metro system. She finds the profiles of the executive board. She scans through the profiles until she locates a middle-aged woman: Drew Allison, VP of Marketing.

She closes her eyes, takes a deep breath, and uses her computer to call the helpdesk number at the bottom of the browser window.

"This is Drew Allison." Her tone has become demanding. "I'm in San Diego for business, and for whatever reason, my Navi won't log me in to the company network so I can get my business email. This is important. I have a big meeting in the morning. It's saying my password is out of date, which makes no sense at all. I even tried going to the intranet manually, and it's not letting me in. Do I even have the right URL for the intranet for when I'm off-site? I mean, I have nothing at all saved here. It's like my Navi forgot I even work for this damn company."

The helpdesk technician is eager to assist. He walks her through the URL for the intranet, supplies her forgotten username, and helps her reset the password. He assures her that her Navi appears to be working correctly from what he can see on his end, and he can't explain why she's not seeing email messages on her end. He suggests that she visit the helpdesk at the San Diego office in the morning.

Mila thanks him and then uses her new credentials to log into the company intranet. With her advanced access levels as a company executive, she's soon searching the Metro camera logs for the van with the X89-Z license plate.

After a while, she gets up to refill her mug with more hot water and brew more tea.

She's yawning deeply when she finally finds the full license plate number.

From there, she pays $30 to run a routine license-plate lookup online. The search gives her the name of the owner of the van. It's Richard Sarran.

A quick search on his name reveals his online profile, complete with photo, confirming that Richard Sarran is Neck.

Further searches on Richard Sarran turn up more pictures—one of them with Televangelist. The name on the caption is Julian Overbridge. They both work for a company called Peake International.

Mila rubs her eyes and opens the document with notes from the jet injector used for Navi installations. While at the hospital, she copied down a username and password and a URL. She types the URL into her browser window and logs in with the copied credentials, bypassing the security screen that says, "Warning! Authorized personnel only. Unauthorized access is a violation of HIPAA and federal data security laws and carries a mandatory prison sentence of ten years."

She types in Richard Sarran and then Julian Overbridge.

A few minutes later, she copies down two Navi IDs.

Neck is Richard Sarran, Navi ID AX02094835.

Televangelist is Julian Overbridge, Navi ID LT05465888.

She stops and taps her fingertips on her keyboard again. Then she searches for Dr. Green at Grady Hospital. She quickly finds his public profile, confirms his full name, and then does some additional research.

Fifteen minutes later, she finds and skims a paper published in a medical journal. Dr. Green and two doctors associated with Peake International did a joint research project on motivation in low-dollar purchasing decisions.

A search on Nurse Honor Thompson shows an association with Waverly Corp, and another twenty minutes of research turns up numerous joint projects between Waverly Corp and Peake International.

Mila glances at the front windows. Dawn has begun to peek in beneath her living room drapes. She stretches, finishes her cup of tea, and goes to bed.

It's early afternoon on Wednesday. Mila is already in the hospital room, working on her silver laptop, a thermos of hot tea at her side, when Phoebe walks in. As soon as Mila glances up at the other woman, her forehead wrinkles. Something about Phoebe's face is wrong. It's slack and staring.

Phoebe asks, "How's Jamie doing?" Her voice is unusually flat.

Mila glances over at Jamie, who appears to be the same as ever—lost in Naviland and perfectly happy to be there.

Phoebe asks again, "How's Jamie?" But she stares past Mila as if she isn't there.

"See for yourself," Mila says, gesturing toward him.

Phoebe glances at her brother, seemingly without recognition. She walks across the room and then back again, muttering under her breath.

Mila tries to work but keeps glancing back at the other woman. She inclines her head as if trying to make out Phoebe's words.

"What are you doing?" Mila finally asks.

"Worrying about Jamie, mostly. And wondering about . . ." She doesn't finish her sentence. Her hands go up to her hair in an uncharacteristic, repetitive motion.

Mila snaps her laptop shut and stares intently at the meandering woman as if trying to solve a crossword puzzle. "Are you feeling okay?"

"I feel funny. My stomach. What are you doing here?"

Mila's eyes narrow. "You didn't drive here, did you?"

"No. Smartcar. What are you doing here?"

Mila lets out a breath. She puts her head in her hands for a moment. "You don't remember."

"I don't remember. I'm . . ." Phoebe's voice trails off.

Mila's face sags. "Oh God."

Phoebe says, "Okay." She stops walking and turns toward Mila. Her gaze doesn't quite make it to Mila's face but stops short, staring out into the far distance with such intensity that Mila turns to look behind her.

Slowly, Phoebe asks, as if thinking of it for the first time, "How's Jamie doing? I haven't seen him . . ."

Mila runs her hand through her hair. "Please sit down. I need to fix this. Somehow." She opens her laptop, finds the name "Phebe Bernhart," taps "Request access," and looks at Phoebe, who's still standing motionless in the center of the room, still staring at that same place. "Your name is misspelled in the system."

"No, it isn't," Phoebe says. The statement restarts her slow movement across the room. "It's P-H-E-B-E. But that's a Biblical name. I don't like it spelled that way. I changed it when I moved here. Phebe Esther is my full name. I hate it. Also, my head hurts."

"Okay, Phebe Esther, can you please approve my access request? And sit down?"

"I'm watching myself sit down," Phoebe says as she takes a seat. "It feels weird. Like I'm not in there."

"Can you please watch yourself approve my access request?"

"Okay." The woman looks down at the floor sadly. "I'm worried about Jamie."

"I know," Mila says through gritted teeth. "Please watch yourself sit quietly now."

Mila works on her laptop, urgency in her movements. Occasionally, she casts concerned looks at Phoebe, who stares into the distance, her face still slack and her gaze still fixed far into the distance.

After about half an hour, Phoebe's eyes glaze, and she slowly begins to slip off the daybed toward the floor.

Mila's eyes widen. "Oh no!"

Phoebe slips onto the floor on her left side. Then her right hand and arm begin to jerk convulsively. Mila jumps up, setting her laptop aside, and pulls Phoebe away from the hard base of Jamie's hospital bed. At the same time, she looks around the room, but she doesn't find what she's looking for. "Jamie! Can you call for a nurse right now, please? Tell them someone is having a seizure."

"Okay," Jamie says. "Really? A seizure?" His gaze focuses on the woman on the floor, and his face brightens with excitement.

Phoebe jerks spasmodically along the length of her entire body, and Mila kneels beside her, watching, her face serious. She grabs the blanket from off Jamie's bed, folds it, and carefully slips it under and around Phoebe's head.

Phoebe makes guttural sounds as her back arches. Mila grabs her laptop and sits next to Phoebe to resume her work, but with increased urgency. "Come on, come on!" she says to her machine.

"Is she gonna die?" Jamie asks with interest.

"Not if I can help it," Mila says tersely.

"What are you doing on your laptop?" Jamie asks.

"Trying to stop whatever her Navi is doing to her."

Jamie laughs. "Her Navi is doing that? Really?"

Mila doesn't answer.

"That's so weird," Jamie says. He studies the jerking form on the floor for a moment. "It looks so freaky, her body doing that. I bet it feels crazy."

Mila continues to work, her fingers tapping rapidly. "Did you call the nurse?"

"Yup. When I was a kid, I had a friend who had seizures. Until they fixed him, I mean. As long as they're breathing and it doesn't last more than five minutes, they'll be fine. Unless they die. Sometimes they die." He consults his Navi. "It's been three and a half minutes."

"This isn't a typical seizure. Be quiet so I can concentrate."

"Okay."

Mila works furiously as another minute ticks by.

Phoebe's face has turned dark red, but the guttural gasping sounds still come.

The door opens and a code team steps in, but the doctor sizes up the situation quickly and holds them back. No doubt they discuss the situation and their options via Navi, but no one speaks aloud.

Mila hits "enter," and code runs by on her screen too fast to track. She types another series of commands and then pushes her laptop aside.

Phoebe's body begins to relax, and at last, she draws a full breath. Her eyes close. Her limbs settle.

Mila takes a long, deep breath of her own.

"Guess the fun's over," Jamie says. "Oh, well."

The medical personnel step in and perform a rapid, silent evaluation of Phoebe's vital signs. Partway through, Phoebe's eyelids flutter open, and she moans.

When they finish, the doctor looks at Mila, recognizes that she doesn't have a Navi, and speaks aloud. "She should be okay soon. She may have some disorientation for up to an hour. Are you a friend or a family member?"

Mila hesitates for the span of a breath. "Friend."

"Do you know if she's ever been diagnosed with epilepsy or any other seizure disorder?"

"No."

"Can you give me her full name so we can check her medical records? Normally, we would find it out from her Navi, but since she doesn't have one . . ."

"Phebe Esther Bernhart." Mila spells out each name for them.

Jamie perks up. "She does, too, have a Navi." He looks at his older sister, and then his expression shifts to puzzlement. "Usually."

The doctor looks back and forth from Jamie to Phoebe to Mila.

"Temporarily deactivated," Mila says.

"I see," the doctor says, although his blank expression suggests that he doesn't. He looks at the data in his display for a moment and then reports, "It's important that she see a neurologist right away and not operate a manual-drive car until she does. Seizures are dangerous but treatable. We would set up an auto-reminder for her to make an appointment, but since she doesn't have a Navi, it would be good for you to remind her later today and again tomorrow. She wouldn't remember if we told her now."

"Understood," Mila says.

The team steps out of the room.

Only Phoebe's head moves. The rest of her body is limp with exhaustion. She looks over at Mila, and something in her gaze seems pleading. It draws Mila as if it were magnetic, and she slides closer. Phoebe reaches out one hand for her, and without hesitation, Mila takes her into her arms.

Tears run down Phoebe's cheeks. She tries to speak, but her words are garbled.

Mila strokes Phoebe's hair with a trembling hand, smoothing it away from her forehead. "I'm so sorry." Tears appear in Mila's eyes, but she blinks them away. "This is my fault. I should have seen it coming sooner."

Phoebe moans. Between long, slow blinks, her gaze traces Mila's face. Mila rocks her slowly. Phoebe's eyes flutter closed, and their breathing rhythms slow, almost coming into sync. When Mila shifts to wipe her eyes, Phoebe starts to try to pull herself into a sitting position. Her right arm gives way. Mila helps her up, and the two women sit facing each other. Then, gradually, Phoebe sags forward onto Mila's shoulder, back into her embrace. "So . . . sleepy," Phoebe whispers.

"Why don't you take a nap, then?" Mila suggests softly. "I can help you onto the fold-out bed."

"Okay."

A few moments later, Mila gently lays a blanket over Phoebe, whose eyes have already closed. Then Mila sits beside her, wipes her eyes, picks up her laptop, and resumes working.

Shortly before ten o'clock, Mila gets up and goes to the telephone at the nurse's station in the hallway.

"Hello?" The same man's voice.

"I just got an email telling me to call."

"Is Ms. Bernhart dead?"

Mila clenches her teeth. "Sorry to disappoint you, but no."

"Her Navi is offline."

"I shut it down temporarily."

Silence.

"I know that you tried to kill her. And I guess I didn't give you enough credit. I didn't think you could affect individual Navis on command. But I stopped you anyway. That puts us at something of an impasse, doesn't it?"

Another pause. Then the man says, "We didn't try to kill her. But let me remind you of why you want to cooperate with us, no matter what happens."

Mrs. Bremer's voice comes through.

"Hello? Who's there?"

"Mom?" Mila straightens up. "It's Mila."

"Mila? Darling, it's so nice to hear from you. Oh, how is school going, sweetheart?"

Mila's voice catches and her eyes glisten. "It's going fine, Mom. None of these classes are hard for me."

"I know, sweetheart. You are so smart. You are as smart as your father was, and he was a brilliant man. Brilliant. He would have talked circles around me if I didn't talk so much in general." She chuckles.

Mila tries to smile. "I know, Mom. You always tell me."

"Well, honey, you got me right before my bath time. These nurses are awful pushy around here about keeping to schedules."

"But they're treating you okay? Mom?"

"Oh, yes, honey, they're perfectly nice. The food here is good, too. We had turkey casserole for dinner. With real turkey, not that soy nonsense. But I've got to go now. Call me tomorrow, okay?"

"Sure, Mom."

The line is quiet again. Then the man returns. "Do you remember now why you want to do what we say and not interfere?"

She clenches her jaw. "I understand."

After she hangs up, she goes directly back to Jamie's room and begins hacking into the Navis of Richard Sarran and Julian Overbridge.

I wake up to silence. I'm aching, exhausted, cotton-mouthed. The room is dark and quiet, but I hear breathing. I sit up slowly, groaning, and discern one sleeping body in a hospital bed and another on the floor under a blanket. Everything seems blurry, and I blink a couple of times, but it doesn't help. I look for the clock in my display, and then I realize that it isn't there, and neither is the icon on the right that's supposed to show me my notifications when I activate it.

< Wake up, Navi. >

Nothing happens.
I wait a breath.
Nothing.
I have that awful feeling of stepping forward only to fall down a step. Never in my life, not since I installed it, has my Navi failed to instantly respond.

< Wake *up*, Navi. >

I see nothing in my display except what my eyeballs show me. And it's blurry. Why is everything blurry?

My heart amps up its rhythm and rate, pounding in my ears. I want my Navi to answer me. I want my messages. I want to know what's happening in the world. I want to know what time it is, what day it is. I'm cut off, alone, helpless.

< Navi? >

< *Navi?* >

< Navi? >

I'm hyperventilating now. I try to get up, and I nearly fall as my right arm collapses under me. I scramble and manage to stand and then nearly fall as my right leg gives way. I lean on the sofa bed. "Oh shit, oh shit."

No reprimand from my Navi.

The body on the floor stirs and then rolls toward me. Mila's face appears. "How are you doing?" Her voice is sleep-raspy.

"My Navi's off. It's not working. You have to fix it. Can you fix it?" My voice sounds stupidly hysterical.

Mila sits up and rubs her face. "Do you remember what happened yesterday?"

"No—what? I feel like shit."

"You had a seizure brought on by your Navi. I disabled it."

My thoughts are a whirlwind. "Well, can you turn it back on?"

Mila rubs her eyes. "Why?"

"Why? Why? Because. Because my arm and leg aren't working and I can't see anything and I don't even know what day it is."

Mila looks at my body and notices how I'm leaning precariously on the sofa bed. She stands up and comes to me. "It's Thursday, early in the morning." She helps me sit down again and crouches next to me. "What's wrong with your vision?"

"Nearsightedness. I'm nearsighted. I think. Or farsighted. Something like that. I don't remember." I'm babbling. "My Navi fixes it for me. Please, can you turn it back on?"

Mila looks at me with concern on her face. "Listen to me, Phoebe. You had a grand mal seizure. Whoever is behind this thing, they hacked into your Navi, and they tried to kill you. It isn't safe for you to have it on. I wouldn't even have been able to turn it off if I hadn't started looking at your Navi a couple of days ago because of those migraines."

"But I need it, Mila. I need my Navi." I'm dimly aware that I'm in a full-blown panic attack, which is ridiculous, but this is my Navi we're talking about. It's my whole world. What am I supposed to do without it?

"No, you don't need it." Her voice is firm.

I try and fail to take deeper breaths.

"What's wrong with your legs?" Mila asks. "Why can't you stand up properly?"

She moves out of the way as I test out various muscles and relay what I discover. The evaluation process calms me down as I shift into nurse mode. "My right arm is weak, and so is my right leg. They don't hurt. I can move them, they're just weak. So, right-side focal weakness." I take a deep breath. "Common side effect of grand mal seizures. It should pass in a few days. How long did it last? Did I stop breathing?"

"Almost five minutes. No, your breathing was fine."

I can't get used to the fact that there's nothing to look at it besides what's right in front of me. And there are no messages coming through.

< Navi, message my Collective: Is anybody there? >

Nothing happens.
I'm alone in my head.
I hate it.
"Mila, please bring it back. Please. I need it. Can't you turn off the dangerous part?"
Mila looks away and sighs.
I wait with bated breath in the uncanny silence and stillness, staring miserably at a world that won't come into focus for me.

She sits down next to me. "I can try to disable the nanobots themselves and nothing else. And add some extra security." Her voice is distant. "It will take me a couple of hours at least."

"Please," I beg. "If nothing else, I need to be able to see. I can't see anything." I hold up a hand in front of my face. I can't even see to arm's length. "I can hardly see you," I start to say as I turn toward her, and then all that I'm aware of is that I can see her perfectly, every millimeter of her beautiful face, because she's so near to me. As my gaze drops to her lips, I realize I could kiss her.

For these precious instants, there's nothing to distract me from taking in her loveliness. The curved lips, the long, delicate line of her nose. The perfectly pale skin, the faint beauty mark to the outside of her left eyebrow that I'd never noticed before. The long blonde lashes, the ice-blue eyes—so imperious as they regard me.

My breath stops as I make full eye contact with Mila. It's like an electrical shock passing through me down into the bottom of my stomach.

Mila is leaning toward me ever so slightly, almost as if that kiss were imminent. She glances down to my lips. I can feel the warmth of her body heat. My stomach flutters again.

Then she pulls away and stands up. "I'll try," she declares as she goes to her customary chair and picks up her laptop. The beautiful details fade into the blur, and I blink to bring them back, but they don't come.

I decide that I'm suffering from temporary insanity. What's happened to my brother, the seizure, waking up without a Navi—these things could drive anyone around the bend. I don't have the energy to think any further about it.

I sit and look around the blur for a few minutes, but too quickly, I can't bear it anymore. The quiet is broken only by occasional small sounds—the air conditioning turning off, footsteps in the hall outside, Jamie shifting in his bed, Mila typing. Nothing moves in my visual field.

"How can you stand to live like this?" I ask Mila.

She gives me a withering look over the top of her laptop screen.

"Sorry," I say. "I didn't think about that before I said it. But this is so *boring.*"

My hands wring themselves in my lap. I have messages that I can't get to, I know. They could be important. I'm missing everything.

"Can you at least tell me the news? I haven't read anything since . . . I guess since yesterday sometime."

"Okay." Mila clicks around on her laptop. "England's sanctions against China have been declared a failure. The bombing in Gaza continues, with ten thousand Palestinians and two thousand Israelis estimated dead. The US has confirmed Monday's rumors of another twenty thousand American troops going to reinforce Israel. The likelihood of another ice age descending within the next fifty years has doubled, and—"

"Whoa, whoa. What kind of news are you reading? I haven't heard anything about any of that."

Mila looks at me blankly. "This is the BBC World News."

I stare, my mind trying to make sense of things. "Why wouldn't I have heard about twenty thousand troops going to the Gaza Strip?"

Mila sighs. "Bubble dweller." It sounds patronizing.

"What are you talking about?"

Mila lowers her laptop lid. "I don't have time to go into this, because I'm bit busy trying to make sure you don't get killed the next time we turn on your Navi. But the short answer is that anyone who uses a Navi lives in an information bubble where your past choices dictate what you are informed about. Haven't you ever told your Navi to stop telling you certain things?"

Of course I have. I've told it lots of things. A couple of weeks ago, I told my Navi to stop telling me sad animal stories.

I look at the floor.

"It remembers everything you've ever told it, and it's always watching, noticing what kinds of messages you stop reading after a few words versus what kinds of messages you respond to. And other factors. Now, you should go back to sleep. Then you won't be distressed about missing your Navi." She opens her laptop again.

There's an entire war going on that I didn't even know about. I wonder what else I don't know.

For the first time in my life, it occurs to me that it was foolish to decide that there were things I didn't want to know.

But I'm too tired. Too tired to deal with any of this. I lay back on the sofa bed with a muffled groan.

"You don't need me to be awake to keep working on my Navi?" She shakes her head while still looking at her code.

I heave a sigh and try to go to sleep. At least when I'm trying to sleep, my Navi is supposed to leave me alone. For the moment, I can pretend it isn't gone.

When I open my eyes again to the sunlight coming in through the drapes, my world is clear, and my clock rests peacefully in the top right corner of my vision. I close my eyes and breathe a sigh of relief. I'd never dreamed how much I would miss my Navi.

I stretch and find that my right side is still weak. I try not to worry about it. It'll get better.

< Read me my messages, Navi. >

Obediently, it starts going through my backlog one at a time. I don't even care that there are a hundred and eight of them. I'll happily listen and respond all morning long.

As I go through my messages, I get up and step over Mila's sleeping body on the floor with a pang of guilt. She probably stayed up all night fixing my Navi. And I should have given her a turn on the foldout bed. I daydream about offering her a back rub as I go downstairs to the cafeteria and get us all breakfast burritos. I've learned that Mila likes hers plain with egg and potato.

On my way up, about half my messages handled, I turn the corner to our hallway and run right into two men in black suits. They catch me and hold me upright.

"Sorry," I stammer.

<< Agent Paulen: Phoebe Bernhart, this is the FBI. You are under arrest for cybercrimes. You need to come with us, please. >>

NINE

They haven't let go of me, though I try to pull away.
A message flashes in my emergency notification panel.

!!! You are being held by the Federal Bureau of
Investigation. !!!

!!! Your cooperation is required. !!!

"What the hell? We haven't done anything wrong."
Handcuffs are going over my wrists, snapping closed. I can't
stop it.
Between the two of them, I catch movement. Two more men
have Mila by the arms and are walking her down the hallway. There's
a sea of dark suits back there.
"Mila!"
She doesn't say anything.
I message my Collective.

< You guys, holy crap, FBI! We're getting taken away
by the FBI! >

!!! You have the right to remain silent. !!!

!!! Anything you say can and will be used
against you in a court of law. !!!

One of the men frowns at me.

<< Paulen: What's wrong with your Navi? >>

< Screw you! Let go of me! >

I try to wrestle free, but I can't.

<< Shannon: Whoa, what? FBI? What???? >>

<< Erik: Like, what did you do?? >>

<< Katie: Who's 'we'? >>

They walk Mila up near me, but she doesn't even meet my gaze.

<< Chris: Do you need help? Not that I could do any-thing . . . >>

"What's wrong with her Navi?" one of them demands of Mila.

<< Alyssa: It's happening right now? Like, right now, right now? >>

Mila raises one side of her mouth in a half-smile. "Oh, that. Sorry. I have some custom programming in place. Would you like me to help you with that?"

<< Robert: Ask for an attorney. Say out loud that you're exercising your right to remain silent. >>

Paulen snorts. "Not if we can help it. Try again, Phillips." Frightened nurses' faces peek around the corner down the hall.

< 'We' is me and Mila. Mila Bremer, since none of you know her. >

"Help us!" I shout to them. "We didn't do anything wrong." The faces disappear.
I finally process what Robert said.
"I want an attorney," I say breathlessly. "And I'm exercising my right to remain silent."

The agent replies nastily, "Then remain silent. Or we'll consider you to have waived that right."

I close my mouth.

> !!! You have the right to an attorney and to have
> your attorney present during questioning. !!!

Frustration is palpable in the room. Apparently, things aren't working out for the agents.

"Okay, shut down her Navi," the other agent growls at Mila. "Now!"

> !!! If you cannot afford an attorney, one will
> be provided to you. !!!

> < You guys, they're saying we can have an attorney. I
> don't have an attorney. I don't know if Mila has one.
> Someone please call one for us? >

"I can't do that without my laptop," Mila says. "And my hands."

"Yeah, right," Paulen says. "Like we're going to give the hacker her computer back."

The men look at each other.

Aziz to other agents:

<< Then what are we going to do? Look, Bernhart has had at least two minutes of unhampered communication and net access already. It'll take a couple of hours to get her to the station and get someone else to hack in and solve it. Can we afford to let Bernhart do whatever she wants in the meantime? >>

Phillips to other agents:

<< Is it better or worse to let the actual hacker have full access to her own machine for several minutes? >>

Robert to Phoebe:

<<What are you under arrest for? >>

Phoebe to Collective:

<< Cybercrimes. I have no idea what they're talking about. And now I can't even ask because I said I was staying silent. >>

Paulen to the other agents:

<< Let's get Bernhart shut down. But we're watching her like a hawk. Phillips, bring Bremer's laptop. >>

Two of the men push the women into an unoccupied room, put Mila in a chair, bring over her laptop, and uncuff her. Mila stretches, rubs her eyes, and then begins to type in a flurry.

Phoebe to Mrs. Jones:

<< I know I'm supposed to take Tobi tonight, but something has come up. I'm not sure when I'll be home again. Can you keep him for a few days?? >>

"So, what settings do you want?" Mila asks, her voice exhausted. "Shut down all communications," Paulen says. "Keep it simple. And keep in mind that we are authorized to prevent your Navi communications from the moment of arrest. So neither of you is to communicate anything to anyone from this point forward."

Phoebe to Collective:

<< Um, guys . . . they're telling us we're not allowed to talk via Navi . . . >>

Phillips to Paulen:

<< We can't make Bernhart comply with that, you know. We can't even tell if she's doing it. I've never seen a Navi locked down like hers is. >>

Paulen to Phillips:

<< I know that. But they don't know that. >>

Mila types furiously, getting access to Phoebe's Navi. In lieu of her normal software, she's working by command line, keeping text flying by.

Paulen to Phillips:

<< Watch Bremer and make sure she isn't doing anything she shouldn't. >>

Chris to Phoebe:

<< Then you probably better not talk. They can review your Navi records later, you know. Go dark, and we'll get you guys a lawyer. >>

Phoebe to Collective:

<< Okay, I will. Thank you so much, Chris. God, I hope I'm not going to jail. >>

Mila looks at the agents out of the corner of her eye and says, "This is going to take a while. You might as well get comfortable. Get some coffee."

Reuben to other agents:

<< Great. Love it when things go smoothly. >>

He sits down.

Mila continues to type furiously. By frequently asking the computer for extendedreports of technical details, she keeps her own commands scrolling up too fast for the agents to catch.

Mary to Phoebe:

<< Good luck, Phoebe! I'm sure it's all a misunderstanding and you'll be fine. Hang in there, and don't let them violate your rights. >>

Aziz to other agents:

<< Fine, I'm going to get some coffee. Anybody else want any? >>

Reuben to Aziz:

<< Yeah, me. Cream and sugar. >>

Paulen to Aziz:

<< Yeah, black. >>

Reuben leans against the door.

Chris to Phoebe:

<< Maintain that right to remain silent, and don't speak without an attorney present. >>

Phillips says, "You'll need to turn off your wi-fi, Ms. Bremer." In between commands devoted to her legitimate task, Mila has entered:

> \text only

> \noconfirm

> \ghostmode

> isearch airport code Zanesville OH

The response comes back:

CMH

She raises an eyebrow at Phillips' comment. "I have to have on my wi-fi or I can't communicate with her Navi." She points at Phoebe.

Paulen to Phillips:

<< Idiot. >>

Phillips says, "Well, remember what we said. No communications."

Paulen to Phillips:

<< Watch for emails or IMs or other internet use. It can't be that hard to tell if she's writing an email. >>

Phillips eyes Mila's screen. She enters more commands, resulting in more status reports filling the screen, so that those lines fly past. It's obvious that she doesn't have an email client, web browser, or IM app open, so Phillips doesn't interfere.

The agent comes back with coffee, which the men accept with Navi'd thanks.

Phoebe has her eyes closed. She's started a calming meditation.

Between legitimate commands, and while keeping the text flying past too quickly to read, Mila looks up three Navi IDs and then types rapidly. She sends a message to Richard Sarran that apparently (but didn't) come from Julian Overbridge, telling him to transfer Mrs. Bremer from wherever she is to an anonymous person, then tells Jerry Armstead to meet Mrs. Bremer in disguise and fly with her to Cleveland, Ohio:

> vmsg nid LT05465888 \use nid AX02094835 \
use voicefile AX02094835 "transfer mrs bremer
to 715 Main arriving 3 pm, allow pickup from
anonymous"

> email nid QW02209200 "email of your mom, explain later"

> isearch first flight ATL -> CMH >1500 hrs

flight 2378 departing 1540

> vmsg nid ZA02897349 \use nid QW02209200
"meet mrs bremer in disguise at 715 Main at 3

> pm, take flight 2378 meet mrs bernhart at CMH explain nothing"

> cmd nid ZA02897349 \shutdown -restart 30m -start 14:45

new msg 2938

> read msg 2938

msg 2938 "Doesn't have. You can leave her a phone message at 740-345-2783. It is a community phone."

> vmail phone 7403452783 \use nid QW02209200 "mrs bernhart your daughter needs you to meet mrs bremer at CMH flight 2378 today critical explain later"

Finally, after requesting more data to fill the screen and hide those commands, she types:

> \ghostmode off

> cmd nid QW02209200 \comms-down

Mila closes the command line window with an emphatic mouse click. "Done," she announces, and she looks up at the agents, her gaze cloaked.

Paulen turns toward Phoebe.

<< Navi, police-check Navi ID QW02209200 status. >>

A moment later, a message pings Paulen.

<< Navi ID QW02209200: communications disabled. Unauthorized third-party programming installed. Further status unavailable. >>

Aloud, Paulen says, "Good enough. Phillips, take Bremer's laptop away and get those cuffs back on her. Let's go."

It takes over an hour for fingerprints and photos to be taken and my purse and possessions and clothes to be taken away in a large ziplock bag. I'm given a green jumpsuit, although I get to keep my flip-flops, which look ridiculous with the jumpsuit. Now it's me and three other women in a dimly lit concrete cell in a federal holding facility. The other women look rough, their expressions cold and closed, like they've been here before. They don't speak to me when I walk in, so I don't speak to them, either. Instead, I play Solitaire and watch a movie from the jail library on my Navi and try not to freak out.

I'm out of touch with everyone I know. I'm missing everything. I can't help Jamie, who still has his Navi in place, trying to turn his brain into mush, and my right side is still hopelessly weak . . . but at least I can keep myself distracted. And if all else fails, I can talk to my Navi, even if it's cut off from everything other than the local jail network.

I tell myself that it's not pathetic to talk to your Navi if you don't have anyone else to talk to.

Waves of cold and trembling keep coming over me, and I keep chasing them away by telling myself that we're innocent, that either this is some kind of wildly improbable misunderstanding or we're being set up and that either way, the whole thing is going to go away as soon as our attorney gets involved. We'll be out of here by the end of the day. Maybe a day or two at the worst. That's what I keep telling myself. We can't possibly have run afoul of the FBI in any legitimate way. Not without even knowing it, for heaven's sake.

Someone comes to the cell, and I straighten up apprehensively. It's a guard unlocking the door. He jerks his head at me. "You got your attorney here. Follow me."

Thank you, Chris. Bless you, Chris.

A few minutes later, I'm seated in a bare, ugly room across from a Mr. Pataky, a heavy man with a bushy mustache. He has a dramatic way of speaking, with a lot of broad gestures. "—it's important that you tell me everything, okay? Nothing you tell me can get you into any more trouble than you're already in, because we have attorney-client privilege. Do you understand what that means?"

He goes on before I have a chance to respond.

"Attorney-client privilege means that anything you say to me is *privileged*, which means I can't divulge it to any third parties, including the judge and law enforcement. It means you're safe to say whatever you need to say. But I don't want to know whether or not you did it, so don't tell me. Do you understand?"

"Yes . . ."

"But here's what you do tell me. You do tell me the truth. Everything that you tell me, tell me the truth." He shakes a finger at me. "Now, what do you tell me?"

"The . . . truth?"

"Right. Okay, now—charges." He glances at something in his Navi. "You are charged with accessory to multiple counts of cyber-crimes. Do you understand the charges against you?"

"No," I say vehemently. "I have no idea what they're talking about."

"Cybercrimes is a catch-all phrase that includes cyber-based terrorism, espionage, computer intrusions, and cyber fraud. That means any of those things—terrorism, espionage, fraud, invasions of privacy—that are done using a computer or a Navi."

He glances at something in his display. "You are being accused of being an accessory to Mila Bremer. You know this woman?"

I'm momentarily surprised, but then, of course he doesn't know anything about what's going on. "Yes, I do."

"What is your relationship to her?"

My mouth gapes open for a moment as I wonder for myself what our relationship is.

"Friends?" he prods. "Coworkers? Spouses? Romantic partners?"

"No, no," I hasten to say. "Um . . . really, acquaintances, at least right up until we started working together on this Navi project."

"Fine. Acquaintances. What was the nature of this Navi project? But *don't* reveal anything that is criminal. Some defense attorneys like to know the whole picture, but I believe I can defend you best if I don't know what you've done. Remember, I don't want to know whether you did anything criminal or not. Is that clear? What *don't* I want to know?"

"Anything criminal we did. But we didn't do anything—"

"That's fine. What was this Navi project?"

"I asked her to help me figure out what was wrong with my brother. You've heard about Hyper-Aggression Disorder?"

"Yes, what about it?"

"Mila had a theory that it was being caused by people's Navis, and I was having her investigate that."

He looks disappointed. "Hyper-Aggression Disorder is caused by problems with some part of the brain—the amig, amid—"

"Amygdalae."

"Right, that, and Navis don't interact with that part of the brain. They're hard—"

"They're not hard-wired," I snap. "Navis can send signals anywhere in the brain, and they are hackable. Mila has already determined that the nanobots used during installation have been deliberately hacked to move into the amygdalae and overstimulate it. You want cybercrimes—that's it, right there. We were trying to uncover it so something could be done about it."

He leans back in his chair for a moment. "Oh, I see. You're after the *real* bad guys." He sounds patronizing.

"In point of fact, yes. And while we're sitting here wasting our—"

He leans across the table. "And you have proof of all this, I suppose?"

"Yes, we have proof. It's all on Mila's laptop. She can show—"

"Then it's already in the hands of the authorities, because her laptop will have been confiscated." He looks again at his display. "I see no prior convictions for you. Is that right?"

Again, I'm openmouthed for a moment. "Of course I have no prior convictions. I'm not a criminal."

"Fine, fine. Now, listen, do you understand that you have the option of being tried before a jury of your peers or before a judge?"

Again, he goes on without waiting for me to answer.

"I explain to everyone that they have the option of a jury or a judge trial. But that's assuming we get as far as trial, which we probably won't. We'll probably plea bargain so you can serve the least amount of time possible. For now, to give us time to develop your defense, you'll plead 'not guilty.' This preserves your right to a trial—whether judge or jury—in the very unlikely possibility that we go to trial. Any objections to pleading not guilty?"

"Of course not, since—"

"You must understand that it doesn't matter whether you're guilty or not, and please remember that I don't want to know whether you're guilty or not. Even if you're not guilty, if we can arrange a better plea bargain than the sentence you'll likely get in a trial—which is probable—then we'll change your plea to guilty. A plea bargain is where you don't dispute the charges, and in exchange, we ask for a concession from the prosecutor. It may result in changing your charge from felony to misdemeanor, or it may reduce the number of counts, which is currently at twelve—"

"Twelve? I have twelve counts against me?"

"Twelve counts of felony cybercrimes, yes."

"Oh God," I whisper. I put my head in my hands, and Mr. Pataky keeps talking to my hands.

"As I was saying, the plea bargain can reduce the severity or number of counts against you, and it's possible, although not terribly likely, that you could end up with time served—which is likely to be a number of weeks or months if we can't get you out on bail—plus a lengthy—"

"*Weeks* or *months*?" It has taken only moments for my house of cards of denial to be blown down by gusts of reality.

"Unless we can get you out on bail. That's a separate issue and one we'll get to in a moment. Now it's time for you to make up your mind about how you want to plea. I suggest we begin with 'not guilty.'" And he falls silent.

I try to disbelieve everything he has said, pretend it never happened. But he's still sitting there, and I'm still sitting in a featureless room wearing a green jumpsuit and shackles. Nothing can make this not be true.

"If I plea bargain, then I don't get a day in court. So how do I tell the judge about what's happening here? That we're trying to uncover some kind of . . . cyberterrorism plot? Something needs to be done about this, and urgently. As far as I know, and as improbable as it may sound, we were the only people in the country who were even on the right track."

"If you plea bargain, you won't have a day in court. You'll have a hearing and be sentenced, and that'll be the end of it."

"Then I don't want to do that. I need to tell the judge—or someone—about what's happening. If they're stopping us, then someone else has to pick up where we left off. Someone has to do something."

Mr. Pataky leans back and rubs his eyes. Then he sighs gustily. "Your friend is also charged with hacking into the Navis of four other people."

I blink at him. "She is?"

He nods.

"Who?"

"I don't know who they are. But there were five altogether, including your brother. And she's being charged with hacking into a national database of Navi IDs, and—"

"Wait a minute. Five?"

He nods. "What about it?"

"Five is the number of patients that I had obtained consent from in order to investigate HAD. What are the names of the people? I'll recognize them if they're my patients."

He reads the names off his display.

"Yes, those are my patients."

"Wait, wait, wait. Hold on." He leans forward and speaks with emphasis. "Are you telling me that all of these people are patients that explicitly granted consent to have their Navis investigated?"

"In writing. I have the paperwork. Well, I had the paperwork when I had access to the internet," I amend. "We could have the hospital send it to you. Does the FBI not know that they were my patients and that they gave consent and that Mila is an approved Navi technician?" I can't keep the annoyance and frustration out of my voice.

Mr. Pataky looks at something in his display while he speaks thoughtfully. "It's not a felony to tamper with the Navis. It's a felony to hack into people's Navis without their consent, but if you've got consent, it's only a misdemeanor. Let me check the statutes. Give me a moment."

I put my head in my hands again and try harder to wish this whole thing away.

Mr. Pataky reads portions of sentences out loud as he scans pages in his display. I don't understand any of them.

"Ah-ha! Here we are. Thought so. It's a misdemeanor. That reduces your charges significantly. If you plea bargain, you can end up with community service or something. Tell me what hospital it is and what the consents are called and everything else I need to know in order to submit a request for those specific documents."

After I do so, he goes on, "Now, look, it's time for your bail hearing in a few hours. You don't speak unless the judge asks you a direct question. I'm your attorney. I represent you, so I'll do the talking. Do you understand that?"

"Yes," I say.

"I'll do my best to get you out on the lowest bail possible. What are your financial resources?"

I shake my head, my mouth dry. "I don't think I have any. Mila does. I can only hope that she would pay my bail as well as her own."

"If not, you can probably get a bail bondsman to cover your bail, depending on the amount. You'll only have to put down 10 percent. How much money does Mila have? Never mind, I'll talk to her next. I'll ask her."

I shake my head again. "A fair amount, I think." I consider the fact that she was willing to pay me $2,500 every week for a time. "At least ten thousand?"

"Well, that's probably not enough to cover more than one of you, assuming it's even enough to cover one of you. But your bail should be lower, since you're only being charged with accessory to the crimes. I'll advise her to bail you out, and then we'll probably arrange a bondsman for her. That's if I can talk them down. We'll see what happens. It all depends on the whim of the judge and the skill of the prosecutor." He stands up and heads for the door. "Watch some movies and take your mind off all this. It's all you can do for now. They'll bring you to the courthouse in a few hours."

The next time I see Mila, we're getting shackled to the same length of chain at the holding facility to be transported to the courthouse. I'm surprised at how urgently I want to reach out to her, touch her, reassure her. Her face is drawn and pale. She looks exhausted. She only glances at me and says nothing.

Another woman is added to our chain, which reach our wrists as well as ankles. She's another tight-lipped woman, emaciated like she's done too many drugs.

They put us into a van like they did after they booked us. A short ride later, we're taken out and escorted into the courthouse through a back door, down carpeted hallways, and then into the courtroom by another back entrance. Once there, a female security guard watches us with casual distrust.

The courtroom is imposing. Everything is designed to intimidate, from the height of the judge's bench to the stone walls and the way sound echoes, making me self-conscious of every cough or shift in position. The floors are blue carpet, and the seal of the United States District Court of the Northern District of Georgia is on the floor and on the wall behind the judge's chair. An American flag hangs behind the chair, too.

The three of us are seated to the side of the courtroom in a small row of chairs. No one is behind the bench yet. No one sits in the few rows of seats in the audience area or in the jury box. A handful of attorneys in dark suits are at two tables in the center of the room, star-ing into their Navis. Mr. Pataky sees us and immediately comes over.

"Remember not to talk," he says to us. "Not one single word. I do the talking unless the judge asks you a direct question, and if he does, keep it brief. A few words, no more. And call him 'sir.'"

I nod, even more anxious. Mr. Pataky's presence here does little to reassure me. On the other hand, I know that if I were here alone, I'd be terrified.

Mr. Pataky goes back to the tables. From the animated ex-pressions, I can tell that the attorneys are talking to one another via Navi. And I'm guessing that it's not about the cases. There's too much chuckling and smiling. These people are trading humorous anecdotes. While we sit here with our lives at risk of being taken away, they're exchanging quips. I hate them.

Another door opens, and a couple of women enter and sit at chairs one step lower than the judge's chair.

The bailiff calls out, "All rise."

Everyone stands up, including me.

The judge enters in his black robes. He looks intimidating, too. He's old, with wrinkles on top of wrinkles and outrageously bushy eyebrows fighting with reading glasses. His expression is as serious as death.

As he walks in, a young woman in a suit—looking mildly em-barrassed—recites, "Hear ye, hear ye, hear ye. The United States District Court of the Northern District of Georgia is now in ses-sion, the Honorable Judge Elliot Keith presiding. We admonish all who have an interest in the business of this court to draw near and pay heed."

"Have a seat," Judge Keith says as he sits down and makes him-self comfortable. I hear that his voice is amplified, and then I notice the microphones suspended from the ceiling in strategic locations around the courtroom.

The judge's voice is cantankerous. "Don't forget, there is no Navi use in my courtroom. You'll get contempt of court if I catch you, so either be smart or be sneaky."

There are a few smiles from the attorneys.

"The United States versus Phoebe Bernhart," the judge says, looking up over his reading glasses.

The sound of my name is like an electric shock. I leap to my feet, my heart instantly in palpitations. Mr. Pataky approaches a lectern in front of the judge's bench and gestures to me to join him. Another man approaches at the same time but stands off to the side. I don't recognize him.

"Don't talk," Mr. Pataky mouths, and I shoot him a glare.

I'm breaking into a sweat.

Judge Keith shuffles paper printouts. Then he looks down at the two men. "Good morning, gentlemen."

They return the greeting crisply and confidently, standing tall. These are two men who seem to have everything under control. No big deal. Of course, their lives and their freedom don't depend on what happens next. My heart is hammering.

"Twelve counts of cybercrimes," the judge says to the other man. "What is the government requesting for bail, Mr. Harren?"

"Your Honor, this is an important case. Ms. Mila Bremer, seated there, is part of the same case." He gestures to Mila, whose expression remains flat.

"Then bring her up here," the judge says irritably.

As the bailiff escorts her up, the judge asks, "Mr. Pataky, do you represent them both?"

"Yes, Your Honor, I do," Mr. Pataky says.

The judge makes a sour face but gestures at Mr. Harren. "Go on."

"These two defendants represent a danger to society on a massive scale," Mr. Harren says and then pauses dramatically. The judge purses his lips and looks at him attentively.

"Your Honor," Mr. Harren goes on, "the FBI executed a warrant and arrested Ms. Bernhart and her co-conspirator Ms. Bremer on direct evidence of their hacking into the Navis of five people and then into a national database of Navi IDs."

He pauses dramatically again, letting the judge draw his own conclusions about the connection between these two acts. "Ms.

Bremer is a loner, an anti-social computer programmer with an axe to grind against society because she is a Nonnie—someone who is unable to have a Navi installed. She is outside of society, and she knows it, and she resents it.

"The FBI intervened before they could execute any cyberterrorism they may have had planned, but it's clear that their capabilities represent a serious security concern for our nation. Bail must be set high enough to keep them away from computers and internet access so that they cannot carry out their full plan."

Judge Keith picks up his pen. "And what is that figure, Mr. Harren, if you'd care to get to my actual question?"

Mr. Harren shuffles his feet. "Yes, Your Honor, I'm sorry. Given the tremendous likelihood that these defendants could carry out substantial cyberterrorism while they're out, we're asking that bail be set at one million dollars apiece."

TEN

I bite my tongue in an effort not to speak. I look pleadingly at Mr. Pataky, but he's looking at the wall.

The judge makes a note and then turns to Mr. Pataky expectantly.

Mr. Pataky lets out a breath and then says calmly, "Your Honor, these charges are nonsense. What Mr. Harren's summary fails to include is the fact that the five people consented."

The judge shoots a glance back to Mr. Harren. "Is that true?"

Mr. Harren replies smoothly. "I'm not aware of any evidence for that claim, but even if it were, the mere fact of hacking into the Navis constitutes a crime. It is a non-consentable offense."

"Your Honor, I would be interested in hearing Mr. Harren explain what court of law ruled that the troubleshooting of a Navi by an authorized technician could not be consented to. Obviously, there must be precedent, or surely my honorable opponent would not have stated it as fact. I'd merely like to know what that precedent is so that I can read it for myself."

The judge glares at Mr. Pataky. "Are you telling me that Ms. Bernhart was merely troubleshooting Navis?"

"I've submitted the consent forms to the office of the attorney general and to your court, Your Honor. The fact is that the people in question are all patients at Browning Charity Hospital. All of them are suffering from a particular neurological malady, and they specifically consented to having their Navis scrutinized by the defendants in order to determine whether the Navis might have some previously undetected problem. My clients were helping these patients. One of them is even Ms. Bernhart's youngest brother. And Ms. Bernhart is a nurse."

"A *fired* nurse," Mr. Harren clarifies. "Terminated only a week ago specifically due to this so-called research, which her hospital had forbidden as a potential violation of the rights of human subjects."

"Not only is Ms. Bernhart a nurse," Mr. Pataky says with a patient tone, "but Ms. Bremer is a licensed and bonded Navi technician approved by the hospital to carry out this research with the consent of the patients and the supervision of a Dr. Kalyani Abadi."

He sighs, and his tone becomes weary. "Your Honor, these two young women have no previous criminal record. While Ms. Bremer is, in fact, a loner, there is no evidence that I'm aware of that suggests that she has any ill will toward anyone. Merely being a loner, is, I hope, not a crime. She just happens to be a cat person rather than a people person. She has been gainfully employed as a computer programmer here in Atlanta for almost ten years, and she supports her elderly mother, who lives in a skilled-care facility.

"And while it's true that she doesn't have a Navi—as someone who eschews the use of a Navi himself, Your Honor, you know that she can still be a part of society."

Mr. Pataky shoots a sly look at the prosecutor, who presses his lips together.

"And Ms. Bernhart here is an upstanding citizen of her community. She has been working as a registered nurse here in Atlanta for over five years. She has hundreds of friends with whom she communicates daily. She has a dog she time-shares with her elderly neighbor, Mrs. Jones.

"These are ordinary people who, at the absolute worst, may have accidentally tread where the law forbids anyone to step, entirely out of their zeal to help. They'll face these charges in good faith. They have no criminal intent, and they'll cause no trouble to anyone while out on bail. Your Honor, we respectfully request that we allow these two young women to return home to their dog and their cat, with bail set at ten thousand dollars for the both of them."

Both men look at the judge and wait. Despite my sick stomach and pounding heart, I admire their lack of animosity. They're civilized about this.

"Gentlemen, this is an interesting story, and I want to hear all the details in a hearing in a few weeks. I want some of these supposed victims up here as witnesses. One of you see to that. In the meantime, I think a few restrictions ought to render these ladies safe enough for society.

"Defendants are not to interact with any of the five patients, are not to approach that hospital, and are not to touch a computer. Ms. Bernhart's Navi is to be disconnected from all forms of communication. The defendants are not to leave the city. Bail is set at twenty thousand dollars each."

"Thank you, Your Honor," both men murmur, and we step away from the lectern.

My stomach clenches with sudden misery. Okay, we should be able to handle that bail amount, probably with a bondsman's help for me, but . . . with no communications and no computers, how the hell are we going to help Jamie?

Mila remains as calm as ever. As we go back through the doors into the hallway, she says in an aside to Mr. Pataky, "I'll pay the bail." He reminds her that we can get a bondsman to supply most of the money on loan, but she says she wants to handle it herself.

She signs a piece of paper that will transfer the money, we both sign our releases with the terms of the bail, and then we recover our personal items and clothes and get changed.

But Mila gets one exciting new fashion accessory: an ankle bracelet. "Don't try to leave the city or remove the bracelet," a disinterested court employee tells her. "You'll have cops on you like buzzards circling roadkill."

Nice visual.

They tell me the same thing, but I don't need a bracelet. I have a Navi with a GPS in it, and all Navis have auto-installed tracking software that the authorities can activate with court approval. So my ankle bracelet is in my brain.

I kind of wish I'd never known that.

They also make good on the judge's decision for my Navi to be disconnected from all forms of communication. It feels like a death knell.

Even though I'm free, I'm hopelessly out of touch. I can't talk to my Collective even to let them know that I'm out of jail. I'm sure there's some way to talk to my Collective via a physical computer, but I was told not to do that, either, even if I knew how. And yet my Collective is the least of my worries right now.

As soon as we see Mr. Pataky again, I say, "The first thing we have to do is get Jamie's Navi shut down."

"I'm hungry," he answers.

We both stare at him. Food is the last thing on my mind.

"There's a cafeteria downstairs in the basement. Let's go down there and talk so that I don't have to talk while I'm starving."

"Fine," I mutter, and we head toward the elevator.

"You can't have anything to do with your brother," Mr. Pataky says as we walk. "You heard what the judge said? You're prohibited from interacting with any of the five patients. You have something called a 'no contact order as a condition of bond.' You signed it, remember?"

"I know," I say through gritted teeth. "But someone has to do something. So if I can't do it, who can? Isn't there some sort of guardian thing?" I dimly remember that coming up with some of my neuro patients in the past.

"Family members," he says as we wait for the elevator. "His parents would be best."

"Do they have to appear in court?" I ask.

"Yes. There's a hearing process."

I shake my head. "They'll never do it. It's a long story as to why, but it's not going to happen. Who else can do it?"

We get on the elevator.

"Wait a minute, what am I missing?" Mr. Pataky asks. "Why doesn't he put in the request himself? He has a right to direct his own—"

"He's been involuntarily committed," I answer. "He's in the neuro ward."

"Ah," Mr. Pataky says.

We get off the elevator and go into a cold, dimly lit cafeteria not much more cheerful than the cell I just got out of. But I'm still glad to be free again. For the moment.

"Then the court probably appointed the facility as his guardian during the confinement hearing," our attorney says. "They'll need to make that decision."

"Okay, but listen to me." I'm getting frustrated and short tempered. And, I realize, hungry. "Someone has to ask the hospital to do it, and I can't. So who can?"

"Oh, that's easy," Mr. Pataky says. "You can ask. You're allowed to call the hospital and ask, so go ahead."

"Consider it done, then," I say. "Mila, will you get me a sandwich and chips?"

She nods, and I go looking for a phone. I soon realize that I have no idea where to find one, since I've been making calls exclusively via Navi for ten years. I ask around until a security guard lifts a phone from behind his counter and puts it in front of me. I do at least know how to dial the numbers.

Ten minutes later, I'm storming to their table with tears welling up in my eyes.

"Jamie's having seizures and hallucinations and blackouts. And they won't take out his Navi."

"Why not?" Mr. Pataky demands as he chews his sandwich.

"They say that they don't feel it would be in his best interest. *In his best interest.* He's dying. It's killing him, and they won't take it out." I try to stop my chin from trembling, but I can't.

"Did you explain the situation?" Mr. Pataky asks.

"Of course I explained!" I shout. People are staring at me, and I don't care. I wipe my face even as I sob, "Are you stupid? Of course I explained. They won't listen to me. And I don't have any proof. Mila, can we prove this?"

Mila shakes her head slowly. "They took my laptop. I've lost all the evidence I had." She slumps back in her chair. "I should have thought to back up my hard drive. But I didn't . . ."

I turn to Mr. Pataky. "Can we ask them to look at the laptop for the proof?"

"Why would they listen to you?" he asks. "You're criminal defendants. *Felony* criminal defendants."

I look for a wall to punch. Luckily for my hands, there isn't one nearby.

"Quit pacing," Mr. Pataky says. "Eat your sandwich. It's faux chicken."

"I cannot possibly eat my sandwich," I say, although I finally do sit down. "Jamie's brain is being destroyed by that thing. We have to do something. What can we do?"

Mr. Pataky eats another potato chip thoughtfully. "I can ask to become his guardian ad litem. Then I can put in the request. But I'll have to ask you to put me on retainer. Guardianship costs are difficult to estimate up front. It depends on whether it's contested and a lot of other factors."

"How much?" Mila asks.

"Two thousand to start with. We'll go from there. Do you have another five or ten thousand more if it comes to that?"

I glare, but Mila answers coolly. "I do."

I could have kissed her.

"Thank God for you," I say with utter sincerity. She tries to smile reassuringly, and I reach out my hand to her. She takes it and squeezes it gently. She feels like a lifeline, like she might keep me anchored in sanity.

"Then I'll put in the request for the guardianship hearing. I'll classify it as an emergency request." He looks at his watch. "It's a Friday, so they'll do it this afternoon. Hold on." He sits back and eats chips slowly while his gaze flutters around his display.

I grab a handful of napkins and clean myself up. "You have to take care of this," I say to Mr. Pataky. "It's important."

"I understand," he replies.

I try to eat my sandwich, but it settles like lead in my stomach.

"So, what else do we need to discuss?" Mr. Pataky asks. He sounds like he's about ready to head off, and I raise a hand.

"Wait, wait," I say. "We have no idea what's going to happen to us."

We have a lengthy and frustrating conversation in which we try to convince Mr. Pataky that we're being framed and he tries to convince us that it doesn't matter. He tells us that all we should worry about right now is beating these specific charges, and he thinks we have a good chance, given what we've told him and the paperwork he's requested from the hospital. His only concern is the charge that Mila hacked into the national database of IDs. When he asks if she has a ready defense for that part, she looks away and says no.

In the end, he says that all the stuff about HAD and what we've learned about what the Navis are doing is all well and good, but, "You're going to have to prove it. So, good luck." Then he gets up to leave.

"Aren't you supposed to help us?" I demand. "Aren't you our attorney?"

He shakes his head wearily. "I'm defending you from the charges you're up against. That's what I can do. Please understand me—I would love to help you prove that HAD is a conspiracy, but I would also love to do an adequate job for the other twenty-seven clients that I'm defending right now, and at some point, I have to go home to my wife, or she'll divorce me. And I don't want to get a divorce.

"I'm happy to answer your legal questions, and I'm happy to make discovery demands and do all those other things that attorneys do. I'm even happy to hire an investigator or expert witness to make your case if that seems to be the thing to do—if you can pay for it, as that would be an expense not covered by my fee. But you have to tell me what evidence we're chasing and where to go get it. If the government has evidence you need to prove your defense or anyone else does, you tell me, and I'll get it. With a court order if need be. But I don't have time to go down rabbit holes. You do that. You give me the path, and I'll walk down it for you. You got it?"

I look at him, dismayed, and he walks away.

"That man is unlikeable," I announce to the table.

"He's just being rational," Mila says.

I look at her and take in her presence. Just the fact that she is sitting there next to me is such a comfort to me. I find myself reaching out for her hand again, and again she takes it. We look at each other for a moment. Her hand is delicate compared to mine, but warm, and it feels lovely.

I find myself in a state of suspended disbelief, postponing until later the questions about why we would be holding hands and what it might mean. As far as I can tell, she does the same.

"What do we do now?" I ask. "We're under arrest for cyberterrorism, framed, out on bail, Jamie and all those thousands of people still under assault by their Navis . . . and whoever's behind it all tried to kill me. And you saved my life, didn't you, Mila?" This last thought has been slow in dawning on me. Embarrassingly slow.

Mila looks down.

"I would have been lost in all this without you," I say.

A faint blush rises up her face, and she keeps her eyes down. She's adorably modest. I admire her for a moment. Without distractions from my Navi, I can enjoy her with my full attention. I wonder at myself. I have never been so entranced with a woman before.

She lets out a slow breath and then says, "Actually, what we need to do right now is call your mom."

Sure, that makes sense—they're probably worried sick about me if they've been trying to reach me—but there's something puzzling about the way she says it.

"What do you mean? And . . . why did you ask for my mom's phone number when the FBI was arresting us?"

"Um," she says and looks away. "I . . . have something I need to explain. Which is going to sound strange."

"Oh? This is going to be good. What is it?"

She stands up, and we both head toward the elevator. Mila seems to be composing her thoughts. After she presses the button, she says, "I . . . sent my mother to your house. I made it sound like you had requested it."

I stare blankly at the granite walls of the hallway and then turn to face her. "Your senile mother? You sent her to my house? Why would your mother need to go somewhere? And why my house?"

"I normally help take care of my mom, you know? When I realized that I was being taken away by the FBI, I . . . I guess I panicked. I wanted to make sure she would be okay. So I had her sent to your house."

I blink a few more times, trying—and failing—to come to terms with this. "You have got to be kidding me. Who decides that sending her senile mother to a stranger's house in another state is a good idea? So that means my parents have been stuck trying to take care of a crazy woman all this time, thinking it was my idea? They're going to kill me."

The elevator finally arrives, and we both get in, though all of that is background to my building outrage.

"You said they were loving and cared a great deal about family and community," Mila says. "You said your mother would do anything to help anyone."

"Yes, they do, and they are, and she would, but . . . my community is insular. They don't like outsiders. They're not going to be happy at all. My dad is going to be pissed."

I realize that Mila's eyes are brimming with tears, and sympathy wars with anger and frustration.

"I'm sorry," Mila says. "I had a matter of minutes to solve this problem before they took away my laptop. I did the only thing I could think of. I didn't have anywhere else to send her or anyone else who could help me."

The raw confession makes sympathy the victor. That . . . and the fact that Mila just loaned me twenty thousand dollars to get me out of jail . . . plus enough to handle my brother's guardianship hearing. That kind of makes up for a lot.

As the elevator doors open, I sigh heavily. "All right," I mumble as I hold open the doors.

"Can we call now and make sure she made it there?" Mila asks with a desperate tone in her voice.

More sympathy sweeps over me. She's been worrying about her mom all this time.

"Of course," I say. "I'll tell them it was my idea, like you said. I'll explain it for you the way you did. We'll figure it out, okay?"

Mila nods, still looking down, and leads the way off the elevator. I follow her out to the lobby, and we find the same security guard and the same phone. I take a deep breath and brace myself as I dial.

"Dad? It's Phoebe." Mila hovers at my shoulder, trying to listen in.

"Phoebe, what in the world has been going on? I haven't been able to reach you in days. And what is the story with this Mrs. Bremer you sent here? Do you know the trouble you've caused us?"

"Do they have her?" Mila mouths at me. I nod, and her eyes close and her face relaxes.

"Dad, can I talk to Mom, please?"

"This is not a matter for your mother. This is my house that you have brought this on. *My. House.*"

"It's also my mother's house," I say through tight lips. Legally, it isn't. Women don't own anything in my community. But I don't give a crap whose name is on the mortgage. "Put her on the phone."

I hear his angry voice in the room on the other side, then a pause, and then my mom's voice on the phone. "Yes, Phebe? What is the story with Mrs. Bremer? Why did you send her to stay with us? Do you know the"—her voice drops to an emphatic whisper— "the *trouble* it has been? And that Jerry person—Armstrong? Armistead?—he wouldn't explain a thing."

I turn to Mila. "Who's Jerry Arm-something?"

Mila's mouth opens as she tries and fails to articulate an answer. Finally, she says, "Armstead. Long story."

"Okay, so I'm sorry, but my friend Mila needed her to have somewhere to go. Because we . . . we . . ."

"Yes, Phebe? What is it?"

The words "we've been in jail" just will not come out of my mouth. But I also can't come up with an adequate lie in time. I take my cue from Mila. "It's a long story. Very long. But basically, Mila and I have been working together on trying to help Jamie, and Mila normally takes care of her mom, and she couldn't while she was helping me, and . . ."

Mila is holding out her hand for the phone. I stare blankly at her and then hand it over. It seems like a terrible idea for her to talk to them, but even she probably can't do much worse than I'm doing.

"Mrs. Bernhart, thank you for taking care of my mother," Mila says in her usual blunt way. "I know it has disrupted your normal routines and caused you stress. I'm sorry about that. We wouldn't have done it to you if we could have thought of a better way to handle it, but sometimes, things like this happen. And I know you want an explanation, but I can't give you one right now, except to say that it's about your family—about Jamie and Phoebe—and we need you to take care of my mother so that we can focus on our work here."

I would kill to hear what my mother is saying in response, but I can only make out the sound of her voice.

"Phoebe loves you, and she doesn't want to worry you when she can take care of things herself," Mila says in response to a question. "But this time, she can't do it alone, and that's why we had to send my mother to you. We knew you would have the compassion and skill necessary to take care of her. Not everyone would."

As I listen, I realize that Mila's bluntness is a perfect match for the plain speech my community and family prefers. Perhaps that's why I find Mila alternately infuriating and comforting. I hadn't even thought about it until now, but I've grown up around people like her.

My mother says something. I can hear the questioning lilt at the end of the sentence.

"It's too early to speculate on what the results might be, but we've had a breakthrough with Jamie."

I hear the sigh from my mother all the way from here. She says something longer. I hear "Jesus" and "serve him."

"Thank you, Mrs. Bernhart. And you don't have to worry about Phoebe. She can be sensible when she needs to be."

I roll my eyes while my mother chuckles and asks another question.

"Mila."

Another pause.

"We will. Goodbye." Mila hangs up the phone.

"Okay, I'm impressed," I say. "You handled that better than I would have."

"Your people like the truth, don't they?" she asked.

"Technically, you left out a whole lot of the truth."

"Well, they like what *sounds* like the truth."

I give her a look. For an instant, I wonder whether she has used— or would use—that same kind of selectivity in what she tells me.

"Thank you," I say to the security guard, who nods and puts the phone away.

We move out past the security checkpoint, out in front of the building where traffic and pedestrians go past. We both take a few aimless steps and then stop and turn toward each other.

I find myself caressing her arm and shoulder and then gently touching her face. And then Mila steps to me and buries her head in my shoulder and wraps her arms around me. "I miss my cat," she says, her voice cracking.

I start chuckling and can't stop. It feels so damn good to touch another warm, living human being. I never want to let her go. Finally, though, I do.

"Well, then, let's go see your cat," I say. "We might as well have somewhere to go while we're trying to figure all this out."

A few minutes later, we're back outside the courthouse after using the same phone again, this time to call an automated cab to take us to Mila's house.

And that's when I get the message on my Navi.

!!! A warrant has been issued for your arrest. !!!

!!! Please turn yourself in to the nearest police
station at your earliest convenience. !!!

"What the *hell*?" I demand.

Mila looks at me, her eyebrows up.

"I got a notification that there's a warrant out for my arrest and I'm supposed to go turn myself in." I stare at her in disbelief.

"Could it be a delayed notification from the earlier charges?" she offers.

"Maybe. God, I hope so. We'd better call Mr. Pataky."

A few minutes later, we're back inside, calling him from the same phone. He answers the call immediately. "Phoebe, I'm glad you called. Bad news. You have a warrant out. There are new charges against you both."

Mila is saying something. I wave at her to tell her to wait a minute, but I speak out loud so she can at least hear my half of the conversation.

"I got the notification. What the hell is going on? What do you mean, 'new charges'?"

"They've added fourteen additional char—"

"*Fourteen* additional charges?"

"Fourteen—and five counts of cyberterrorism."

"How is that even *possible*?"

"The FBI brought new evidence to the attorney general's office that your Ms. Bremer introduced the Hyper-Aggression malware into the Navis of those five people."

As Mr. Pataky talks, I look over at Mila, uncomprehending. This isn't happening.

"The bail is going to impossible to meet this time. I can guarantee, with five counts of cyberterrorism, they're going to ask for maybe two million dollars for each of you."

I swallow. How are we going to prove our innocence from a jail cell? All my hopes are evaporating.

Mr. Pataky will get the Navi uninstalled from Jamie. I grasp onto that idea. Even if we're in jail waiting for our trial, Mr. Pataky will take care of Jamie.

"—waiting more than a few hours before you go turn yourselves in. Maybe three hours. Are you still at the courthouse? You can turn yourselves in there right now."

"No," I lie instinctively.

"Is she there with you now?" he asks.

Mila is looking at me intently as if she's trying to discern what's going on by reading my facial expressions. There's no hint of guilt on her face. No fear.

"Is she there now?" he asks again.

"Yes. Yes, she's here."

"Tell her everything I've told you. Do it now, out loud, so that I can hear it and have it on record."

My throat is dry, but I swallow hard and get out the words somehow. "There's a warrant out for each of us. The FBI brought in new evidence that you . . . caused HAD with those five patients. We have to turn ourselves in within a few hours."

"Three hours," Mr. Pataky corrects.

"Within three hours. Bail will probably be set for two million dollars each, maybe more."

Mila looks away, out through the front windows of the lobby. "What time is it now?"

I glance at the clock at the top right of my vision. "Two thirty." She nods.

I stare at her. I wish she weren't so damn difficult to read. I wish I had any sense at all that I understood her.

"Ask her if she has any ready defense for these charges," Mr. Pataky is saying.

Tentatively, trying to make it sound offhand, I say, "He's asking if you have a ready defense for these charges." My heart is in my throat. I want her to say yes.

She doesn't even think about it. "No," she says. "Nothing."

"All right," Mr. Pataky says. "I'll contact you after the guardianship hearing. It's at three." He hangs up without waiting for my response.

Mr. Pataky's words echo through my mind. *Ask her if she has a ready defense.* Suddenly, I realize that I don't know this woman at all. She is almost entirely a stranger to me.

Until a moment ago, I would never even have considered the possibility that Mila had done anything wrong. I asked her to help me, after all. She's been helping me. Why would she help me if she were involved?

Maybe she only offered to help so she could tell me what she wanted me to hear. It's not like I understand anything she's doing with her laptop.

Mila turns and looks directly at me. I feel pierced by her gaze.

"You're wondering whether the charges are true. Whether I did something to those people."

I open my mouth to answer, but I can't think of what to say.

"The charges aren't true," she says. "I didn't do anything to them. I am trying to help."

I close my mouth.

I think back over everything that's happened. Mila came to help me of her own accord, yes. But she also saved my life when I had that seizure.

Saved. My. Life.

My ears burn.

We walk silently out to the curb and wait for another automated cab. As if by silent agreement, we continue our plan to go to Mila's house, even given all that's happened.

I find myself wanting to take her hand again as we ride together in the passenger compartment, but I've offended her. Anyway, wanting to hold her hand is an urge that I shouldn't be having, and that leads me down a line of thought I'm not ready to go down.

Instead, I replay the whole strange series of events in my mind—everything that has happened in a couple of weeks. I feel like I'm coping pretty darn well, all things considered, and I wonder if I'm in a state of shock. Maybe I'll feel functional only for now and then have some kind of PTSD afterward. At least we have good drugs for PTSD now. Even some promising Navi treatments.

I break into a cynical laugh at the thought of using a Navi for mental health, now that I know everything I know, and Mila looks over at me in surprise. "Nothing," I say. "Kind of overwhelmed by it all."

When we arrive at her apartment, before Mila can even unlock the door, we hear piteous mewing from the other side. Mila gets the door open, and her legs are immediately assaulted by a beautiful gray cat who does her utmost to trip her. Mila steps inside and then kneels to smother her with attention.

I glance around. I've been curious to know how Mila lives, and I'm somewhat surprised to find that it's artfully decorated and cozy, though somewhat minimalistic. I'm immediately enchanted by the presence of physical books on bookshelves and a physical upright piano against the wall in the dining room. It makes sense, though. She can't call up a Navi keyboard or read books on her Navi, though she could use an ebook reader. I'm reasonably sure they still have those.

"Person-Phoebe, meet cat-Phoebe," Mila says from the floor.

I kneel on the floor. "It's nice to meet you," I assure cat-Phoebe, who answers by delicately sniffing my hand and knee and then throwing herself on her side and purring vigorously.

"Her purr is so loud," I remark.

"Yes," Mila said, and I note the second smile I've ever seen from the blonde woman. "It's one of my favorite things about her."

We're both in a daze, I think. We sit there on the floor and pet the cat, not talking. I soon realize that there's nothing to do here other than play the piano and read the books, neither of which we make any move to do. There's no TV, no radio, no computer. Unlike at the hospital or at the jail, there's no local database of movies and music for me to pull up on my Navi, either. It's so quiet.

But the message refuses to leave my display:

!!! A warrant has been issued for your arrest. !!!

I'm not allowed to forget about it for even a moment. Even with all other communications disabled, I still get this message burned into my brain.

"Two and a half hours of freedom remaining," I tell Mila. "I feel like there's something important we ought to be doing with this time, but I can't think of what it ought to be."

She nods. "It's like I'm . . ."

"Paralyzed." We say it at the same time and then grin wanly at each other.

Her phone rings. She gets up and answers it, a land line in her kitchen. I hear a few quiet words, and then she hands the phone to me. "It's Mr. Pataky again."

My heart jumps. He's out of the hearing about Jamie. I take the phone. "Hello?"

"Phoebe," he says.

Just from his tone of voice, I know something has gone terribly wrong.

TEN

Fifteen minutes later, I lay on my back on Mila's floor, tears of anger leaking from the corners of my eyes. Cat-Phoebe has decided that she likes me, and her chin rests on my hip bone. I can feel the purring through my jeans, and it may be the only thing keeping me sane. My body is rigid with tension. Mila sits cross-legged nearby, sipping some tea.

"Something is *happening* to us," I say adamantly. My stomach clenches in helpless rage. "Someone is . . . *doing* something to us. This can't be accidental. For the hospital to block Jamie's transfer of guardianship . . . these charges against us . . . the FBI . . ."

Mila straightens and tilts her head as she gazes at me. "Something is happening to us," she repeats thoughtfully. She tilts her head again the other way as if she's thinking intently.

"Don't you think?" I ask.

"Yes," she says calmly. She leans back against the base of the sofa and closes her eyes. I can't read her expression.

"So what can we *do*?" I sit up and stare at Mila accusingly, as if she's supposed to have the answer. Cat-Phoebe objects to my sudden movement with a mew. I say, "We're about to be back in jail, and I can't help Jamie, and—" I don't think I can go on without bursting into tears, so I stop.

An idea strikes. I scramble up to my feet. "Let's call Dr. Abadi."

The phone call goes straight to voice mail. The brusque, tense recording says, "This is Dr. Abadi. I'm unavailable due to a family emergency. Messages will be returned in a day or two."

I groan, but I leave a message anyway. I don't know what else to do. "Dr. Abadi, it's Phoebe Bernhart. I'm sorry to bother you. I hope you're okay. Look, something has to be done to continue our work on HAD. We're being framed, and they wouldn't bother to do that if we weren't on the right track. By the time you get this message, I'll be back in jail, so it's up to you to do something. *Please* do something. Please tell everyone. Tell the CDC and the World Health Organization and everyone you can think of. I know it sounds crazy, but if you tell everyone, maybe someone will believe you and look into it. Something has to be done. It's up to you now."

I hang up. "Crap. I hope she's okay. Maybe someone in her family has HAD, too." I groan. "What now?"

Mila lets out a long breath. "In two hours?" She shakes her head and rubs her face tiredly. "That's only enough time for us to make arrangements for our pets and pay up our rent and bills . . . you know, get ready to go back."

I contemplate the fact that I'm expected to waltz over to the nearest police department and give myself up. Put all my things back into a plastic baggie. Step into a green jumpsuit again. Put out my hands for the cuffs. Voluntarily resign myself to futility and helplessness.

I stand up and pace the small living room.

There has to be another way. I refuse to accept that this is where it ends for me, that it's in other people's hands now to find the cause of HAD and to get treatment to Jamie before he dies from the grand mal seizures. While I'm helpless. Unable to help him. Unable to do a damn thing.

My stomach clenches again, so hard I nearly double over, and I brace myself on the back of a chair.

Jamie is my responsibility. I brought him out here into "the world." It's my job to protect him from it.

This is everything my father ever warned me about. This never would have happened back home, where we would have had the resources of the entire community to rely on. When hundreds of people are on your side, you don't have to be afraid of the world. You stay out of it, and it leaves you alone.

And just like that, I know what we have to do.

My breath is taken away by how much there is to do and how quickly we have to do it.

"Mila, do you have a carrier for cat-Phoebe? We'll take her to Mrs. Jones. She can take care of both Tobi and the cat. We're going to have to cut off your ankle bracelet. Do you know how to do that? Because otherwise, we'll have to find a computer somewhere to look it up. And you have to disable the app that they're using to track me with my Navi. And then Jamie's. Jamie's, too, or they'll follow us through him."

Mila looks up at me, her eyes wide. But, to her credit, she doesn't ask me what I'm talking about it. She's smart. She understands everything in an instant.

Changes in expression flicker across her face. She's considering this. Whether she's going to do it.

I sink to my knees in front of her. I plead with her silently. But I don't need to say anything. She understands what's at stake. She understands that I have no other options.

"I don't know how to remove the bracelet, no." She brings up her ankle and looks at it, feels it. "It's plastic. It's so flimsy, it feels like I could cut it off with kitchen shears. But I don't know much about it. You're right, we should look it up."

She straightens up and thinks for a moment. "There's a computer at a library down the street, but we should buy me another laptop. I'll need it. I'll be useless to you without it."

I nod vigorously. I should have thought of that.

"Disguises," Mila says. Now she's talking as fast as I am. She suddenly seems energized, even frantic, but then, so do I. I'm shivering with anxiety. "We don't pack any of our own clothes. The moment we take off the bracelet, they'll be looking for us, so we have to be in clothes they won't recognize. And we'll need wigs—several wigs. I don't know where a wig store is, but there's a big Goodwill down the street that I shop at all the time. What are your sizes?" She rushes to a kitchen drawer to get a pencil and a pad of paper and writes them down as I tell her.

I start making a list of things to do on my Navi display.

- Disguises and wigs
- Get Mila a laptop
- Jamie's meds
- Jamie
- Cat-Phoebe to Mrs. Jones

"First, we do everything that doesn't look suspicious," I say. "Taking cat-Phoebe to Mrs. Jones would seem like a perfectly reasonable thing to do. We do that first. Going to Goodwill won't raise any red flags. You might as well pack your toiletries, since you're here, and I'll grab mine when we take cat-Phoebe to Mrs. Jones." I'm nearly hyperventilating, I realize. "Oh my God, we have so little time to do all of this."

"Was five thirty the absolute deadline?" Mila asks.

I check the time. It's three thirty now. I try to recall how Mr. Pataky said it. "I don't think so. He initially said something like, 'you don't have more than a few hours.' Then he said three hours. I think he said that to be on the safe side. We might still have three hours left, or even four hours. I don't know."

"Let's call the courthouse and ask," Mila says.

"What? Really? Ask?"

"Why not?" Mila shrugs. She picks up her land-line phone on the kitchen counter and dials. I go back to composing my list while I pace.

- Money (is there untraceable money anymore?)
- Fake IDs?
- A private manual-drive car—not Mila's
- How to get off ankle bracelet?

I'm feeling overwhelmed and intimidated when Mila comes back.

"I told them that I found out about the warrant and asked how much time I have to make arrangements for my elderly mother and my pets. They said they would hold off until seven thirty. They were perfectly pleasant about it."

I exhale and nod. I look at the time. It's three forty. "Almost four hours. Okay, then this might be doable. What happens at seven thirty?"

Mila shrugs. "I guess they send cops to pick us up."

I nod. "I've been making a list of things to do. Mila . . . I can't tell you how embarrassed I am to have to ask this . . . but you know I don't have any money. And we're going to need some. We might need a lot."

Mila nods as if she's already thought of this. "I'll have to empty my accounts, because they'll freeze them as soon as we go AWOL. But we'll have to do that as one of the last things, because it'll get their attention."

"Is there any such thing as untraceable cash anymore?"

"I don't know. But I do know who to ask. I need that laptop computer first."

Time rushes by with alarming speed. Mila packs up her few things in five minutes, but then it takes another fifteen minutes to put cat-Phoebe into the carrier. There are a few things in life you cannot rush, and getting a cat who has all of her claws into a small box is one of them. So now it's four o'clock.

"Laptop first," Mila says urgently.

We head to a DigiBox, and Mila buys the cheaper of the two laptops they still offer. I'm surprised, but she explains that her task will require little computing power. She also gets solar chargers and battery packs, since my family doesn't have electricity. She asks whether the national wi-fi covers my community, and I assure her that it does—I've noticed it on my few return trips since I got my Navi. She pays with her credit card, and we head back to the car. "Aren't they going to be able to trace this laptop back to us?" I ask.

She shakes her head. "Not really. I just have to be careful where and how I connect to networks, and I have to keep changing my MAC address. But just to be sure, I'll also install a special-purpose rootkit to remove any tracking software and automatically route all traffic through anonymizing routers."

I just shake my head and keep walking.

Once in the car, Mila opens the laptop and connects it to the car's charging port. "I'm connecting to another server in Thailand I still have access to from an old contract job. From there, I'll reach out to find someone who can get us anonymous cash cards."

By now, it's 4:25.

I drive to the Goodwill and go in for an armload of clothes in both our sizes, paying no attention to styles or colors. This takes twenty-five minutes.

Mila reports that she has a contact for the cash cards, and she dives right back into her work. "I have to be ready to shut down your Navi and Jamie's."

It's a good thing nationwide wi-fi was put in years ago. Otherwise, we'd be seriously handicapped while we tried to do all this.

I continue driving. Because Friday-afternoon rush-hour traffic has kicked in, it takes thirty-five minutes for me to get cat-Phoebe to Mrs. Jones and then another fifteen minutes to extricate myself from Mrs. Jones, who is eager for company and determined to sit me down for a cup of coffee and some pastries. I tell her that Jamie is in the hospital with HAD and I'm spending all my time there right now. I spend eight minutes grabbing my toiletries and sundries from my apartment, and now it's 5:48.

Our next stop is the nearest Diva Dimension, which takes twenty minutes to get to with this traffic. I'm practically hysterical with stress by the time we get there. Then, while Mila continues to work on her computer as fast as she can, I go in for an armload of wigs, skull caps, hair pins, and makeup. It's 6:25 when I come out.

I have intense anxiety. My chest aches and I'm dizzy from constantly hyperventilating. But there's nothing to be done about it.

We're starving, and brains don't work well without fuel, so we stop at a drive-through for soy burgers. While we sit in the car in the parking lot and eat our burgers and fries, she looks up how to remove an ankle bracelet. Thankfully, that only takes about four minutes.

"Any sharp blade will do it," she says. "But the alarm goes off within ten seconds. And they recapture ninety-nine percent of offenders within forty-eight hours. We'll have to move fast. Plus, tampering with it will add another felony charge. Of course, all of that will also apply to me disabling the tracking on your Navi."

I think my stomach would be doing flips if it weren't already weighed down by the fast food. Instead, it gurgles.

"On the up side, they sometimes spend as long as four hours trying to reach the 'offender' before they declare them AWOL. Oh, and if the cops can't find us, federal marshals will be sent after us to get us back. But not private bounty hunters, from what I can tell. We didn't use a bail bondsman, and those are the guys who hire the bounty hunters to get their money back."

I rub my face and let out a long, slow breath. This is getting too real. And now I'm acutely aware of the fact that I asked Mila to do this for me. For my family. And we're putting everything at risk.

"Mila."

She looks at me.

I don't want to say this, but I have to say it. "You don't have to do this. I have to go get Jamie out. I have to risk it, because he's going to die if I don't. But you don't have to go with me."

The truth is that I can't possibly do this without her, but still. Now that I'm fully aware of the consequences, I can't ask her to do this for me.

She faces forward again. I gaze at her profile, thinking—irrationally—that she's beautiful from every angle. Her curly blonde hair slips forward, covering her face, and she smoothes it back.

"They won't let me program anymore if I'm convicted of cyberterrorism," she says thoughtfully. "So I have to prove that we're being framed. And I can't do that from a jail cell."

I shouldn't be surprised at how pragmatic she is, at how mechanically she sees the world. I should know this about her by now. For a moment, I wonder if all her thoughts are in binary. Just 1s and 0s in there. Nothing human.

But then she takes my hand and turns to gaze at me, and my heart skips a beat. Her voice low, she says, "And I don't want Jamie to die."

Tears well up in my eyes. I am so damn grateful right now. I squeeze her hand and murmur thanks, and she squeezes back.

I catch sight of the time in my display. "It's 6:40," I say, my voice strangled.

She takes a deep breath and thinks for a minute. "I think it's about time for us to go AWOL. We've done everything we can do legally and without drawing unnecessary attention. So getting all my money out is the next thing to do, and that's when they'll take an interest. That will be our cue to take off the bracelet and get disguised."

We both sit and study one another's faces for a moment. I think both of us are looking for some sign in the other that we're going to back down. This is our last chance.

Whatever we're looking for, we don't find it. And while Mila continues to work on her new laptop, I drive us to the nearest branch of Mila's bank—Dash Bank. I grin at the apt name, and I thank God that Dash Bank has late-night hours on Fridays.

She hurries in and comes back five minutes later with four money cards. "They would only let me take out ten thousand dollars. Let's go now. I've made arrangements to meet my contact at the Super Seven off 278."

It takes an alarming eighteen minutes just to get there. She gets out before I've even come to a complete stop, and she hurries back, panting, exactly three minutes later.

"Done. These money cards are anonymized."

It's 7:28.

"Now is the time to go AWOL," Mila says breathlessly. "I will shut down your Navi first, since it will take longer. I will take off my ankle bracelet after that."

About ten minutes later, Mila mutters something in frustration. "I forgot that you depend on this device to correct your vision. Give me a few more minutes."

I chew my nails and try to stop hyperventilating.

It takes a few more minutes, and then my Navi is gone. Everything in my display vanishes. I can still see, though.

I hadn't been using my Navi for much since I got out of jail this morning before the bail hearing, but I still want it back. Like, *right now.*

Actually, I had been using it consistently for one purpose. "Now we need to buy a watch," I say.

Mila and I look at each other and laugh, though there's hysteria in it.

Out of necessity, I set aside my mourning for my lost Navi, and I start driving to a used-car dealer. Mila keeps working on the money cards in the meantime. While we're on the freeway, though, she takes a knife out of her backpack, slices through the ankle bracelet, and tosses it out the window.

I shake my head.

I cannot believe what has happened to my life. A couple of weeks ago, I was a run-of-the-mill nurse with of an attitude problem who talked to her Collective 24/7 and was addicted to coffee. Now I'm a suspected terrorist on the run.

We stop on the way to put on wigs and makeup and new clothes. I'm impressed by how different Mila looks as a brunette with too-dark lipstick and dark sunglasses. She's still drop-dead gorgeous, but in a different way. For my part, I'm now a curvy redhead with too much blush.

I take us to the shoddiest car dealer I can find that's close by—the kind that has faded, sagging paper pennants and a hand-lettered sign that says, "Bad credt, no credt, drive away 2day."

I park a block away, and Mila goes in for the kill. As I watch the poor guy who owns the place gesticulate wildly out in the parking lot, I'm dying to know how Mila's coming across. I can imagine how she looks—this too-calm, too-beautiful *chica* with too much makeup who wants to buy a car right now and doesn't care what car it is and will overpay him by five thousand dollars from an untraceable money card if he will give her the car right-now-please and then kindly forget she ever existed.

I'm pretty sure she makes an impression. I don't think his operation is legal to begin with, though, so I'm also pretty sure he's not going to tell anybody about us. And her disguise is good.

We drive both cars about six blocks, and then I leave Mila's in a big parking lot. Mila slides over into the passenger seat of the new car, and I take over driving. It's a silver Honda. Can't get much more nondescript than that. And it doesn't have plates, and it's a manual-drive car, so there's no ID associated with it.

It's killing me that all this has taken so long—and that I don't know how long it's been, now that my clock is gone. I'm in a serious hurry to get to Jamie. If they suspect that I'm going to try to break him out, then they'll put security in place.

We arrive at the hospital, and this is where things get tricky. But considering that I have years of experience in hospitals, it's not as tricky as it might otherwise be.

We don't have the time or the knowhow to hack in and get me the right kind of access to Jamie's floor or records or anything else. So, we do it the brute-force way, the we-will-be-so-damn-lucky-if-this-actually-works way.

First, we loiter at the entrance until the security guard is distracted. Normally, all visitors are checked in—and employees are badged in—by Navi, but Mila doesn't have one and mine is nonfunctional. I figure Nonnies are typically supposed to sign in physically with the security guy, and after that, I honestly don't know if there's any other security in place for them.

So once the guard is distracted by chatting with someone, we swagger in like we own the place. We go up to Jamie's floor, go to the locker room and change into some scrubs we casually steal out of a locker, grab an unattended stretcher on the way up to Jamie's room, and close the door.

I've been expecting some sort of alarms or some sort of security around Jamie, but there's been nothing. I guess they didn't expect an in-person attack from the cyberterrorists.

Jamie is out like a light. Judging from his slack expression and nonresponsiveness, I'm guessing he's under sedation. That's good for us. It irks me like crazy that I can't check his medical records before removing him from the hospital, but I can have Mila check all of that for us as soon as we get clear. The important thing is that he's not on any life-saving equipment. I can see for myself that he's only on saline, and I can safely remove that IV myself.

We transfer him to the stretcher, and while Mila wheels him out to where patients are transferred by ambulance, I go to the dispensary, loiter until I'm reasonably sure no one else is in there, and then pull every drug I can think of that Jamie might need in the next few days. I put everything into a paper sack and head downstairs.

I keep expecting people to stop me and demand to know who I am and what I'm doing, but I realize after a while that everyone is too busy with their Navis to *look* at me. All they catch sight of in their peripheral vision is a person in scrubs moving purposefully down the hallway. Because I effectively don't have a Navi, I don't even register on any other level.

In some sense, I don't exist.

By the time I get back downstairs, I understand why Mila isn't the most . . . sociable person on the planet. She's been treated as if she doesn't exist for the past ten years.

Right about the time I get to the exit where Mila should be, our luck runs out, and I hear raised voices. I run the remaining dozen yards.

Mila is standing between three hospital employees and the stretcher, and the employees are yelling for security.

I don't stop running. I hurtle directly into the employees and send everyone sprawling. I feel like a bowling ball that made a strike, and I think I caught an elbow in my left eye, but there's no time for that now.

"Run!" I yell to Mila.

She turns, wide-eyed, and starts pushing Jamie at a fast trot out into the parking lot, the stretcher wobbling dangerously. I shove down the people around me who are trying to stand back up, and I yell apologies at the same time—I'm not too good at being a violent criminal, apparently—and then, when I see reinforcements showing up, I turn and run, too.

We parked close and left the car unlocked, and so we shove Jamie unceremoniously into the back seat, Mila jumping in on top of him. I kick the stretcher away, jump in the driver's seat, and start the car. Thank God I still remember how to drive a manual car from before I got my Navi. People are on us, tearing the doors back open, and I gun it.

We squeal away with people tumbling off the car, two of the doors swinging wildly and dangerously.

Please, God, don't let anyone have gotten hurt.

I swerve to the right and gun it to make my door swing in, so I can catch it and close it. As I correct back to the left, I hear Mila slam the other open door.

I drive like an absolute maniac, checking my rear-view mirror all the way, to the nearest big parking lot, which is about five minutes away. I stop and park in the rows of cars.

No one is behind us—not yet.

Mila transfers to the front seat and opens her laptop. I know she's disabling Jamie's Navi. Otherwise, they'll use his GPS to track us down. They're probably doing that already.

I saw her pack a small toolkit in her backpack while we were at her apartment, and now, it's apparent to me how freaking smart she is. I dig inside it, find a Phillips-head screwdriver, and go out and transfer the license plates from a Hyundai to ours. Then I transfer the plates from a Toyota to the Hyundai.

The owners of the Hyundai will take forever to even realize their plates have been changed out, and meanwhile, the plates that get reported missing from the Toyota won't be the ones on our car.

While I'm at it, I take two magnetic decals off other cars and transfer them, too. Now we support Ekindorff for Senator, and we're fans of the Snake Charmers.

People pass by occasionally, but no one is paying any attention. Everyone is always looking into their Navis. How have I never realized that before?

I look in the car window at Mila. "Almost there," she says. "Go ahead and drive."

I check in on Jamie first. He's been roused by all the activity, but he's too heavily drugged to register anything that's going on. I lay him down in the backseat and try to get him at least somewhat secured by the seatbelts.

Then I drive again.

I take random side roads away from the hospital until Mila declares only a few minutes later, "It's done. We're off the grid."

Then I drive to the nearest freeway and get on, heading north toward home—toward Zanesville, Ohio.

Night is falling, and clouds are moving at an easy pace across the darkening sky. The moon is a slim crescent over my left shoulder. Jamie is snoring softly in the backseat, while Mila stares into the glow of her laptop screen. And maybe we're going to be okay.

Forty-five minutes later, Mila receives an email from a name she doesn't recognize.

> Dear Ms. Bremer,
>
> I want to sincerely apologize to you for how things have been handled so far. Acting directly upon your mother was an egregious error in judgment, and those responsible have been terminated. I've taken this matter over myself, and I assure you that things will be different now.
>
> I know that you have no reason to trust me, but I believe that we might be able to quickly develop a mutually beneficial relationship if you'll give me the chance. I invite you to contact me from an anonymous email address to discuss further. Please reach out to me as quickly as possible. The situation is escalating rapidly.

Sincerely,

Slava Knyazev
Director of Sales and Marketing
Peake International

A few minutes later, after some furious internet research, Mila responds.

I've verified that this email came from your Navi ID, but it could be spoofed. Why should I believe it's you? Are you really so stupid as to message me from your own Navi?

She flips back to a browser window. Her voice level, she says to Phoebe, "News headlines are flooding in now."

She reads from her screen. "'Indicted Cyberterrorists Skip Bail.' 'Arrest Warrants Issued for Suspected Terrorists.' 'Cyberterrorists Abduct Hospital Patient.'"

"All news people love the word 'terrorist,'" Phoebe comments drily.

"They have pictures of us and Jamie and this car."

"In its original condition, or as it is now?" Phoebe asks with some alarm.

"Original, minus the plates and magnetic decals," Mila replies. She pauses for a moment and then reads again. "'Rioting at Government Detention Centers Overnight. An undercover reporter with the Associated Press reported earlier today that some violent patients at government detention centers have been cuffed to steel bars and left without bathroom facilities or medical treatment. In response, members of the public have armed themselves and made attempts to breach the defenses of these facilities, apparently with the agenda of breaking out family members imprisoned there. Guards defending the facilities have shot and killed sixteen people. Another thirty-five have been hospitalized with minor injuries related to the use of tear gas, smoke bombs, and riot gear.'"

Phoebe winces. "Jesus."

"There's nothing else the government can do," Mila says calm-ly. "These are dangerous patients, and there aren't enough drugs or padded rooms to go around. What choice do they have?"

Phoebe doesn't answer.

A reply from Slava Knyazev comes in for Mila.

> Ms. Bremer,
>
> Smart question. Naturally, I'm not sending this th-rough my company's network. And of course I don't have the Memory app running. That means the only data stored from my Navi is from the past three days, as required by law enforcement and medical person-nel. However, I and all my colleagues have a slightly illicit program running which will delete all the con-tents of my Navi upon my command if necessary, such as if I were taken into custody by law enforcement per-sonnel. So we can consider this conversation private on my end—which is why I suggested that you write to me from an anonymous email address on your end, for your own protection.
>
> And I'm not worried about your turning over these messages to the authorities yourself. With no cor-roborating evidence, we can claim that *you* created these messages. It would be your word against ours, and given that right now all the evidence about HAD is pointing at you, I'm fairly confident that we'd win that round.
>
> But there's another reason I'm not worried, Ms. Bre-mer. I'm not worried because I'm certain that you are smart, rational, and willing to consider a solid deal.
>
> Am I right?
>
> Again, I urge you to get back to me just as quickly as you can. The window is closing.

Sincerely,

Slava Knyazev

Mila doesn't reply, and she says nothing to Phoebe. She closes the email window.

Mila tells me that our original bail has been revoked, and new warrants for Failure to Appear have been issued. I'm glad my Navi can't give me the warning messages. They'd probably stack up until they obscured my vision.

I quickly realize how damn lucky I am to have Mila. The first thing she has us do, once we're about an hour out, is stop off in a secluded spot and set up a live video shoot with the camera on the laptop. She gets video of our car sans the plates and magnetic decals and of us sans disguises and then integrates that footage into the live Navi display of a convenience store clerk about an hour southwest of Atlanta.

He "sees" us walk in and look around. Because he's been watching the news—and he's not terribly bright—he immediately yells, "Hey! Are you Mila and Phoebe?" We know this because we're watching his feed. So we "run away." He runs after us and "sees" our car speeding away. And then he notifies the police, exactly as we'd hoped.

Half an hour later, the news reports, "Suspected Cyberterrorists Spotted at Shell Station."

"I'm laying a false trail that will show us heading straight to the Mexican border," she tells me, not a little proud of herself. "Reynosa."

I am dumbfounded that this is even possible.

"You know," I say, "if you had half a mind to be a cyberterrorist . . ."

She grins just slightly. "This trick is only going to work so many times and only for so long. As soon as they look at the footage closely, they'll see that it was a shoddy cut-and-paste job. I don't have time to do it well enough for it to stand up to scrutiny."

"What else are you able to do?" I ask, still marveling. For a moment, she looks like a technology goddess. What could be off limits to someone who can get into anyone's Navi and make them see and hear anything she wants?

Her grin fades. "That's really about it," she says. "Consider me a one-trick pony for now. I have to have the right footage to insert, and I have to have a Navi ID in the right location, and there can't be any other people around to disconfirm my added footage. It's a very limited technique."

"I'm still impressed," I say. "Honestly, it's a little scary. Is it that easy to hack into people's Navis, or are you just making it look easy?"

She grins again. "I'm brilliant, remember?"

I just shake my head.

In addition to Mila's digital wizardry, every time we make a stop for gas or food or the bathroom, we wear a different disguise, and we never go in together, since they're looking for two women traveling together. I periodically switch out license plates and magnetic decals. I especially like to trade out political sentiments. The guy who parks with a "Guns, God, and Glory" decal and drives away with a "Greenpeace" one is my favorite.

An hour or so later, Mila reads, "'Cyberterrorism Death Toll Tops 5,000.'"

"Jesus. Really?" I say.

"'The world's worst cyberterrorist attack on record has now killed 5,011 people, the Centers for Disease Control and Prevention reported this evening, with approximately 15,000 total patients. In New York City alone, there have been 315 homicides, 174 suicides, and 358 hospital deaths that are attributable to what was termed Hyper-Aggression Disorder, now called Eve.'"

"'Eve'?" I blink.

"Viruses and malware get names, sort of like hurricanes, but a lot less organized," Mila says. "Whatever takes off in the media, usually."

I shrug. "Well, we're women and we're supposedly evil, so I guess 'Eve' makes sense."

"Eve wasn't evil," Mila says absently. "She just chose knowledge over blind obedience. Here's the rest of the story: 'Officials estimate that the number of homicides and suicides is 400% above normal throughout the United States as a direct result of the malware allegedly promulgated by two women from Atlanta, Phoebe Bernhart and Mila Bremer. No motive has yet been determined for the two women. Any tips . . .' etc. etc."

A sigh slips out of me as I think about what's going on. "I guess the good news is that now that everyone knows what's causing it, they can stop it. Right? We no longer have to save everyone. We just have to clear our names now."

Mila shakes her head. "I was just reading some more articles about that. Yes, people know it's the Navis now, but what can they do about it when the numbers are so high? A couple of cities started sending cops door-to-door to shut down people's Navis using their law enforcement overrides, but first, some cops got shot by people who think that Eve is a government conspiracy designed to take away people's Navis—"

"Holy crap," I say.

"—and secondly, it didn't work. The malware resides in the security module, which is not disabled by police measures. I'm confident that whoever created Eve designed it that way."

"Why don't they send Navi technicians? They should be able to shut them down or remove them entirely, like you did to mine and Jamie's."

"Some cities are working on that, but realistically, there just aren't enough technicians to go around. With billions of Navis and only thousands of technicians, it would take months or even years to accomplish that. We need a software fix."

"That's what I meant a minute ago. Surely they have lots of people working on that now."

Mila shrugs. "They don't know what Eve does, yet, let alone how. It took me days to figure it out. It's going to take them at least twice as long as it took me, and then they still have to write the patch. It could take weeks."

I nod slowly. Mila is not a humble person, but she's not bragging, either. She's being honest. "And by then," I say, "the death toll could be ten thousand, or twenty thousand, or more."

"Yes."

I glance over at her. Something about her perfectly calm demeanor annoys the hell out of me. I want her to sound as upset as I feel. But she doesn't. Not for the first time, I wonder whether she even cares about all these people.

"So why don't you tell them?" I ask. "Release what you know to the internet. Help the people who are working on it."

"That's my plan," she replies. "But I have to reconstruct my evidence first."

"Why? Can't you just explain what you've learned? Help them find it for themselves?"

"It will be much more efficient for me to reconstruct the evidence and present it in an orderly way than for anyone else to reverse engineer my assertions. Preparing the information will also give it plausibility. I don't think it will take me very long. Perhaps a day or so."

I'm not entirely thrilled with this reasoning, but again, I have to bow to Mila's expertise. This is her world, not mine.

We stop and hack into a new person's Navi on occasion, continuing to lay the false trail, until Mila insists that we stop and sleep in the early morning. "It only takes ten hours to get to Zanesville," she says. "But it takes sixteen hours to get to Reynosa, so there's no need for us to hurry. And we need to keep our minds sharp."

"Can we hack into the Navis of the people chasing us and see what they're doing?" I ask. "It would be awfully handy to know where they're looking so we can go the other way."

She shakes her head. "I already tried that. The security on Navis for federal agents is a lot better than for regular people. I don't have time to figure it out. But we can keep watching the news. As long as they're looking for us along the route to Mexico, we should be fine."

We park along a residential street in a mid-sized city and recline our seats. As I fall asleep, I think about Jamie. Mila looked up his medical records for me earlier and read them off to me. It turns out he's not drugged. He slipped into a semi-comatose state all on his own late last night.

His pulse and breathing have remained steady and strong, but I haven't been able to rouse him enough to eat or drink. I try not to let it worry me, but honestly, it terrifies me. Mila already confirmed that she shut down his Navi entirely, so whatever it was doing to his brain should have stopped, and that means he should be getting better soon. I don't know what it means that he's not.

All along, I've been telling myself that once the source of the problem was removed, Jamie would heal naturally and go back to normal—back to the person he used to be. And I can't afford to entertain any other possibilities.

After Phoebe falls asleep, Mila replies to the email from Slava Knyazev. She sends the message from her mab287a239@anony.net email address.

I'm listening.

Slava:

Ms. Bremer,

Then I will get to the point.

First, I want to assure you that we want this whole thing to go away. I want you to understand that we never intended for anyone to get hurt. You may laugh, but it's true. Our highest priority is profits, and in our line of work, we need a robust economy and at least marginally healthy society to ensure those profits. This epidemic was unintended, and we are working hard to fix it.

Now, I've watched our previous videos with you. It's clear to me that you don't care about money, luxury goods, vacations, or any of the other things those thugs offered you. I also understand that you don't care about people other than your mother—and I apologize again for the tactics used with her previously—but the point is, I'm not going to waste time appealing to your humanitarian instincts.

It seems to me that what you do care about is programming. Good, clean, fast code that does its job. And you're very, very good at it. Is that about right?

Sincerely,

Slava Knyazev

Mila:

Yes.

Slava:

I know that you had to work your way up from being a Navi technician. At the risk of offending you, and I apologize in advance, I know it took you years to even be considered for a programming job, only because you can't have a Navi. You've never been treated fairly, despite your brilliance, because of your "disability."

If you were to help us fix HAD, and if you were to be revealed as the one who solved it—but of course, you find that the true perpetrator is someone else, not us—then imagine the opportunities that would open up for you. Imagine the status associated with being the coder who solved HAD. Having your genius rec-

ognized. Being able to pick your projects and your fellow coders from here on out. Does that interest you?

I know I'm dreaming. The all-night diner swims in front of my vision, rippling in black and white and then breaking into random spots of color. Every table is filled with people. They all stare into their Navis without expression, occasionally lifting cups of coffee to their lips. A procession of waiters bring trays of food, which also waver and ripple.

I know that something terrible is going to happen, and I can't stop it.

My disguise is slipping. I feel my wig dragging down my face, and I try to put it back, but the tangles of hair fill my hands. I throw the wig aside, hoping no one will notice. My makeup is melting. I wipe my face, and my hands come away covered in thick, waxy red lipstick and too-bright pink blush. I must look like a clown.

Every face lifts up just slightly in unison as they all receive the same bulletin in all their Navis at once. Then every face turns toward me.

Recognition blossoms. "That's her. That's the one. That's Eve!"

From beside me, Mila looks at me with disinterest. "They're going to kill you," she says dispassionately. "What else can they do?"

They stand and walk toward me, their movements robotic and their faces blank. I try to get up, but Mila holds me down with inhuman strength. Then, at the last moment, she simply disappears.

As they tear me limb from limb, I feel the ligaments rip and the joints give way. I feel the flesh and skin pull apart. I scream.

Mila shakes me awake. My body is calm, my breathing restful. She shows no sign of alarm. "It's getting light out," she says. "We should go."

While we grab a fast-food breakfast and I struggle to forget my harrowing dream, she tells me that, according to the news, the authorities have projected that we're heading to the Mexican border and checkpoints have been instituted in a tri-state range to intercept us. It makes me chuckle, thinking how frustrated they'll be when we somehow manage to slip through.

Then Mila goes back to work. She tells me that she's tracing the logs to find where the malware has been either installed or given new directions from "command and control" servers. "If we can find the point of origin, then we can identify the companies responsible," she tells me.

With Mila working, Jamie tuned out, and my Navi turned off, it's quiet in the car. I have no one to talk to and nothing to distract me. At first, I spend all my mental energy trying to forget my dream, but at last it releases me, and then, as the miles wear on, I find myself thinking more—and more deeply—than I've had time for in years. I'm not sure that all that mental activity is adding up to anything, but it feels different. I decide, after a while, that it feels good. Looking around at the world and letting my own thoughts tumble through my mind . . . it's calming.

I find myself thinking about my Collective, wondering how everyone is doing. I wonder if they miss me, if they're worried about me.

Perhaps somewhat belatedly, I also think about Mr. Pataky. He's going to be upset at us for running away like this. As difficult as he could be, I realize I don't want to disappoint him. I hope he doesn't fire us as his clients. He seemed like a good attorney.

And, wow, are we going to need a good attorney.

ELEVEN

At last, late in the morning, the sun blinding me and making me wish my Navi's auto-sunglasses feature was working, we exit I70 into Zanesville, about fifty miles from Columbus. As I recognize the old landmarks, my heart starts to flutter in my chest. I realize that perhaps I should have warned Mila about my community. Actually, I could have spent the whole trip trying to prepare her and it might not have been enough.

"Mila, just to tell you a few things about my family . . ."

She doesn't look up from the laptop.

"Plain people are insular and deliberately under-educated. They know nothing about the outside world—nothing about popular culture or history. A lot of them don't even know who Gandhi was or JFK or anything.

"They're religious and strict about it. Almost anything you can think of to do is considered a sin. Recorded music, dancing, drinking, photos, watching TV. Cursing. Art. Jewelry, makeup, having your hair down. We'll need to adopt plain dress as soon as we get there."

"They seemed fine to me on the phone," Mila says, seemingly unaffected by my litany of warnings.

I cast a look over at her. I take note of her modest attire, her lack of jewelry or makeup, and the fact that I've never heard her curse. She doesn't listen to music or own a TV, either.

Still, I shake my head.

"You don't understand. We're going to be treated like second-class citizens because we're 'worldly.' We don't belong in their community. We're sinners, and we're going to burn in hell. So . . . don't expect a warm welcome."

She glances over at me. "Then why are we coming here?"

"Because they don't have Navis or even smartphones. They don't have computers of any kind. They don't even have electricity. They're off the grid. And they're also kind of notorious for passive resistance to the authorities in situations like this. I'm hoping they're going to be willing to hide us."

Mila doesn't comment, and I don't say anything else. I scan the farmland and gardens on either side as I drive up to my parents' house, looking for people I recognize. But it's hard to distinguish them from each other with the plain clothes—the long, full dresses, aprons, and caps on the women, and the dark pants, white shirts, and suspenders on the men.

I both love and hate coming home, but mostly, I hate it. Certainly, if they weren't my family, I'd never come here.

I pull up into the driveway behind the carriage my parents drive. The house is large, two-story, and wood-framed—identical to all the others in this community. "Stay here with Jamie for a minute," I say. "I'll ask for help to come get him."

I'm already feeling resentful and upset as I approach the back door. But what can I expect? They've never forgiven me for being who I am. And it isn't my fault that I wasn't born to be like them.

I knock on the door, and in a few moments, my mother answers it. Her eyes widen. "Phebe!" she exclaims. "Where is he?"

By the way she says it, I know that she already knows. Probably some busybody in town—from normal society—recognized the name Bernhart from the news and then told someone in the Plain community, and the word spread.

"He's in the car," I say. "I need Dad's help to get him in. He's not doing so well."

Mom pushes me past me and hurries out to the car. Mila is standing by it, but Mom ignores her to open the door to the backseat and slide in partway, trying to get a good look at her baby boy.

Dad is walking up the driveway to the house. He's always come home from his work at the carriage and harness shop for lunch. His face, always sober, darkens when he recognizes me. He takes in the whole scene, with the car and the stranger and Mom half in the backseat. "Is James in there?" he asks.

I nod.

"Then help me with him," Dad says.

I usher Mom to the side and Dad pulls Jamie out, holding him up under the armpits. I catch him by the knees. It's awkward, but we get him into the house. Mom hurries a few steps ahead of us and puts a coverlet and pillow on one of the sofas in the spacious living room, and we lay him down there.

"Blood pressure cuff and thermometer?" I ask of Mom as I check his pulse and pupils again. My people are big believers in do-it-yourself doctoring. She brings both items. A minute or two later, I report, "His vital signs are still good. Bring me some water, Mom." I've been trying to get water into him every few hours, but he hasn't taken any yet. Getting him rehydrated is my most immediate concern.

"So, what's wrong with him?" Dad asks.

I heave a sigh. I guess it's time to face the music. I'm opening my mouth to speak when Mila interrupts. I look up to see her hovering at the entrance to the room.

"There's a third wave," she says. "Of Hyper-Aggression Disorder. It was first reported on the news last night. It's affecting new patients as well as many of the old ones. Symptoms are much more severe. Hallucinations, blackouts, and seizures are appearing in as many as sixty percent of the third-wave patients. Jamie is one of them."

As I stare at her, open-mouthed, wondering when she was planning to tell me this, she steps toward my father. "I apologize for intruding in your home. My name is Mila Bremer. I'm the one who spoke to you on the phone yesterday."

My mother is so startled that she almost drops the water she brought me. "Your mother! That's your mother upstairs!"

Mila nods. "May I see her?"

"Of course, of course," Mom says. She puts the cup of water on the coffee table and leads Mila away.

"Why did you take him out of the hospital?" Dad asks me.

"They wouldn't let us take out his Navi," I say as I try to get Jamie propped up with his head steadied by cushions. His eyes flutter as I do so. "And the Navi is the cause of the problem. That's what's causing HAD. We had to get him out of the hospital so we could treat him."

I open his mouth and carefully put in a trickle of water. His eyes open briefly, and he swallows. I breathe a sigh of relief and give him some more.

"Why are they saying you're some sort of terrorists?" Dad's brow is wrinkled. He doesn't understand anything about the outside world, but he doesn't trust me entirely, either. I can see that in his expression, and it hurts.

"We were trying to fix it, Dad. Nobody else knows that it's the Navis. Whoever's responsible for this thing, they knew we were on to them. They tried to get us out of the way."

He crosses his arms, still looking down at his youngest son. "The world brings nothing but trouble."

I don't say anything. Jamie stops drinking water and tries to look around before drifting back off.

Dad looks at me coldly. "And you've brought that trouble to my house, Phebe Esther."

I swallow hard. "But I need your help, Dad. And we help each other. It's our way, to help each other."

He remains cold. "You've left our ways behind."

I take a deep breath and think hard before I speak.

"But you haven't."

I bite my lip before I can say anything else that might make things worse.

We look at each other for what feels like an eternity.

Then he looks me up and down, and his distance is supplanted by everyday disapproval. "Go put on some proper clothes, and then you can come down for lunch."

When I pause at the open door to Mrs. Bremer's room, I feel like I'm intruding. The rooms in my parents' house are large, and in this room, there are several chairs to the side of the bed, where the three of them are sitting and chatting pleasantly. Mrs. Bremer appears to be in both good spirits and good health, with rosy cheeks. She's wearing some of my mother's plain clothes, including the cap.

When she sees me at the door, she waves me in. "Why, hello, there! Come on in, join the fun."

"Actually, Mrs. Bremer, it's time for lunch. I need to get Mila and myself dressed properly."

Looks of alarm on the faces of the other two tell me that I've misspoken somehow.

A shadow crosses Mrs. Bremer's face, and she looks around in confusion. "Is Mila here?" she asks.

Mila shakes her head at me, a tiny but emphatic motion.

"Um . . . no? . . . No, of course not. But you know . . . *she* looks a lot like Mila, so I . . . got confused?" I'm improvising the best I can, given my level of fatigue and tension, but everyone beams at me approvingly, so apparently, I'm on the right track.

"Oh, I *know*," Mrs. Bremer says. "Doesn't she? If she were only a few years younger and didn't have that long hair, she'd be the spitting image of my girl. Tell me, how do you know Mila?"

My brain freezes, and I stare helplessly.

"From college," Mila supplies. "Phoebe and I were both seniors when Mila was a freshman. We were all students together. Of course, now we've graduated, but Mila hasn't yet, or she would have come with us to visit."

"Oh, of course." Mrs. Bremer smiles.

"But you heard Phoebe. It's time to go down to lunch. I'll go get dressed and be right there." Mila gets up and escorts me from the room.

Once in the hallway, I take over and lead her to my bedroom. "I know you said she was senile, but I didn't realize she didn't even know you. Oh my gosh, Mila."

I look back at her and remember how I messaged her about Jamie a couple of weeks ago. *He doesn't know me anymore,* I said. And when she didn't reply, I thought she didn't care. No. She understood too well.

"My name is Margaret for now." That's all Mila says.

I wonder why she doesn't keep explaining to her mother who she really is. I guess it got too painful after a while. Or maybe her mother doesn't deal well with the news. Some senile patients don't.

I take her to my room and find some print dresses that will do, even though they're too short for her. They're only just past the knee, which is almost scandalous in my community. I give her an apron and show her how we put our hair into a bun and secure it under the cap.

"Why do you wear the caps?" Mila asks.

"It's Biblical," I say. "First Corinthians 11:5: 'But every woman that prays or prophesies with her head uncovered dishonors her head.' And since we never know when we might need to pray, we have to have our heads covered at all times."

I'm surprised that I remember the exact Bible verse. Apparently, at least part of my brain is still working, even if it's only the part that remembers Bible trivia.

We work our way downstairs. We're both so tired that we're starting to weave when we walk.

Mila stops in the doorway to the dining room when she sees that they've pulled out the card table and set it against the wall with place settings for us. My parents set places for themselves alone at the big table. They even took away the other chairs.

I was excommunicated when I left the community, and, of course, Mila and her mother have never been anything but worldly, so we're not considered suitable for sharing a table with godly folks.

I've fought this battle before and lost—painfully. I don't feel like fighting it again right now, so I sit at the card table and gesture for Mila to join me there.

Maybe now she understands what I meant by "second-class citizens."

She glances up and asks, "What about my mother?"

"We take her a tray, dear," Mom says, her eyes downcast.

That's a good way to skirt the issue. I was wondering how they explained this treatment to a patient with senility.

Mila nods. She surveys her lunch hungrily—there's real chicken and homemade dumplings and green beans—and is about to dig in when I put out my hand to stop her. My father clears his throat, and we bow our heads as he says grace in his funereal tones.

"Bless, O Father, Thy gifts to our use and us to Thy service, in Jesus's name. Amen."

Lunch starts out without anyone talking, only the sounds of the clinking of silverware and plates and glasses breaking the silence. I think my parents have too many questions that they expect might lead to an argument. By and large, our community is nonconfrontational. They try to avoid harsh words, though, of course, they define "harsh" in their own way.

As usual, I can't read Mila's expression.

Eventually, my mother asks the questions she can't help but ask. "Is James going to be all right? Do we need to call a doctor to come see him?"

"I'm seeing some improvement," I answer. "He woke up and took water while ago, and his vital signs have been steady. If he continues to improve, and if he starts eating today or tomorrow, I don't think we'll need to call a doctor."

"And you got the . . . Navi? . . . out of him so that it's not hurting him anymore?"

Evidently, my dad has caught her up. I glance over at Mila, who answers impassively, "Yes, ma'am, we shut it down. There shouldn't be anything causing him harm now."

"Thank you, Jesus," my mother whispers.

More silence passes.

Mila seems more distant than I'm used to. She rarely meets my eyes anyway, but I don't think she's looked right at me all day.

Our meal is nearly done when my mother asks, forcefully, as if the words are tearing themselves out of her, "What kind of trouble is this you're in, Phebe? What's going to happen to you? Are you going to go to jail?"

My father puts a hand on my mother's hand and gives her the look that means *Be silent, woman.*

"Answer the question, Phebe Esther," Dad orders.

I inhale sharply and put down my napkin a little too aggressively.

It's all the years of putting up with the judgment and the institutional misogyny of this community. It makes me over-reactive to their every word and gesture. I know that. But I can't help it.

Before I can speak, Mila answers calmly. "We're here because we needed a safe place where we could take the time we needed to prove our innocence, and when Phoebe thought of a safe place, she thought of you."

Damn. I couldn't have said that better. And it's true. I glance over. They're both looking down, absorbing this thought.

"If we can find the right evidence," Mila goes on, "we may be able to convince the authorities to drop the charges against us. A lot depends on the judge and how angry he is that we ran away."

"We heard rumors from the folks in town," my father says. "They said you were trying to get out of the country. They saw you headed to Mexico."

"I laid a false trail," Mila says. "Trying to lead them away from here and your family. Phoebe wanted us to be as careful as possible not to put any of you at risk."

Also true. And, I note, she anticipated that need without my even mentioning it.

My father puts down his napkin and looks into the distance. "People have been asking us about you. We haven't known what to say." He looks over at us—no, he looks at Mila.

"We know you will tell them the truth," she says. "We wouldn't ask you to do anything else."

He nods slowly.

I'm going to keep my mouth shut from now on. Mila's got this. She's on the same wavelength as my parents.

"And you want our protection," Dad says.

"All we ask is that, if the authorities come here, you don't give us up to them," Mila says, her voice barely audible.

"Of course not," my mother interjects.

"And please don't mention us on the phone, in case your phone lines are tapped."

"We won't," Mom says. "We don't even have a phone. Only our bishop does."

My dad gives her a look, but he doesn't argue with her. He composes his thoughts. "There's a Saturday-night social here tonight. We're next in the rotation, so we're going to have it, and you all need to attend. Word will already have spread about that car in our driveway and us carrying in James. You know how it is around here—busybody women peeking out of their windows at everybody, minding everybody's business but their own.

"So I'll speak to folks, ask them for their forbearance. But I can't predict how they'll react, and I can't promise you that they'll keep their peace. It's possible that you'll only have a few days. Maybe not even that long."

He looks old and tired suddenly, and my heart sinks. I know Jamie and I have been a trial to him and to my mother. I know it's affected their status in their community to have only five children and then to lose two of them to Satan. And now here we are again, making it even worse for them.

"I'm sorry," I murmur, surprising myself. But they don't respond, and I realize I said it quietly, and maybe they didn't even hear me. And then I don't know what else to say, and we finish our meals in silence.

After lunch, Mila politely offers to help with the dishes, but I quickly interrupt her to ask her to go out to the living room with me to check on Jamie. Once we're there, kneeling at his side and checking his temperature, I explain quietly that we're not allowed to help with any of the chores. "It's part of our being damned," I say. "They can't accept anything from our hands. It's like our sin is contagious."

It's one of the things I hate the most about visiting my parents. The only thing I liked about my community—the only thing I took with me into my adult life—was an appreciation for the routines and demands of physical work. It's why I became a nurse and not a Navi worker of some kind. I like doing things with my hands, and when I come back, I'm forced to sit here, useless, only a witness to those routines that speak of home to me.

At least this time I can tend to Jamie. He and I are both damned, after all.

"And that's why we can't sit at the same table with them?" Mila asks quietly.

"Yeah. Partly. The other part is shunning. By treating me like I'm worthless, they're trying to pressure me to come back."

I debate whether to tell her the story, but it slips out of me whether I mean for it to or not. "Once, on one of my early visits home, I deliberately set a place for myself at the big table while no one was paying attention. This was when my three younger siblings still lived here, including Jamie. And I sat down and started eating with them. And when they realized their mistake, they couldn't do anything about it, because we're pacifists, so they couldn't force me to get up, so instead, they all got up and came into the living room to eat without me."

And I sat at the big table in there alone and cried while I ate. But I leave that part out, because I don't think I can tell it without crying again.

Mila doesn't say anything.

Mom brings a cup of broth and a few dumplings and another cup of water. I offer both to Jamie. He takes some water, and he rouses at the taste of the broth. He takes several spoonfuls and one dumpling, and then he's out again. But it's progress.

I just don't know if he's ever going to be a normal person again . . . my *brother* again.

We carry Jamie upstairs and get him comfortable in his old bedroom. Then my mother continues her work in the kitchen, no doubt getting ready for the social tonight. Mila grabs her laptop and heads to her own room.

"I wish I could help," I say. "But without my Navi . . ."

"I know," she says.

Instead, I go downstairs to take care of the car.

First, I just stand there and stare at it blankly for a while. My mind has been through too much already. But I can't leave it here. It's a dead giveaway. In fact, I can't safely leave it anywhere within sight.

I think about trying to get it painted tomorrow, or trying to park it in someone's barn, but I decide that damaging it is probably the safest and fastest way to disguise it. I drive to a secluded dirt road where I get it dusty, use my keys to vigorously scratch long lines on all of its sides, and kick in one of the mirrors.

I take it to a residential area and park it under a tree between houses. Then I walk two blocks, where I've arranged for Dad to pick me up in the horse and buggy, and I ride home in the back, where I can't be seen.

It's not among my best-laid plans, but I'm exhausted. I can only hope that no one has it towed before we need it again and that no one bothered to make note of me leaving it there and walking down the street to be picked up by Plain people. I also hope that law enforcement won't notice it.

I figure, with the entire US population entranced by its Navis, the odds are in my favor.

When Phoebe leaves the house, Mila opens and rereads the emails from Slava Knyazev. Then she types a reply, and a series of emails go by as quickly as Mila can type and Slava can think.

Mila:

> I'm already well on my way to fixing HAD without you, so I don't think I need this deal you're offering me.

Slava:

Wouldn't it go a lot faster if you had full access to all of our code?

Mila:

You're offering to give me that access?

That must mean you need my help to do this.

Slava:

"Need" might be an exaggeration. But just as you can solve this a lot faster with direct access to our code, we can solve it a lot faster with the help of a genius programmer like yourself.

I believe you want HAD to go away, just as we do. This would truly be a mutually beneficial arrangement.

Mila:

You're really telling me that HAD was unintentional and now it's out of your control *and* you can't fix it?

Slava:

Again, "can't" is an exaggeration. It's just taking us more time than we had hoped. Otherwise—as much as it pains me to say it, and as much as it's going to annoy me when you tell me what idiots we are—yes.

Mila:

You all are idiots.

So how did you manage to "accidentally" cause an international neurological epidemic? If that wasn't the intended function of the malware, what was? It looks purposeful, how it sends the nanobots to the amygdalae and overstimulates them.

Slava:

You're right, that was the intended function of the program. It just wasn't supposed to do it quite so strongly. A
bug was introduced that affected the calibrations, and
that resulted in the unforeseen consequences. Which
we regret, I hasten to add.

Mila:

The amygdalae control visceral emotions, like fear and
anger. That must mean that your original goal, before
the bug was introduced, was to manipulate those feelings.

Slava:

Fear and anger, yes, but also joy.

As much as people like to pretend that they're rational,
their decisions are usually emotional. That goes double
for purchasing decisions. Nudge up joy when people
make certain purchases and dial up anxiety when they
abstain, and suddenly, people's behavior is a lot more
profitable. And they don't even notice. There's no real
harm.

Increased profit was the entire purpose. The rest was
accidental.

Mila:

Just out of curiosity, out of all the Navi users, how
many have your original program?

Slava:

Approximately 70 percent. It's lucky for everyone that
we roll out new code in stages, just in the event of some
bug such as this one. We were able to stop the rollout
when the first symptoms appeared.

Mila:

> Why did it change so much on the third wave? Why
> is it suddenly so much worse?

Slava:

> Had to make it look like real terrorism. The sympto-
> mology of the first two waves was too bizarre, too at-
> tention-getting. If we simply fixed it, someone would
> have gone looking for why it happened to begin with
> and maybe found our little program, as you're doing.
>
> But if it's clearly about destroying human lives, then
> when we fix it, nobody will dig any deeper. Especially
> when we supply them with a bad guy. We've already
> got some excellent Unabomber types picked out to
> choose from. Assuming the bad guy we give them
> isn't you, of course.

Mila:

> You keep saying that you want to "fix it." Do you mean
> removing your behavior modification software? Or
> correcting the bug?

Slava:

> The program itself is far too successful to remove, but
> I'm assuming that won't bother you too much, Ms.
> Bremer. People are sheep, right? *Someone* has to tell
> them what to do. Does that sound familiar?
>
> Now, I'd feel a whole lot better about spilling my guts
> like this if I knew that we had a deal and that we were
> on the same side. So, do we have a deal?

> Again, you walk away from this a hero, with your pick
> of the best programming jobs for the rest of your life,
> and we both get to bring about an end to all of this
> quickly. Is there really any good reason you can't say
> yes to this, Ms. Bremer?

I'm taking an unplanned nap on the sofa when knocking at the back door wakes me. Instantly, my system floods with adrenaline, and I'm practically falling all over myself trying to run up the stairs while my father calmly passes by to open the door.

When I recognize the voice of my oldest brother, Jonas, I sheepishly come back down the stairs.

Then I decide that perhaps I should tell Mila that folks are gathering, so I go upstairs to do that. It's also a good way to buy some time while the warmth fades from my cheeks and my heart palpitations settle down.

When I knock and step into her room, she snaps her laptop closed and looks up with a poker face.

"It's my brother Jonas," I say. "We should go down."

Something about her expression stops me. "What's wrong?" I ask.

Her face remains blank. "Just stressed," she says. "I'll be down in a minute."

With a nod, I head back down. If she needs space, I figure I should probably give it to her.

Jonas and his family are the first to arrive. The rest of my siblings and their families soon follow. They've even brought all the kids over. It's the first time I've seen them since I left home years ago. Some of them weren't even born yet. Normally, the kids aren't allowed around me or Jamie—us being the dangerous, worldly ones—but I suppose it's different since there's a social here tonight.

At any rate, they give us cordial and curious—though not friendly—greetings, and then the women go to the kitchen and prepare food while the men set up the living room, leaving Mila and me to sit awkwardly on the steps in the living room and watch.

Although I've seen this routine unfold dozens of times during my childhood, the quick transformation of the room is still impressive. The room swarms with sober males in nearly identical dark slacks and white shirts and suspenders, all ages working together. They clear all the furniture into a side room and set up dozens of folding chairs. The three- to five-year-olds help by putting a hymnal in each seat.

"Is it church?" Mila asks me quietly.

"No, it's fun," I say, and I chuckle sarcastically. "Plain people think that getting together to sing hymns is the most fun there could possibly be. Who needs movies or nightclubs or football?"

Mila looks thoughtful. "No piano accompaniment?" she asks.

"No. Musical instruments are of the Devil."

She nods, looking disappointed.

Knocks continue to come at the door, and people continue to flood in, the women bearing covered dishes. They look at Mila and me curiously, but they don't speak to us, which is fine by me. In fact, I'm pretty sure I'm giving off an effective "don't talk to me" vibe.

Since everyone is punctual, the room is full in about fifteen minutes, and then everyone is filling their plates from the kitchen and taking seats.

"Well, let's get our food," Mila says and gets up to go into the kitchen. Reluctantly, I follow. Then we take our plates back to the stairwell, and I pick at my food while I worry about everything.

My father gets everyone's attention by tapping his plate with his fork. I struggle to tune back in. The chairs have filled up, I realize, and people have finished their meals.

"Good evening and God bless you," Dad says, and the group returns the greeting. "I'll get right to what you're all wanting to hear. As several of you no doubt know by now, we have several guests in our home. My daughter Phebe Esther and my son James are here.

And my daughter's friend Mila Bremer and her mother have joined us as well."

As our names are given, there's a slight stir and some horrified looks directed at us. I look down, feeling my cheeks grow warm. I'm used to being a pariah here, but this is much worse. I wish I could take Mila's hand, but of course I can't.

"You all have heard the rumors. It's true that Phebe and Mila have gotten into some worldly trouble. Something to do with this aggression disorder they're talking about out in the world and those Navis. I've spoken with Phebe and Mila, and I'm clear as to their innocence. They're only here seeking a safe haven while they attempt to clear their names so that they can . . . go back." I can hear that those last few words are painful for him to utter.

He looks down before he goes on, and then he speaks slowly and deliberately.

"You all know 1st John 3:17. 'But if anyone has the world's goods and sees his brother in need, yet closes his heart against him, how does God's love abide in him?' And you know Galatians 6:2: 'Bear one another's burdens, and so fulfill the law of Christ.' And perhaps most relevant in this case, Romans 15:1: 'We who are strong have an obligation to bear with the failings of the weak.'"

Ouch, Dad.

"This is worldly trouble that has no place here. Let's keep that trouble where it belongs, at a distance. If anyone comes here in search of Phebe and Mila, I ask you to follow Paul's exhortation to 'obey God rather than men' and send them away unsatisfied."

There is quiet from the group for a long moment.

My father's voice drops. "And, as many of you have heard, my son James is unwell. We don't know what ails him or how to cure it. And so we ask for your prayers at this time."

Heads bow in unison. A few moments into the silence, I find myself praying, too, for the first time in years.

Dear God, if You exist and if You can be bothered to care about these things, would You please, please, please save my brother and make him a normal pain in the butt again? Please? I will never, ever complain about him again if You could . . . please . . . bring him back to us. And please help us get out of this mess we're in.

My eyes are brimming with tears when my father says, "Amen." The word echoes through the group, and I mutter it, too.

My father pauses for a moment. "I have one more thing to ask of you. Because of Mila and Phebe, the authorities may come here looking for Jamie. Are there any among you who would open your house to our son to keep him hidden and safe?"

Most of the people have blank faces, but I see an older lady, Sister Friesen, nudging her husband in the ribs repeatedly until finally he says, albeit grudgingly, "We'll take him in."

"God bless you for that," Dad says.

Then a middle-aged man stands. I remember him—Brother Tillitzki, a decent, hardworking man. "With respect, Brother Bernhart, and I'm reluctant to even mention this, but I feel I ought to . . . I got the word through the postman this afternoon, and they're saying your girl and this other person, Mila—that they killed a woman last night on their way out of Atlanta."

Murmurs rise up, and I exchange shocked glances with Mila.

Someone asks, "Who did they say they killed?"

"I don't remember the name exactly. Some foreign-sounding name. It was a woman doctor."

A woman doctor with a foreign-sounding name . . .

I'm on my feet, blurting out, "Dr. Abadi?"

Brother Tillitzki shifts uncomfortably and nods. "Yes, that was it."

"Oh God!" I cry out.

Mila stands and supports me as my knees almost give way. "What happened to her?" Mila asks the man. Her voice is steady, but her face is pale.

Brother Tillitzki seems to have trouble getting it out. "Shot to death in her own home."

Various people call out to God or utter prayers. I struggle to hold back tears. She had two young children, I remember—a boy and a girl.

"Are her children okay?" I ask through my choked-back sobs.

"Well, I don't know that," Brother Tillitzki says uncomfortably. "But the postman didn't say anything about that, so I'm going to guess they're all right."

"We didn't do it," Mila says steadily. "They're blaming us because they're trying to get us out of the picture. It's all part of the same scheme."

"Look at them," my father pronounces soberly. "You can see from my daughter's reaction that she had nothing to do with this. Look at these two girls and use your common sense. These are not the sort of girls who *shoot* people."

I realize it's to my advantage at this particular moment that I can't stop my tears, and that makes me feel even weirder about it. I'm usually the strong one.

The women look at their husbands, who nod slowly.

After a long moment, one of the elderly men, whose name escapes me at the moment, stands slowly, his frame both rigid and fragile. He speaks slowly, in a gruff voice. "First Corinthians 1:10: 'I appeal to you, brothers, by the name of our Lord Jesus Christ, that all of you agree, and that there be no divisions among you, but that you be united in the same mind and the same judgment.'" He looks around. There's not a sound in the room.

Brother Tillitzki sits down, looking relieved to be done with it.

Finding no disagreement, the elderly man sits, too.

My father picks up his hymnal. "We'll start with #152."

He takes his seat, and the room fills with the sound of hymnals opening. I glance up in time to see my mom escort Mrs. Bremer to a seat. She's beaming with pleasure to see all these people.

Moments later, voices break out into song.

Twelve

Mila to Slava Knyazev:

You killed Dr. Abadi.

Slava:

Yes. I'm sorry about that. Pinning HAD on you three and then killing you was the original plan. That was before I took over the project yesterday, on Friday. And I can still save you two, but I wasn't able to save her.

Mila:

Then why did you try to kill Phoebe Wednesday? You hadn't started pinning HAD on us yet.

Slava:

Tried to kill Phoebe Wednesday? You mean her seizure? That was an accident. Actually, we're not entirely sure what happened. It was probably a side effect of the aversion programming we added with the second wave of HAD. We wanted to discourage people from doing too much work on Navis while we tried to solve the problem. We're still not sure how Phoebe withstood the migraines up to that point or how the seizure occurred.

I apologize for that seizure, by the way. We may not have intended it or foreseen it, but it shouldn't have happened.

By the way, they're saying that your attempts to hack into my Navi tonight have been skillful. I agree that it would be very useful for you to be able to get in. I consider myself fortunate that Peake has invested in extra security for its executives. But listen, this is going to go so much easier for all of us if we just work together. We can bring about an end to this whole thing, and fast.

So do we have a deal?

Mila taps her fingertips on the keyboard, thinking. Then she closes the email conversation.

That night, as soon as everyone goes home, we move Jamie over to the basement of Sister Friesen's house. The big farmhouses out here are spaced out to give room for the gardens and farmland, but there are usually one or two neighbors a short jog away, and Sister Friesen is the nearest neighbor to the west. My father and Brother Friesen take Jamie over unceremoniously in a wheelbarrow, which irks me, but we don't have a stretcher, and he doesn't have any spinal injuries, so I can't complain.

I explain to Sister Friesen that I'll come over every two hours during the day to check on him and do the caretaking, but she convinces me to alternate shifts with her so that we each do it every four hours during the day. She says she'll check on him once during the night as well. People around here are savvy and self-sufficient, so I just tell her what needs to be done and what to watch out for.

After I do the caretaking for Jamie, I go back home. Mila has already gone to her room, so I miss telling her good night. I can see from under her door that the light is on, but I don't want to bother

her while she's working. I go in my room and throw myself across the bed and stare at the ceiling.

My schedule has been thrown off by the short sleep last night and then this afternoon's accidental nap. And it's too quiet here. I have no Navi, there are no books to read, and there are no chores I'm allowed to do. I'm desperate for distraction. But I eventually find myself at my old desk with a pen and paper in hand, doodling while I think. It feels satisfyingly rebellious, wasting paper and ink on something that is of no use and no glory to God.

I think, of course, about Dr. Abadi.

It seems like they've taken the gloves off, whoever "they" are. And that's part of what's bothering me, I realize as I shiver with anxiety. I don't know who "they" are.

I remember some of the crackpot theories that people put out there in the past couple of weeks—the government, big corporations, foreign governments, terrorists, domestic terrorists. The list of possible crazies is pretty long. Whoever it is, it seems clear now that they want to put an end to what Mila and I are doing. And they'll kill us for it.

They'll *kill* us.

I've been a little distracted by the threat of prison lately—silly me—but of course that's not the worst thing I have to worry about here. That seizure I had wasn't an accident. Mila told me that.

Oh my God . . . those migraines I was having . . . Did they really have anything to do with caffeine or rebound headaches, or were the people behind this thing already trying to stop me?

I put my head down on the paper, too demoralized to even doodle. Of course. If I hadn't been so distracted by the work we were doing with Jamie, I would've put it together. They only started as soon as I started trying to help Jamie. And although I've always been prone to headaches and even mild migraines, I've never had migraines that severe or that frequently before.

They were already in my head. Trying to stop me.

I wonder why they even bothered to shoot Dr. Abadi. They could have fried her brain like they tried to do to me.

But no, they might have had a harder time pinning it on us that way. I wonder if they managed to get my fingerprints onto the gun somehow.

I feel deadened and numb by the realization that Dr. Abadi faced that particular, terrifying death because of us.

I realize I'm shivering—it's colder up here in Ohio—and I get into bed and try to go to sleep. But I keep thinking about Dr. Abadi and Jamie and Navis and green jumpsuits and Mr. Pataky and the escape from the hospital and Greenpeace magnetic decals and red wigs and Brother Tillitzky and everything else, and it's no good.

Sometime after one in the morning, I get up to go to bathroom, and as I tiptoe back down the hallway—the floors creak too much in this old wood house—I can see from underneath the door that Mila's light is still on.

I can't help myself. I tap and say, "It's Phoebe."

I hear soft rustling sounds and the snap of Mila's laptop closing. "Come in," she answers.

I enter and close the door behind me. "I can't sleep," I whisper. "And we have to be quiet. Sound carries in this house."

"I can't sleep, either," she says, matching my volume. "Come sit." She moves her laptop to make room for me on the bed.

"I can't stop thinking about Dr. Abadi," I say as I climb under the blanket to try to stop the shaking that's partly from the cold and partly from anxiety. "She was murdered, right? I mean, obviously she was murdered, but I mean . . . it's the people behind all this, right? The same people?"

"I think so," Mila says distantly.

"They're going to come after us, too, aren't they? I knew the police would come, but these other people, they'll come, too."

"I don't think they'll find us soon," she says, not looking at me. "I think the trail I laid was convincing enough for the moment. And no one here has a Navi that can be hacked into or tracked. I've been spoofing my own connection to other servers all over the world, so they won't be able to pick up on the fact that suddenly someone here is on the 'net."

"You're brilliant," I tell her for the second time.

She only shakes her head slightly. "Do you trust the people here not to give us away?"

I have to think about that one for a few minutes. "Not a hundred percent, no. People here are . . . It's a different world. Plain people are so thoroughly out of touch with the real world that their own petty issues are all that matter to them. This community split from another one twenty years ago over whether, according to the Bible, men have to shave their beards or not. Seriously, these people decided that they couldn't worship under the same roof with men who didn't *shave*."

Mila nods slowly.

"So, if someone has a bone to pick with my father, they might tell just to be vindictive. Or because they think it's the wrong decision and they can't live with it. Hell, we may have the bishop here tomorrow telling my parents that they have to kick us out or be excommunicated themselves."

Seeing Mila looking increasingly worried, I touch her hand. "But . . . I don't think they will. Honestly. I'm venting because I get so frustrated with these people. But . . ." I let out a slow breath and lower my voice again, as it has been creeping up in volume. "Probably they won't. I mean, that's the whole reason I came here, right? They're good about uniting against the outside world. And you heard my dad. He made a good argument."

With a sigh, Mila sets her laptop aside. She lies down, pulling the blankets up, and I do, too, a foot or two separating our bodies.

"God, I can't even believe that this is happening," I say. "I'm not . . . this isn't me. Jesus. I'm not a criminal. I'm not even some . . . civil disobedience–type person. I've never broken the law on purpose before. And it's freaking me out to be *between* the good guys and the bad guys, in this muddy middle ground."

"You're with the good guys," Mila says. In answer to my questioning look, she explains, "Now that Jamie's safe, you keep talking about clearing our names. But you know this isn't about that. You're trying to stop this thing. You're trying to save the lives of all of the people who have been affected."

I nod. "Of course that's true. I can't think straight right now, that's all."

Looking down, she says, "You care about people in a way I wish I could. I know I'm supposed to, but . . ."

I stare at her, wishing I knew what to say. "You do, too, care," I say.

She stares at me helplessly, and a twinge of doubt hits me. "Okay," I say, "so maybe you're a bit out of practice."

I grin reassuringly.

She studies my face for a moment, and her expression shifts. "Honestly, though," she says. "I feel like something in me is broken. Or maybe just . . . deeply asleep. But maybe . . . I think maybe something about you is waking it up."

I stare at her, touched and totally at a loss for words this time.

When she speaks again, her voice is unexpectedly soft. "I'd feel better if you stayed here tonight. I'm not used to sleeping alone."

I must have a funny expression on my face, because she suddenly breaks out into muted laughter. "Cat-Phoebe," she splutters as quietly as she can. "Usually, cat-Phoebe sleeps with me."

My face heats up.

"You're blushing," she says.

"Am not!" I insist, absurdly, since my face is practically aflame. I hide my face with the blanket for a second, but that's even more absurd, so I pull it back down. I can't believe I was thinking about Mila and sex and got caught doing so, and now I can't seem to stop.

"*Anyway*," I say, "that's fine. I can be cat-Phoebe tonight, I suppose."

She nods. "Okay. Then we should try to go to sleep. It's late."

She rolls away, blows out the kerosene lamp, and then rolls back onto her back and pulls up the covers. She chuckles again once or twice before settling down.

I roll onto my back as well and study the ceiling, letting my eyes adjust.

I can sense that she's still wide awake, and I know I am. But I try to settle my breathing and relax. I'm so exhausted, I should think that I would be able to fall asleep now. But there's something about the nearness of Mila that makes me want to stay awake to savor it.

I feel and hear Mila shift. She's rolled over to face me, and without thinking, I turn to face her.

Her eyes are still open, too, and we study each other. It's so much darker here than in the city, but enough moonlight comes in through the curtains above the bed to allow us to see each other in shades of gray.

I admire her eyes, her lips. Her gaze skips around my face, too, and I wonder what she's thinking. I don't want to speak, to break the spell of this suddenly intimate moment. I grin again, remembering the misunderstanding about sleeping alone. I *am* thinking about this woman and sex. I am. I can't seem to help it.

I find myself shifting closer, nearer. And then she lifts up the blanket as if it were an invitation, and I slide over, right next to her, the blanket over us both, and then our bodies are intertwined, her leg over mine, my arm over hers. I feel a sense of rightness I cannot remember ever feeling before. In an instant, I forget everything else.

She looks at me, and I at her. I'm wondering if she feels this same pleasure. There's something in her eyes I've never seen before, but I don't quite recognize it. She glances at my lips, and I glance at hers, and then I bring my lips to hers, or perhaps she meets me halfway, and then my whole world is her warm kiss.

Her lips are so soft and smooth, more so than any man's I've ever touched, and smaller, yet more full. So perfectly kissable. Her breath has the scent of sweet mint from her toothpaste.

A few small kisses, each one longer than the others, and then we're both pulling away and looking at each other again.

She releases a slight sigh—the tiniest moan—and it sounds like desire.

My breath catches, and suddenly I'm hungry for more—more kisses, more Mila. I pull her to me. She returns my kisses with a like hunger, and we press our bodies together. I feel her breasts against mine, her hips against mine, the tantalizing hollow between her legs where normally by now I would feel the swell of a certain part of a man's anatomy against me. But this is unlike any moment I've shared with a man. There is desire, but there is no hurry, and I kiss her lips again, nibble them this time.

A few more languorous, luxurious kisses, and then she parts her lips, and I part mine, too, and the sweet tip of her tongue enters my mouth, making me draw a quick breath before I bring my tongue to taste hers.

Hungry for more, I raise one thigh to that hollow between her legs and press it against her, finding it astonishingly hot there. A like heat has blossomed within me. She moans softly as I press against her.

I caress her shoulders, her back, the perfect curve of her waist, that luscious place where the hips begin, and she does the same to me.

Suddenly, the fire flares up, and we roll over between the sheets, our bodies pressed together, breathing hard, kissing hard, as if with enough passion, we could blot out every bad thing that has happened in the past few weeks.

Moments pass with delicious kisses and her sweet, small tongue and our bodies intertwined, as much of us touching as possible at each moment, gasping with pleasure.

Then she pulls away, and I see a tear running down her cheek. My heart stops. "What's wrong?" I ask in a whisper.

"I don't know what we're doing . . . what this *is*," Mila says, her voice choked with tears.

"Shhh . . . shhh." I relax and lay down with her, holding her. "It's okay. I don't know what this is either." I feel my own stab of panic. "I don't know either."

She buries her head against my chest, and I stroke her hair. Suddenly, I'm terrified that this has been all wrong. "You don't . . . You don't like it? Us . . . kissing?" If she says no, I'll be crushed.

"I like it," she whispers. "But I don't understand it."

My heart soars. *I like it,* she said.

"I don't understand it, either," I whisper back to her. But when I dip my face down to hers, she kisses me again, this time tasting of salt. Then she pulls away again.

"I'm afraid," she whispers.

Hearing those two words—so out of character for this remarkable woman—suddenly all I want is to protect her, to earn her trust, to be worthy of her. "I won't hurt you, Mila. I'll never hurt you." I mean it with all my heart, although I also have this sense that I'm stepping off a bridge into some dark chasm and I don't know what's there—but whatever it is, I won't let it hurt her. I won't.

She seems to think on this for a while, and then she nestles against me again and kisses me again. The passion has calmed now, and we cuddle and kiss with exquisite pleasure but without urgency. A sense of peace—of rightness—takes over me. I never, ever want to let her go.

Finally, she whispers, "We should sleep."

I nod and kiss her cheek affectionately, which draws a smile. I stroke her hair until her eyes close and her breath evens out and her body relaxes.

Eventually, a series of sleep twitches run through her body, and her breath deepens. And at some point, sleep takes me, too.

As dawn creeps through the windows, Mila lifts her laptop over Phoebe's sleeping body, opens it, and types, "What happens to Phoebe if I agree to this plan?"

Slava Knyazev:

> We know you value Phoebe. Consequently, we need her as collateral—a way to ensure that you will uphold your end of the bargain. Let us take her—without harming her, of course—and when you've completed your end of the deal, we'll release her. Again, unharmed. You will note that even the idiots you dealt with previously did not harm your mother, and I can guarantee you no less.

> You already hold a great deal of evidence that could implicate us. We will hold Phoebe. In this way, we will be able to trust one another.

I also have an extra incentive for you.

I know that not being able to have a Navi has significantly hampered your programming career. Well, ENI
has some promising experimental technology that is
allowing previously non-Navable people to get Navis.
It's been kept under wraps because they've wanted to
ensure they were first to market, and they're still a long
way from marketing it. But because of my connections
there, I can get you into the top-secret pilot program.
I confirmed it less than twenty minutes ago.

If you help us, you can get a Navi—one that I personally guarantee will be free of our little enhancement.
Within a few weeks, you can have a Navi. I promise it.

When I wake up, I'm alone in the bed. I think of Mila's soft lips
and touch, and I'm struck with certainty that she'll be upset that we
did that and now . . .now . . . I'm not sure what, but something bad.

I get up and shower while I worry.

As I do, I note that it's been several days since I've been able to
check my messages. I've lost the intense cravings and the itch to see
what I've been missing, and now I just worry that there's something
important I need to know about. I'm painfully out of touch. The
good news is that everyone who's truly important to me is right here
with me, in this house.

Suddenly, my heart rate doubles.

Everything I care about is right here in this house.

We're all sitting ducks here. All they have to do is come here
and shoot us all. My people are pacifists, for God's sake. How are
they supposed to protect themselves, let alone us?

I'm too alert now, and I go from window to window looking for
any suspicious strangers. I don't see anything amiss, but I have to
sit on the bed and try to talk myself back down. It doesn't work. It's
clear to me that we have to leave right away. Today.

I get dressed and go down to the kitchen with butterflies in my stomach for at least two different reasons.

Mila is alone in the kitchen, buttering toast, somehow captivating even in a print dress and cap. I stop at the doorway to the kitchen, too anxious to approach.

She glances up at me, and her sober expression doesn't change. I'm tongue-tied. She finishes that piece of toast and starts on another, methodical, still silent. It's hardly a warm welcome, yet she isn't yelling at me, either.

She puts down the last piece of toast and lays down the butter knife, looking down at the counter, and some expression flickers across her face that I don't consciously recognize but suddenly understand. She's afraid of how I might react to what happened between us last night.

I hurry over to her, and she turns to me and puts her head on my shoulder as I take her in my arms. We hold each other in silence, swaying slightly.

I luxuriate in the sensation of holding her. It feels as if all my anxiety and tension are drained right out of me, leaving comfort in their place—comfort and an intense awareness of her presence.

I try to remember the last time I held another person. I've had a few short-term boyfriends, but those relationships were via Navi. One of them was interested exclusively in Navi sex. I guess it's been over a year since I've even hugged another person. Did it always feel this amazing, or is it only this amazing with Mila? I can't remember.

"Someone will come in soon," Mila whispers, and we release each other reluctantly. Just in time, too. We hear footsteps, and we break eye contact and quickly move to opposite sides of the kitchen as my mother comes in to cook breakfast.

While I remain behind to take care of Jamie and Mila opens up her laptop, everyone else goes to church. Unlike the Old Order Amish, our community has separate buildings for church, albeit simple wooden structures to prevent idolatry. They sing hymns and listen to a sermon by the local bishop. For them, the afternoon and evening will be taken up with quiet Bible study, as there can be no work on Sundays.

Mila says that she's still trying to find "command and control" servers for the malware—the servers that tell it what to do, but she's having no luck.

"They've rewritten the code to point back to me, and it's all me, everywhere I look. All the logs point to me. All the command and control software is now on a server that supposedly only I have access to, that I used some months ago on a subcontract. I can't find the original code anywhere, and that means I can't prove what the code used to be, or find the companies who did it."

She looks at me, but I have nothing to offer. All I can do is shake my head. "Keep trying," I say pointlessly. "We need you."

For my part, I spend the afternoon over at Sister Friesen's house, trying to get some sort of response out of Jamie. I sit him up, give him water and more chicken and dumplings, and try stimulating his hands, feet, and face. He wrinkles his face and tries to swipe at my hands, which is something, at least. But his eyes refuse to focus, he doesn't even try to speak, and I can't get him to hold a cup or a book.

He seems so far away, locked so deep inside. To imagine that he might stay this way forever, that maybe he's not locked away but truly *gone* . . . It turns my stomach. And with Mila having no luck with the code . . . I can't bear to think about it, so I lay him back down and tuck him in to rest, and I go outside to take a walk and clear my mind.

That's the only reason I see them coming.

I'm passing behind our garden, about halfway back to my parents' house, and there they are: the two SUVs that are slowing down as they approach my parents' driveway. I know that they're here for us.

I run as fast as my suddenly weak legs will carry me. Precious seconds go by before I'm throwing open my back door and screaming to Mila.

Thank God, she's working downstairs in the living room. She snaps her laptop shut and then we're both dashing out of the back door, to the corner of the house, then we stop and peek around the corner.

The SUVs are parking and men are stepping out with serious expressions and guns strapped to their hips. A couple of them are wearing vests that say "US Marshal" on the back. I close my eyes in a moment of relief. The authorities won't kill everyone they run across. They're after Mila and me. They can gain nothing from hurting my parents. Nor Mrs. Bremer. There's no *reason* to hurt them.

They aren't looking this way yet, so I grab Mila's hand and we run behind the cover of tall tomato plants in the garden to the barn a few dozen yards away. We stop at the corner and look back, gasping.

Two of the men are going to my parents' front door. Three are spreading out around the house, looking up at it and also scanning the surrounding land.

We run through pasture with tall grass waiting to be cut to hay to Sister Friesen's house. I throw open the back door, and we stumble in. I shut the door and lock it. I peek out through the curtained window in the back door. No one yet.

As we run to the basement door, Mrs. Friesen's two youngest boys come running to see what the commotion is. "Lock the front door!" I scream-whisper.

They look at me blankly for a moment. In this community, crime is unheard-of. But kids are obedient, too, so they recover quickly and run to the front door to lock it.

As we open the basement door, Brother Friesen comes down the stairs to see what's happening.

Knowing that every second is critical, I say, "Don't open the door to them! No matter what!" I half-drag Mila down into the basement and shut the door without another word.

We both lean against the door facing each other, listening intently and trying to catch our breath. I think I'm panting from terror at least as much as from running. I look down the stairs at Jamie on his cot below. He only stirs slightly.

"They've looked through your house by now," she says quietly. "They'll be fanning out, looking through your property, looking for any signs of us."

"Thank God my people are so tidy," I whisper. "All our clothes and toiletries are put away, our beds are made . . . there should be no sign of us. And thank God I hid the car."

She looks at her laptop as if to be certain it's with her, and she nods.

A terrible thought occurs to me, and I grab her arm in a panic.

"What about your mother?" I ask. "They'll know we're here because she's here."

Mila shakes her head. "She doesn't know who I am, remember? She'll tell them Mila isn't here. She doesn't have a Navi to ID her with, either, and she may not even know her own name, depending."

I nod slowly. Turns out senility can be handy sometimes.

The knock at the front door makes both of us jump. "Don't answer don't answer don't answer don't answer," I whisper. "Please, God, don't let them answer."

I hear no sounds from upstairs. Then, more knocking. A male voice from outside. "US Marshals. Open up! We need to ask you some questions."

We are sitting ducks down here, I realize. If they open that door and let them in, we *will* be caught, and we *will* be leaving here in handcuffs.

The knocking comes a third time—louder and more insistent.

The sound of the door opening comes to our ears. I think I squeak in terror, and Mila clutches my arm to quiet me. We stare at each other, barely breathing.

"Whatever it is you want, you'll find no help here," Brother Friesen says. "You'd best move along."

"We're US marshals. We're looking for these women. Have you seen them?"

"I said you'll find no help here."

"Does that mean you've seen them?" The tone is distinctly irritated now. I can imagine the man with his marshal's vest, his guns strapped to his waist, his badge on a lanyard, and his authority disregarded.

"Move along. You'll get no help here."

A female voice interrupts. She sounds African American. "Have you two little boys seen either of these women?" she coos.

The older boy answers. "Matthew 25:41: 'And he shall say to them on the left hand, depart from me, ye cursed, into everlasting fire.'"

I have to press my hand to my mouth to keep back the laughter.

"Oh really?" the woman asks. Oh, she sounds mad. "Oh, is that what you think? That we're damned? Because you—"

Her partner interrupts her, his tone clipped. "Mind if we take a look inside?"

"You'll need a warrant to enter my home." Brother Friesen's tone remains level.

Mila and I clutch each other. This is it. If they have a warrant . . .

"If you hear anything about these women, you'll need to let us know," the other man says, his tone furious.

No response.

Then the door closes again, and Mila and I embrace each other, both of us gasping in relief. We wait as long as we can stand it, and then we crack the door open. Brother Friesen and his two youngest sons stand by the window, looking outside. Staying low, we creep out to join them. We can't help but watch.

"They've knocked on three more doors," Brother Friesen observes quietly. "Two people have answered but have not let them in." He sounds satisfied.

As we watch, the marshals approach a large family walking from one house to another. Keeping pace with the family, the marshals speak to them and flash the pictures of us. As far as I can tell, the Plain people don't even respond. Man, woman, and children, they just look at the authorities with sober gazes and keep walking.

The body language of the marshals is agitated as they stalk back to their car.

Mila and I squeeze hands.

"Thank you," I say to the Friesens.

Brother Friesen nods, and I think I detect amusement in his expression. He walks tall as he escorts his sons back to the "quiet room," where they spend their Sundays in prayer.

"We should go back into the basement," Mila says. "And then we need to be careful about moving around in the open. They're going to assume that we might still come here—if they don't think we're here already—so they'll set up a perimeter and keep watch."

I nod.

And this suddenly seems like an excellent time to clutch Mila's body against mine and kiss her.

Mila to Slava Knyazev:

> So the offer is the carrot. And the marshals—and making us your fall guys—are the stick. But what happens to your plan if they actually catch us?

Slava:

> You're smart. You won't get caught.

> Time is up, Ms. Bremer. I've been very patient with you and provided a lot of answers. I need an answer from you now. Right now.

Something in Mila's posture catches my attention, and I look up from my book. Her expression is bleak.

"What's wrong?" I ask.

She lets out a breath as she makes a couple of clicks. "'Trail of Fugitive Cyberterrorists Lost,'" she reads, her tone subdued. "'US

Deputy Marshal Tom Lyons, who is heading up the manhunt, told ABC News this morning that he suspects that the fugitives never headed south. 'We have reason to believe that the supposed sightings from earlier were digitally created . . .'" Her voice trails off.

"We knew it could only last so long," I say, hoping to comfort her. "You said you didn't have time to make it stand up to scrutiny."

She keeps reading. "'Mr. Lyons states, "We're following all possible leads to determine their whereabouts. If you think you may have sighted either of the suspects or the brother in any part of the country, email wanted@usdoj.gov immediately. We will act promptly on all tips."' They don't know where we are. If they had any idea, they'd say so."

I nod. "What else is going on out there in the world?" I hate to ask. I don't really want to know.

"There are all these do-it-yourself videos coming online for how to remove Navis at home using everything from electromagnets to thin wires. Dozens of people have killed themselves or given themselves brain damage by accident. Naturally, officials are telling people not to attempt to remove their Navis themselves, but everyone knows there aren't enough technicians to go around."

She shrugs bitterly. "And a number of patients who went from second-wave to third-wave, like Jamie, have been released back to hospitals from the detention centers. Many of them are in bad shape after as long as seven days there. Dehydration, hunger, diabetic comas, stuff like that."

"Thank God I kept Jamie out of those places," I say fervently.

She nods, but she still looks bleakly unhappy.

"How's your work going?" I ask.

She shakes her head and closes her laptop. "I still can't find anything that doesn't just point right back at me. I can't tell you how weird and frustrating that is."

She looks at me, and I wish I knew what to say. But I know so little about any of this.

Then, suddenly, the way she's looking at me changes, and she lunges toward me, her eyes wide. "You!" she exclaims.

I pull back. "What?"

"Sorry—but your Navi! You've been disconnected from the network since Thursday, when we went to jail. That was . . . that was before the third wave. You have the original programming in your brain. Don't move!" She flips open her laptop and starts typing furiously.

I don't move. I suddenly have a very valuable brain, and it feels very strange.

After I start to get a cramp in my right foot, I ask if I'm allowed to adjust my position. She barely glances at me. "Yes, of course. Sorry. You can move a little. Just don't leave the room until I've copied down your programming."

Mila to Slava Knyazev:

Give me until tomorrow.

I ask the Friesens to set us up with two cots down in the basement and to tell my parents that we need to lay low. They bring us down trays for dinner, which I appreciate immensely.

Mila works hard into the early morning hours, her brow permanently furrowed, before I insist on interrupting her. "You can hardly keep your eyes open," I say. "Listen, your brain will work better if you let it rest for a while."

"Almost out of time," she mumbles in protest, but she lets me take the laptop off her knees and close it.

We slip into pajamas and brush our teeth and push the two cots together so that we can at least put our arms around each other. But with Jamie nearby—even if he's asleep—and with Mila exhausted, we don't make out this time. She closes her eyes and snuggles up against me with a tired grin.

I gaze at her and stroke her hair. As I do, it amazes me that I'm so privileged as to touch this beautiful woman. Who am I to deserve this? To be worthy of her attention? She's like a goddess. I'd be lucky to be her handmaiden, let alone her lover.

I take in her beauty for a long while, savoring each detail from the way her long eyelashes curve to the pale freckles barely visible on her cheeks. I'm captivated. And when her eyes suddenly open and she whispers, "I don't want to lose you," my heart skips a beat.

I smile at her—a huge, stupid smile. And then I say, "Then don't. Solve this thing." My voice turns wry. "After all, what are the odds that they'll let us share a cell in federal prison?"

She grins slightly. Then her face grows serious again. "I will. I am. That's for sure. But . . . I mean, I don't want to lose you like this. Like we are right now." She seems to hunt for the right words. "You're present. You're here with me, not off in"—she grimaces— "Naviland. I don't want you to go back." It sounds like a plea.

I gaze into her ice-blue eyes and I don't want to refuse her anything, ever.

I speak cautiously, as if she might be a wild animal I could enrage by accident. "I noticed when we were on the run that since I didn't have a Navi, it was like I didn't even exist. It must be hard for you, not to be . . . seen. I would think that, when everyone else got Navis when we were teenagers, it must have felt like you were being left behind."

Her eyes well with tears, and when she speaks, her tone is harsh and bitter. "I *was* left behind." She blinks back the tears. "But here . . . with you . . . it's like I exist again. Like I've . . . become visible again."

"Mila made visible," I say thoughtfully. "I like that." I slide my top leg over hers, craving that extra bit of closeness. "Okay. But . . . I can't promise not to have my Navi turned back on at all . . . I need it, you know?"

She looks unhappy. "You really want it back, given everything we know now?"

I sigh. "Not right now, not immediately. The thought terrifies me, actually. But . . ."

"Human nature being what it is," Mila supplies, "once the immediate danger has passed, people will want them back."

I nod. "Nothing like Eve has ever happened before, and people will implement safeguards against it happening again. The response will be better and faster next time. And let's face it—Navis are unbelievably useful."

Mila shrugs sleepily. "The only time in history that humans have ever stopped using a new technology because it was too dangerous was after Hiroshima and Nagasaki. Otherwise, we adopt it and forge ahead. Every time. No matter the cost. It's how we operate. Like manual-drive cars. I only feel safe driving mine because I'm almost the only one on the road. But people drove their own vehicles for decades, and *millions* of people died—more than from any plague or war in history. And yet we didn't stop."

She looks unhappy, and I nod, thinking about everything she's said. She's not wrong. "Mila, I'll never ignore you for my Navi when we're together, okay? I promise. I'll turn it off entirely when you want my attention."

She looks thoughtful, and I worry.

"Is that enough?" I ask hesitantly. I'm trying to imagine life without a Navi compared to life without Mila, and if I have to— *have* to—I think . . .

She smiles and kisses me. An errant curl of blonde hair falls in front of her eyes, and I sweep it back for her.

"That's enough," she says.

I let out a breath in relief. I was about willing to do it, but I'm so glad I don't have to.

"You might have to remind me sometimes," I admit. "Early on, especially. Until I get used to it."

"It's a deal," she says.

She strokes the back of my shoulder down to the curve of my waist and hip and then back up, her eyes closed again. I close my eyes, too, lost in the sensation, savoring it. I listen to the sound of our breath and of Mila's fingertips along the cotton sheet.

"Do you wish I could have a Navi?" she asks. "Do you wish you could talk to me inside your head like you do with everyone else?"

I furrow my brow while she continues to slowly stroke my side.

"I don't know," I say at last. "I can see pros and cons. I guess I would have the same fear you do, of losing you to Naviland. But being more-or-less telepathic with each other, that's pretty cool, too. I guess I don't know."

She nods, her expression grave, and then grins slightly. "I thought I didn't even . . . *like* people," she says. "You know, in that way. I guess I just don't like men."

I chuckle quietly. "I do like men. So I guess I like both." I shake my head. "But, honestly, no other woman has ever turned my head like you have. I've never even thought about . . . this . . . with any other girl."

"Really?" She looks pleased.

"Really."

She seems to think on that for a bit. "Does your family approve of same-sex relationships?"

I roll over and look at the ceiling, my smile gone. "No," I admit. "Not at all. Actually, it's one of the greatest sins you can commit. I mean, they already think I'm going to hell, but if they knew about this . . . about us . . . I don't think they would even let me visit anymore."

Mila rolls over, too, looking up at the ceiling.

"I wish I could make them understand," I say. "That they don't have to be afraid about my soul. I don't know what I think about God, but I *am* sure that he doesn't care about who we have sex with." I rub my eyes. "You know, my mother told me once that God hates low necklines. I don't think God gives a crap about low necklines or anything else like that. If He even exists and if He's good and if we're His children, then He ought to want us to be happy."

"So you don't believe in hell?" she asks.

I make a restless motion. "No. I don't think I do. It's just one story out of one old book. And it doesn't make *sense*. I wish I could make them understand that. It's like . . . it's like they're little kids who are afraid there's a monster in the closet because someone told them there was one in there. I wish I could make them understand that there's no monster there to be afraid of, but I can't. I can't help them stop being afraid."

"Mmm," Mila says.

"It's the worst part of my leaving home. They have to be afraid for all of us."

Mila turns over to face me again. "You know, when Jerry Armstead brought my mom here, he offered to stay and help get her settled in and such. Your parents weren't friendly toward him. They acted like they couldn't wait for him to leave. But they didn't react that way toward me."

I turn toward her, resettling myself on my pillow. "How do you know all that? Oh, I guess you've messaged him on your laptop."

She nods, and I pick back up the thread of the conversation. "That's weird, that they treated him that way. Well, not that weird. I mean, I told you they were insular. They seem to like you quite a bit more than they like most people."

Her eyebrows go up and then back down as she considers this. "He's black," she says. "Do you think that could have anything to do with it?"

My heart sinks. "Oh. Yes. It could." I hate to admit it. "Plain people are not always super accepting of people who aren't white. They aren't used to it. It's not their culture. They descended from white Europeans, and they've kept to their own for centuries."

Mila turns over restlessly. "I was disappointed for him. That he was made to . . . feel like that."

"Please convey my apologies when you get a chance," I say. "My utmost apologies. They're ignorant people." I'm mad now.

Mila stretches and seems to consider the ceiling. "I like them, actually," she says. "Despite everything. I like it here."

"No Navis," I comment.

"No Navis. And my mother is happy here—much happier than in the Lovely Pines rest home. Do you . . ."

She trails off, and I cock my head to prompt her to go on.

"Do you suppose she could stay here? When all this is over"

It's my turn to raise my eyebrows. I have to think about it for a moment. "Usually, I would say no. But they do like you a lot—a surprising amount, given all the trouble that's come along with your visit. I think that maybe, when all this is over, you could ask. There's no harm in asking."

"I'd pay them, of course," she says.

I nod.

"It wouldn't be for the rest of her life," she goes on. "She's been stable at this level of senility for some time, but she will deteriorate. Once she becomes too difficult, she'll have to go back to a nursing facility. But she might get a few happy years here."

I look over at her to make sure she's okay, but as usual, her face is inscrutable. I squeeze her hand in sympathy.

As I lay there in the Friesens' basement, Jamie's faint snoring a few feet away, I feel like I ought to be overwhelmed, that I should have a hundred things swimming through my mind, but Mila's presence is so soothing that it clears everything else away.

Soon, we're both asleep.

THIRTEEN

We stay down in the basement all the next day, making me restless and sleepy at the same time. Sister Friesen brings us our meals on trays again, even including an afternoon snack.

I continue to nurse Jamie, who's shown no improvement at all. When he fails to eat more than a few bites of the afternoon snack of apples and crackers, I decide that he's not eating enough. We can't keep him here for more than a few more days.

As I'm staring at him in misery, Mila stops her work and performs one of her catlike stretches. I've learned that these often precede an announcement, so I turn to her. She has a Cheshire-cat grin.

"Do you have it?" I ask.

"Yes." She puts down her laptop and comes over to me to kiss me.

I return it eagerly. "Thank God," I say. "So what's the story?"

She hops up, goes to her canvas backpack, and takes out two silver thumb drives.

"I'm going to save the files down to these drives so that we each have a copy."

She puts in the first thumb drive as she talks. "I was able to trace the logs that were stored in your Navi back to the original command-and-control servers and then find who was in control of those IP addresses. We were lucky that you had untouched, original code in your brain. Yours may be the only Navi in the world that still has it."

"So who's behind it?" I demand impatiently.

"ENI is involved, as I suspected. So are at least four other large corporations—conglomerates, I should say. Peake International, Big Wave, Kimberley Corp, and AmeriTaste—fast foods, convenience foods, cigarettes, Navi entertainment apps, casinos, toys . . . A lot of what they used to call vice stocks."

I try to put two and two together. "Why would vice-stock companies shred people's brains? What do they have to gain?"

Mila half-shrugs as she hands me the first thumb drive and inserts the second one. "I can only tell you that the command and control servers are at those companies."

"Could someone have created Eve somewhere else and made it look like it was coming from there?"

She shakes her head and takes out the second thumb drive. "No. It's definite. I'm following a trail, and the trail stops there." She gestures at the thumb drive I'm holding. "Put it somewhere you won't lose it. If I somehow lose mine, our freedom could depend on that."

I tuck it into my bra.

"As soon as I finish saving this down, I'm going to release the files to the net. Once it's public knowledge, our attorney can use it in court to exonerate us and get the right people charged."

"How come we can't send it directly to Mr. Pataky?"

"I'm no attorney, but from what I could research, the fact that we got this data illegally means they can't use it in court unless it becomes public knowledge first. Once it's out there, they can use it."

"You don't think we should go straight to the media? Give a journalist our side of things?"

"No time. That can be the next step, but we need to get this out there now. Okay, look, let me show you how we know where Eve started from." She waves me over to the computer.

She points out various files and folders and then runs commands in a black text box and points out the results, but I don't fully understand what she's showing me.

In a window that's open behind the black text box, among many other folders, a folder titled 'MBremer' catches my eye. I point to it. "What's that?"

She looks at it for only an instant. "I'm not sure," she says casually. She hesitates an instant too long before saying, "Probably my personnel file. These are ENI files."

That doesn't sound right. The other filenames aren't people's names.

She starts closing windows. Her voice is pitched high as she says, "So, the next thing we need to do is release the files. I'm trying to decide the best place. I'm thinking that probably we ought to go with Wikileaks . . ."

She stops and looks at me, because I'm staring at her, my forehead wrinkled. Something is wrong. She's hiding something from me.

She goes back to her computer, turning her face away. "I'll publish these files on Wikileaks, I think. That's the easiest thing to do, and probably . . ."

I swallow down a sick feeling in my stomach. "Mila. What's in that folder?"

She looks at me, and, from her expression, as blank as it is, I know that she's trying to keep something from me.

"I don't know, actually," she says. "It's probably nothing."

"So let's find out," I say. It comes out cold and harsh, because I don't know what she would want to hide from me, but whatever it is, it can't be good.

She clicks on the folder. There are video files. Lots of them. Two of the file names have a "!!!" prefix.

She hesitates, looking at me.

I stare back at her. Waiting. And trying to ignore that fact that my heart is pounding and my stomach feels sick.

She clicks on the first "!!!" video.

It shows Mila opening the door of her apartment to three visitors in suits.

"We need you to play bit dumb for us," one of them says. "Stop being quite so effective at figuring out what's going on. And at some point, we may need you to pass some misinformation to Ms. Bernhart."

She refuses, but not because she doesn't want to lie to me—not because she has any moral objection. In fact, when they ask, "Why are you objecting to our request? Do you care about this woman, this Phoebe Bernhart?" she says, "Of course not."

No, she refuses only because "I don't feel like doing you any favors."

They hit her under the jaw with a jet injector, have a short but fierce argument over what to do, tell her that her mother has already been taken away, and then extract whatever they injected through the corner of her eye. Then one of them says, "One more thing. We may need you to exert some influence on Ms. Bernhart. So we suggest you get close to her, just in case you need to be able to persuade her."

One of the other men says, "See if you can get her . . . interest." He leers at her.

Then the video ends.

I can't think. I can't even tell what I'm feeling. It's as if lightning has struck me, and I'm already dead. I'm just waiting to realize it.

I reach over Mila, who has gone still, to click the link to play the other "!!!" video. It's dated a week or so before the first one. In this one, Mila sits at a table in a nondescript, corporate-looking conference room. The cameraman and another man watch her.

> "So, yes, I know what you're doing," Mila says. She's cold and distant. "But I would like to point out that I don't care, so this is a waste of everyone's time."

> "Oh?" says the man. His hair spikes out over his ears, despite the copious hair gel. "So tell us, what do you think is going on?"

> "You're manipulating the nanobots to do things that they aren't supposed to do—go places in the brain they aren't supposed to go." She sounds like she's reading off a grocery list composed of foods she doesn't much like. "Which, yes, goes well beyond what a Navi is FDA-approved to do and violates about half a dozen—"

"And what makes you believe all of this?"

"Don't play stupid," Mila says sharply. "I'm smart. I looked at the code I was working on and observed some bits and pieces of the code assigned to my co-workers, and I put it together."

The spiky-haired man turns to the cameraman. "Is that possible?"

The cameraman shakes his head. "Only if she's a freaking genius."

"I happen to be a freaking genius," Mila says dryly.

Spike makes a face. "So, what do you think we're doing with the nanobots?"

"I don't know, and I don't care. I only pointed it out to my supervisor because it amused me that I solved the puzzle. Otherwise, I have no interest in having this conversation."

"You don't care? What if we were—oh, I don't know—trying to manipulate people's behavior on a large scale. Mind control. Taking away their free will. That wouldn't bother you?"

Mila closes her eyes briefly. "Let me try saying this again more plainly. No, I don't care. I have no use for people. And people, just so you know, have no use for free will. People are mindless idiots. Somebody's got to tell them what to do. Might as well be you."

Spike breaks out into derisive laughter. "You know, you're a real piece of work. You really don't care, do you?"

"You've got it, and I only had to say it three times. Very good. May I go now?"

I turn to Mila, who stares at the screen, unmoving, and I wait without breathing for an explanation, but nothing comes. She closes the video window, and then she looks at me. There's a challenge in that look, not an apology.

My mouth twists into a rictus, and words freeze in my throat.

And then a message pops up on her screen. An email notification. One line:

> Do we have a deal, Ms. Bremer? Do we get Phoebe?

Mila looks at the notification, too, and she says nothing. Nothing.

At first, I can't speak at all, and then I'm surprised at how measuredly I ask, "What the hell is all this?"

But the calm disappears in an instant, and suddenly I'm standing over her, screaming, "What the *hell* is all of this? Explain it! Now!"

Mila's face twitches. "You weren't—this isn't—this isn't a good—"

"You were going to *give* me to them? To whoever is behind this?"

"No," she says. "No, I wasn't. I was just—"

"You're *talking* to them? Negotiating?"

"Listen, it's not—I didn't—look—" She turns to the laptop and hammers out a message.

> No, no deal. Screw you. You don't get Phoebe.

She hits "send" and then turns to me. "See? No deal. I'm not doing it."

"That doesn't fix it," I say incredulously. "That doesn't make it all go away. You *knew*. You knew all along. You kept all this from me."

"No . . . I . . ." She gives up and stares into the distance.

Tears are in my eyes, and my chest is tight. I'm losing my mind. Another message pops up.

> I'm sorry to hear that, Ms. Bremer. I really am. Time for Plan B.

My mind refuses to process the words. "What *is* all this?"

Mila just shakes her head. "That was probably a mistake," she murmurs.

I turn away. "I can't take this, Mila. I can't deal with this. Get away from me. Just get away."

She gets up, closes the laptop. When she looks at me again, I remember her cold, harsh face and her voice snidely saying, *You've got it, and I only had to say it three times.*

I scream again, "Get *out*!" and my throat is raw and my fists are clenched and I am full of terror for what I'll do if she doesn't—

She grabs her canvas backpack and disappears up the stairs.

I turn away. Jamie's eyes are open, but he has no expression.

Tears are spilling down my cheeks, and I wipe them away with hands that are shaking violently. My throat stings.

I pace aimlessly.

She was spying on me. She was keeping information from me. She knew all along.

She knew. All. Along.

And she didn't care. Right from the beginning.

Her mother had been kidnapped by these . . . these corporate thugs, and Mila sent her . . . here.

To my family.

She led them to my family.

She was negotiating with them, talking to them, and keeping all of it from me. Lying to me.

I'm crying as I pace, but I don't have the luxury of grieving this . . . horrible mistake. My family is in far more danger than I realized.

"Plan B"—that can't be good, whatever it is.

I pull the thumb drive out of my bra. Is this worthless? Does it make any sense that she would have pulled down incriminating information when she was part of this?

God. She *worked* on the code that destroyed my little brother.

I double over, my stomach clenching so that I think I might get sick. But I don't.

I have no idea what might be on this drive and I have no way of finding out, because I don't even have a computer.

I force myself upright and I wipe my face and I go upstairs.

I look around, but she isn't there. The front door hangs open. I look down the road both ways. Nothing.

I don't know how to do this without her.

But I have to now.

Resolute and terrified at the same time, I walk through the field and behind the garden to my parents' house, seeing nothing around me as I go. I'm haunted by Mila's cold, sarcastic tone on those recordings. I can't reconcile that woman to the one I was lying next to last night, thanking my lucky stars I was privileged to touch.

I go upstairs, avoiding my mother, and change into my regular street clothes. I pack up my few things and go downstairs, where I'm unexpectedly confronted by both parents. Dad is home from work.

I open my mouth to explain, and I burst into tears instead. Mom walks me to one of the living room sofas and sits down with me while I sob. To my surprise, she puts her arms around me and rocks me as if I were child again.

It takes me a few false starts while she patiently holds me. Finally, I sob out, "Mom . . . we're not safe. None of us is safe. They might come anytime. These . . . awful corporate guys are behind everything and they were going to kill Mrs. Bremer and that's why Mila sent her here and . . . they might come here and try to hurt all of you."

My mother sits me up and takes my hands in hers. She bows her head and prays—I can tell by the way she closes her eyes and the expression on her face. I've seen it so many times. It calms me immediately, as it always has.

She lets out a deep breath, opens her eyes, and steadily says, "Phebe, we're pacifists, you know that. God giveth and God taketh away. If it's our time—"

"No, Mom!" I wail. "You have to run away. Hide. Something. Please!"

My father paces, his expression stormy. He says nothing.

"Mom, please don't let them hurt you. I couldn't live with myself." I'm hysterical again already, but I can't help it. "Please . . ."

My tears are contagious, and her face crumples. "Oh, Phebe. Why did you ever have to leave? Why couldn't you stay here with us?"

"Mom, I can't. I can't live here. I *can't*." The words come out of me with tremendous weight. I've never said these things to her. We've never had this conversation.

She struggles to compose herself, looking away. But I can tell from the look on her face that some part of her understands, no matter how much she tells herself that it's wrong of me. "I wish . . ."

I throw my arms around her and squeeze as if, with the force of my hug, I could press happiness into her. "I wish I could be here," I say miserably. "I wish I never had to leave."

And I leave it unsaid that if God was just, if He was fair, He would have made me so I could stand to be here, so that I didn't have to break my parents' hearts every single day. But He didn't. And I can't do anything about it.

At last, I tear myself away from my mother. "I have to go," I say brokenly. "Mila said there was evidence on this drive she gave me, and I have to go try to get it to a computer so I can tell the world. So that I can clear my name. And hopefully, I'll draw their attention when I go. Draw them away from you. Just be safe. Please, please be safe."

I gather my things, and my father presses a money card into my hand. Since Mila took the other cards with her, I accept it gratefully.

As I'm opening the door to leave, I nearly jump out of my skin, because a man stands there in front of the door. I quickly register that his stance is uncertain, that he's nervous about being here.

He says, "Oh, I'm sorry. I didn't mean to surprise you. Mila sent me over . . . asked me to help keep an eye on things."

From behind me, Mom says, "Jerry Armstead? I thought you went home after you brought Mrs. Bremer here." She steps up to the door and I give her room.

"Oh, well . . ." He looks embarrassed. "See, Mila's not real good about asking for help when she needs it, but I knew something serious was going on when she sent me here incognito with her mama. So I kind of stuck around town, just in case. I just wouldn't feel right, walking away. I had some vacation days saved up anyhow."

My heart leaps in my chest even as I wipe away the last of my tears. "Jerry, thank you for being here. Do you have a car here?"

"Yes, I sure do. I rented one. It's right out front. Right out there."

"And you have a Navi?"

"I sure do have a Navi. Yes, I sure do."

I speak quickly, my words tumbling over each other. "As soon as I'm away from here, I need you to call the police. Tell them that Mila Bremer and Phoebe Bernhart are here. That's all you need to say. Then, take my parents and Mrs. Bremer and Jamie in your car and get them away from here as fast as you can. And then I'll contact you as soon as I can. Hopefully, this will all be over in a few hours." Then I add, belatedly, "Please?"

He almost laughs, but then he sobers. "I will. Of course. That's why I'm here."

He looks at my parents, and I think everyone is aware of their hesitation. Their discomfort.

Then my mother raises her hands. "Thank you, Jesus," she says.

From behind us, my father says, "'Behold, I am going to send an angel before you to guard you along the way.'"

Jerry laughs, but he looks pleased and relieved. "Well, I don't know about an angel," he says. "A servant of God, at my best, I hope. I sure aim to be, anyway."

Then something he said a minute ago strikes me. "You saw Mila? Just now?"

"No, she sent me a message. She said she had to leave, but you all might need help, so that's why I came."

I take a breath. "Do you trust Mila?" I ask him.

"Of course I do. She may be odd, but she's good people. Why do you ask?"

I shake my head. "No reason." I don't know what to say. I don't want to tell him that he's wrong about her.

I end up having Jerry take me to our stolen car, which is still there, before he calls the cops and takes the others away. When I see the car, it occurs to me to wonder how Mila is traveling. Then I realize that I never told her where I'd parked our car.

I can't make up my mind whether I'm worried about her or not. My anger and hurt war with my fear.

Rubbing my face wearily, I focus on my task. I need to get to a computer that's on the net, look at what Mila put on the drive, try to make heads or tails of it, and then, assuming I can figure it all out, I'll try to do what Mila said—release the data on Wikileaks. It feels like a long shot, but it's all I've got.

I decide to go to the John McIntire public library in Zanesville, because libraries usually have computers. I drive in a daze, my stomach sick with anxiety, not even able to take in my surroundings. I try not to accidentally run any red lights or kill any pedestrians on the way.

This town is small, maybe twenty thousand people. I get to the library, a couple of blocks from the river, within a few minutes.

As dusk begins to fall, I park, step out of the car, walk about ten steps toward the small building—and then tires squeal nearby.

One of the US marshals' SUVs is a few yards away.

It doesn't even properly stop before the doors swing open and the barrels of guns flash. and strange men bark commands to get down—but I'm already running, not toward the library anymore, because I'd be cornered in there, but past it, toward the woods on the other side of the parking lot.

Sirens approach, and then gunfire cracks. My heart lurches, and I'm panting hysterically and running as fast and as erratically as I can without stumbling.

Why the hell are they shooting at me? I'm supposed to be a cyberterrorist, not a serial killer.

And then I realize I probably ought to be dead by now if they're at all competent with guns, because a lot of shots have been fired and I'm confident that I have zero ability to dodge bullets.

I slow down enough to turn and see that there's a black SUV caddy-corner to the brown one and that five men in that SUV are shooting the marshals dead.

I run. And run.

The horse-drawn buggy stops in front of the lone Greyhound bus station in Zanesville. Mila gets out from where she was hidden on the floorboard. "Thank you," she says to the driver, and the buggy pulls away with the clip-clopping of horse's hooves.

She changed into her ordinary street clothes from her backpack while she was in the buggy. Her eyes are still red from crying. She has a thousand-yard stare, her shoulders slumped.

A single Greyhound bus waits at the bus stop, its engine running. Mila steps up into it. There are only three other passengers. She opens her laptop to show the driver her ticket, and when he nods, she takes a seat by the window. As the bus sets off with a jerk and a roar, she opens her laptop in her lap.

Sirens approach from behind them. She looks out of the window, but she can't see anything from this angle.

The bus picks up speed as it starts onto the Y bridge over the river that runs through the center of Zanesville.

Then there are sounds like firecrackers, and the front of the bus drops with an alarming lurch and swerve.

Startled shouts come from the other passengers as they hit the backs of the seats in front of them.

A hard impact accompanied by a forceful crunching sound jolts the bus from one side, throwing everyone and everything into the neighboring seats. The jolt knocks the laptop out of Mila's lap.

Seconds later, another impact slams the bus much more violently than the first one, this time on the left front corner.

The bus rolls onto its side with a tremendous crash and the shattering of windows.

Everything flies into the air—people and luggage, Mila's laptop—roughly colliding with the walls, seats, and roof of the bus.

Mila's right arm slams against the hard edge of an overhead compartment.

The bus slams, jerks, and skids before it comes to a rest on its side.

Mila lies across the sides of two seats, motionless like all the other passengers.

Then she rouses and tries to pick herself up. She cries out as she puts weight on her right arm. Instead, she uses her left arm.

More gunfire erupts from outside, and sirens close in as the other passengers begin to stir and groan.

Fast-fading sunlight comes in from the windows directly above them, but they reveal only darkening sky.

Mila finds her backpack between two seats and slings it onto her back, crying out again as she puts her right arm through the loop. She climbs over seats toward the shattered front windows.

Along the way, she stops as she sees her laptop between seats, open, the hinge broken, the screen shattered and dark. She gives it a forlorn look and then moves on, leaving it behind.

Before she gets to the windows, she can see that the headlights illuminate no road ahead of them. Too far below them is a river.

She looks back, but there's no back window in this bus. Her only other option is overhead.

As others begin to get up or call for help, she scrambles one-handed up the horizontal seats to one of the broken windows and looks out.

Immediately, rough hands grab her by the shoulders and torso, and two men in black outfits pull her out.

She screams as they grab her by the arms and pull her down off the bus amid the shouts of angry men and sirens and gunfire.

While three more men hang out of windows to exchange fire with the half-a-dozen police cars and the tan SUV that have all come to a stop some yards away, Mila's captors shove her into the back of a black SUV. They pull two of their own, now dead, back in from the windows, and the SUV squeals away past the bus.

I make it to the woods to the west of the library. I don't look back. With any luck, they've all killed each other by now, although I doubt it. It looked like those guys in black were slaughtering the marshals.

I dodge and weave among the trees while I angle to the north. I know that the river is close. I have some vague idea of either finding a boat or simply jumping into the water and letting the current take me away. The light is fading into twilight, and I hope that will help me. Thank God I'm not wearing white.

I'm also suddenly grateful for my Navi forcing me to run on every one of my days off for the past however many months.

Within a hundred yards or so, I emerge into what looks like an abandoned train yard, with dozens of rusting train cars. I climb into a boxcar, which I figure ought to give me enough cover that I can look back.

For a few seconds, I don't see anything. But then light glints off fast-moving metal inside the woods.

Panting, I look forward. Past the train car graveyard is a set of train tracks and then, a few dozen yards away, the river. There's a big house, and there's a large, white boat tied up at a private pier. The space between here and there is flat and open, so I can't go that way. But they'll also know that, so they'll know I'm here in the train cars, and they'll search all the cars until they find me and kill me. If they're smart, they'll split up and shoot me when I run.

I climb out the front of my boxcar and find a ladder at the far edge. I climb up to the top edge of the car and then bend to the side so I can peek around the side of the boxcar.

I'm extremely grateful that only two of them come out of the woods, but two still feels like a lot when they both have guns and I don't.

I hear the whistle of a train and twist to look. From this height, I can see a train coming from the north. It's not moving all that fast, probably because it's coming through a town.

I look back at the two men. They split up as they approach. One comes toward the left of my car, close, and the other veers wide to the right. Once they're quite close, I pull myself up and over onto the roof and, staying as flat as I can, roll toward the back of the roof. I stop on my back, staring up into the darkening sky.

Now that I'm here, I don't know how long to stay. If I wait too long—if they go past the train car too far—they'll be able to see me up here.

So I stay up there until I can't stand it anymore, and then I peek over the edge on the back side. I don't see anyone. I climb down the ladder. All I can hear is the whistle and roar of the oncoming train—closer now—and I try to jump down quietly.

My breathing is harsh, my throat dry, my heart pounding, as I lean down and look under the boxcars to look for legs.

I find one pair to the far left. Where's the other one?

I hear a hollow clang close to my right, and I startle like a hunted deer.

I climb up into the box car and run straight through it, leaping out the other side, landing hard and painfully, and then pick myself back up and make a mad dash for a large, rusted tank car.

I hear the crack of a gunshot, but I feel no impact.

I run past the tank car, and there it is immediately to my right—the oncoming train on the outermost of three sets of tracks. I turn back, and there the men are, right behind me—and with no better options available to me, I try to run across the tracks in front of the train.

I know I won't make it even as I'm midway across. The train's whistle and the squeal of brakes is deafening, the headlamp is blinding, and I'm throwing myself forward when I feel myself caught and spun as if I were a rag doll.

Fourteen

Mila has her head up enough to see another black SUV pass them going the other way and spin out across the two-lane bridge. It stops, and more gunfire breaks out. The cops and marshals are momentarily stopped. Then, one man grabs Mila's head and doubles her over onto the seat. She screams as if in agonizing pain.

The vehicle goes down an incline, turns a left, goes a surprisingly short distance, and pulls into what seems to be a large garage. The car doors open, men jump out, and a large door motors closed behind them. Flashlights cut swaths into the darkness in a large, echoing space.

A man and a woman grab Mila and drag her out of the SUV. She screams again, and the woman smashes her elbow into Mila's ribs. "Shut up," she says. Doubled over, Mila chokes and gasps for breath as she's half-dragged along. She doesn't resist.

Someone drapes the SUV with a tarp, and another man runs up some stairs toward a large window on a top floor while the woman takes Mila into an interior room.

The woman shoves Mila roughly onto a metal folding chair and steps away as another man flips the lights on.

This person has a soft look, with too much padding on his bones, and he wears a dull, gray suit and carries a small briefcase. He's not with the others. His face is tight and agitated, and his breathing is too fast.

Mila sobs in the chair, clutching her ribs and her right arm and making no effort to get up.

"Mila Bremer, you pain in the ass," the man says with pent-up feeling, and he slaps her across the face.

She cries out and hangs her head.

"You led us on a wild goose chase," the man snaps. "Across the whole damn country. But then, you know? As soon as we looked for your mother, there it was. Flying from Atlanta to Cleveland under her own damn name. You're not that bright after all, are you?"

The mercenary woman stares at them both with her lip curled and her arms crossed.

"And it was all no thanks to you, wasn't it?" the man shouts at the mercenary. "I thought you people were competent!"

"She's here, isn't she? Still alive. And so are you."

"Thanks to luck," he snaps. "What the hell was that stunt with the bus? You nearly got her killed. And you weren't supposed to draw this kind of attention. We told you not to draw attention! How the hell are we supposed to cover this up now?"

The mercenary woman shrugs with an eyebrow raised. "Yeah, well, that was before the targets ran for it *and* the US marshals showed up. It kind of all went to shit after that. If you had told us about the marshals, that might have come in handy. Makes me wonder if this is your first damn rodeo."

The man turns and kicks at Mila, missing. "You couldn't just accept our deal. You just had to turn this into one big, hard-to-cover-up *wreck* of a situation."

The mercenary rolls her eyes. "You need help with this pathetic woman or can I go make sure we're not all about to be killed? There are only three of us left on Alpha team, you know."

The suit slams his briefcase down on a table and opens it. Inside is a jet injector and a gun.

He goes over to Mila and grabs her face, forcing her to look at him. "You're not going to fight me, are you?"

"No," Mila sobs. "P-please don't hurt me."

The man lets go of her face and surveys how she's clutching her arm and ribs. He grabs her right arm roughly, twisting it. Mila voices an ear-piercing shriek. He looks at the arm and sees inches of bruising already evident. "Broken. Ribs, too, huh?" he demands. He slaps her torso, and she chokes and doubles over.

He turns to the mercenary with satisfaction. "No, she's not going to give me any trouble."

The woman smirks and leaves the room, closing the door behind her.

"You're going to give us the confession we need to make all this go away, aren't you?" the man says coldly. "We've got it pinned on you already. We just need a confession and a very tragic suicide in a standoff with law enforcement, and then I don't know what the hell we're going to do about the rest of it yet, but I guess we'll figure that out as we go along, won't we? Because what choice do we have, Ms. Bremer?" His face reddens as his voice reaches a scream. "*What choice have you given us?*" Rage boils visibly within him, so strong it might break loose. He snarls under his breath as he pushes it down.

Mila cries quietly, her head down again, trying not to draw his rage.

The man turns back to his briefcase and picks up the jet injector, and already, Mila is on her feet, holding her metal chair with both hands and swinging it viciously at the man's head.

I lie in the grass as the world settles down around me. I don't even try to get up. My nurse training kicks in, and the first thing I do is assess the damage. I think I got hit on the left leg as I was trying to leap away from the tracks. My left knee joint feels wrong and maybe the hip joint, too. Even though everything still moves like it should, which means nothing's dislocated, the joints feel loose. I've probably screwed up some tendons. Recovery is going to suck, but nothing hurts yet. My body's in shock.

The train is still braking, the wheels squealing. For the moment, my pursuers are on the other side of the train.

I look behind me. That house and its tied-up boat call to me less than a hundred yards away, but I'll never make it across that wide, bare expanse of grass.

From my angle on the ground, I see the pumping legs of one of my pursuers as he runs up and tries to jump onto the ladder of a moving boxcar from the other side. It's a three-foot vertical, and he doesn't quite make it high enough. His legs flail and come forward to counterbalance his weight and get pulled into the wheels directly below the ladder.

I can't hear anything over the squealing of the wheels, but I get a fine mist of blood on my face.

I feel nothing now. Later, I'm sure I'll be horrified. For now, what matters is that there's only one left.

I look to my right. The tracks branch out to a set of five, and not far down are two more trains at rest on their own tracks.

I try to get to my feet, but I simply can't put weight on my left leg. Some primal part of my brain tells me it's not an option, and that means something is broken after all. I feel down my leg and discover that putting pressure on the shin makes me scream.

I cast about for something—anything—that might help, and I'm lucky to find a discarded piece of metal by the tracks. I use it as an impromptu crutch and hobble toward the other trains, my heartbeat thudding in my ears.

The way my left leg feels, I'm going slow—so slow, it's like moving through waist-deep water—but the train is still braking, and I don't have far to go.

I see freight cars with ladders that only go halfway up. There's a series of cars loaded down with enormous metal tubes, but if I go inside those, I'll be a sitting duck. And if I go into an engine, I'll be cornered, and it's too easy for him to glance into them to see if I'm there.

I'm at the first train now. There's a tank car with a catwalk around the outside. I want my legs off the ground so he can't see where I am, but I don't think I can climb up there and down again. I hobble past this car. Ah. The next train is pulling double-decker flats of smartcars. I look behind me. The first train is almost stopped. I'm out of time.

I hurry as best I can to the double-decker flat, open a car door, pop the trunk, and look around one last time. I can't see anything from here, but I don't see my pursuer. I climb into the trunk and pull it almost closed. I put the tips of three fingers into the gap and pull the lid down until it hurts. I don't want to be stuck in here, but I also can't risk him seeing that the trunk lid is tilted up.

Now, all I can do is hope, because now I've trapped myself. If he checks every train car and every smartcar methodically until he finds me, I'm dead.

The metal chair crashes down on the man's head, and he crumples.

"My arm is bruised, not broken," Mila says, and she hits him again. "And my ribs are just sore."

He's still conscious but stunned, his hands on his head but not protecting it well enough.

"And I had less than five minutes to get my mom away from you people. Not enough time to construct a false ID that would stand up to the TSA, okay?"

She rotates the chair and hits him with the edge of the chair back, and finally, he goes unconscious.

"And it's a good thing I don't need you awake," she finishes.

She looks around, opens the door briefly, and peeks down the hallway. Seeing no one, she checks rooms before she finds an old desktop computer in the third room. After ensuring that it has wi-fi, she goes back for the man.

After two failed attempts to transport him, she goes back to the computer and searches for "how to drag an unconscious body."

Seconds later, she goes back to the first room, rolls the man onto his back, and kneels behind his head. First, she gets her arms under his shoulders and raises him up onto her lap, and then she gets her arms around his waist and stands up, lifting his upper body with the strength of her legs. Then she drags him slowly down the hallway.

She goes back for the metal chair, too, just in case.

Sitting at the desktop computer, she launches into a flurry of activity. First, she pulls out a USB drive and quickly installs the exploit she used to hack into other Navis from her laptop. With the exploit, she gets into the Navi of the unconscious man besides her, who she confirms is Slava Knyazev, and from his Navi, she intercepts the messages and Navi IDs of all three corporate mercenary teams currently hunting them.

She watches until she finds what she needs—messages from the man who's hunting Phoebe.

His name is Michael, and, according to the messages he's sending his fellow mercenaries, his situation isn't good. He's hiding from the cops and US marshals that are closing in on the train yard, and he's still trying to find Phoebe at the same time. But apparently, the other mercenary team somehow got away from the cops on the bridge and are coming up in the woods behind the cops and marshals. Things are about to get ugly.

She sends a quick message to Tom Lyons, the US deputy marshal responsible for their manhunt.

> vmsg nid CT09372380 "Dear Tom. This is Mila Bremer. The corporate mercenaries are right behind you. I think you might want to address that. Phoebe and I will turn ourselves in soon, I promise. Meanwhile, please don't get killed."

While she moves on to trying to hack into Michael's Navi, she watches the communications between Tom and the rest of the marshals and cops. He's not dumb. He sends a small team to scout the area behind them while he continues to advance with the rest of his men.

This is a problem, but it's a problem that solves itself as soon as the scouting team finds the mercenaries and all hands turn to trying to defend themselves.

At last, Mila gains access to Michael's Navi, and she sends him a quick message.

> display emmsg nid LS03984703 "Excuse me, Michael. This is Mila Bremer. I'm inside your brain.

And I would like to suggest that you stop hunting Phoebe now."

The message appears in Michael's emergency notification panel, highlighted with triple exclamation marks.

Michael's video goes still. Then he gives his Navi the command to turn off.

Mila grimaces and turns it back on.

> display emmsg nid LS03984703 "No, no, Michael. You're not in control now. I am. Now, let's see how well you can dodge cops and shoot helpless women when you can't see. Oh, and let's take away all your communications, too."

> godark nid LS03984703

> cmd nid LS03984703 \comms-down

Michael's display goes black.

> vmsg nid LS03984703 "Now, listen. You might want to consider the fact that I know where you are—currently, crouching behind a green van—and I can relay that to the cops who are all around you. Give that some thought. Also, think about the fact that if you make me happy, I might let you go. I can hear you, so say, 'Yes, ma'am' when you agree to do what I say."

She hears him curse.

She turns her attention to Slava Knyazev, still on the floor next to her. He's sleeping peacefully. She shakes her head.

Reluctantly, Michael says, "Yes, ma'am."

Mila nods, her face still tense. She gives him his vision back. Then she orders him to take the bullets out of his guns and throw them away and then throw away the guns. Next, she makes him look at his ankles, wrists, waist, and pockets to show her that all of his weapons have been discarded.

> vmsg nid LS03984703 "You can tell from the
gunfire that the authorities are busy, so go ahead
and start looking for Phoebe again. And repeat
after me, loud enough for her to hear you: Mila is
in my head, and she says . . ."

Curled up in the car trunk, I have plenty of time to think about the situation and start worrying about Mila. I don't want her to get hurt. I'm unspeakably angry at her and I don't think that I could ever forgive her for what she's done, but I still don't want her in the hands of these men.

I also have plenty of time for my leg to stiffen up and start to hurt in earnest, all the way from ankle to hip, and maybe up toward my ribs, too.

I nearly have a heart attack when I hear a man's voice only a few yards away. He's speaking in a rough and reluctant tone of voice. ". . . I'm not allowed to hurt you. Mila says she's sorry about what happened earlier. She says she finally figured it out. Do you remember how that one day she wanted to go to the ER and get an M-MRI because she thought she'd had a Navi implanted, and now you know from the first video that they did inject something that they used to make her cooperate?"

I listen intently.

"So apparently, the same thing happened earlier, after that conversation she had with those guys at her office in the second video, only that time they wiped her memory. She remembers that day. She got sick and she didn't know why. So she really didn't know about Eve or what it was doing."

Muddled as the explanation is, it makes perfect sense.

"And so far as the message about giving you to them, she admits that she was considering their offer, but only up until the point where they wanted you. She would never have given you to them. After that, she was just stringing them along to buy time."

I open the trunk a crack and look out. A man with his dark hair in a ponytail and black combat fatigues is looking around, unarmed. He goes on in an increasingly disgusted tone of voice. "Mila admits that she was a huge jerk on both of those videos that you saw. She feels like she's been changing over the past couple of weeks. She says that she didn't think that she cared about people. But that was 'before Phoebe.' She says that you're showing her what she's been missing. She says you're teaching her to how to care . . ." He makes a face and heaves a sigh. ". . . and she wants to keep learning."

I'm half-crying and half-laughing as I open the trunk. "Um, a hand here?" I call to the pony-tailed thug.

As he comes over, I say, "By the way, I'm going to want to hear all that straight from her. Sorry, dude, but hearing it from your ugly mug isn't quite the same."

He grunts in annoyance. "She says she'll be happy to say it in person, too." He looks like he would rather be almost anywhere else right now. As he helps me out, he says, "Mila wants to know how you got hurt."

"Oh, I got hit by the train," I say casually. Then I start laughing, because what else can I do?

"Are you going to be okay, she wants to know."

"Yes, I'll heal up."

"She says the cops will only be distracted for so long, so we have to go now. She's telling me to lead you to her. And she says to tell you my name is Michael."

"Thanks, Michael, and thanks for not killing me," I say wryly. "How'd she manage that?"

"No comment," he says grimly, which makes me chuckle.

We hurry south along the river as fast as I can hop on one leg, breathlessly debating where we should cross the river. There's a dam coming up soon, but Mila insists that it wouldn't be safe for me to go across the top of it.

Then we see it and exclaim on it at the same time—another train has stopped on the train trestle that crosses the river before the Y bridge. "We can cross on the trestle on this side of the train and it will block line of sight from the bridge," I say.

"Good, because there are still a dozen cops on that bridge," Mila tells me through the man.

We cross the train trestle without incident, although by now I've discovered at least five more places where I hurt. The right side of my head is tender, my right hip is almost as unhappy as my left hip, and I think even my sternum is somehow bruised. But all I can do is clench my jaw and keep moving.

I ask Mila via Michael whether she's released the data yet. "Not yet," Michael relays. "She says she's been distracted with staying alive and keeping you alive and keeping the cops busy with the mercs."

A few minutes later, we've been guided to a tire factory. Mila dismisses Michael at the door and sends him away. I duck through the door just as the clatter of helicopters approaches overhead.

About the time I determine that I have no idea where to go and can't possibly get there by myself even if I did, Mila comes through a stairwell door. She stops in front of me, and we grin stupidly at each other for a moment before we both reach out to each other for a hug. I teeter, and she catches my weight and steadies me.

"Sorry, my leg is pretty messed up," I say, laughing and crying at the same time.

"I'm sorry you got hurt."

We look at each other, and both of us tear up. I stroke her face. "I was so mad at you," I say with a shuddering laugh.

"I know," she says. "But I couldn't figure out how to explain everything all at once, and at first, I couldn't understand why I didn't remember that second video. I got overwhelmed, and I couldn't figure out what to say. I'm not good at emotions and explanations all at the same time."

I wipe a tear from Mila's cheek and can't help but chuckle. "I would say that I'll try to remember that the next time you seem to have utterly betrayed me, but I'm kind of hoping there won't be a next time."

She just nods. "Let's get upstairs and upload the data."

Our progress is slow, with Mila carrying half my weight and steadying me as we go. My whole body hurts more and more as the shock wears off.

As we go, Mila says, "I messaged Jerry Armstead. He says our family members are safe. They're having dinner at a cafeteria outside Cleveland right now."

"Thank God. Mila, thank you for sending him. Where did you even find him?"

Mila shrugs and shakes her head. "He's a hero, that's all. He worked security at my mother's nursing home, and he insisted on helping. Without him, my mother would be dead."

"Without him, I think my whole family might be dead," I say.

Once we're upstairs in the office, she eases me into the softest-looking office chair. Then she opens up Wikileaks.org and starts uploading the data in one large file.

As Mila writes a few paragraphs explaining the data, I notice a body on the floor. I start to get up to go check his vital signs, but then my own body reminds me that I was just hit by a train. "Mila?" I ask, pointing.

"Bad guy," Mila says. "Tell me if you see him move."

"Is he okay?" I ask. "And did you do that to him?"

Mila glances at me with a little shrug, and my eyebrows go up.

"I think he'll be okay," she answers. "I just hit him on the head with that chair over there . . . um . . . a few times."

I shake my head. "Head injuries are bad. Help me up so I can make sure he's not dying."

"He's a bad guy," Mila says. "And this one deserves a little brain damage if anyone does."

"I'm a nurse," I retort.

"You're injured," Mila says, "and he could be faking it, waiting for one of us to get close enough to grab. Help will be here very soon, I promise. Let me finish this. I'm almost done."

I'm too exhausted and overwhelmed to argue. I space out while I keep an eye on the guy's breathing.

In another few moments, Mila finishes her post of the explanation and the data. "With what I've explained here, they'll unpack the data, analyze it, and explain it in laymen's terms in short order. Then it will hit the media, and then they'll finally be able to fix Eve."

"So that's it?" I ask. "We're home free?"

"No," she says with characteristic bluntness. "We're going to go to jail again first. How soon we get out depends on the judge, Mr. Pataky, and luck."

We hear sirens outside. "There they are," she says. "I told you help would be here in a minute. I'll tell Tom what room we're in." In response to my questioning look, she says, "Tom Lyons, the US deputy marshal. I've been keeping him busy taking out the remaining mercenaries with the promise that we'd turn ourselves in afterward."

I catch her hand as she turns back toward the computer. "I'm not ready," I protest with a laugh. "There's so much we need to talk about."

"We'll have time," she promises, squeezing my hand. "We'll have all the time in the world."

It sounds like a promise that she'll be there with me. I like the sound of that.

She finishes typing a message to Tom, and then she turns back to me. "I understand you being mad," she says gently. "I didn't like the Mila I saw in those videos, either."

"I've never understood you—not at all," I say with a wry laugh. "But I did think that you didn't care about people much, and it frustrated me. Do you really think you've changed because of me? You meant that about 'before Phoebe'?"

"I meant it," she says. She rolls her chair right next to mine, takes my face in her hands, and kisses me warmly.

I was important enough to her to change how she sees the world. I'm thrilled. I kiss her back, and we don't even stop when Tom and the rest of the marshals open the door and tell us to put up our hands. As if by silent agreement, we raise our hands and keep right on kissing.

Jail is, in fact, where we go next, although we get a trip to the hospital on the way. We're put in separate ambulances and don't see each other at the hospital.

Exhausted beyond endurance, I wait through X-rays and examinations with my hands cuffed to the bed rail and an army of cops nearby. A doctor eventually confirms what I'd suspected—damaged ligaments, strained muscles, and a broken tibia. To be specific, it's a nondisplaced partial oblique fracture, which is very lucky. A simple cast takes care of it. Then I hobble to jail on crutches.

There, weeks pass with Mila and I still cut off from the world and from each other, waiting for our fates to be decided by forces outside of our control.

Other than my twice-weekly physical therapy, I spend much of my time listening to meditation recordings or music from the prison library. I have no desire to watch movies, even though I thought I would. I expected to want to lose myself for a while and forget everything, but instead, my brushes with death have made me want to immerse myself and remember everything.

What I want is to stay in reality even when it's nothing special—to watch the beams of sunlight lengthen on the wall across from my cell as the day draws to a close, taste the cold, metallic water from the fountain, and track the way my cellmates gradually relax in my presence as the time goes by until we're sharing stories from our lives. Talking to people who share the same physical space with me for days at a time—all of us free of distracting Navi messages—is like rediscovering a foreign country where I once lived and didn't know I missed.

Real life is steady and reassuring, I find, not like the ephemera of Navi communications.

I also relearn how my body feels when I stretch and the way my brain gradually wakes up in the morning—how pre-sleep thoughts pop back into my mind while my dream images diminish—and what it's like to follow the same train of thought for twenty or thirty minutes at a time.

I find memories. Real ones, not the videos preserved by my Navi, which I can't access while I'm in jail. These recollections are unsteady and fleeting, and I'm not sure I can trust their accuracy, yet I find unexpected depth and meaning in them. Maybe it's simply that I have time to reflect on them.

My own mind is like an old friend I'm getting to know again, and I find myself to be much better company than I remembered. When I first got my implant as a teenager and first heard that slightly mechanical voice in my head, I felt an overwhelming sense of relief: never again would I be alone, trapped with my own thoughts. But now it seems to me that my Navi was its own sort of trap.

And yet, the novelty of such insights can only last so long. After I'm firmly grounded in reality, and then that reality remains the same week after week, I become restless. Bored and agitated, I find myself watching movies in my Navi again, but only one or two a day, just to break up the monotony.

Above all, I miss Mila. I have so much time to think about our tumultuous few weeks together. I couldn't have predicted anything about it, from our unlikely meeting through a car accident to kissing passionately in my old room at my parents' house. Yet I have a sense that I can predict what will come next. I think that Mila and I are going to last well beyond all this drama. There's just something in my heart that tells me so. But I can't wait to see her again and make sure of it.

The only visits I get are from Mr. Pataky, who, despite being cantankerous about our disappearance, remains willing to represent us.

On the first visit, he tells me that Eve has been patched and that no new cases of HAD have occurred, thanks to the information Mila released on the internet.

On the second visit, he tells me that they've devised a new treatment for those already afflicted by Eve: putting the patients in a coma and lowering the temperature of their brains until there is virtually no brain activity—a profound state of rest. It turns out that the brain is adaptable enough to heal from nearly any injury given enough time, and the freezing method shortens the time needed from months or even years down to a couple of weeks. It's mostly working with the younger patients. The elderly don't seem to have the resilience necessary.

They're trying it with my brother, whose condition has remained unchanged up until now. I cross my fingers till they hurt.

Mr. Pataky also tells me that the government is beginning to dismantle the detention centers and has initiated three separate investigations into the abuses of human rights that happened there. But as Mila said, what else could they have done with those patients? Nevertheless, high-profile officials will pay with their jobs and possibly their freedom for the crime of not predicting and preparing for something no one saw except in hindsight.

Other new information has confirmed what I later learn Mila already knew: Eve was merely a visible symptom of an underlying disease, because the original purpose of Eve was to modify people's behavior and make it more profitable. Then they got greedy and tried to increase the effects, and they accidentally introduced a bug that made the stimulation far too strong. That was the first wave. When they tried to fix it, they failed and only spread it further. That was the second wave.

And the third wave . . . that was for us. For me and Mila. By then, we'd learned too much and exposed too much, so they decided to make it look like terrorism and then blame the whole thing on us.

It turns out that I'd had Eve for months. Most people did. We just didn't know it.

"They were watching everything we did, deciding when to reward us and when to punish us?" I ask Mr. Pataky at one point, aghast.

"No," he says, looking forlorn. "They didn't need to. Our Navis did it for them."

"Are *you* giving up your Navi?" I ask him.

He snorts, his usual, brash personality reasserting itself. "Of course not. Too useful."

In fact, according to Mr. Pataky, Navi usage is down a whopping three percent. I'm reminded of Mila's comment about nuclear weapons and human nature. Perhaps those who didn't get HAD feel immune or just think it won't happen again. But what can I say? I'm among those who isn't giving up her Navi.

On his third visit, Mr. Pataky tells me that the conspiracy has been fully mapped. Slava Knyazev, Director of Sales and Marketing for Peake International—the body on the floor in the tire warehouse—conceived of and oversaw Eve all along. He was the only one in the executive suites of any of the involved companies who knew what the program did. The rest only knew that it was a program that "incentivized" folks to buy their products. Mr. Knyazev thought it best not to reveal anything else, for the purposes of plausible deniability. The other companies loaned their resources to the "incentive program," knowing that there was something a bit unusual and very profitable going on and willing to leave it at that.

"Will they really escape liability because they didn't know?" I ask.

"Not by a long shot," Mr. Pataky says. "They were responsible for doing their due diligence, and they didn't do it. They're not going to get away with that."

I ask how the bad guys knew about our work at Browning Charity Hospital in order to turn us in to the FBI. According to Mr. Pataky, Mila says it was Nurse Honor Thompson, planted there by Dr. Green, who was in the pocket of Peake International.

It creeps me out to know that all these people were watching us and plotting against us while I was obliviously popping Tylenol and Dramamine, lost in my Navi and worrying about my brother. What an idiot I must have seemed. At least they're both being charged for their collusion.

I'm profoundly disappointed when I learn on that third—and final—visit that the attorney general isn't dropping the charges against myself and Mila. Mr. Pataky cuts me off when I try to argue. He points out that we did, in fact, commit multiple crimes. "You'll get a chance to talk to the judge," he says, "so save it for him." The important thing, Mr. Pataky tells me, is to plead guilty and hope for a good plea bargain. Even then, he says, we'll probably still face several years in prison, but that'll be better than the alternative.

I spend my remaining jail time in a self-blaming funk. Somehow, I'd dreamed that we might walk away from this heroes. By the time they come to take me to court, I've convinced myself that I was a naïve fool to break the law and even more of an idiot to involve Mila. I can never make this up to her.

Once again, Mila and I are connected to the same length of chain. She looks much better this time than the previous time. She even smiles at me, and I return her smile weakly.

Once again, we're called first to appear before the curmudgeonly Judge Elliot Keith. The same man—Mr. Harren—stands to our left, with Mr. Pataky at the lectern.

The judge surprises me by speaking to us directly, his tone irascible. "Ms. Bernhart, Ms. Bremer, you made us assurances that you would reappear in court on your scheduled date. Instead, you chose to leave town and cost multiple states many thousands of dollars for a manhunt across state lines. You kidnapped James Bernhart from where he was receiving appropriate treatment, exposing him to needless risk of harm, and you committed multiple counts of cybercrimes in an attempt to do what should have been left to the authorities. I understand that you're both pleading guilty to all charges. Is that correct?"

"Yes, Your Honor," we both mumble. I don't know about Mila, but my heart has sunk to my toes. This sounds really bad.

He turns to the prosecutor. "Mr. Harren, do you have sufficient evidence to substantiate these charges?"

Mr. Harren clears his throat. "Yes, Your Honor. We recaptured the defendants in Zanesville, Ohio. Ms. Bremer has turned over her laptop and shown us all evidence of her hacking during their absence and of how she hacked into the central Navi ID database prior to leaving town. It is undisputed by numerous eyewitnesses that Ms. Bremer accessed the Navis of multiple people without legal authorization to do so. Video cameras at Browning Hospital clearly show their kidnapping of James Bernhart, and he was also recovered in Zanesville, Ohio."

The judge turns back to us. "Do you understand that by pleading guilty, you lose your right to a trial, and you lose your right to appeal certain decisions of this court?"

"Yes, Your Honor."

"I understand that the attorney general is prepared to suggest certain punishments for these crimes. I am not obligated to follow his recommendations. Should I so choose, I may sentence you, Ms.

Bernhart, to anywhere from . . ." He checks the papers in front of him. "Anywhere from thirty-six months to . . . all told, one hundred and sixty months, which works out to just over thirteen years. And you, Ms. Bremer, could receive anywhere from six to forty years. However, if I do not follow the recommendations of the attorney general in your sentencing, you will have the option of withdrawing your guilty plea and going to trial and preserving your right to appeal. Do you understand all of this?"

We mutter our agreement. My heart is hammering so hard, I feel dizzy.

"Ms. Bernhart, it is my understanding that you kidnapped your brother from the hospital because you felt that his care was inadequate and you had exhausted all legal recourses available to you. Is that correct?"

I nod, my mouth too dry to speak.

"Is that a yes, Ms. Bernhart?"

I clear my throat. "Yes," I say. "Sir. Your Honor." I wince at my stumbling.

"Both of you, it is my understanding that you jumped bail not to avoid prosecution, but in order to research Hyper-Aggression Disorder and find those responsible. Is that correct?"

I look at Mila, who says, "Yes, Your Honor. I knew that I could do it faster than anyone else working on the problem and that I could not do it from a jail cell."

"Ms. Bremer, that decision was not yours to make," the judge says tartly. "By making this decision on your own, you placed your own wisdom superior to the wisest heads involved in our government and judiciary. Do you think you know better than all of us?"

I wince again. This is Mila we're talking about. Humility is not her strong suit.

"It was my idea, Your Honor," I interject. "It's my fault."

"Thank you, Ms. Bernhart, but I'd like to hear from Ms. Bremer," the judge says.

My cheeks heat up.

Mila says, "I understand that I should have made an effort to pursue a remedy within the law." It sounds rehearsed, but the judge seems to accept it.

"That is correct. Next time, try having a little faith in the system. You might be surprised." The judge turns to me. "Ms. Bernhart, do you have anything else to say on your behalf before I accept your guilty plea and decide your sentencing?"

I let out a long breath. I rehearsed all sorts of arguments while I waited in my jail cell over the past weeks, but eventually, every argument fell apart on me. "No, Your Honor. Just that I really was trying to help Jamie and all the other victims of HAD."

He nods and directs the same question to Mila. She simply says, "No, thank you, Your Honor."

"Very well." Judge Keith turns back to Mr. Harren. "I understand you have certain recommendations?"

My heart hammers even harder as Mr. Harren shuffles his feet. He seems much less dramatic in today's proceedings than the last time we met. The wind seems to have been taken out of his sails, but I'm not sure what that means yet.

"Yes, Your Honor," Mr. Harren says. "Given the instrumental role that Ms. Bernhart and Ms. Bremer played in exposing the conspiracy behind Eve and bringing about a rapid cure for the disorder, and given that their goals were clearly noble ones, we feel it would be unreasonable to require them to serve time beyond that which they have already served.

"On the other hand, we recognize that they committed serious crimes when they took matters into their own hands, and we want to be sure that we get their attention and make it clear to everyone involved and everyone watching that this kind of lone-wolf activity is not appropriate. We feel that a conviction, time served, and a lengthy probationary period should be adequate to ensure that."

My heart skips several beats. They're not sending us to prison?

The judge turns to Mr. Pataky. "Are you in agreement with these recommendations, Mr. Pataky?"

"I am, Your Honor. I reiterate what I said in our last meeting. These are ordinary, upstanding citizens. They were caught up in dramatic, once-in-a-lifetime events. I don't expect that any of us will ever see them in court again, unless it's to testify against Peake International."

The judge sighs. "Very well. Then I sentence the both of you to time served and to five years' probation. You are required to maintain gainful employment for the duration of your probation, and if you commit any crime during that time, your probation will end and I will see you in this court again. Do either of you wish to revoke your guilty plea and go to trial?"

"No, Your Honor," I say, hardly able to believe it. "Thank you, Your Honor." Mila echoes my words.

"Then this court hereby accepts your guilty pleas. The sentences stated are to be entered into the record. Dismissed."

A huge grin takes over my face. I believe I get a lot of credit for waiting until we are out of the courtroom to kiss Mila.

Mr. Pataky seems to be in a hurry to move us out of the courthouse, and I'm okay with that, even while I struggle with the crutches. I'm so busy thanking him that I don't even register the crowd outside until I'm on the courthouse steps and the roar of applause and cheering gets my attention. I look around—and then I see the signs.

"Welcome Back!"

"Mila and Phoebe Rock"

"We Love You"

They're shouting our names.

Well, I'll be damned. We're coming home heroes after all. With my eyes wide and one hand over my open mouth, I survey the cheering faces. I recognize some of these folks. There's Sara from Grady Hospital, and Abhay and Derrick, and Deonte. And others from my Collective—Ian, Shannon, Wayne . . . I hobble on my crutches from person to person, hugging them and mumbling incoherent words of happiness.

And then I see a particular face, framed with shaggy blond hair, in the front line of the crowd, and my heart just about stops.

It's Jamie. He's thinner than I'd like to see and he's in a wheelchair, but he's sitting up, fully alert, shouting my name, and holding up a sign that says, "That's My Sister."

I burst into tears as I hurry to him. I lean over to hug him, and we both squeeze each other like crazy while people around us erupt in shouts and air horns and God knows what other noisemakers. I'm too busy crying to speak. Someone hands me tissues, and I wipe my face.

"How do you like your party?" Jamie asks with a mischievous grin.

"You did all this?" I ask. "How did you even know we were getting out today?"

He shrugs nonchalantly. "Mr. Pataky said the odds were good."

I punch him on the shoulder. "I should have known you would do something big and loud and obnoxious." It's not a complaint, and he knows it. He laughs at me.

"Just wait for the Hummer limo pickup," he says. "And the ceremony with the mayor of Atlanta giving you the key to the city. And the fireworks display that'll write your names in the sky."

I'm open-mouthed and red-faced with embarrassment—and happiness. I fall back on punching him again. He laughs and punches me in return.

Ah, yes. I have my brother back.

Epilogue

In what seems like no time at all, we're back home with Tobi and cat-Phoebe, settling back into a normal life.

I suspect that, with felony convictions on our records, it will take us a long time to get work again. After a discussion with Mila that is long and very frustrating but entirely logical (on her side), I finally agree to let her support me out of her savings.

As it turns out, however, the government is willing to overlook our felony convictions, considering the good we did. Mila ends up in network security with the Department of Homeland Security, and I end up at the CDC, researching the possibility of future outbreaks of "disease" caused by Navis. Both departments also give us the time off we need to testify at various trials.

More importantly, by the time it has all settled out—by the time everything has died down—Mila and I have settled into the coziest, happiest relationship I've ever known.

Mila's lack of a Navi makes me continually aware of whether I'm fully present with her or not, and just by being present, the quality of our time together is much better than I've ever experienced before.

When we're together with my Navi off, we curl up on the sofa, listening to cat-Phoebe purr, looking out of the window at the vivid colors of the flowers and sky and trees and cars and people, and just absorbing it all—just feeling that we're together and safe and alive, just putting all of our attention into those beautiful moments.

I've discovered that feeling another person's warm body against your own is a form of bliss that nothing can replace, but only if it's mindful—only if you're fully aware and present and putting every bit of yourself into it. And now I can do that.

THE END

Acknowledgments

This novel required a lot of research on numerous topics, and I am indebted to the lovely people who shared their time and knowledge with me:

A big "thank you" to Dr. Dennis Fehr for his insight into Plain people society. Thank you, Dr. Jeffrey D. Schlitt and Chris Lewis, for your legal insight. Thank you so much, Dr. Reeta Achari and Dr. Gerri Hanten, for information about the functioning of the brain. Thank you, Abhishek Mathur, for electronics knowledge. Thank you, Dan Crocker, for law-enforcement information.

Thank you, Shannon Winton, Alyssa Everett, and Dr. Dominick D'Aunno, for your knowledge about psychiatric wards and how hospitals work.

For giving me advice about technical details and hacking, thank you to Ryan "Iggy" Harrison and to several redditors: @ iagox86, several anonymous folks, and one redditor after whom I have named a character, as promised.

Also, thank you to those who helped me with the writing process:

Thanks go to my critique group, Team Gargoyles—Shannon Winton, Alyssa Everett, Chris Lewis, Wayne Basta, and Ian Everett—for reading at least four versions of the first chapter, not to mention reading the rest of it.

Thank you to all my beta readers—Katie Kim, George Wright Padgett, Antha Adkins (whose critique was remarkably thorough!), my mother, Janet, and my mother-in-law, Lisa.

Thank you to Josh Mitchell for being my editor (if you see anything wrong, it's because I secretly reverted your changes—mwahaha!) and for supplying the jokes about HAD.

Thank you to my publisher, Jason Aydelotte of Grey Gecko Press, for publishing me a second time and for putting up with me in the meantime!

And finally, thank you, most of all, to my readers! If you like my work, please review this book online and post the review on social media—it's the single most helpful thing you can do—and please sign up for my email fan club at www.hchritz.com to get exclusive content and special offers directly from me.

About the Author

H.C.H. Ritz has a degree in theatre from the University of Houston and directs community theatre in her spare time. Originally from rural Mississippi, she has lived in Houston, Texas long enough to have turned into a city person. She is married to a wonderful human being and has a young son and a tortoiseshell kitty named Roxy Underfoot.

Connect with H.C.H.

Email:	hchritz@gmail.com
Facebook:	facebook.com/HCHRitz
Web:	hchritz.com

Support Indie Authors & Small Press

If you liked this book, please take a few moments to leave a review on your favorite website, even if it's only a line or two. Reviews make all the difference to indie authors and are one of the best ways you can help support our work.

Reviews on Amazon, GoodReads, GreyGeckoPress.com, Barnes and Noble, or even on your own blog or website all help to spread the word to more readers about our books, and nothing's better than word-of-mouth!

http://smarturl.it/review-absence

Recommended Reading

The Year of the Hydra
by William Broughton Burt

Could a dark agenda be woven into the architecture of China's most sacred ancient temple? An agenda that only Julian Mancer is seeing? Or is Julian off his meds again? If the structure were in fact a doomsday device awaiting an astronomical tripwire—could Julian stop it?

Julian is determined to discover the answer, as soon as he concludes a far more pressing matter involving a sixteen-year-old girl with a *most* intriguing mutation.

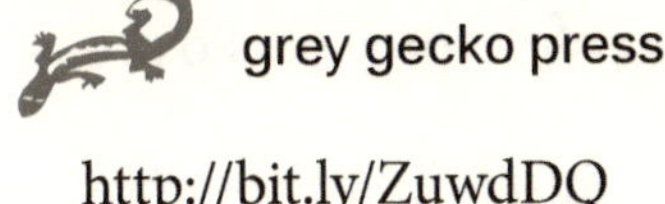

grey gecko press

http://bit.ly/ZuwdDQ

Recommended Reading

For over a hundred and fifty years, the rarest and most valuable substance in the solar system has been mined from the only location where it exists in significant quantity: Jupiter's largest moon, Ganymede. For all of this time, the remote mining outpost has been serviced by clone slaves who are drugged into mindlessness, and all of it has been monitored, controlled, and administered by the artificial intelligence known as Prinox.

But what happens when a failed rescue mission causes a small band of escaped clones to begin questioning their lives, their society, and their very existence? Hunted by deadly killing machines, confused and scared, these renegade slaves are about to find out—for better or worse—just what it means to be human.

Spindown
by George Wright Padgett

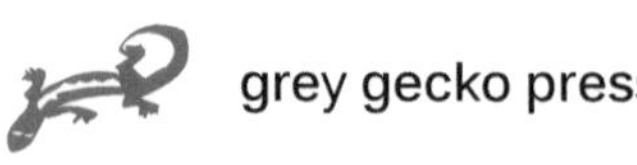

http://bit.ly/Z8gu6O

GREY GECKO PRESS

Thank you for reading this book from Grey Gecko Press, an independent publishing company bringing you great books by your favorite new indie authors.

Be one of the first to hear about new releases from Grey Gecko: visit our website and sign up for our New Release or All-Access email lists. Don't worry: we hate spam, too. You'll only be notified when there's a new release, we'll never share your email with anyone for any reason, and you can unsubscribe at any time.

At our website you can purchase all our titles, including special and autographed editions, preorder upcoming books, and find out about two great ways to get free books, the Slushpile Reader Program and the Advance Reader Program.

And don't forget: all our print editions come a free ebook!

www.GreyGeckoPress.com

9 781938 821790